LORD OF FORTUNE

DARCY BURKE

ZEALOUS QUILL PRESS

LORD OF FORTUNE

Dashing adventurer Penn Bowen is dedicated to preserving Britain's history and his carefree, bachelor lifestyle. He's happiest when he's in pursuit of knowledge and the occasional liaison with the right woman. So he's more than a little perturbed when the wrong woman inserts herself into his latest quest—proving that a valuable artifact in Oxford's museum is a fake. Amelia Gardiner is smart and capable...and determined to prove that Penn is wrong about the treasure her grandfather found.

Amelia won't allow Penn to denigrate her family's legacy, and she certainly won't join the ranks of women who throw themselves at his feet. As secretive and dangerous factions infiltrate their hunt, Amelia and Penn must work together to stay one step ahead. But passion ignites between them and suddenly their alliance is more than a simple convenience. When peril strikes too close, they'll risk everything they hold dear: family, honor, and a chance for the greatest treasure of all—love.

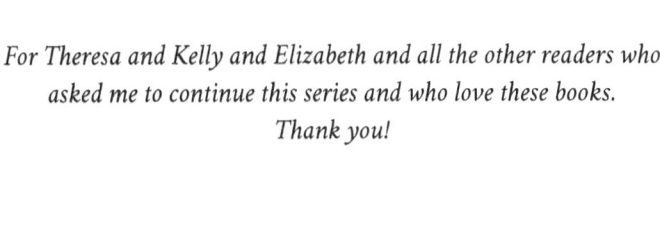

For Theresa and Kelly and Elizabeth and all the other readers who asked me to continue this series and who love these books. Thank you!

CHAPTER 1

August 1819, Wiltshire, England

A fine sheen of sweat beaded across Penn Bowen's forehead as he dangled from the rope and reached for the slick side of the cave. The lantern his assistant hung from the opening fifteen feet above him cast a meager glow into the large space, but he'd known he'd be operating in the near dark. It was no worse than he'd managed before. In fact, it was a bit better than some of the situations he'd found himself in.

He scanned the wall of rock, left to right, top to bottom, searching for the small opening that would lead him to his prize. A darker spot drew his eye about five feet to his right and above his head. He squinted into the inky dark to confirm it was what he sought. Damn, it was *very* small.

Clenching his jaw, he swung toward the wall, aiming for the hole. The rope felt as sturdy as it had when he'd lowered himself a few minutes before. He was also comforted by the presence of his very capable assistant, Egg, who would ensure Penn didn't drop the fifty or so feet to the cave floor. Most of it was likely sandy and soft, but there were rocks too, and he'd no desire to end his adventures in such a fashion.

A few feet short of the hole, he grasped a small outcropping of rock and brought himself flush against the cool limestone. Finding purchase with his hands and feet, he let go of the rope, though it remained tied around his waist—a measure Egg had insisted upon. Tentatively, he sought another handhold to bring himself closer to the hole. It was a bit of a stretch, but he managed to wrap his fingers around another, albeit smaller, outcropping. Now to get his lower half in the same direction.

He searched for another foothold, his boots scraping against the coarse rock. Finding a small shelf, he put his right foot there and took the left one off the other foothold. A cascade of dirt fell down the hole through which he'd descended, distracting him momentarily. His boot slipped from the rock. He hung suspended for a few seconds, his heart launching into his throat and his pulse beating at a frenzied pace.

"Sorry about that!" Egg's voice boomed into the cavern, further disrupting Penn's concentration.

Penn didn't know what had caused the disruption of earth, nor did he care, so long as it didn't happen again. He closed his eyes for a bare moment and willed himself to move. He found his footing once more and successfully brought his left foot to perch beside the right. He exhaled and told himself to hurry the hell up.

The hole was just above his head now. Holding on to the rock with his left hand, he reached up with his right and slid his hand into the opening. It barely fit. It was a good thing he hadn't worn gloves, an argument he'd won with Egg earlier. "But the rope will burn your 'ands!" Egg had insisted.

"I can grab rock much more easily with my bare fingers," Penn had said. "I'll take the potential rope burn." As if it mattered. Penn's hands were not the manicured, pampered hands of a scholar or worse, a nobleman. His were the rough and ready appendages of someone who lived the most of each moment, experiencing as many adventures as possible. But of course, he was *also* a scholar, just not the typical sort.

The hole was cold and narrow. He met a bit of resistance at the top and pushed his hand past it. The rock dug through his flesh, slicing through nerve and sinew. He winced and silently swore. Egg would berate him for not wearing gloves.

Just when he feared he wouldn't be able to reach back any farther without jeopardizing his position, his hand plunged into a void. Opening his fingers, he felt around—there was a ceiling to the hole, but the bottom had fallen away. Pressing himself tight against the rock so that the rough surface abraded his cheek, he stretched his fingers and felt down into the void.

And found what he was looking for.

Relief coursed through him, and he smiled as he wrapped his fingers around a cold metal shaft that was maybe six inches long. Clutching the artifact in his fist, he withdrew his hand cautiously, going slow lest he scrape his hand again. When he reached that spot, he couldn't get past it. Fisted, his hand was now too large. *Hell and the bloody devil.*

Sweat broke out along the back of his neck. Urging calm, he loosened his grip, careful to retain hold of the artifact between his thumb and fingers. It was exceptionally lucky that this piece was narrow, but then it would have to be in order to be placed in this spot in the first place.

He continued, aware that he was likely going to reinjure

himself. The rock cut into him once more, creating a new wound so he would have two. *Spectacular.*

Once past the obstacle, he tightened his grip on the artifact and quickly pulled his hand out. Though tempted to look at it, he didn't, instead stowing it into a pocket sewn inside his waistcoat.

Confident the item was secure, he gripped the rope with his right hand, then withdrew his left to climb. "Coming up!" he called to Egg. He pulled himself up, hand over hand, as the slack curled from his waist.

The light above him moved as Egg withdrew the lantern from the hole. A moment later, Penn reached for the edge of the rock. Egg's hand came over his, and he grabbed the back of Penn's waistcoat, hauling him into the upper cave.

The rock scraped over Penn's midsection and thighs. Egg let go, then helped him turn and sit up. No sooner had Penn withdrawn his legs from the hole than Egg demanded, "What the bloody 'ell did you do to your 'and?" He reached for Penn's right hand, but Penn scrambled to his feet.

"Nothing. Well, barely anything," he amended, knowing Egg would argue with him. Egg would argue with the Regent if he thought he was right. And Egg almost universally thought he was right. "Never mind it now. Just take care of the rope, will you?"

Egg frowned up at Penn from his five feet six inches, his weathered face carved with deep canyons from the years he'd spent outdoors. His dark eyes narrowed, and he muttered to himself as he set about looping up the rope.

"I found it, if you care to know." Penn removed the artifact from his coat and moved closer to the lantern. He squatted down and placed the item on his left palm.

There were etchings in the gold hilt of the iron dagger, deep and quite legible. Indeed, the hilt didn't look right at all. Penn frowned.

"And there it is," Egg said softly. He was always as thrilled as Penn to unearth a new treasure. *Always.*

"Yes, there it is." The words hadn't come from Penn or Egg.

Penn closed his hand around the dagger and rose to his full height. He turned toward the mouth of the cave where a lone figure blocked the entrance. Due to the daylight behind him, the man was unidentifiable. However, the cock of his pistol was not. Make that two pistols, for he held one in each hand.

"Thank you for taking care of the difficulty of finding it," the man said. "Please have your companion deliver it to me."

"Why not me?" Penn asked, his mind racing. His small knife was tucked beneath his waistcoat, but he couldn't reach for it without prompting the stranger to perhaps shoot him. Egg, however, had a knife at his side, and the stranger wasn't watching him as closely. He'd be able to employ it while Penn pretended to deliver the artifact. Which, of course, he had absolutely no intention of actually doing.

The stranger, whose face was mostly covered by a neckerchief, trained a pistol between Penn's eyes. "Your companion looks far more amenable. Send him, or I'll start shooting."

He thought Egg looked more amenable? Penn wanted to laugh. Egg was as surly as they came. Or could be, at least. "I don't think you will," Penn said softly, hoping to unnerve the man with a lack of concern while edging forward. "Why on earth would you want a silly old dagger?"

The man barked out a laugh. "Do you take me for a fool?"

This miscreant knew the value of this find, that it was an important treasure that could change the face of history. This knowledge was highly guarded—only a handful of people were informed. Which meant this man was either one of them or an associate hired by one of them. Whoever he was, he would leave here empty-handed.

Penn clasped the dagger. "Indeed I do if you intend to steal this from me."

"Must I really shoot you?"

Penn looked askance at Egg. "D and C," he whispered. *Divide and conquer.* They'd done this many times.

Egg gave an infinitesimal nod.

"Now," Penn breathed as he darted to the right while Egg went left.

One of the pistols fired. Penn thrust the dagger back into his waistcoat as he scrambled along the edge of the cave. Reaching the mouth, he dove for the man, hitting him in his midsection and wrapping his arms around his back. They both went sprawling backward through the entrance into the light of day.

"Oof!" The villain landed with a thud and an exhalation. He lifted his arm—likely so he could take another shot—but Penn knocked the pistol from his hand. The other pistol was gone.

Penn stared down at the man, eager to see if he knew the brigand. The cloth covering his face had dislodged, exposing his features. Penn's breath caught as he took in the unfamiliar face and the softness of her—*her*—body imprinted on his.

"What the bloody devil are you doing?" Penn thundered.

"Get off me!" she shrieked, raising her arms to push him away. Gone was the deep, clearly affected voice from the cave. Her tone was still darker, grittier than most females, but it was *unequivocally* female.

Penn ignored her struggles even as she landed several blows against his chest. "Egg, do you have the weapons?" he asked.

"I do now, sir." He came abreast of them and sucked in a breath. "Blimey, it's a woman!"

Penn took in the soft arc of her cheekbone, the lush curve of her lip, the sparkling green of her eyes, and the blonde curls peeking from beneath her hat. "So it is."

"She nearly shot me," Egg complained, his voice climbing. "Bullet whizzed past my ear, it did. If I were any slower..." He shook his head.

She glared up at him, her eyes nearly as dangerous as the weapon she'd fired. "Get. Off. Me."

"Are you going to try to kill us again?"

"You have my weapons," she hissed.

Penn lifted a shoulder. "So you say, but there might be more. Perhaps I should verify for myself." He patted at her coat, and she renewed her efforts to beat him away from her.

"What are you doing? Don't touch me!"

"I'm making sure you aren't still armed. Forgive me if I don't trust you."

"I'll forgive you nothing, you scoundrel!"

He felt down her abdomen. Despite the bulk of her men's costume, she was quite slender and, as he'd recognized a few moments ago, soft. He grazed his hands over her hips, and his body seemed to realize he was astride a beautiful, curvaceous female. Beautiful? Oh yes, she was stunning. But then so were wolves, and Penn had no desire to tangle with one of them either.

He pushed himself to the side and stood, offering her his hand to help her up.

She glowered at him and rose on her own. "You're despicable."

"And you're a thief."

"Would-be, actually," Egg clarified, ever the stickler for accuracy.

"I'm not sure I believe that," Penn said, keeping his gaze

glued to the blazing-eyed virago. "I'm sure she's stolen from others."

Egg snorted. "I'm not. She's a fairly good shot, but she didn't plan very well. Much better ways to steal—or at least try to—from you, sir."

"Please enlighten me," she said.

Penn had to admire her courage and her determination. More importantly, he had to wonder how in the hell she'd come to be here. "Who are you?" he asked.

"That doesn't matter. All you need to know is that dagger rightfully belongs to me." Her hands tightened into fists at her sides, and as the gloves pulled over her slender knuckles, Penn wondered how he'd ever mistaken her for a man.

Penn stared at her a moment, then laughed. Egg joined in. Amused and curious, Penn said, "I can't begin to imagine how you arrived at that fantasy, nor can I puzzle how you even know about this artifact." He sobered, narrowing his eyes at her. "How *do* you know about it?"

She lifted her chin, her gaze coated in frost. "That doesn't matter either."

Perhaps not, but it would bother him. Penn liked to have answers. "Well then, if you'll excuse us, we'll be on our way." Penn nodded toward Egg, who tucked the pistols into his waistband.

"I'll just grab our things." Egg turned and disappeared into the cave.

"You will not." The spitfire lunged forward and grabbed Penn's elbow. "That dagger is mine."

He dropped a perturbed look at where her fingers wrapped around him. "Unless you'd care to disclose why you think that, this interview is over."

Her jaw clenched tight. "I can't let you take it."

"I'm afraid you have no choice. If you'd care to share information about how you even know about this treasure, perhaps we might come to an arrangement." It was a bald-faced lie since he had no intention of relinquishing his find. But he was keen to learn her role in this.

As she opened her mouth to speak, the all too familiar sound of a pistol cocking filled the air. Penn looked past her as she released her hold on him and spun about. Make that multiple pistols. Four men approached them, their weapons poised to shoot and the lower part of their faces covered with neckerchiefs so that only their eyes were visible beneath the shadows cast by the brims of their hats.

"Bloody hell," Penn muttered. "Friends of yours?"

"No." The tension weighing that single word was enough to tell him that she wasn't with these new arrivals.

Penn hoped that Egg was somehow aware of what was happening and would stay in the cave until he could find a way to turn the situation in their favor. In the meantime, he'd try to talk their way out of whatever was going on.

Wait, "their" way? Was he referring to himself and Egg, or was he including this unknown woman?

Penn smiled at the quartet of masked men. "How can we help you, gentlemen?"

One of the men—the leader, apparently—raised his weapon toward Egg, who'd emerged from the cave still holding the woman's pistols. Unfortunately, another of the men went and relieved him of the weapons.

The leader answered Penn's question. "You can hand over the dagger."

Damn, they knew about it too. So much for secret treasure. "I didn't find it."

The speaker snorted as a rather large fellow standing a little off to the side growled. "We know you're lying, Mr. Bowen," the man said. His tone held the sophistication of a learned man. He was no hired thug. He also knew who Penn was.

"I'm afraid you have the advantage," Penn said. "And you are?"

"Not leaving until you hand over the dagger," the man said pleasantly as the large growler took a few menacing steps forward. This put him rather close to the lady. She stiffened.

Penn moved to her side, close enough that he could feel her against his arm. She might be a thief, but he wouldn't allow her to be harmed.

"Who is she?" the man—clearly the leader of the foul group—asked.

"Does it matter?" Penn asked nonchalantly.

"Take her."

Growler pounced like a cat, moving far more quickly and gracefully than Penn ever would have wagered. His hand curled around the woman's arm, and he dragged her away from Penn. He stuffed his pistol into his waistband and withdrew a long knife from a scabbard at his side. With another growl, he pressed the blade against her neck.

Every muscle in Penn's body tensed. He was finished pretending to be pleasant. He snarled at the leader. "Release her."

"Give me the dagger," he responded blandly.

When Penn hesitated, the leader nodded toward him. "Search him."

As the other two men holstered their pistols and advanced, the growler tipped the woman's hat from her head, revealing her mass of golden curls. Strands cascaded down her back while the bulk of it stayed wrapped in its knot at the back of her skull. She twisted in the brigand's arms, and he tightened his grip, forcing a cry from her throat.

Penn lunged toward her just as the other two men grabbed him by the arms.

"Can't we just shoot the lot of 'em?" the growler asked

hoarsely. "Maybe not her. At least not yet. She smells nice." He sniffed her hair and dragged his lips across her forehead.

Penn moved quickly, surprising the men who'd grabbed him by elbowing them swiftly and dashing forward. The leader's pistol came up. "Stop!" he yelled.

A pistol shot rent the air, but Penn didn't turn. He dove for the growler, knocking the large man—and the woman—to the ground.

"Bowen!" The sound of Egg's voice broke through Penn's haze of fury. The distraction was enough for the growler to gain the upper hand. He hit Penn in the jaw and flipped him to his back. The leader stood over him then, his pistol aimed at Penn's head.

"We've shot your man. Give over." He looked at the woman. "You—find the dagger and give it to me. Otherwise, I'll let my man have you."

"You're despicable," she spat.

Penn couldn't see her, but he heard the venom in her tone and imagined the fire that must be sparking from her green eyes, just as when she'd called him the same adjective. He wasn't sure how he felt about being judged the same as these villains. His thoughts turned to Egg and what his wound might be, but he didn't dare move his gaze from the gun pointed between his brows.

"You all right, Egg?" he called.

"Just a nick on my arm," Egg answered.

Penn exhaled with relief, but it was short-lived since their situation was utterly untenable.

"How about I give him more than a nick?" the leader offered. "And we'll take your lady friend here with us." His dark eyes narrowed, and he bared his teeth for a brief moment. "Give me the goddamned dagger."

Anger spilled through Penn's veins. Trapped, he slipped

his hand into his coat and pulled forth the dagger. "I'll get it back."

The man reached down with his left hand and pulled the artifact from Penn's grip. "Highly unlikely, but you're welcome to try." His mouth spread into a condescending, malevolent smile.

"I'll do more than try," Penn promised.

"Bind them," the leader said, taking a step back.

The other three men sprang into motion, one of them dragging the wounded Egg to where Penn lay in the dirt. The growler pushed the woman next to Penn as another of the men pulled Penn to a sitting position. Egg dropped beside Penn, and their arms were pulled behind them and bound together at the wrist. Penn tested the rope, but it held fast.

"And their feet," the leader bade as he turned the dagger over in his hand.

As the three men bound their ankles together, the leader looked down at Penn. "This is quite a find, thank you."

"You're a bastard and a coward," Penn said, gritting his teeth as the man tying his feet pulled the rope extra tight.

"No and no, actually. Come, gents." He holstered his pistol and turned away.

Two of the men followed him immediately while the growler lingered a moment. He leaned forward, his face a few inches from the woman's. "Next time, my pretty." He flashed her a smile that was missing several teeth before backing away and jumping to his feet.

She was close enough to Penn that he felt her shudder.

"Are you all right?" he asked.

"Fine." The word was strained, and Penn didn't believe her.

Penn turned his head to his assistant, who was tied to his right. "How is your arm?"

"It 'urts, but it'll clean up all right, I imagine. So long as we get ourselves out of this mess."

"Someone will come along," the woman said.

Penn appreciated her optimism but didn't think it was well placed. "I doubt that. We are quite a ways off the road." A thought occurred to him, and he turned his head toward her. "Does someone know you're here?"

She nodded. "My maid."

"Your maid. Have you no man to assist you?"

"My coachman is back at the inn. He just doesn't know precisely where I am."

"He should."

"This was a discreet errand," she snapped.

Penn laughed derisively. "A fool's errand, you mean."

She pulled at her bindings, which caused Penn to fall toward her and Egg to fall on Penn.

Egg grunted. "Watch yourself!"

Penn caught the scent of honeysuckle and sunlight before jerking away from her. "We are tied together," he said. "Your movements affect ours. Please be so kind as to not cause Egg pain."

"Where's your knife?" Egg asked.

It was tucked into a leather scabbard secured to the inside of his waistcoat. "In its usual location, which will be impossible to retrieve given the state of our hands."

"Where is it?" the woman asked.

Penn turned his head and was greeted with the intensity of her emerald stare. "My waistcoat."

She eyed his chest. "It can't be very large."

His lip twitched. "It's bigger than you think."

"Can I use my mouth?"

She seemed to have missed the humor in his double entendre given the innocence of her question. Only there was nothing innocent about his sudden reaction. Unexpected heat sparked in his belly, and he struggled to recall what she was going to use her mouth *for*.

The knife.

"I suppose you could try." It was the only plan they had. He angled toward her as best he could. "It's on the left. My left." The side closest to her.

"I need to move a bit closer. Egg—is that your name?—I'm going to move now, if you could brace yourself."

"Egbert Howell, ma'am."

"I am Mrs. Forrest."

Mrs. "Where in the devil is your husband?" Penn asked.

She twisted at the waist. "I am a widow."

"You undoubtedly drove him to his early demise." Penn chided himself for making light of her situation. He blamed the disaster this day had become. "My apologies," he said softly.

"Something like that," she murmured before bowing her head. Using her chin and nose, she nudged at the waistcoat to get to the scabbard. Thankfully, it was rather accessible.

The feel of her against him in such an intimate fashion only served to stoke the dormant fires in Penn's gut. It had been months since he'd lain with a woman, so it made sense Mrs. Forrest would arouse him.

A moment later, just as he grew uncomfortable because his body was beginning to respond to hers in a rather inappropriate manner, she lifted her head. Gripped in her teeth was the slender hilt of his knife.

Penn grinned. "Brilliant! Drop it behind you so that I can grab it and cut us free."

She turned her body back to a more natural position, and he realized she might have incurred more than a bit of discomfort. After a moment, she turned her head, moving her chin to the edge of her shoulder. She dropped the knife.

"It's in my hand," she said.

"Well done." He didn't bother keeping the admiration from his tone. Thieving had clearly given her some useful skills.

"Where's your hand so I can deliver it to you?"

"Let me find you so you don't stab me," he said. "I'm not wearing gloves."

"You're taking the fun out of this."

He smiled in spite of himself. She was skillful *and* brave. And witty. Also beautiful. She was, in a word, dangerous.

Penn sobered as he searched for her hand. His fingers grazed her sleeve. Moving down, he encountered her glove. A few more inches and he clasped the knife.

"Egg, give me your hands."

"What about mine?" Mrs. Forrest asked.

"I won't risk cutting you," Penn said.

"I *am* wearing gloves. And neither of you are. It makes sense that you should cut my restraints first."

It did, in fact, make sense. Nevertheless, he wasn't going to. "Egg?"

"Here." The assistant thrust his hands into Penn's.

Sweat dappled Penn's brow as he worked at Egg's bindings. It took a few minutes of blind navigation and several minutes more of awkward sawing, but Egg's hands soon came free of the ropes. He exhaled. "Thank you, sir."

Mrs. Forrest made a sound of irritation.

Egg quickly untied his feet, then set about freeing Penn's hands.

"What happened to helping ladies first?" Mrs. Forrest demanded.

"*Are* you a lady?" Egg asked. "I'm not sure."

She let out a distinctly unladylike expletive under her breath, but Penn caught it.

As soon as Penn's hands were free, he shook them vigorously to restore feeling, then leaned forward to untie his feet. When he was finished, he turned to Mrs. Forrest.

Her eyes narrowed when he didn't immediately release her. "What are you waiting for?"

"I'm contemplating whether I ought to untie you."

"You're as beastly as they were."

"No, I'm not." He moved to her back and untied her hands. He lowered his head and spoke next to her ear. "I may be a scoundrel from time to time, but I am *not* like them. If you get to know me, you'll find that out for yourself."

As soon as her hands were loose, she scooted away from him and untied her own feet. "I have no plans to do either."

Penn climbed to his feet. "Pity. I was hoping you might tell me how you knew about the dagger."

Her shoulders crumpled, and her face lost a bit of color. "The dagger."

"Don't fret. It was a fake anyway."

"A *what?*" She stared at him with incredulity, her jaw hanging open.

"A fake."

"How can you know that?"

"The hilt and, more importantly, the markings on it were too new."

She surveyed him with great skepticism. "I ask again, how can you know that?"

"Mrs. Forrest, I am an antiquary with a great deal of knowledge and experience. I am trained to recognize artifacts and determine their authenticity. That artifact was absolutely a fabrication. But then I am not surprised, since its counterpart, currently residing in the Ashmolean, is also a sham."

He didn't think it was possible for her to look more shocked, but her jaw dropped farther and her eyes practically fell from their sockets.

"Are you talking about the Heart of Llanllwch?" Her pronunciation of the Welsh was impeccable, and he couldn't suppress a flash of admiration.

He nodded. "I am. It's a fake."

She drew herself up to her not unimpressive height. "It most certainly is *not*."

"And how can *you* know *that*?"

"Because my grandfather found it, you cretin."

CHAPTER 2

*A*melia stared at the man while thoughts of murder barreled through her. He didn't actually mean to accuse her grandfather of fraud, did he?

"I can see why that would be distressing for you, but it is, alas, a fake." His tone was as condescending as his pitying gaze.

Yes, he actually meant to accuse Grandfather of fraud.

She crossed her arms over her chest and glared at him. "Prove it."

His dark blue eyes glittered in the afternoon sun. "That's precisely what I mean to do. After I tend to Egg." He turned and strode toward the cave. The older man, Bowen's assistant, had gone to where he'd dropped their belongings— two bags, a length of rope, and a lantern.

"Let's see about your arm," Bowen said.

Egg scoffed. "It's nothing." He picked up the bags with his uninjured left arm and attempted to lift the lantern with his right. Wincing, he let go, but Bowen caught it before it tumbled to the ground and started a fire in the dry grass. After putting the lantern out, he frowned at his assistant.

"It's not nothing. Drop the bags and sit."

Egg grimaced and directed a dark glower toward Bowen. "It's not as bad as your hand!"

Amelia's gaze dropped to Bowen's hands, and for the first time, she noticed the back of one was sliced open and covered in dried blood.

"That is an utter fallacy," Bowen said calmly. "I know you don't want me to touch it. You're such an infant." He knelt beside the older man and rummaged through one of the bags. Withdrawing a flask, he handed the vessel to Egg and bade him to drink. Next, he took out a cloth. "Remove your coat."

Amelia walked toward them. "You can't mean to tend the wound here?"

Bowen arched a brow as he looked up at her. "Do you have accommodation nearby?"

"In Burrington, yes. Haven't you?"

"We do not."

"And you say I didn't plan very well," she muttered.

"*I* didn't say that," Bowen protested. "Egg did."

She lifted her gaze heavenward before kneeling next to him and giving his arm a light shove. "Let me."

After a moment's hesitation, he scooted to the side.

"What are you doing?" Egg asked, his voice heavily laced with doubt.

It was hard to see the depth of the wound with his clothing in the way, but the bleeding had slowed to a trickle. "Trying to determine if you require sutures."

"You're skilled with that?"

"I've stitched a few people here and there." Amelia's grandmother had taught her old remedies, and between them, they'd cared for their retainers as well as a few neighbors. She poked at the wound, drawing a sharp hiss from Egg.

"Watch it," he scolded.

She glanced over at Bowen. "You're right. He is an infant." She stood abruptly. "It would be best to clean and dress the wound properly. Burrington isn't far on horseback. I saw your mounts tied near the road." She inclined her head toward where the animals were in plain sight. Her own horse was on the opposite side in a copse, hidden.

"You're offering help?" Bowen asked, his head cast at a skeptical angle. "After you threatened to shoot us?"

"She did more than that," Egg said. "She nearly nicked my ear off."

Amelia winced. "As you said, *nearly*. If I'd wanted to, I would have." She was wholly exaggerating. She'd never meant to shoot at them at all. She'd brought the pistols for defense—she was a fair shot—never imagining she'd encounter someone trying to steal her grandfather's treasure. Panicking, she'd acted out of desperation when she'd pulled a neckerchief over her face and threatened them. Looking back, she felt a burst of pride at her daring, along with a blaze of fear over what she might have done if her aim had been a bit more true. Couple that with the horrifying intentions of the man who'd held a knife to her throat, and she was surprised she wasn't shaking in distress.

Unsettled, she tried to find the bravado she'd shown earlier. "Are you coming or not?" She pivoted toward the road.

"We're coming," Bowen responded. He helped Egg to his feet, then bent to pick up their bags.

Amelia swept up the lantern.

Bowen's gaze conveyed a mix of gratitude and wariness. He retrieved the rope, and they started toward the horses. Amelia stole several glances at him. He bore the dark complexion and accent of a Welshman. His hair was also dark, but his eyes were a striking blue, like the lapis her grandfather had given her on her tenth birthday.

"Today has not gone as I planned," Bowen said. "Beginning with you. How did you know about the dagger?"

She took solace in the irritation buried within his tone, glad to have stopped him from taking her grandfather's dagger, even though it had ultimately been stolen. "My grandfather found it, as he did the heart."

Bowen was quiet for a few steps, then said, "I wonder, did he know they were fraudulent when he found them, or did he believe them to be real? I should like to ask him, if I may."

Amelia ground her teeth to keep her emotions at bay. "You can't. He died this past spring." Despite her efforts, the loss swept through her. She moved faster, hoping Bowen didn't see her disquiet.

Bowen bowed his head. "My condolences. If your grandfather found these items, why is one in the Ashmolean and the other hidden in a cave?"

They'd reached Bowen's and Egg's horses, and Bowen set his items down to help Egg mount.

Amelia put the lantern next to the bags. "If you think I'm going to share information, you are mistaken." Again, she relied on bravado. The truth was she didn't know.

"I see. And here I thought you wanted to be helpful."

"Offering to tend Mr. Howell's arm has nothing to do with sharing secrets." If anything, she felt beholden to Bowen for saving her from certain disaster with that brigand. And if she could glean something helpful into the bargain, so be it. "However, perhaps I ought to demand information from you in exchange for my assistance."

Egg snorted. "I don't want your 'elp, then, especially if you're going to call me 'Mr. 'owell'."

Bowen turned to her once he had Egg situated. "Please call him Egg. I know it seems unlikely, but he *will* be more cantankerous if addressed too formally. Now, what do you want to know?" he asked politely. And perhaps with a bit of challenge.

She stiffened her spine. "Why do you think the heart is fake?"

He bent to pick up their belongings and began tucking them into Egg's saddlebags. The rope and lantern went on Bowen's horse.

He flicked his deep blue gaze toward her while he worked. "As I told you, I'm an experienced antiquary. I work at the Ashmolean where the faux heart is stored."

She clenched her fists and bit back a scathing correction.

He continued, "I've seen a depiction of the heart by a source who would know what it looked like, and the heart in the museum doesn't match."

"In what way?"

Ignoring her question, he glanced about. "Where's your horse? We can continue this conversation as we travel. Egg's wound may no longer be bleeding, but it requires attention."

She didn't disagree. "Across the road." She hurried over the dirt track and mounted her horse with the assistance of a rock. When she met them in the lane, Bowen swept his gaze over her.

"I was going to say I should've offered my help, but it seems you don't need it."

No, she didn't. She'd been managing quite well on her own for some time now. Not alone, precisely, but her grandfather had been ill the last few years, and she'd spent the majority of her time caring for him.

She pushed his attention back to what she wanted to know. "Tell me why you think the heart in the museum isn't the real artifact."

"It's painted, and the rock beneath it isn't tourmaline."

"Why does that prove anything?"

"Because in the picture I've seen, the heart *is* tourmaline. It also isn't gold, and there are no jewels adorning it."

"That's just one depiction. If you're any kind of antiquary at all, you know that stories change over time. The more stories are copied, the more they become legend instead of fact."

"You're correct. However, this particular illustration was made directly from a source that would know what the heart looked like."

She stared at him a moment. "A source from King Arthur's time?" She laughed then, amazed that this man would believe such nonsense. "You're not saying he actually lived?"

Bowen slid her a quick glance from beneath the brim of his dark brown hat. "You're saying he didn't? If you think that, why do you care about any of this?"

"Because it mattered to my grandfather, and I promised him." She wished she hadn't said that. None of this was any of Bowen's affair. Except he'd made it his affair by sticking his nose in it and trying to steal the dagger before she could get to it.

"What did you promise?" he asked softly.

"That I would keep it safe." She wasn't able to keep the dejection from her voice.

"If it makes you feel any better, there's no way you could have retrieved it from the cave. I had to dangle from a rope and cut my hand to bits to get it." He'd donned gloves after she'd left him to retrieve her horse, but her gaze flicked to his hands, recalling his injuries.

She begrudgingly appreciated that he was trying to improve her disposition. "Because the heart my grandfather found doesn't look like the picture you saw, you think it's fake. That's a fairly weak argument for such an *experienced* antiquary."

"I tested its use. It doesn't work. Therefore, it is a counterfeit."

If she'd been walking, she might've tripped. As it was, she gripped the reins a bit too tightly, and her horse sidestepped. Amelia whispered soothing words before darting a look at Bowen. "You did what?"

"You do know what the heart is purported to be?" he asked. The condescension had returned to his tone.

"Of course I do. With the heart in one's possession, the bearer is supposed to be able to make someone fall in love with them. And the dagger was enchanted as a counterbalance, to prevent the spell from working." She was quite familiar with the story, but it was just that: a *story*.

"Exactly right. However, the heart in the museum has no effect."

She laughed loudly. "Of course it doesn't."

He shook his head. "I am bemused by you, Mrs. Forrest. You were intent to find the dagger, and yet you have no regard for it."

"You said it was a treasure," she said. As had her grandfather. She didn't doubt it was an artifact from legend, but again, that was all it was—a legend. "The crown jewels are treasures, but they don't cast spells. I am bemused by *you*, Mr. Bowen. I would think your education and experience would keep you from believing such nonsense."

"I can see why you would think that. However, I know such *nonsense* to be true."

They were nearing the outskirts of Burrington. She slowed her horse and stared at him. "Preposterous. Did you see proof?"

"No, but I trust those who did."

"And what, pray tell, did they see?"

"I don't think we're sharing our secrets today, Mrs.

Forrest. Or so you said." He kicked his horse toward town. Egg gave her a smug look as he rode past.

Stifling a groan, she quickened her pace and led them toward the inn where she was lodging. A dozen questions formed in her mind, followed by a dozen more. How she wished she could talk to her grandfather. She was sure he could answer every one of them. At least he could have before he'd become lost in his mind so much of the time.

A groom met them in the yard of the inn. "Good afternoon, Mrs. Forrest. Did you have a nice ride?" He'd grown used to seeing Amelia dressed in breeches and riding out every morning for the past five days. That first morning, his eyes had widened, but he hadn't said a word. Now he didn't even seem to notice that she was not garbed as she ought to be.

"Yes, thank you." She didn't wish to tell him of the brigands they'd encountered. "I met some friends along the way, and one of them sustained a minor injury that I'd like to tend to. I don't suppose you have additional lodging for them tonight?"

He helped her dismount and took the reins of her horse. "I think the other room is vacant, but ask Mr. Tarleton to be sure, of course." He looked toward Mr. Bowen, who had just climbed to the ground.

"We'll do that, thank you," Bowen said as he helped Egg from his horse.

Amelia preceded them into the dim interior. She glanced back at Bowen, wondering if he'd clear the low ceiling. He had to duck through the doorway but had a few inches between the top of his head and the wood beams that ran the length of the common room at intervals.

Mr. Tarleton, the innkeeper, came from a back room, his ruddy face breaking into a smile. "Ah, Mrs. Forrest. Your maid is on an errand, I believe."

"Thank you, Mr. Tarleton. Allow me to introduce Mr. Bowen and Mr. Howell. They require lodging for tonight."

"The room across from yours is vacant." He looked to Bowen and Egg. "It's a bit smaller but sufficient for the two of you."

"Thank you."

"Would you have warm water brought up to their room? I need to dress a wound on Mr. Howell's arm."

Alarm flashed in the innkeeper's gaze. "Nothing serious, I hope?"

Amelia offered a pleasant smile. "Not at all. Just send up some water and a bit of spare toweling if you have it. Thank you, Mr. Tarleton. While you do that, I'd be happy to show the gentlemen to their room."

"Thank you, ma'am." Mr. Tarleton inclined his head and disappeared from whence he'd come.

Amelia turned to the stairs. "This way." At the top, she led them along the short corridor to the room on the left. Opening the door, she saw that it was indeed smaller. The roof pitched on the front of the inn, causing a lower ceiling and less space. There was one bed and a pallet in the corner. Amelia's room had a larger bed and a smaller bed instead of a pallet, which her maid, Culley, used.

She gestured to the small table near the cold fireplace. "Sit while I fetch my things."

Bowen set down the bags he'd brought up from the horses and moved to the hearth. He leaned his bicep against the mantel and looked at the older man. "Sit, Egg."

Amelia hurried to her chamber and fetched the salve from her bag. Upon her return, she surveyed Egg, sitting rather morosely in the single chair. "Off with your clothing, then."

Penn dropped his arms to his sides. "I beg your pardon?"

"I was talking to Egg," she said, noting the spark of

interest in Bowen's gaze. "I can't very well tend his arm if he doesn't remove his coat and shirt."

"Of course not." Bowen threw his assistant a dark look. "Don't be difficult."

Egg muttered something under his breath that sounded suspiciously like "No more than you can be" and Amelia wondered at the nature of their relationship. They were clearly protective of one another, but she sensed they liked to bicker.

Grumbling, Egg removed his coat, wincing as he eased it from his arm. Amelia offered assistance, peeling it back from his appendage with care. "You'll 'ave to 'elp me with the shirt too, I'm afraid." His expression and tone were more akin to someone who'd had to ask for assistance climbing the gallows.

She gave him a wide smile and was pleased to see it surprised him. "Happy to." Grandmother had always told her to be kinder to the people who were grumpiest, for they needed compassion the most.

He pulled the shirt from his waistband, and she drew the linen over his head. Egg was a mass of compact muscles and hair. So much hair. And all of it gray.

Separating the fabric from his wound proved a bit troublesome and he gritted his teeth as she finally worked it free. "There. That wasn't so bad, was it?" she asked.

He gave her a sour look but said nothing.

"You're being difficult," Bowen said, refolding his arms and glowering at Egg.

"You know it's my way."

"Indeed I do, but you could endeavor to be indifferent if not pleasant. For Mrs. Forrest's sake. She may have tried to shoot you, but she *is* helping you now."

"'Tis the least she can do."

Mr. Tarleton arrived with the water and some toweling.

After they'd assured him they could handle things, he bustled from the room.

Amelia lightly touched the angry flesh around the tear. "A handful of stitches ought to do it. Can you manage, or do you need spirits?"

"Just get it over with," Egg said hoarsely.

"You need whiskey," Bowen said, turning to one of the bags he'd brought up. He thrust his hand inside and produced the same flask from earlier, which he handed to Egg. "Just drink the lot. You'll sleep better."

"Aye, I will." He took a long, deep draught.

Amelia prepared her needle, and Bowen fetched a lantern to provide light. Egg grimaced and let out the occasional hiss as Amelia cleaned the wound and sewed it together. When she was finished, she applied the salve.

"What's that?" Egg asked suspiciously, wrinkling his nose.

"It will stave off infection from the wound." Amelia plucked up some of the toweling provided by Mr. Tarleton and used it as a bandage. "Try to keep it clean," she advised.

Egg rose from the chair, his face gray. "I'm going to lie down."

Bowen tried to help him, but the older man pushed him off. "Leave me be for now." He went to the pallet and practically fell upon it.

Amelia looked at Bowen's injured hand. He'd removed his gloves at some point, and now she could see the damage. "Let me tend to your hand."

With a nod, Bowen gestured to the door.

Amelia put the jar of salve in her pocket and picked up the basin of water. "Will you grab the toweling? I need to go get fresh water." She preceded him from the room and went downstairs to empty and refill the basin. When she climbed back up to her room, she found Bowen sitting at the small table, his hand lying palm down atop the scarred wood.

Amelia set the basin of water down and frowned at the cuts scored into his flesh. They'd stopped bleeding long ago but were caked with black-red blood and grime. "Was the rock made of razor blades?"

"Something like that."

She picked up a scrap of cloth and dipped it into the water. "Where was the dagger?"

"Stashed in a hole. It was a bit above my head, so I had to reach for it, and I couldn't see. The passage was rather narrow at one point—that's where I encountered the razor blades."

Amelia had to admit she couldn't have obtained it on her own, not the way he described the endeavor. Gently, she began to clean his wounds. "How did you know where to find it?"

Her grandfather hadn't given her the specific location—just that it was in a cave near Burrington. He'd been too confused in his last months, and unfortunately, he hadn't told her about it until then. Why had he kept it secret?

Bowen eyed her while she cleaned his hand. He winced as she worked to scrub the last of the blood off. "I'm not inclined to reveal my sources, but in this case, I suppose you deserve to know."

"How magnanimous of you." She immediately regretted the sarcastic comment. "My apologies. I should be grateful to know whatever you care to share." She spread salve over his scrapes and cuts, careful not to cause him discomfort.

"And I am grateful for your ministrations."

"I should also thank you for your assistance with that repulsive brigand earlier."

"Whatever our differences, I would never allow you to be assaulted or degraded." He delivered the statement with a sincerity that made it sound like a vow.

Their eyes met for a moment, and something flashed

between them. Something that made Amelia's belly pitch in a way it hadn't in quite some time. She refocused her attention on his hand.

Bowen cleared his throat. "I work with a gentleman at Oxford—his name is Carlton Burgess."

She paused in reaching for another bandage and blinked at him. "I know him. Not *him*, but his name. My grandfather asked me to write to him after he died." Realization dawned in her mind, and with it came a mix of frustration and sadness. "Grandfather asked me to forward a letter to him." It had been sealed, so she was unaware of the contents, nor had Grandfather revealed them to her.

Bowen had the grace to give her a look of sympathy. "That letter included the location of the dagger."

"That's how you found it."

"It's what I do." He gazed up at her, his blue eyes bright and vivid in the light from the lantern on the table. "I go out and find things of historical importance."

She wrapped the bandage around his hand. "Did my grandfather know that? Did he ask for you to find the dagger?"

"No. He asked Burgess to find it and keep it safe."

That made no sense. "But he asked me to do the same! When did he write that letter? Was there a date?"

His eyes flickered with a bit of surprise. "You're rather astute, aren't you? Burgess and I noticed that detail because it was dated March 1809."

She felt defeated. "So long ago?" She shook her head. "And he never told me about it until just before he died. He was out of his mind by then, really. I wasn't entirely sure I believed there *was* a dagger, but he was so insistent. I had to at least look. I was ready to give up—today was the last day I planned to search the caves."

"It was our luck that you happened upon us?" he asked.

"I'm afraid so." She turned and went to her bed where she perched on the edge.

"And both of our 'luck' that those brigands came along when they did. I wonder how *they* learned of the dagger?"

"I'd like to know that too." She had a suspicion but wasn't sure she wanted to share it with Bowen. They'd reached some sort of truce, but they weren't pursuing the same thing. He wanted to prove the heart was a fake, to discredit something that had defined her grandfather's life. And she wanted to prove the opposite. Yet with each revelation today, she began to doubt her grandfather. If he'd kept the dagger from her for so long, what else hadn't he told her?

"I'd also like to know why they'd steal a fake dagger," she said.

"I think it's likely they don't know it's a fake. As far as I know, I'm the only person who thinks the heart in the Ashmolean isn't the real one. And you're the first person I've told."

She felt a bit of relief. "I appreciate you not publicizing your suspicions until you can prove them."

"It will be hard to do that until I find the real artifacts."

"That's what you intend?"

He nodded as he stood from the chair. "Thank you for seeing to my hand."

She gestured toward the salve on the table. "Take that—for you and Egg."

"Are you sure?"

"I have more at home."

He picked up the bottle and curled his fingers around the glass. "And where is that?"

She narrowed her eyes at him. "I don't think that's something I wish to share with you. I believe our association has reached its natural conclusion."

He took a step toward her, and she came off the bed, a

burst of energy shooting through her. "I don't think so," he said softly, but with distinct intention. "Your grandfather had secrets, and I'd like to help you unravel them."

She scoffed at him. "Only because you think it will help you."

He squared his shoulders, facing her from just a few feet away. "I won't lie to you. Yes, it would help me, I think. I'm going to find the real heart, whether you share information with me or not."

His pledge reminded her that they were at cross-purposes. "You may not lie, but you'll withhold information."

"Not if I think it's important to your safety." Cross-purposes, but in an apparently friendly way—if he were to be trusted, and she wasn't sure that he was.

She folded her arms over her chest. It was the only thing she could do to put something between her and him. She couldn't back up, not with the bed behind her. And why did she want to retreat? There was something predatory about his demeanor, but not threatening. It was…unsettling. But not unpleasant. *Damn.*

She lifted her chin. "You aren't going to find the heart because it's already been found."

He lifted a shoulder, his gaze boring into hers. "Perhaps, and if that's the case, so be it. I can't say I'll mind working with you."

Was that supposed to be a compliment? A flirtation? No, it was an honest statement. She wasn't sure this man flirted. Regardless of what it was, a delicious shiver raced down her spine.

"I haven't agreed to that," she said.

"No, but if you want help finding out what else your grandfather didn't tell you, I'm offering my assistance. Starting with the letter he sent to Burgess. I'll share it with you."

"If I agree to work with you?"

He gave a single, slow nod. "It won't be so bad."

"What do you expect me to do?"

"I'd like access to your grandfather's things—books, letters, anything you may think is important. Or not. Everything, actually."

Reviewing his library and small collection of antiquities was precisely what she intended to do. Which didn't mean she was ready to share them. Maybe she'd find the answers she sought without seeing the letter he'd written to Burgess. "I'll think about it."

The tension in his frame—and there'd been a great deal of it—loosened. But not entirely. His eyes gleamed before he turned from her. "Do that. Good evening, Mrs. Forrest."

When the door closed behind him, Amelia sagged against the bed. What a puzzling, unnerving man.

And attractive.

Shaking that assessment from her treacherous mind, she went to her bag and pulled out her grandfather's journal. She'd brought it with her because it contained a picture of the dagger. She opened to the page and traced her fingers over her grandfather's drawing. He'd written nothing about it save the illustration. It was damnably frustrating.

She flipped a few pages and read the entry she'd committed to memory.

The Order will stop at nothing to find the treasures. Why? They proclaim they are protecting them, but there is something off. If only I'd been able to read the book. I feel certain it would provide the answers I seek.

She'd wondered at what the Order could be, but after today, she thought she knew. Those men could be from the Order, whatever it was. If they wanted the treasures so desperately, it made sense that they would take one at gunpoint.

Did Bowen know anything about this Order? Or the book her grandfather referenced? She'd been on the cusp of asking him, but couldn't bring herself to expose all her secrets. They were engaged in some sort of dance of information.

And maybe something else?

No. They were interested in these artifacts that were important to her grandfather. Nothing more.

Could she bring herself to work with him?

She wasn't sure. Just as she wasn't as sure as she wanted to be that the heart and dagger her grandfather had found were the real artifacts. And that made her angry.

No, for now, she would cling to their authenticity. Penn Bowen was wrong. He was also arrogant and smug.

And attractive.

Stop that!

He was wrong, and that was all that mattered.

CHAPTER 3

*T*ypically up at dawn or shortly after, Penn was surprised to be jolted awake by the sound of movement in the hallway. He'd intended to be waiting downstairs when Mrs. Forrest descended for breakfast, assuming she planned to have breakfast before departing. He wanted to know the results of her deliberations and whether she would agree to give him access to her grandfather's things.

Penn leapt from the bed and hurriedly washed and dressed. Egg was oblivious to Penn's actions—and noise—but then he'd imbibed enough last night to ensure he slept until mid-morning at least.

Rushing down the stairs, Penn came upon Mrs. Forrest seated at the table in the common room. Her green eyes flashed with surprise as they met his.

"Good morning, Mrs. Forrest," he greeted, placing his hand on the chair opposite hers. "Do you mind if I join you for breakfast?"

"I suppose not." Her tone was tinged with regret, and he suspected she'd been hoping they wouldn't cross paths this morning. But then if that had been her intent, why not leave immediately? Again he wondered where she lived. Perhaps she needed sustenance before embarking on a long journey.

He sat down and offered her a pleasant smile. "Do you have a full day of travel ahead?"

She narrowed her eyes briefly but was prevented from answering by the arrival of the innkeeper with a plate of ham, eggs, and some rather scorched toast. Her expression softened into a smile as she looked up at Mr. Tarleton. Penn was unaccountably jealous of the man.

"Thank you. The toast is perfect."

She liked burned toast?

The innkeeper turned a cheerful grin toward Penn. "Can I get you something, Mr. Bowen?"

"The same as Mrs. Forrest, although if you could toast the bread just a bit less, that would be lovely."

"Of course." Mr. Tarleton inclined his head and took himself off.

Mrs. Forrest tucked into her meal without giving Penn a second thought. Perhaps she was in a hurry after all.

"You didn't answer my question." Penn doubted she would, but he had to try. She might think their association was finished, but he was convinced to the contrary. Her grandfather had possessed knowledge of the heart and dagger—even if his artifacts were fake—and Penn meant to obtain it.

She glanced over at him. "No, I didn't."

Penn let out a frustrated breath. "Mrs. Forrest, we can help each other."

She swallowed a bite of eggs and pierced him with a dark stare. "How can you help me?"

"Your grandfather's letter, remember?" Since it seemed that wasn't enough to entice her, Penn pressed forward. "In my field of work, I research, I dig, I find answers. I will help you determine what your grandfather was doing with this fake heart and dagger." He knew that troubled her.

She gritted her teeth. "They aren't fake."

He relaxed back in his chair, confident he'd found a way in. "If you are so confident, don't you want me around so that you can crow that you were right all along?"

She stared at him a moment, her features relaxing—not in the way they'd done with Tarleton, but they lost a bit of their animosity. "I know what you're trying to do."

"Find answers."

She leaned forward, her gaze glued to his. "And if you find the *real* heart"—the disbelief in her tone was palpable—"what will you do with it?"

"Put it in the museum, of course."

"Where the heart my grandfather found currently resides. You'll discredit him."

Penn stifled a scowl. She'd managed that rather neatly. "I will do my best to ensure your grandfather retains *some* credit for the entire affair." Penn had no idea what that would be, but he was certain the man would somehow help them, even from beyond the grave. He'd known enough to find a fake heart and a fake dagger, and the fact that he'd put one in a museum and kept the other hidden was a mystery begging to be solved.

And Penn couldn't resist a mystery.

Playing his trump card, Penn removed a piece of parchment from his coat. "Allow me to prove to you that I'm earnest in discovering the truth—whatever it may be." He unfolded the paper and laid it flat on the table before sliding it over to her.

Her eyes rounded briefly before she snatched up the paper. Now her features betrayed the most vulnerability she'd ever displayed. She held the parchment lovingly, her lips parting as she scanned the letter.

Penn had read it a dozen times. Aside from providing the location of the cave where the dagger was hidden and urging his friend Burgess to keep the artifact safe, it mentioned protecting his family, which at the time had included his son and granddaughter, from the Order. Penn watched her reaction carefully.

She read it a second time, more slowly, her gaze trailing over the paper before she set it back on the table beside her forgotten breakfast. "Thank you. May I keep it?"

"Yes." That was all she had to say?

Picking up her knife and fork, she returned her attention to her plate.

Penn wasn't going to let the matter go. There was too much at stake. "Since you don't seem the least bit inquisitive, I have to assume you know all about this 'Order.' Would you mind enlightening me?"

She gave him a shrewd look. "You're telling me you *don't* know about the Order?"

He'd meant it when he'd said he wouldn't lie to her. Not unless it would keep her safe. And while he'd no reason to trust an organization that prized secrecy and the suppression of knowledge, he didn't think they posed a threat. At least not yet. "I didn't say that. I want to know what you know."

She stared at him a moment, and then the warm lilt of her laughter unexpectedly filled the space around them. "If this is how our partnership would work, I think my reticence was well-founded."

"Does that mean you're considering a partnership?"

"On the contrary. I think this only demonstrates that it wouldn't work—for either of us. Not when we're intent on keeping our guards up."

She had a point. He ought to have just come out and told her what he knew of the bloody Order instead of trying to learn what she knew first. "I am used to dealing with individuals with far less scruples than you. Forgive me for not giving you the benefit of the doubt." He inclined his head. "Let me begin again." He glanced at the letter next to her plate. "Your grandfather mentioned the Order. Are you familiar with that organization?"

She hesitated, and his frustration grew. "A bit," she said at last. "A very *little* bit. I've seen it referenced elsewhere—don't ask me where just yet. I may be *considering* a partnership with you, but that doesn't mean I trust you."

"Of course not," he murmured in a mix of admiration and irritation. "Are you aware the full name is the Order of the Round Table?"

Her gaze flickered with interest. "I am not. The Round Table…as in King Arthur?"

"Yes. The Thirteen Treasures were items gathered by Arthur and his knights for one of their own—Gareth—so that he could win his bride."

"And the heart and the dagger are treasures." She set down her fork, apparently ready to completely abandon her meal. "The heart is anyway. I'm not sure the dagger is considered one of them or if it and the heart constitute one of the thirteen."

"There is some dispute as to what makes up the thirteen, and in some versions, the heart doesn't even exist."

Now she looked truly surprised. "I didn't realize that. I grew up listening to the legend of Ranulf and Hilaria. She used the heart to make Ranulf fall in love with her, but he loved another and didn't wish to fall prey to the heart's spell. So he had a witch enchant a dagger to use against the magic of the heart, thus preventing him from falling in love with Hilaria. The witch's spell is supposedly carved into the dagger. Were you able to read it?"

"I didn't have a chance." Bitterness made the words come

out harder than he'd intended. Softening his response, he said, "You know the story well."

"Well enough to know that Ranulf was an idiot," she said somewhat crossly. "He married the selfish and prideful Maud, while Hilaria married his younger brother, who'd fallen madly in love with her. Hilaria grew to love him too, and they lived happily ever after. Ranulf regretted his choice, as well he should have."

Penn enjoyed watching her animated expression change as she'd relayed the tale. "You're a romantic."

Her brow pleated for a moment. "Not particularly."

He wasn't sure he believed her, but he'd have to take her word for it since he barely knew her. Though he hoped they were rectifying that.

He did?

Did he hope to know her better? Certainly, if it meant gathering information he needed to find the real heart and dagger. As to that—he needed to convince her to accept his partnership, especially if the Order was involved. "The Order's primary objective is to keep the Thirteen Treasures —and really anything to do with them—from being found or publicized. They want them to remain a legend."

"But one of them is in a museum."

He lifted his right shoulder. "Or not."

She rolled her eyes and pursed her lips. "Does the Order agree with that assessment?"

"I can't say for certain—let me be clear: I am *not* a member. Members are, for the most part, descendants of the knights."

"How can that be possible if it's all a legend?"

"The Order wants everyone to *think* it's all a legend. I didn't say they believed that."

Mr. Tarleton returned with Penn's breakfast. Thankfully, the toast wasn't blackened.

After the innkeeper left, Mrs. Forrest shook her head. "That seems ridiculous. What is their reasoning?"

"That the treasures are too powerful, that if they were to be found, they would cause strife and conflict." He sliced off a piece of ham and brought it to his mouth.

"War?" She stared at him a moment, and her shoulder twitched as if she suppressed a shiver. "My grandfather told me once that he gave the heart to the museum because it was far too valuable to keep. He feared someone would steal it."

Penn relaxed slightly. Her sharing such a thing with him was progress.

Her brow furrowed once more and stayed that way as she spoke. "What he said in the letter... Was he afraid of this Order? Do I need to be concerned?"

It was the perfect opportunity to bind her to him, to encourage her reliance, but he'd also said he wouldn't lie. "You do not need to be afraid. Concern, or wariness, is always a good thing. Even if you decide to associate with me."

She gave him a dark but curious stare. "And what do I need to be wary about with you?"

He didn't think she meant any sort of innuendo, but his brain took that route automatically. *Lout.* "I don't plan to steal anything from you. I merely want to share information so that we may get to the heart—pardon the pun—of the matter."

She rolled her eyes again, but this time, the edge of her mouth ticked up with humor. He suppressed a smile before taking another bite of ham.

After he swallowed, he said, "I only meant that being guarded will serve you well. That said, you *can* trust me."

She let out a short laugh. "One of the first things you said to me was that you didn't trust *me*, and now you expect me to trust you?"

He *had* said that, blast. And he'd meant it. Did he trust her now? Not completely. But then the list of those he trusted completely was quite succinct—his parents and his sister. "How about we give it a try?"

There was something about her... Something he wanted to discover. She, like all women, was a mystery. The difference was that he wanted to investigate this one.

She studied him, her eyes narrowing slightly before she answered. "I'll think about it. Where can I find you if I decide I wish to share information?"

Damn. He'd hoped he'd persuaded her completely. "I'll be near Bath at a friend's house." His father's friend, Baron Septon, lived several miles outside Bath. He was a leading antiquary—if not the premier antiquary in all of the United Kingdom.

"Bath?"

Her instantaneous response and the surprise in her reaction provoked him. "Do you live nearby?" He would bet his collection of Roman coins she did.

She hesitated, perhaps debating whether to reveal the truth, but ultimately did so. "Just outside."

His lips curled into an appreciative smile. "How fortuitous. It is all but guaranteed we shall meet again."

A scowl flickered across her features, but she tamped it down. "Nothing is guaranteed, Mr. Bowen. I should think yesterday's events would be a perfect example." She rose from the table, and he jumped to his feet with her. "I'll send word if I wish to speak with you."

"I'll try to be patient." And he'd fail, but he wouldn't tell her that.

"Good day, then." She started toward the door, but turned and said, "I do hope Egg is feeling better today. Make sure he uses the salve." Then she departed the inn, and Penn quashed the urge to watch her leave, or worse, follow her.

There was no need. He knew where to find her. He'd give

her two days. Including today? He forked a bite of eggs without answering himself, thereby giving himself latitude. *Two days.* He could wait that long to continue his quest.

And what if she refused him? What if she never meant to see him again?

Well then his quest would simply become far more challenging, because he planned to win her over.

Penn never surrendered.

∽

*R*eplacing the book upon the shelf, Amelia frowned at her grandfather's library. What had she expected to find? She was familiar with the contents of his bookshelves, and there was precisely one book that contained mention of any of the Thirteen Treasures. It was a compendium of medieval romances her grandfather had transcribed for himself, including the story of Ranulf and Hilaria. Of the treasures, perhaps her grandfather had only cared about the heart and the dagger, which made sense since he'd found them.

Or found fakes.

The doubt Penn Bowen had planted in her mind drew her lips into a grimace. Damn him.

She turned and surveyed her grandfather's small but cozy study. Everything in here was familiar and yet she felt as if she were looking at it all with new eyes. She drifted to the worktable in front of the window where he would lay out his books and antiquities. A handful of ancient iron tools cluttered one corner, while a large piece of chipped pottery sat in another.

How she wished she'd talked to him more about his interests. But she'd been too busy with her own life until coming to live with him five years ago. And then her father had died, which had prompted her grandfather's decline. One thing she *had* learned—life was short, and the time with loved ones even more fleeting.

Which was why she was weary of being a spectator, first with her own matters and then in others. She went to the desk where she'd begun to work in recent weeks and found the last letter she'd received from Lady Spier in Bath. As chair of the Ladies' Antiquities Society, she'd contacted Amelia after her grandfather's death to extend her condolences. And to invite Amelia to their next meeting.

Amelia had sent a thank-you note but declined their invitation. Another invitation had arrived a month later and a third while she'd been in Burrington. It was the third—which she'd read just that morning—that she picked up. Their meeting was today. Amelia could go and find out how they'd known her grandfather and why they'd invited her. Perhaps they could also tell her about Penn Bowen or the mysterious Order. Or both.

Clutching the missive in her hand, she left the office and went in search of Mrs. Talmidge, her housekeeper. Amelia found her dusting in the small sitting room at the front of the cottage.

A motherly woman in her middle fifties with dark gray hair and bright blue eyes, the housekeeper looked up as Amelia entered. "Do you need something, Mrs. Forrest?"

"I should like to go into Bath this afternoon for an appointment. Has Horatio returned from accompanying Mr. Talmidge on his errands?"

"Just a bit ago. I'll let him know to ready the carriage. When do you wish to leave?"

"Within the hour, thank you."

"Dare I hope you're attending a social engagement of some kind?" Mrs. Talmidge's mouth curved into an expectant smile.

"Yes, in fact." Amelia enjoyed a rather close relationship with the staff. They were like family, probably because most of them were. Mrs. Talmidge was married to the caretaker, Mr. Talmidge, and the groom who also served as coachman and footman was their son Horatio. Amelia's maid, Culley, was Mrs. Talmidge's niece. Only the cook, Mrs. Jermyn, wasn't related to the Talmidges, but she and Mrs. Talmidge had worked together since they were fifteen, so they might as well have been sisters.

The housekeeper's smile broadened. "How lovely. I am so glad you aren't spending too much time in mourning. Your grandfather wouldn't want that."

Amelia glanced down at her dove-gray gown, one of only a few she owned that would satisfy mourning costume. She didn't see the point in investing in any. "I'll just get ready. Please let Horatio know I'll be down shortly."

Mrs. Talmidge gave a brief nod before disappearing from the sitting room. Amelia followed her out and went upstairs to prepare for her departure.

Less than an hour later, Horatio steered the coach into Sydney Place. It was a fashionable address, and Amelia had to assume Lady Spier came from wealth. Or had married wealth.

Horatio opened the door and helped her down. Amelia took a deep breath and formulated the questions she wanted to ask. She prided herself on organization and order, which made this mystery surrounding her grandfather and his findings so troubling. It was difficult not to be able to lay her hands on proof that what he'd found was *real*.

As she reached the top step in front of the door, the portal swung open, and a tall stately butler welcomed her inside. "Good afternoon," he intoned, his deep voice carrying through the large marbled foyer.

"Good afternoon." Amelia kept her voice soft, feeling a

trifle intimidated by her formal surroundings. She'd been in elegant settings before, but she came from a simple back-ground. "I'm Mrs. Forrest. I'm here to attend a meeting."

"Of course. Please follow me." He turned on his heel and led her toward the back of the foyer, where he took a sharp right. Pausing at the threshold of a well-appointed sitting room, he said, "Mrs. Forrest has arrived."

Three women were seated, and one of them stood. "Thank you, Blessing."

Blessing? Amelia slid a glance toward the butler as he turned and left.

The woman came forward, drawing Amelia's attention once more. "We are so delighted you've come!" She paused in front of Amelia, her full lips spreading into a welcoming smile and her gray eyes twinkling. Blonde curls framed her face, and Amelia realized they had met before, at some social event within the last few years, though she couldn't place exactly where.

Amelia bobbed a brief curtsey. "Thank you for the kind invitation, Lady Spier."

"Oh, you must call me Andy, which is short for Androm-eda, of course—all my friends do, and I've decided we shall be friends. Come and meet the other members of the Society. Well, the ones who are here. We're missing one, I'm afraid, but she was recently wed, so she has an excuse for her absence."

"An exceedingly poor one, if you ask me," one of the other women said a bit sourly. She was clearly a relative of Andy's, with the same strong chin and similar golden hair, though hers carried a bit of red that gave it a coppery tone. Gold-rimmed spectacles framed her hazel eyes as she looked Amelia over.

"You would say that, committed spinster that you are," the

third woman said softly, but with a warmth that said they regularly spoke to each other in this manner.

Andy laughed. "Forgive my sister, Mrs. Forrest. Selina is quite right about Cassie's spinsterhood. Allow me to present Miss Cassiopeia—Cassie—Whitfield and Mrs. Selina Ashcombe."

"It's a pleasure to make your acquaintance," Amelia said, inclining her head to them.

"We're so glad you've finally come," Mrs. Ashcombe said. "You must call me Selina—I've decided that we'll be friends too."

Amelia didn't remember the last time she'd felt so welcomed. Maybe never.

Cassie narrowed her eyes. "I suppose that means we'll be friends as well, so you should call me Cassie. I daresay you'll like me best." She gave her sister and Selina a superior look that caused them both to laugh.

At that moment, Amelia couldn't imagine liking any of them more than any other. They were, sadly, the first friends she'd made in years and she'd do nothing to alienate any of them. Why had she waited so long to accept their invitation? "I've been in mourning," she blurted.

Andy's forehead creased in sympathy. "Of course. We were so sorry to hear of Mr. Gardiner's passing. He was a revered member of our community."

"He was?"

"At one time," Andy said. "Come and sit. Would you care for tea?"

Amelia nodded as Andy led her to the settee where Selina sat. "Yes, thank you."

Selina set to pouring her a cup and asked if she cared for milk or sugar.

"Just sugar," Amelia said. "I must apologize, but I'm not at all certain what your…organization does or how you know my grandfather."

Andy nodded, her gaze warm with empathy. "I understand he was ill the last few years."

"Yes." Amelia accepted her teacup from Selina and took a small, tentative sip. It was an excellent, aromatic blend, unlike anything she'd ever tasted. "This tea is extraordinary."

"Cassie is very particular about tea. She likes to create her own." Andy, who'd retaken her chair, looked to her sister, who sat in a matching chair adjacent. "Which one is this, dear?"

"I call it sunlight harmony. It has a distinctively summery flavor. Perfect for today."

Indeed it was. The day was bright and warm and beautiful—the best of summer. "It's delicious," Amelia said, taking another sip. "So is this an official meeting?"

"As official as we ever get," Selina said, grinning. "We should explain ourselves." She looked to Andy, who was clearly the leader.

"We are the Ladies' Antiquities Society, dedicated to the discovery and preservation of antiquities." That sounded a bit like the purpose of the Order Penn had told Amelia about. Penn? She really ought to think of him as Mr. Bowen. "We are not to be confused with the London Natural Society of Antiquities."

Cassie snorted. "How could we be? They don't allow women."

"So true," Selina said dispassionately. "But then that's why we started our own group." She gave Amelia a definitive nod. "And ours is better."

Amelia laughed. How could she not? These women were utterly delightful. "Do you actually go out and search for artifacts?" She'd tried and failed. If only she'd met these women before she'd undertaken to find the dagger. Regret curdled in her gut.

"Yes," Andy said. "Generally speaking, we do not possess the smooth hands and manicured nails of a cultured lady. Particularly at this time of year."

Selina nodded in agreement. "We don't care much what other people think. I'm married, Cassie is a spinster—as you know—and Andy is a widow."

What a lovely attitude, and one that Amelia supported. "I am also a widow." More or less. In two years' time, it would be official.

"I lost my husband eight years ago," Andy said. "How long has it been for you?"

"Five." Lost was an apt description in Amelia's case. "And we didn't have any children."

Andy gave her an encouraging smile. "Neither did we. I miss Cecil from time to time, but it's been long enough, and our union was so brief that I don't even think of him every day." Her smiled faded, and she looked around at her friends. "Is that ghastly?"

"Not at all," Amelia said. "I don't think of Thaddeus every day either." And when she did, it was to say "good riddance." "How long has your Society been together?"

"Twelve years," Cassie said. "Andy and I founded it when I was just fifteen and Andy was seventeen."

"And whatever provoked you to do so?" Amelia asked. "Aside from the fact that you couldn't join the London one."

"Why should men have all the fun?" Cassie scoffed. "I've always liked to dig and read and go adventuring. This is why I'm a spinster."

Andy sipped her tea and gave her sister a long-suffering look. "I do believe Amelia comprehends." She turned her attention fully to Amelia. "Now, let us return to your dear grandfather. I was acquainted with him several years ago—

before he stopped going out. I know of his antiquarian pursuits and his achievements. I wondered if you had perhaps inherited his interest?"

She didn't think she had, but after her adventure to Burrington, her mind was changing. "Yes, I think I might have." The words came out slowly, as if she'd just come to that realization. And perhaps she had.

Selina clapped her hands together. "Wonderful!"

Cassie sat forward in her chair and pushed her spectacles up her nose as she studied Amelia with keen interest. "Tell us what you've done."

"Er, done?"

Cassie nodded. "What you've discovered or researched. We write papers and publish them under an alias. We could help you share what you've learned—that is our overarching purpose."

"So they won't know we're women," Selina clarified.

Certain she'd stepped into the deep end of a pond, Amelia tried to find a suitable answer. She settled on the truth. "I haven't discovered or researched anything. I've only come upon this…interest recently. This week, in fact."

Cassie's brightness dimmed just a bit, and she inched back on her chair. "Oh."

Andy rolled her eyes at her sister. "Don't be like that. Amelia has come to us with an interest, and who better to guide her? I know you were hoping she might be able to share stories with you, but—"

"Well, I can share one story," Amelia interjected before she could censor herself. Three pairs of eyes turned toward her expectantly. Perhaps she shouldn't have said anything. Liking these women and wanting friends wasn't the same as trust. She'd trusted too easily once, and it had buried her in trouble. "My grandfather discovered something extraordinary—it's in the Ashmolean Museum."

"The Heart of Llanllwch, yes," Andy said. "We know all about that. It's an astounding achievement. We wondered if he found anything else of note."

Were they pursuing specific information? What if they were somehow linked to the Order? Except their women-only society and disdain for the general antiquary community seemed to infer that they were on their own. She couldn't see an ancient organization like the one Penn had described as something they would be involved with. Still, she should be wary. Hadn't Penn advised her to do just that?

Taking his advice grated, but she had to grudgingly admit he was right.

Andy's eyes widened. "Oh my goodness, you think we're trying to ferret information from you. Please accept my deepest apology. We want nothing of the kind."

"That's not entirely true, sister," Cassie said pertly. "We always want information. However, we want it for the sake of knowledge—nothing more." Cassie smiled at Amelia, which softened her features.

Selina turned toward her on the settee. "We suspect your grandfather also found the dagger, which goes along with the heart. Are you familiar with the tale of Hilaria and Ranulf?"

"Quite." Amelia relaxed slightly. "My grandfather did find the dagger, and I only recently went in search of where he'd hidden it. Unfortunately, someone else found it first and it was stolen."

Three sharp intakes of breath filled the room, followed by a rather unladylike curse from Cassie. "Do you know who it was?" Cassie asked, her eyes narrowed in what seemed to be a mix of anger and determination.

Before Amelia could answer, Blessing returned to the doorway. "You've another visitor, the proxy for your missing member, I believe."

Andy blinked. "Ah yes, I forgot."

"Do you know who found and stole the dagger?" Selina pressed.

Amelia jumped at the opportunity to query them about Penn. "I wanted to ask you about this individual—the one who found the dagger. I suspect he's a well-known individual in antiquarian circles."

Blessing's deep voice sounded from the doorway once more. "Mr. Pennard Bowen."

Amelia turned her head and rose from the settee, aghast. "Him."

CHAPTER 4

*P*enn could scarcely believe his eyes. Standing on the other side of the settee, her eyes wide and her lips slightly parted, was Amelia Forrest. Her blonde hair was dressed with artful curls around her heart-shaped face, and a lace-edged dove-gray gown encased her thoroughly feminine form. How had he *ever* mistaken her for a man?

He executed a deep bow. "Mrs. Forrest." He realized he'd done that wrong. He ought to have bowed first to his hostess, who also outranked everyone else in the room as a dowager viscountess. He corrected his mistake and went to where Andy sat. "Lady Spier."

"Do stop with that nonsense," Andy said, swatting her hand at him. "You're family."

"Family?" Amelia's question rattled the air.

"Not really. His sister is our missing member, so he's *like* family," Selina explained.

"Are you saying *he* stole the dagger?" Cassie asked loudly.

Penn looked at Amelia sharply. "What did you tell them?"

Amelia's shoulders stiffened. "Nothing yet." She clasped

her hands together in front of her waist. "He didn't steal it, but he found it before I could."

"You couldn't have found it on your own," he said.

Cassie scowled at him. "Why, because she's a woman?"

Penn should've expected Cassie's reaction—he'd walked right into it. "Because she was ill-equipped and yes, because she's a woman. I had to dangle from a rope and cut my hand to ribbons to reach it." He held up his gloved hand, which had hurt quite a bit yesterday but had drastically improved once he'd applied Amelia's salve regularly. Between him and Egg, they were nearly out of the stuff. His hope that she might provide more began to wither beneath her so-far frosty reception.

Cassie snorted again. "Let the record show that I didn't agree with including him as proxy."

Andy threw her sister an overly patient stare tinged with annoyance. "Cate said he had important news to share."

"Important to whom?" Cassie grumbled.

"You were right," Amelia said to Cassie. "I do like you best."

Cassie immediately brightened and adjusted her spectacles as she sat a bit taller.

And now Amelia was aligned with the man-hating termagant. Wonderful.

"What news are you sharing?" Amelia asked.

Penn looked around the room. "Is the meeting in session, then? Did you start without me?"

"I'd forgotten you were coming, actually," Andy said. "I do apologize. But no, we hadn't officially started. We were just getting to know Mrs. Forrest."

"You must call me Amelia," she said.

Penn wanted to thaw the air between them. He took a step toward her. "Does that include me?"

She narrowed her eyes at him. "It does not."

"Pity," he murmured.

Andy waved Penn toward the settee. "Do sit."

"Yes, there's plenty of room," Selina said, scooting to the farthest side of the settee. That left the rest of it for Amelia and Penn. To sit next to each other. She looked around, seeming to assess her options. He was certain she was contemplating dragging another chair over to avoid sitting beside him.

Penn moved forward and stopped near her. "I won't bite," he whispered. "Unless you want me to."

"Stop it," she hissed. She motioned for him to move past her and sit in the middle.

Penn waited for her to sit, and when she did, noted that she sat as close to the end as physically possible.

"Perhaps you wouldn't mind starting at the beginning," Andy said, looking between Amelia and Penn.

"Certainly," Penn began.

Cassie flashed him a perturbed glare. "Let Amelia speak first."

Penn briefly dropped his gaze to the floor. "Of course." He turned to face her, wondering what she'd already told them.

She kept her gaze fixed on the sisters. "I went in search of the dagger my grandfather hid. Before he died, he asked me to find it. Unfortunately, he gave me an imprecise location. I looked for a few days but found nothing until I happened upon Mr. Bowen after *he'd* found it."

Cassie pinned her shrewd gaze on him. "And how did *you* find it?"

"I had *precise* directions. Provided by Mr. Gardiner—Mrs. Forrest's grandfather."

"You had more information than his relative?" Cassie asked incredulously. "That hardly seems fair."

"It seems my grandfather drafted a letter several years ago to a friend of his at Oxford. Since then, his health declined so much that I daresay he may not have remembered the dagger's location. In hindsight, it's a good thing he sent that letter."

Penn was a bit startled by her attitude—and impressed. He'd taken her to be in possession of good sense, and he was pleased to see this verified. He gave her an encouraging smile even though she wasn't looking at him.

"So you were able to go right to the dagger?" Andy asked. At his answering nod, she continued, "Then it was stolen."

Penn leaned closer to Amelia and spoke in low tones. "Are we disclosing the entire story, including the bit where you tried to shoot Egg's ear off?"

She turned toward him then, and the brilliant green of her eyes made his breath catch. There was a fire in the depths, and the word the stone had always brought to his mind simmered there now: *passion*.

"I suppose we must," she murmured before turning her attention to the women. "In my search for the dagger, I happened upon Mr. Bowen and his assistant, Egg. I tried to recover my grandfather's property."

"Don't leave out the part about being dressed in men's clothing," Penn offered.

She gave him a droll look. "I was confident you'd mention it."

Selina laughed. "How splendid. You simply *must* join our Society." She looked over at the sisters. "Assuming you both agree."

"I do," Andy said, her eyes glowing with mirth. "How did you try to recover the property?"

"With my pistols," Amelia said. "Unfortunately, they didn't take me seriously, and I was forced to shoot at Egg."

"She barely missed him." Penn held up his hands to show a scant few inches between them. "But she did make it up to us by tending our wounds. It happens that Mrs. Forrest is a skilled nurse in addition to her other...talents." He felt he'd just barely uncovered what those might be and longed to peel back the layers of the secretive lady.

"Amazing," Andy said. "She should be a member, don't you think?" She turned to her sister.

"Since she says she's interested in continuing her grandfather's pursuits, I would agree." Cassie seemed far less enthusiastic than the others, but that was merely her demeanor. Penn had known these women for several years, since they'd invited his younger sister Cate to join their ranks. They were smart, curious, devoted to antiquities, and fiercely loyal. On occasion, he'd wished he could be a member too. They were a far less stuffy and self-important organization than the London Natural Society of Antiquities, of which he *was* a member. What he wasn't a member of—and neither were any of these ladies, as far as he knew—was the Order of the Round Table.

Penn picked up the thread of their tale. "Before we could resolve the issue of the dagger's ownership, we were accosted by brigands. Four men of varying...er, charm."

Amelia turned her head sharply, and he heard her swift intake of breath. "Not one of them possessed an ounce of *that*."

"You are correct. I misspoke. I only meant to relay that at least one seemed of a higher class than the others."

"Have you any idea who they were?" Selina asked.

"The Order," Cassie spat. "I'd stake my copy of Caxton's first edition of the *Canterbury Tales*."

Penn let out a low whistle. "That's quite a wager. My father doesn't even have a first edition."

Cassie's generous mouth spread into a smug smile. "I know."

It was hard not to laugh at Cassie's reaction. She did pride herself on her small but spectacular collection of rare books and antiquities, as well she should.

"I think I have a copy of that already," Amelia said slowly, drawing every head in the room to turn toward her. "And a second edition—with the woodcut illustrations."

Andy sat forward in her chair, her gaze keen with interest. "What else is in your library?"

"A variety of things. I'd be happy to have you come look at it some time. If that's what you...do in this...club."

Andy gave her a warm smile. "We most certainly do, and we'd be delighted. Now, no one need give up their rare books on account of the blasted Order. Penn, do you think it was them?"

"It seems likely. Unfortunately, I can't ask Septon because he's traveling at present." Penn had arrived at Septon House late yesterday to find that he wasn't at home. It was frustrating not to be able to ask him about the dagger and Jonathan Gardiner, yet convenient since Penn would be able to search for information without Septon peering over his shoulder. He planned to do just that later, but first he'd wanted to come to this meeting on the off chance they might know of a Mrs. Amelia Forrest or at least Jonathan Gardiner. Instead, he'd been far luckier and found her here in the flesh.

"Septon?" All three of the members of the Society said his name in near unison.

"He *is* a member of the Order! I knew it." Cassie's voice was triumphant as she shared satisfied looks with her sister and Selina.

Penn held up his hand. "Let us pause a moment. How much do you know about the Order?"

"Only what Cate told us in a letter," Andy said.

"She sent you something in *writing* about them?" He swallowed a curse. He'd talk to his sister when she was back from her wedding trip to Cornwall.

"Don't be angry with her. She wanted to warn us about this secret group. She didn't confirm Septon's membership, but you just did. We have long suspected there was more to him than simply a passion for antiquities. Since you opened the door, you may as well tell us what you know."

"I'd intended to." He explained the group to them, detailing what he'd laid out to Amelia the day before.

"Knights of the bloody Round Table," Selina muttered. She pinned Penn with a skeptical stare. "Cate has persuaded Andy and Cassie that these Thirteen Treasures are real, but I'm not certain I believe that." She waved her hand. "I know about the heart in the museum, but it can't possibly be used to make someone fall in love."

"I thought that once too, but they are real—everything about them is real." He looked at each member of the Society before continuing. "This is what my sister wanted me to share with you. She found Dyrnwyn."

"Of course she did." Cassie's tone rang with pride once more, but this time for her friend.

"And is the sword magical?" Andy seemed to hold her breath.

Penn was sorry Cate wasn't here in person, but she'd been adamant that he tell them. She hadn't wanted to make them wait. "Cate said it burst into blue flame when our cousin picked it up."

"Kersey?" Cassie asked sharply. "Doesn't that mean he's a descendant of one of the knights?"

"Of Gareth, yes."

"How extraordinary," Andy breathed, sitting back in her chair, her expression turning contemplative.

"Cate saw this?" Selina asked.

Penn nodded. "And you trust her as much as I do."

"Perhaps more," Selina said softly.

Penn smiled as he gave her a pointed stare. "That, I'm

afraid, is impossible." The bond he shared with his sister, despite the fact that they shared no blood, was unique and unbreakable.

Selina inclined her head. "So the heart may actually provoke someone into falling in love?"

Penn looked sideways at Amelia, expecting to find her watching him. He wasn't disappointed. She wanted to know if he would tell them he suspected the heart in the museum was a fake. He wouldn't. Not until he found the real one and could prove it. "Yes, it likely does do that."

"Which means the dagger would prevent the spell from working," Cassie said. She looked at Amelia. "Why would your grandfather put the heart in the Ashmolean but hide the dagger?

"That is a question I can't answer, unfortunately." The note of disappointment in Amelia's voice pulled at Penn. He knew what it was like to have questions that you could never answer. Questions that ate at you and kept you up at night.

"What a shame." Selina peered around Penn at Amelia with a comforting gaze.

"What about the person he wrote that letter to?" Andy asked. "Would he—or she—know more about your grandfather's intentions or thought processes?"

That was an excellent notion and one Penn ought to have thought of. He turned to Amelia. "We can speak with Burgess, if you'd like."

"I *would* like that, thank you."

"What of Septon?" Cassie asked. "He has to know something, particularly about the theft of the dagger. Do you think you can get it back?"

"I hope so." Insofar as it could possibly help them find the real heart and dagger—*that* was what Penn was in pursuit of. He also supposed he wanted to get it back for Amelia. Fake or not, it had belonged to her grandfather, and she wanted it.

Yes, he'd get it back for her. He gave her a look that held a silent promise. "We'll find it."

She blinked at him. "We'll?"

It seemed she still hadn't decided they should work together. Dammit, what else did she need to know to accept that he could be trusted?

Penn glanced around at the other women. "Perhaps you could tell Mrs. Forrest that I am both trustworthy and loyal."

"It's true," Cassie said. "As far as men go, he is one of the —*few*—good ones."

"I would trust him with my life," Andy said. "His sister is our dearest friend, and we've known them for years. In the antiquarian community, Penn is greatly admired."

"I appreciate your votes of confidence; however, there are things you don't know." She paused, perhaps weighing whether to tell them the rest. "He believes the heart in the museum is a fake. He seeks to discredit my grandfather. While it may seem reasonable for us to align our efforts to find the dagger, we are at cross-purposes."

"Oh dear," Selina said.

"I see," came Andy's response.

Cassie shrugged. "Then it probably is a fake. I highly doubt Penn means to discredit your grandfather; however, the truth must out." Amelia pursed her lips, and Cassie added, "And now you won't like me best anymore." She sighed.

"On the contrary, I value your candor," Amelia said. "You will understand when I say that I must still decide for myself."

"Of course," Andy said hastily. "And please allow us to assist you in any way that we can. Indeed, how can we help?"

Amelia stood, surprising everyone, and Penn jumped to his feet beside her. "I think I've learned all I can for today," she said. "I look forward to you coming for a visit to survey my grandfather's library and antiquities collection, small though it may be."

"Size doesn't matter," Cassie said, completely missing the subtle, humor-filled look her sister and Selina exchanged.

Amelia coughed. "Yes, well, thank you for the tea and your kind invitation."

"I'll walk you out," Penn offered. He was encouraged when she said nothing and simply strode toward the door.

Everyone said good-bye, and Penn trailed Amelia from the town house. She descended the stairs and walked straight to her coach, where her coachman waited.

Penn touched her elbow to stop her from leaving. "Amelia —*Mrs. Forrest.*"

She swung around. "You are too familiar, sir."

"Haven't we moved past all this?" He didn't bother keeping the exasperation from his voice. "So our goals aren't exactly aligned. I am not going to humiliate your grandfather. Perhaps we'll find that he knew the heart was a fake. Perhaps he hid the real heart somewhere. Who knows what we'll find, but we have to at least look."

"Actually, we don't—at least not for the heart. The dagger is another matter. Will you really help me find it?"

He rested his hand over his heart. "With my dying breath."

She rolled her eyes. "There's no need to be melodramatic."

"Perhaps not, but it seems a little levity might be in order." He moved closer and looked into her eyes. "I am not your enemy."

"Neither are you my friend," she said softly.

"I'd like to be. Let me demonstrate my earnestness in helping you. Yesterday, I gave you the letter. Today, I invite you to dine with me tonight at Septon House, where, together, we can search for clues about the heart and dagger."

Her eyes flickered with surprise before darkening. "This sounds a bit scandalous."

"It's only dinner."

"And sleuthing."

He grinned. "And sleuthing."

"All right."

Had she just agreed? He wouldn't ask for confirmation, lest she change her mind. "Septon House is an hour away, near Bradford on Avon. If you like, you can spend the night as well."

Her blonde brows arched high enough on her forehead he feared they might fly away. "That is more than a *bit* scandalous."

"Only if we allow it." He shouldn't have said it, but he couldn't help himself.

"You're flirting." Her eyes narrowed. "You must stop. We have a tenuous affiliation and nothing more. Do not make me regret it."

He held up his hands in surrender. "I promise I won't."

She climbed into her coach then, and the coachman closed the door behind her.

Penn watched as they drove away. He'd never looked forward to a dinner more.

~

*A*s her coach pulled into the drive leading to Septon House, Amelia wondered for the hundredth time if she hadn't made a mistake. Because she and Penn *were* at cross-purposes. Because she was going to the home of a man who belonged to this mysterious and perhaps dangerous Order. Because she and Penn would be *alone*.

And she'd packed a bag since it looked as though it might

rain. She didn't want to get stuck in bad weather late at night.

She reminded herself—also for the hundredth time—that Andy, Cassie, and Selina had made a point of praising Penn. She'd gone to their meeting to see if they knew him, and if so, if he could be trusted. She had her answer. At least according to them.

If she were honest with herself, and she really tried to be after what she'd endured, she had to admit he'd demonstrated a keen interest in proving his helpfulness and trustworthiness. He had given her Grandfather's letter, and he'd invited her here tonight. Hopefully, it would be worth her time and effort.

The coach came to a stop, and her maid jolted instantly awake. She rubbed a hand over one eye and blinked. "We're here?"

"Yes."

"Sorry, didn't mean to fall asleep." Culley gave Amelia a sheepish smile.

"Don't apologize. It's a perfectly good time to nap."

The door opened, and Horatio helped Amelia step down into the graveled drive. A fat drop of rain landed on her sleeve, causing her to hurry toward the door. The butler welcomed her inside.

"Good evening, Mrs. Forrest. I trust you had a pleasant journey. I can show you to your room, or if you'd like to join Mr. Bowen in the library, I can show you there instead."

She was anxious to see if her trip had been in vain. "I'll join Mr. Bowen, thank you, and you can show my maid, Culley, to my room."

Culley had come in behind her and now rushed forward to help remove Amelia's pelisse. She also took Amelia's hat and gloves before the butler motioned for a footman to show her upstairs. The butler then bowed to Amelia. "If you'll just follow me."

She trailed him through the entry hall and into perhaps the grandest room she'd ever seen. The large, elegant drawing room contained many antiquities: tapestries, pottery, weapons, and probably many other things she didn't have time to see.

They moved into an even larger room with wide windows on the opposite side. Bookshelves lined the massive space, and Penn stood on a ladder halfway up one wall, his arm extended as he reached for a book.

"Mrs. Forrest has arrived."

Penn turned his head and smiled. "Excellent, thank you, Peverell. Do let us know when dinner is served."

The butler bowed before taking himself off, leaving them precisely as Amelia had both expected and feared: alone. Why was she afraid? Because he flirted with her. No, because she *liked* it.

Penn clutched the book in his hand and made his way down the ladder. "I'm so glad you came." He strode toward her but stopped at a respectable distance. His expression darkened. "Is something amiss?"

"Nothing you aren't already aware of. I'm doing my best to put aside our initial meeting—and the fact that you want to defame my grandfather."

"I want to do no such thing. Anyway, if I can overlook your trying to shoot me, surely you can move past any reservations you may have about me. Especially after meeting with the Ladies' Society today."

He made a valid point. "Clearly, I am trying to do that; otherwise, I wouldn't have come," she said. In an effort to change the topic, she looked around the library. "This is quite a collection."

He followed her gaze. "It is. My father is a renowned

medieval scholar who collects and translates rare books, but even his library isn't this large."

Amelia walked toward one of the walls of books. "How old is Septon that he's accumulated such a huge collection?"

"He's in his late fifties, but he inherited a large portion of this from someone he knew at Oxford."

She turned to look at Penn. "Not a relative?"

"No, a friend."

"How generous." She finished her stroll to the bookshelf and walked along it until she reached a cavernous fireplace where a low fire burned.

Penn followed her. "It's my understanding the man had no heirs, and he knew Septon would value it as much as he did—if not more."

She turned to face Penn. "Do you know if this man was a member of the Order?"

"I don't, but I've wondered. The members are either descendants of the knights, or, as in Septon's case, they are scholars with an exceptional knowledge and understanding of Arthurian lore. I know this man—Pritchard—was a mentor to Septon. It's possible he recruited him into the Order."

Amelia shook her head as if that might somehow sort all the new information invading her brain since she'd met Penn Bowen two days ago. Had it just been two days? Everything seemed so different. She could measure time before encountering him and after. Put like that, their meeting seemed a significant event.

"This is all so much…bigger than I realized," she said. "To think that my grandfather was somehow involved with this secret group is difficult for me to comprehend. His was a gentle, peaceful soul. He always seemed quite content with his books, his herb garden, and his family." Her happiness and that of her father had been supremely important to him.

"We've no confirmation that your grandfather was involved with the Order at all."

It was time to share at least some of what she knew with Penn. "I don't know whether he was involved, but he was aware of them."

Penn took a step toward her, his eyes widening. "In what way?"

She nodded. "He had a journal—I've brought it with me—and there's one entry that mentions the Order." She recited it from memory:

The Order will stop at nothing to find the treasures. Why? They proclaim they are protecting them, but there is something off. If only I'd been able to read the book. I feel certain it would provide the answers I seek.

"So that is why you didn't seem surprised when I brought it up. What book is he referring to?"

"That I don't know." And the more she thought about it and tried to determine what it might be, the more she was convinced it was important. "It's a mystery we'll need to solve."

He took another step toward her so that they were barely two feet apart. "*We.* I like the sound of that."

There he went, flirting again, or at least infusing his words with heat and the hint of innuendo. And there went her body responding—a warmth building in her chest and a pleasure suffusing her limbs. It had been so long since a man had paid her attention. It was only natural she would feel flattered. It meant nothing.

She put her mind to the matter at hand. "I searched my grandfather's library when I arrived home from Burrington, but nothing stood out to me. There's nothing to do with the Thirteen Treasures at all, save a collection of medieval romances he transcribed, including Ranulf and Hilaria."

"Did you also bring that by any chance?"

"I did."

His gaze sparked with admiration. "You are going to be quite good at this. Hunting for antiquities, I mean."

"Is that what we're doing?"

He lifted a shoulder. "*I* am. I'm looking for the Heart of Llanllwch."

She narrowed her eyes at him and clasped her hands. "Well, *I* am keeping an eye on you and will gleefully say, 'I told you my grandfather's was real,' when you fail to find it."

"I almost look forward to that," he murmured.

Straightening her shoulders and stiffening her resolve against the onslaught of his magnetism, she moved to a glass-fronted case which held several artifacts—pottery, jewelry, a very old-looking manuscript with faded color illustrations that must have been strikingly beautiful when it was first produced. "There are so many books. How can we ever hope to find the book my grandfather wrote about in his journal?"

"If you wouldn't mind allowing me to read it, I might be able to find some clues that weren't noticeable to you."

She didn't take offense because he was far more knowledgeable than she. "I wouldn't mind. Would you like to read it now? If you find something, we could discuss it at dinner."

He gave her a slightly sheepish smile that was quite endearing. "I was hoping you would say something like that. I'm a fast reader, so unless it's a multi-volume saga, I should be able to complete it quickly. I can ask the staff to hold dinner for a bit."

"That would be fine. I'd like to go upstairs for a respite. I'll have the journal—and it is just one, slender book—sent to your room."

"Excellent."

She nodded and began to pivot when he stopped her. "I'm quite glad you're here, Mrs. Forrest. I do believe this will be the start of a wonderful adventure."

She peered at him, honestly curious, but also a bit in awe. "Is that what all this is to you—an adventure?"

"Of course. All of life is an adventure. I wouldn't have it any other way."

She'd never thought of it like that. She supposed she'd had her fair share of "adventure," if one wanted to think of some of the mishaps that had befallen her that way. In fact, it sounded far more palatable. So much so that she decided right then to adopt that notion. From now on, she was on an adventure, and she meant to make it grand.

She allowed a small smile to curl her lips. "See you at dinner."

CHAPTER 5

*A*fter pushing dinner back an hour, Penn had furiously read through Jonathan Gardiner's journal. He could see why Amelia thought there was nothing informative inside, but one thing in particular stood out to him, and he looked forward to discussing it with her.

He met her at the top of the stairs and was once again struck at how he ever could have mistaken her for a man. She wore a dark green evening gown with black trim that draped her quite feminine frame to perfection.

"Good evening, Mrs. Forrest. You look stunning."

"You shouldn't say such things. But thank you." Her gaze trailed over him, and while she didn't repay his compliment, he caught a flicker of appreciation.

"I only speak the truth. May I escort you to dinner?" He offered her his arm.

She curled her bare hand around his sleeve. "I didn't see the point in wearing gloves."

"Me neither."

As they started down the stairs, she launched right into

what he most wanted to discuss. "Did you manage to read all of the journal?"

"I did." It chronicled several years from his time at Oxford as a young man to when he settled on his farm and started his family. Penn wondered if there were more volumes. "Is this his only journal?"

"No, but it's the only one that contains anything to do with the treasures," she said. "There does seem to be a gap, however."

"Years when he didn't keep a journal?"

She nodded as they reached the bottom of the staircase. "Starting in 1777—when my father went to Oxford. The next journal picks up in 1780."

Penn wasn't sure what that meant, but they had to treat it as important. "If it's not in his library—and I'm assuming you've looked extensively—where could it be?"

"I've no idea, which is quite frustrating."

"Mmm, yes. Well, we'll keep it in mind. I wanted to ask you about something in the journal I read. Your grandfather writes about his studies at Oxford. He traveled to Wynnstay in Wales."

"Yes, I recall him telling me about that. He went to see the gardens. They were designed by Capability Brown."

"Are you certain that was the reason he went?"

They moved into the breakfast room, and she withdrew her hand from his arm, turning to face him. "He told me so. Are you saying—again—that he's lying?"

He reacted to the note of irritation in her voice. "No, no. I only meant to make absolutely sure. Wynnstay boasts an extensive library, much of which was once owned by William Maurice. He was a collector and antiquary."

Her lips parted in surprise. "You think my grandfather went there to conduct research."

"Perhaps. I find it rather coincidental. And I always investigate coincidences." He moved to the small table. "I hope you don't mind dining here. It seemed silly to use the formal dining room for just the pair of us." He held her chair in invitation.

"I don't mind at all." She took her seat, and the footman poured wine for both of them. "Do we need to go to Wynnstay?"

Penn sat but didn't immediately answer. He waited until the footman departed. "Forgive me, but I wish to conduct our discussions out of earshot of the staff. I wouldn't want them reporting what they've heard to Septon."

She gave him a shrewd look. "You're rather suspicious. I like that."

Penn didn't try to contain his laughter. "Do you? I'll keep that in mind. To answer your question, no, we don't need to go to Wynnstay. At least, not yet. I'm trying to recall what is in their library."

She stared at him. "You know the contents of their library?"

"Some of it. Remember, my father is an expert on rare and ancient texts. I know far more about books and libraries than anyone would probably care to."

"*I'd* care to. I find all this fascinating."

"Do you?"

They were interrupted by the arrival of the footman with the first course. After serving the soup, he took himself off once more.

Penn studied her as they ate. She was a remarkable woman, unlike most he encountered. Oh, there was no shortage of women who wanted to spend time with him, but those who actually shared his interests were few and far between. "What is it that fascinates you?" he asked.

She thought for a moment before answering. "The mystery, I suppose. And learning new things. I always thought it would be marvelous to go to university. My father and grandfather loved studying at Oxford."

"Did you attend a school?"

"Not formally. My father and grandfather took a hand in educating me. I'm afraid you'll find me more bookish than most females."

"How utterly charming," he murmured while a smile curved his lips.

A faint blush stained her cheeks, and she directed her attention to her soup.

"Your grandfather didn't share his love of antiquities with you? Or is it just that he didn't share information about his discoveries of the heart and dagger?"

"He did share them with me, but I was more passionate about botany and medicine."

"Such as the salve you gave us. You specialize in such things?"

"Yes, I suppose I do." She set her spoon down. "I keep meaning to ask how Egg is faring."

"He's as cantankerous as ever, which means he's just fine."

"Where is he now?"

"Visiting his sister. When I come to Septon House, he always swings a bit south to check in on her. He'll join me in a day or two unless I send for him sooner."

"How did he come to work for you?"

Penn swallowed the last of his soup as he nodded and set his spoon beside his bowl. "We met at a pub in Oxford and became friends, if you can imagine. He worked as a cabinet-maker, and when I went on my first excursion in search of an artifact, I needed someone to act as groom. He was agile and wiry and slightly better tempered than he is now. He's worked for me ever since. I suppose he's a sort of valet too."

She laughed softly. "Now, that I have trouble imagining."

Penn grinned. "He hates it when I call him that."

The footman came back and removed the first course, then replaced it with the second—lamb chops with peas and potatoes.

Once the footman had gone again, Amelia asked, "Is there something of import in the Wynnstay library? Something my grandfather would have been interested in?" She cut into her lamb.

Penn spared some attention for his meal but found he was far more interested in conversing with his lovely companion. "Probably a great many things, but we are, of course, focused on the heart and the dagger—the tale of Hilaria and Ranulf."

"Aren't there other tales involving the heart and dagger?"

"Actually it's the only one that contains the dagger and the legend behind it." As he chewed a bite of lamb, he pondered the story's origin.

"You look very serious all of a sudden," Amelia said, drawing his attention.

He sipped his wine. "I was just trying to think of where the story came from—the first time it was recorded. Many old texts were written down by monks and then copied by other monks—and sometimes antiquaries."

"When was this story recorded?"

"I'm not entirely sure. My father would know." He searched his memory but came up blank and frustrated.

"Should we go back to the library and see what we can find? Surely Lord Septon has something that would at least spur your memory."

"Actually, what we should do is go to his secret library upstairs."

She paused in eating, a spoonful of peas arrested on the way to her mouth. "*Secret* library? And you have access to this?"

"I know where he keeps a key." He was suddenly impatient to be done with dinner.

She finished swallowing and dabbed at her mouth with her napkin. "Would it be terribly rude if I asked if we could go now?"

His admiration for her grew. "Not at all. In fact, I was hoping you would say that." He stood from the table and held her chair while she got to her feet.

As they were about to depart, the footman entered, his brow arched in silent question.

"We weren't terribly hungry," Penn said. "But it was delicious, thank you."

He escorted her from the room and started quickly toward the stairs. She kept up, and when they reached the first step said, "You are far less formal when you're in a hurry."

He winced, realizing he hadn't offered her his arm. "I spend a great deal of time away from polite society. It's not a fair excuse, just an explanation. My apologies." He presented his arm.

She laughed softly, the sound tickling the hairs along the back of his neck. "It's not necessary. I was merely making an observation. Please, let us continue." She started up the stairs without taking his arm. He couldn't decide if he was disappointed or appreciative.

At the top, she looked at him. "Now where?"

"This way." He led her to the left along the gallery to a branch of corridors. They continued along until he turned to the right. At last, he held open the door to a small office. Light from a sconce in the hallway filtered into the room, but Penn would need to light a candle or a lantern. "Septon has a larger office downstairs, but he uses this one for more private discussions and research." He went to the desk and found a lantern, which he lit with alacrity. The room illuminated, and he saw Amelia standing just inside, her gaze sweeping the chamber with interest.

"This is his secret library?" she asked.

"No, I need the key for that." He went to the desk and reached beneath it for the hidden button. Finding the small depression, he pressed, and a slender compartment opened from the underside. Inside the velvet-lined drawer lay a key. Grasping it between his fingers, he withdrew the brass implement and moved out from behind the desk.

"Where is it?" She turned back toward the door.

"This way." He strode to a large painting painted in the last century featuring a man surrounded by his hounds. He found the keyhole—hidden in one of the dog's eyes—and slid the key inside. Feeling the mechanism click, he withdrew the key, then gently pushed on the frame.

"It's *here?*" Amelia had come up behind him. "How clever. Or suspicious."

Penn laughed. "I'm sure it's a bit of both. Septon guards his secrets quite closely." And those of the Order. Penn still had to work out how to take the dagger back from them. Though it was fake, he'd promised Amelia he'd get it back for her, and he meant to do so.

The secret library was little more than a closet. There was no window, and it was dark save for the light from the office behind them. "We need the lantern." Penn quickly returned to the desk and fetched the light. Bringing it back into the library, he set it on a locked trunk that also served as a table.

She gestured to the trunk. "What's in there?"

"I don't know, actually. Septon invited me into this library for the first time just after I started at Oxford. A few years later, he showed me where the key was kept and invited me to use it for research, while also swearing me to secrecy." He hadn't even told his sister, though she'd learned of it herself. Septon hadn't been so generous with his knowledge with her, nor had he invited her to make use of it. They'd discussed this when he'd seen her last, and Penn regretted that he'd kept it from her. He'd told Septon to stop treating her as if she wasn't as smart or committed to antiquities as they were. Since she'd found the lost sword called Dyrnwyn, Septon had finally—and thankfully with enthusiasm—agreed. He drew his attention back to the present. "He's never showed me the contents of the trunk."

She peered at him. "Doesn't that make you especially curious?"

"Of course, but I've been unsuccessful in trying to open it."

"You've tried?" She shook her head. "Of course you have." She looked around the small space. "What are we looking for?"

"Anything to do with the Thirteen Treasures." He went to one of the shelves and pulled down a book from the midsixteenth century that was in remarkably good condition. "This was copied from the Red Book of Hergest. It's not the entire contents, but much of it. I recall that it contains Arthurian romances."

She stood close to him—there was no other choice in the tight space. "They're all love stories? I didn't realize that."

"Oh no, that definition is more recent. The term romance is used in this way to specifically describe a story that recounts the adventures of a knight—it comes from France in the twelfth century, I believe." He suddenly recalled that Septon kept a list of Arthurian romances and where they originated. He turned and went to a different shelf, his gaze traveling over the spines until he found what he sought. It was a slender volume with black binding, if he remembered correctly.

Seeing one that matched that description, he pulled it

down and flipped it open. But it wasn't the right book. Stashing it back on the shelf, he continued his search.

"What are you looking for now?"

"A list of Arthurian romances." Another thin black book drew his attention. He pulled that down and, when he peeked inside, smiled. "This is it." He went back to the trunk and, seeing the other text, handed the black book to Amelia. "Hold this." After he returned the sixteenth-century book to the shelf, he took the list and opened it atop the trunk.

She moved very close to him so that their sides touched. "I can't understand some of this."

"It's Welsh, some of it quite old. Septon is a stickler for using the original name of a text, even if it's been translated into English, but see, he also lists the other names it might be known by." Penn pointed to one particular entry, his fingertip barely touching the parchment, which had the Old Welsh name followed by medieval Welsh, French, and English. "And this is the text where it originated." Penn moved his finger across the page to the name of the book.

"And this is who wrote it?" She pointed at where it said "By" followed by a Welsh name.

Their fingertips collided, and they both looked at each other sharply, as if a magnet had drawn their gazes to connect. The moment held, and ultimately, Penn forced out a "Yes." He was unaccountably warm all of a sudden.

They returned their attention to the list, both withdrawing their hands to their sides. It wasn't long before her indrawn breath filled the space and sent Penn's pulse climbing.

"Look." She pointed at one of the entries near the bottom of the page. It read "Ranulf and Hilaria." Their eyes must have traveled across the page at the same time, because they both read the originating text aloud: "The White Book of Hergest."

"That's it!" She sounded so buoyant, so excited… Penn didn't remember sharing a moment of discovery that was more alluring. But then Egg wasn't Amelia. In *any* way.

He turned toward her slightly, his gaze meeting hers. At this proximity, he could see the scattering of gold flecks shimmering near the inner ring of her emerald irises. The book on the trunk fell away, and right now, the only thing crowding his mind was her. "You have the most extraordinary eyes."

She blinked, briefly shuttering them to his view, and he realized he'd said that out loud. *Damn.* He'd meant what he'd said earlier about not having much experience in polite society. Sometimes he said things he really oughtn't.

"Thank you," she said softly. "You know so much about all this. I feel rather…dull."

He leaned closer. "I just said you were extraordinary, and you feel dull? How can that be?" Her lips parted to respond, and he realized his error. "I complimented your eyes, but it's much more than that. We haven't been acquainted long, but you strike me as an exceptionally intelligent person. In that way, you remind me of my sister. It's a pity Oxford doesn't allow women."

She looked up at him, the light of the lantern splashing across the elegant planes of her face. "I can't even imagine having that opportunity."

"And that is a crime." The smallness of the space, and their proximity, infused him with heat. Or maybe it was just because of her. Rather, his attraction to her. He wondered what it would be like to kiss her.

"What is the White Book of Hergest?" Her question should have jolted him away from his errant thoughts, but he was too far gone.

Even so, he could answer. Maybe if he did, he could stop himself from doing what he wanted. "An old Welsh text, similar to the Red Book—they're named for the color of their bindings." He was intent on her mouth and its color, so pink and lush. Her lips had to be soft as down. Softer maybe.

"Is it here?" she asked, sounding rather breathless, which only fed Penn's desire.

"The Red Book is at Oxford. I'm not sure where the White Book is, but we'll find it." At the moment, he could barely remember why…

Penn bent his head as her lids began to sink, and her delicious lips parted…

The sound of a man clearing his throat—*loudly*—filled the room like an explosion. Penn jerked back and noted that she did the same, moving to the other side of the trunk.

Worse than being caught in a near kiss, the interloper, though he wasn't really one at all, was none other than the owner of this secret library: Lord Septon.

CHAPTER 6

A hot wave of embarrassment shot up Amelia's neck and threatened to set her face aflame. She prayed the dimness of the small room would make it hard to see the depth of her discomfiture. A moment later and she might have been kissing him…

Her gaze strayed to Penn, but he was staring straight at the man who'd entered. The man who *had* to be Lord Septon.

"Septon, good evening," Penn said, sounding far more at ease than Amelia felt. How was that possible? Or fair? "May I present Mrs. Amelia Forrest? She is the granddaughter of Mr. Jonathan Gardiner, a recently deceased antiquary you may have known."

"Of course I knew Gardiner." The baron bowed to Amelia. "It's a pleasure to make your acquaintance, Mrs. Forrest."

Amelia dipped a curtsey and murmured, "Good evening."

Septon turned his attention back to Penn. "Peverell told me you were here and that you'd disappeared from dinner. When I couldn't find you, I wondered if you might be here."

His gaze dipped to the open book on the trunk. "Looking for something?"

Penn closed the book gently. "We've found what we're looking for." Now he dashed a glance toward Amelia, and she couldn't help but note his use of the word "we." Penn turned and replaced the book where he'd found it.

"I look forward to hearing all about it. Artemisia is downstairs in the drawing room. Join us for a nightcap." He offered a welcoming smile before turning and exiting the small chamber.

Amelia finally let out a deep exhalation. She looked over at Penn. His brow was creased, and his lips were pressed into a flat line. "What's wrong?" she asked.

"He doesn't like that I brought you here, I think." He turned toward her, and his expression softened. "Don't let that trouble you. Everything's fine. Hopefully, he'll be able to tell us where we can find the White Book of Hergest. Come, let's go downstairs." He gestured for her to precede him from the tiny library.

Amelia did so slowly, moving back through the doorway into the office. Penn followed her, drawing the portrait closed behind them. As he turned to insert the key into the dog's eye, she wondered what she was doing. She'd become wrapped up in the prospect of an exciting adventure and lost sight of her original quest—finding her grandfather's dagger and keeping it safe.

"How will the book help me regain the dagger?"

Penn turned from the portrait. He opened his mouth, then closed it again. It was a moment before he spoke. "It won't," he said with measured care. "But I promise we will find it."

"You've said that. Am I to understand that trying to prove the heart my grandfather put in the Ashmolean is fake takes priority?"

"No, we're doing both at the same time. And Septon can likely help us with both matters." Penn went to the desk and returned the key to its hiding place. He looked up at her as he finished, straightening his coat. "I apologize if I...caused you concern in the library."

Concern? He'd caused her heart palpitations and a considerable rise in temperature, but, surprisingly, not a bit of concern. She'd been ready—nay, *eager*—to kiss him. And that *should* concern her.

"Not at all. Let us go downstairs, shall we?" She turned and exited the office without waiting for his reply.

He caught up to her as they made their way back to the gallery.

"Is Artemisia Lady Septon?" Amelia asked.

For the first time in their acquaintance, Penn looked slightly uncomfortable. "Er, no. She's his mistress. They've been together for several years now."

How odd. "Why aren't they married?"

"Because her husband is still alive."

How outrageous. "And their relationship is simply accepted?"

"Lady Stratton—her husband is the Earl of Stratton—was desperately unhappy in her marriage and began to fear for her safety. She'd fallen in love with Septon and decided to leave her husband."

Amelia could scarcely believe such a scandal—to do with an earl, no less. "Stratton allows this?"

"Stratton is an inveterate blackguard. Think of the worst man you've ever known and multiply his sins by a factor of ten. It's probably still not bad enough to equal Stratton, but it's close."

Amelia blinked as they started down the stairs. "I see why she left." Her mind strayed to the worst man she'd ever met, and she nearly stumbled. She'd gotten rather good at not thinking of her husband, but when he did enter her mind, she invariably suffered a shock of anger and deep regret. Still, she wouldn't have left, not like he did.

They entered the drawing room to find Septon standing near the fireplace and Lady Stratton seated on a settee, her dark blue traveling skirt pooling around her feet. It seemed they hadn't changed from their journey, but then Amelia supposed her and Penn's presence had been a surprise. But was it an unwelcome one?

Lady Stratton was a striking woman with an elegant bearing—a long, aquiline nose defined her face along with a pair of pale gray eyes that shone with welcome. Her dark hair was liberally streaked with gray, and Amelia would estimate her age to be somewhere in her late forties. "Good evening, Mrs. Forrest. We're so pleased to welcome you to Septon House. And you are always welcome, of course, Penn." She greeted them as if she *were* Lady Septon.

Septon was exceptionally tall, and his hair, of which he had plenty, was entirely gray. His eyes were also gray, but a darker, flintier color than those of Lady Stratton. "What can I get you to drink, Mrs. Forrest? Madeira, sherry, whiskey, something else?" he offered pleasantly.

"Sherry, please."

Lady Stratton patted the settee beside her. "Do come and sit."

Amelia glanced at Penn, who nodded almost imperceptibly, before taking a place on the settee.

Penn went to the sideboard where Septon was pouring drinks. A moment later he delivered a glass of sherry to Amelia, then took up a position behind a chair opposite their settee, a glass of whiskey cradled in his hand.

After giving Lady Stratton a sherry, Septon took a chair angled near the settee and sipped his own glass of whiskey.

He looked over at Penn. "What were you able to find in my private library?"

The ownership in his tone was unmistakable, and Amelia suffered a pang of doubt at being there.

"Allow me to start at the beginning," Penn said.

"Yes, do," Lady Stratton said. "But would you mind sitting so I don't have to strain my neck?" She smiled sweetly.

Penn came around the chair and sat down. He took a drink of whiskey. "I found the dagger, but it was stolen from me"—he glanced at Amelia—"*us*—and we want to recover it."

She noticed he said nothing about wanting to prove the heart in the museum was a fake. Why would he keep that from Septon?

"There were four thieves—three were obviously hired brigands, but one was a well-spoken gentleman. I wondered if he is a member of the Order."

Septon's brows arched briefly. "You want to know if I'm aware of the theft. Or behind it." His tone carried a hint of dispassion. "I'm aware you don't like the Order or our mission, but we aren't common thieves."

A loud bark of a laugh escaped Penn's mouth. "Tell that to my parents, who were accosted by the Order when one of them sought to steal the decoding glass. Though it was more than twenty years ago, I'm sure you remember it."

Septon's nostrils flared. "Your point is valid. At least it was. After that unfortunate incident, we've changed our procedure."

Amelia leaned toward Septon. "Are you saying it wasn't the Order who stole my grandfather's dagger?"

"It wasn't the Order, but neither is it your 'grandfather's dagger,' my dear." He gave her a smile that bordered on patronizing, but she refused to let it bother her. "The dagger is an historical artifact. It belongs to history."

Penn snorted, drawing Amelia's attention. "How convenient for you to say that, and yet the Order seeks to 'protect' the Thirteen Treasures from the public. I would argue that does nothing to preserve history and everything to bury it."

"Yes, I'm aware of your opinion on the matter, and we must accept that we disagree. Rest assured that the Order had nothing to do with the theft of the dagger." He frowned. "This is most concerning."

Amelia would agree. She'd been concerned about the Order, particularly given the note her grandfather made in his journal, but if it wasn't them... "If it wasn't the Order, who could it have been? Who else would even know about the dagger, let alone where it was located? It's not a famous treasure. It's only ever mentioned in the story of Ranulf and Hilaria."

"That's correct," Septon said. "The only people who would even think to look for the dagger would be people familiar with the Thirteen Treasures and the dagger's place in their lore."

"Most—if not all—of those people are members of the Order," Penn said sternly.

Septon gave him a scolding look. "You aren't."

Penn pressed his lips together but said nothing.

Septon turned to Amelia. "I know it must be distressing to lose this artifact that your grandfather had found. I wish I could tell you that it could be easily recovered, but tracking it down will be most difficult. I fear it may have been taken by the Camelot group." He sent a dark look toward Penn, whose lips moved in an inaudible curse.

Amelia looked between the two men. "What is the Camelot group?"

"A rogue faction inside the Order," Penn answered before Septon could. "They're made up of only descendants of the knights. They hate having people like Septon in the Order, and they hate hiding the treasures. They'd rather put them to use."

She blinked at both men. "Do they have a specific use in mind?"

"Not that we're aware of," Septon said. "They *are* a dangerous group, however. Led by a dangerous man—Timothy Foliot." The baron sipped his whiskey before turning his steely stare on Penn. "I'd wager some very valuable pieces in my collection that he's behind the theft of the dagger."

"Which means it will be difficult to regain, but not impossible. Cate was able to recover Dyrnwyn."

"Thanks to Kersey." Lady Stratton spoke for the first time. "He gave it to her."

"The transaction wasn't quite that pleasant," Penn said, prompting Amelia to wonder what had happened and why Lady Stratton would care. And she clearly cared as evidenced by the color leaching from her face. "As I was saying, it won't be impossible to get it. We simply need to find Foliot."

Septon released a hollow laugh. "I can tell you exactly where he is—holed up at his estate near Glastonbury. That won't help you, however. He will never grant you an audience."

Penn lifted a shoulder. "Everyone has a price."

Amelia's head spun. It certainly sounded as though it *might* be impossible to recover the dagger. And if it was fake, did it really matter? "If you're convinced it's an imitation and trying to recover it would be dangerous, why bother?"

Penn swiveled his gaze to hers. "Because it belongs to you."

Warmth spread through her, and she worked to keep a smile from lifting her lips. His words made her ridiculously happy.

"Hold on," Septon said, pitching forward as he looked sharply toward Penn. "You say it was a fake dagger anyway?"

Penn tossed back the rest of his whiskey and set the empty glass on the table next to his chair. "The carvings on it aren't more than four hundred years old."

Septon visibly relaxed, his shoulders sinking back against the chair. "It isn't fake, for the dagger was made much later than the heart. The story of Ranulf and Hilaria is the only one that contains it, because the dagger was enchanted relatively recent to the midfifteenth century, which is when the White Book of Hergest was compiled."

Amelia, still quite skeptical, looked at the baron. "So it's not from the same time period as the Thirteen Treasures, but it counteracts the power of the heart to compel someone to fall in love with someone else."

"Yes." Septon turned his whiskey glass in his hand and looked down at the amber liquid briefly before glancing between Penn and Amelia. "Upstairs, you were researching the White Book of Hergest."

It wasn't a direct question, but it was still a query. Now would Penn reveal his insistence that the heart was a fake? Amelia quickly had her answer.

Penn rested his hand on the arm of his chair as he pinned Septon with a direct stare. "I believe the heart in the Ashmolean may be an imitation. To prove it, I'm going to find the real one."

Septon leaned forward and set his glass down on a low table situated in front of the settee with a loud clack. His dark gray eyes narrowed slightly as he looked at Penn. "Why would you think that?"

"It's painted, and I'm not entirely sure it's tourmaline."

"It *is* tourmaline, and it was painted at one point to disguise it from those who sought to steal it."

"And yet my grandfather stole it anyway." Amelia hated

thinking of it in those terms, but what else could it be but theft?

"How did that even happen without the Order knowing?" Penn asked, suddenly animated.

"Sometimes these things happen," Septon said evenly. "Despite our best efforts."

"Or, maybe the Order allowed him to take a fake artifact while the real one is kept somewhere safe."

Amelia heard the irritation in Penn's tone but also the note of truth. That actually made sense—if she believed everything she'd learned so far about the Order. And the one thing she accepted as absolute truth was that they couldn't be trusted—she would never forget what Grandfather had written in his journal.

Septon inhaled deeply before saying, "That's a rather cynical view."

"And likely accurate. I'm going to find the real heart."

Septon shook his head. "If you're planning to start with the White Book of Hergest, I regret to inform you that it's been missing for several years."

"Bloody hell." Penn exploded out of the chair and stalked behind it. He kept walking, making a circuit to the fireplace and back.

Amelia clenched her hands together and angled herself toward Septon. "Missing?"

"Do you know what the book is, Mrs. Forrest?" he asked. "It was written in the middle of the fifteenth century, much of it by Lewys Glyn Cothi, who studied at the St. John Priory at Carmarthen."

"Carmarthen is where the heart was found," Penn said from near the fireplace.

"Yes. I believe your grandfather tracked it there."

Some of the pieces of the puzzle that they knew began to connect in her mind. "My grandfather visited Wynnstay. Is it possible he studied the tale of Ranulf and Hilaria in the White Book of Hergest there? Unless the book has been missing for a very long time."

"No, it hasn't, and it *was* at Wynnstay before it was lost. Yes, I would guess Gardiner did study it there." Septon's brow furrowed.

"What is it?" Lady Stratton asked.

"I've seen the book myself, and I didn't think it would lead anyone to find the heart—or the dagger. However, now I must wonder." He pounded his fist on the arm of his chair. "Bloody travesty it was lost."

Penn had walked back toward Septon's chair as he'd spoken. "How was it lost?"

"It was sent to a bookbinder in London, and a fire in Covent Garden destroyed the man's business, including the White Book. That was in 1808."

"Not so long ago." There was a bead of excitement in Penn's voice. Amelia didn't know him terribly well, but he liked the hunt—no, he probably loved it, fed off it—and this information was something he could chase.

Septon reached for his glass. "Mackinley was the bookbinder if you want to go to London to try to speak with him."

"You said the fire destroyed his business."

"It did, but he's rebuilt."

Amelia looked up at Penn. "But if the book is lost, what's the point?"

His eyes gleamed, and the corners of his mouth ticked up. "Don't give up too easily. Until Mackinley himself tells me the book burned up, I will keep a bit of hope alive." He turned to Septon. "It's curious, isn't it, that the book may have led to the heart and it burned in a fire."

Septon held up his hand. "Don't even think of laying this on the Order. We would *never* destroy an antiquity."

"That I believe," Penn said.

Septon drank the contents of his glass before getting to his feet. "I think this is a bit of a fool's errand, my boy. I'll be thrilled if you find the book, of course, but the heart in the Ashmolean is real. It's been handed down from female descendant to female descendant. The Order has always tracked it."

"Until it was taken by Jonathan Gardiner." Penn gave his head a shake. "I don't think the Order is as in control of everything as they'd like. If they were, they'd have the dagger and they'd have Dyrnwyn." He said the last with a bit of superiority.

"In a way, we do have Dyrnwyn," Septon said softly. "You're just keeping it safe for us." He held his hand for Lady Stratton. "Come, my lady, let us retire."

Amelia stood along with the countess. "Thank you for allowing me to visit."

Lady Stratton gave her a warm smile. "Any friend of Penn's is a friend of ours."

They all said good night, and their host and hostess left the drawing room. Amelia wasn't quite ready to call it a night, and since Penn wasn't heading toward the door, it seemed he wasn't either.

"When are we going to London?" Amelia asked.

Penn chuckled. "Tomorrow morning, unless you think that's too soon."

"Not at all. It's probably unwise for us to travel together, however." She'd meant it from a sense of propriety, but given what had nearly happened upstairs, she realized there were perhaps deeper risks. "I'll go in my coach."

He inclined his head. "We'll stay at my brother-in-law's town house in Mayfair. He's the Earl of Norris."

"Your brother-in-law is an earl?" She'd never met an earl.

"Yes." Penn moved toward her. "You look concerned. Don't worry, he's a nice enough fellow, if a bit stodgy. He was in the army. Anyway, he won't even be there. He and Cate are still in Cornwall for another week or so, I think. And then, I believe, they'll return to his estate in Wootton Bassett.

That made her feel slightly better, but only slightly since Penn was suggesting they stay together. Although, wasn't that what they were doing now? She'd come here knowing full well they'd be staying at Septon House. Together.

But that had been before he'd almost kissed her. Before she'd *wanted* him to kiss her.

Penn took another step, lessening the distance between them. "You seem hesitant. I want you to come."

"I *want* to come. I just wonder if it's what I *should* do."

"Of course it is. We're on a journey to find the truth. You want that, don't you?"

"I do." Even if it meant that her grandfather had found a fake heart. He'd been passionate about the story of Ranulf and Hilaria, perhaps inspired by a visit to Wynnstay and a viewing of the White Book of Hergest. To find that missing tome, to see and touch the pages that had sent him on a life-long adventure, was an opportunity she couldn't resist. "I do," she said more firmly. "But, we must…" she searched for the right words, "behave appropriately."

His dark blue eyes sparked as he drawled, "Haven't we?"

Longing pulled in her belly. No one had ever looked at her the way he was looking at her now. It made her feel beautiful, desirable, and completely singular. As if she were the only woman in the world—his world.

She struggled to answer. "Yes. For the most part." Did she have to draw attention to what had happened, or almost happened, upstairs? "Let's avoid small spaces." There, that should make it clear.

He edged even closer to her, until there was scarcely six inches between them. "Does it bother you to be too close to me?"

"No." She answered far too quickly—and honestly. "What bothers me isn't at issue."

"Why? If it doesn't bother you, why stop doing it? Dare I hope you may even like it?"

Oh, this was too familiar. And yet…he had a point. She wasn't some green, unmarried miss who needed to preserve her reputation. Still, kissing would change their relationship and affect their objective.

She straightened her spine and held herself stiff. "I should like to maintain a professional working relationship. We are on a quest to find the White Book of Hergest, and I would ask that we focus on that. I bid you good evening." She turned on her heel and hurried from the drawing room before she lost herself even further in the smoldering heat of his gaze.

Later, as she tossed amid the lonely bedclothes, she wondered if she was embarking on a colossal mistake or a life-changing adventure.

CHAPTER 7

*P*enn suppressed a smile as he glanced at the woman next to him in the coach. Amelia surprised him at nearly every turn. Although, he shouldn't be any longer. She'd proved herself to be curious, eager, and nearly fearless.

Only *nearly* because she was clearly afraid of what might happen between them. If they were too close. As they were now while they traveled the streets of London from Mayfair to Bow Street, where they would meet with one Hamish Mackinley.

They'd departed Septon House in separate coaches early the previous morning, without even saying goodbye to Septon or Lady Stratton in person. It was just as well. Penn had grown up with Septon, considered the man a friend, but all this secrecy to do with the Order and their insistence that the Thirteen Treasures stay hidden was almost enough to damage the relationship. Even now, Penn doubted some things Septon had said last night—the fact that Amelia's grandfather had found the heart and delivered it to a museum without the Order intervening just didn't sit right.

Last night, they'd stayed at an inn in Andover, arriving late and taking supper before retiring to their rooms and leaving even earlier this morning. Dawn had barely broken when they set out for London. Penn included staunch travel companion among Amelia's outstanding qualities. "Thank you again for coming out straightaway." They'd left his brother-in-law's town house almost as soon as they'd arrived.

"I'm just as eager as you are to learn what we can from Mr. Mackinley." She peered at him askance. "You should know that about me by now."

Yes, they were getting to know each other fairly well. "You are correct. I won't ever underestimate you again."

"I did want to talk to you about something." There was a weight to her tone that gave him pause.

He hoped it wasn't the issue of their attraction or whatever she wanted to call it. Or not call it. She couldn't deny it, but then that was likely why she'd felt compelled to set rules for their relationship. He'd never liked rules.

She brushed her hand along her skirt, drawing his attention briefly to the barely perceptible curve of her thigh beneath the layers of fabric. "How much do you trust Lord Septon?"

Had she been reading his thoughts? "I've known him most of my life," he said carefully. "He and my father are friends. Even so, I know there have been times my father might have cheerfully choked him."

"Such as the time the Order put him and your mother in danger?"

"Yes, that was one such time. They'd found an antiquity that ultimately led them to the only contemporaneous writings about King Arthur and his knights—a poem written by a sixth-century monk."

"That was the document you mentioned in Burrington? I

didn't know such a thing existed." She paused briefly before cocking her head to the side. "Why is that?"

"Because the Order insisted the poem remain secret."

"But they didn't find it—your parents did. Or am I misunderstanding?"

"You have the right of it. Septon was able to convince my father that publicizing such a thing would cause problems."

"But *you* aren't convinced."

He shook his head. "I think knowledge belongs to everyone. When my sister found the flaming sword—called Dyrnwyn—I wanted to put it in the Ashmolean, but Septon, as a member of the Order, of course disagreed. He was insistent that people would fight over it."

"Isn't that what's happening in the Order? This Camelot faction has formed and now there are problems."

Penn couldn't dispute what she said. "So you agree with Septon?"

"I didn't say that. But perhaps his fears and those of the Order are well-founded. Who do these treasures really belong to? I admit I am distressed to think my grandfather stole the heart."

"I don't see it as theft. He was trying to share the heart with the people of England when he gave it to the Ashmolean. I think of him as liberating an important historical artifact."

"Liberating?" She was quiet a moment and glanced out the window. "Are we nearly there? I've only been to London once, and I scarcely remember it."

"Just once?" Penn had visited on many occasions, particularly to spend time in the British Museum. "What a shame. I wish we had more time. I'd take you to see the Rosetta Stone and the Elgin Marbles."

She turned toward him, her sharp inhalation spiking his awareness of her. "That would be wonderful."

"Next time," he promised.

"There likely won't be a next time, Mr. Bowen. But perhaps we won't be able to learn anything to help our cause and our journey will end here. I shall take the opportunity to visit the museum before I return home."

The coach slowed. "Try to be more optimistic, Mrs. Forrest," he said softly. "About everything. I intend there to be a next time." He gave her a pointed stare as the vehicle came to a stop. He reached for the door. "We're here."

As he quickly climbed down, he wondered what the hell had gotten into him. He never planned for future encounters with women, and yet he hadn't been able to stop himself with her. Perhaps she was right, that they ought to focus on keeping things professional. He turned and held up his hand to help her out.

She took it, but there was wariness in her gaze. When she was on the ground, he said, "I didn't mean to overstep. I get rather excited about things in the museum. I would very much like you to go there someday and if I'm able to join you, so much the better."

"Because you're an expert in these things?" she offered helpfully.

He smiled, knowing that she knew he was trying to rectify a potentially awkward situation. "Just trying to keep things professional."

"Which I appreciate." She turned toward the building they'd stopped in front of. "Mr. Mackinley's Bookbindery."

"Let us see what we may learn." He offered her his arm, and they went into the small shop.

The scent of parchment and leather filled Penn's nose as the door closed behind them. A large man, both in height and breadth, stood behind a wide table, where he could stand to do his work. He looked up. "Good afternoon."

Penn moved farther into the shop. "Good afternoon. Are you Mr. Mackinley?"

"I am," he answered in a dark, throaty burr. He looked down at their hands. "Did you bring a book?"

"No, we came to ask about a book that was in your possession some years ago. Around the time of the fire."

He exhaled—it was a sound of deep remorse. "If I had it before the fire, it's gone."

Penn grimaced, hating to think of such a treasured object incinerated. "We're hoping you might be able to tell us about it. The book, I mean. It was rather distinctive—the White Book of Hergest."

Mackinley grunted. "Every so often, one of you Oxford types comes in here asking about it."

Surprised to hear this, Penn stepped toward the table. "They do?"

"Most of them are far younger than you—maybe still in college. They think they'll somehow be able to find a lost masterpiece. They fancy themselves heroes maybe."

"Well, that *would* be rather heroic." Amelia had come forward to join Penn. She offered Mackinley a wide smile that would have disarmed even the most cynical of men. "We'd like to ask you about the manuscript itself, specifically the story concerning Ranulf and Hilaria. My grandfather used to tell me the tale when I was a child. It holds a great deal of sentimental value for me."

Mackinley, who was probably nearing fifty, was not immune to her charms. He smiled in return. "I do remember that manuscript, of course. The Williams-Wynn family are excellent clients. Their library is extensive. I was quite devastated when that book was lost." He grimaced and shook his head.

"I'm so sorry," Amelia said, taking another step toward the table and resting her gloved fingertips upon the edge.

"Such a tragedy."

"Indeed it was. The theatre was a complete loss, of course. That's where the fire started." His gaze clouded, and it seemed he was chasing a memory.

Penn moved to Amelia's side, and they exchanged glances before he said, "Is there any chance you recall anything special about the story in the White Book?"

Mackinley nodded, returning to the present. "Yes, back to your wife's request."

Penn and Amelia exchanged another glance, but this one was far more charged. She opened her mouth, likely to correct him, but Penn shook his head gently, urging her to remain quiet. It was best not to draw attention to their alliance. Despite her widowed status, he wouldn't want their activities to reflect poorly on her.

"I'm afraid I don't recall anything special. That story was written like all the others, but I will say it's one of my favorites too." He gave Amelia another smile.

The door opened once more, and Mackinley's gaze moved past them to the new arrival. "Afternoon, Mr. Edwards. I'll be right back with your book." He looked back at Penn and Amelia. "Please excuse me."

As Mackinley disappeared through a doorway into the back of the shop, Penn moved away from the table. Amelia joined him, her forehead creased.

"Well, that wasn't helpful," she said, sounding as disappointed as Penn felt.

"Not terribly," Penn said, frowning.

A slight man with a stooped back followed Mackinley from the rear doorway. While Mackinley went to meet with Mr. Edwards at the table, the other man, who was at least twenty years Mackinley's senior, his head topped with a shock of bright white hair, ambled toward Penn and Amelia.

"Hamish wanted me to see if there was anything else I could help you with?"

"I don't think so," Penn said.

The man squinted at Penn. "I heard you asking about the fire and a book. The White Book."

"You worked for Mr. Mackinley then?"

"I was Mr. Mackinley first," he said, his eyes twinkling. Though he and his son weren't the same in stature, they shared the same rich brown gaze. "He's right—young men come in from time to time asking about that book. The first one came not long after it arrived to be rebound. I remember because he was an odd fellow. He was a bit older than the Oxford gents that came in after the fire, but not old enough to be bald. Yet he was. He asked to see the book, but we told him we weren't a library and sent him on his way. I thought it strange that he knew we had the book at all, let alone had the nerve to think he could look at it."

Penn's pulse picked up at this information. It could be nothing, but then again, it could be something. It was certainly more than they'd had five minutes ago. "Did he ever come back?"

"Not that I'm aware of. The fire was a few weeks later, I think. And about that fire... It started at the theatre. Some say by arson, but how can we ever know?" The elder Mackinley shrugged, his eyes narrowing slightly as he added, "There was a extreme lack of water—the main was shut down because there was an issue with the flow, and they were working on repairing it. Terrible luck since the theatre was completely lost, along with several other buildings including ours." He shook his head. "It was awful, but that didn't stop people from stealing while others fought the blaze. Several people were arrested."

Arson? Was there a chance the fire was set as a distraction so someone could steal the White Book? It was a bit of a stretch, but given what Penn knew about the Order and Camelot, he'd believe almost anything. "Is there any chance you remember the name of the person who wanted to borrow the White Book?" Penn held little hope but had to ask.

He shook his head. "My son might. I never forget a face, but he's better at names."

Penn glanced at Amelia, who gave him a subtle nod. "We'll ask him when he's finished, thank you."

A moment later, the customer left with his book, and the elder Mackinley went to the table. "I was just talking to these folks about the fire. Do you remember that gent who came in before—he wanted to look at the White Book that belonged to the Williams-Wynn family."

Confusion marred the younger Mackinley's features for a moment before his eyes widened briefly. "Yes, I remember him now. I think he came in twice, actually. The second time, he asked about bookbinding—said he was interested in learning the trade. He asked an overabundance of questions. I found it strange because my father hadn't been particularly polite when he'd come in the first time." He cast his father a look that revealed the fondness between them. It reminded Penn of his own father, whom he admired and loved.

"It's extraordinary that you recall all that," Amelia said. "Thank you for sharing it with us. I don't suppose you remember his name? If you even got it at the time."

"I'm sure Father told you I'm excellent with names. Of course I remember it, especially since it seemed perfect for someone interested in books—Foliot, the word folio is tucked in there."

Penn heard Amelia's intake of breath but didn't look at her. Later, he'd explain the necessity of maintaining their composure in order to keep their secrets close.

"Do you know him?" Mackinley the younger asked Amelia.

"No. You're right, that's a very interesting coincidence with his name." She smiled her dazzling smile again, and Penn decided she'd already learned the lesson he was going to teach. Yes, she was incredibly quick-witted.

Mackinley smiled in return. "I thought so too."

"Well, you've been most helpful," Penn said, offering his hand first to the elder Mackinley and then the younger.

"Our pleasure," the elder said.

Penn escorted Amelia from the shop and back into the coach. Once inside, she settled herself on the seat and apologized. "I shouldn't have gasped like that. It's important we don't reveal things."

He sat next to her, and the coach moved forward. "You covered for it very well. I'm beginning to think you were born for this sort of thing."

A pretty blush bloomed in her cheeks. "So what do we do now? We have to assume the book was lost to the fire."

"Do we? I wasn't entirely convinced before, and now I'm even less so. It could be that after Foliot was denied access to the book, he went back the second time to learn all he could about the shop and how they did business."

She gasped again, her eyes widening. "So he could go back and steal it?"

"That's what I would do."

Her lips parted. "You've actually done that?"

"A time or two. Not to steal anything, but to obtain information."

"That's a form of stealing, isn't it?"

He couldn't tell if she was offended or simply asking a question. "I don't think so, but we could dispute that for some time. I accept that a certain ambiguity is necessary in this profession."

"What profession? I thought you worked for a museum."

"I do, and my job includes obtaining artifacts for the museum, which sometimes necessitates me to search for them. And searching requires information. On occasion— such as now—that information is hard to ascertain." He waited for her to respond, and when she didn't, said, "I find it ironic that you're questioning the gathering of information when you shot at Egg in order to get the dagger."

She blushed again. "Yes, well, we've been over that. I do understand why you would gather information in whatever way you could. It seems as though you regularly court danger."

"I wouldn't say regularly. How about occasionally?"

There was a bit of silence before she asked, "Is this one of those times?"

"No." Not yet. But now that he had confirmation Foliot was involved, things would become…challenging. He gazed at her intently, hoping to reassure her. "I won't let anything bad happen to you. If I think things are too dangerous, I'll say so. You have my word."

She nodded before turning her head toward the window. It seemed they'd finally arrived at a place of trust. He was glad.

"You never did say where we're to go next," she said, returning her alluring gaze to his.

"I need to talk to Kersey." Penn had grown up with Gideon—or Kersey, as he was usually called.

"Who is that? Lady Stratton mentioned him."

"He's her son. Viscount Kersey and apparent descendant of Sir Gareth, Knight of the Round Table. He was working for Foliot, and he stole the flaming sword from my sister after she found it." His voice hardened as he recalled the tale that her husband Elijah had told him.

Cate hadn't wanted Penn to know the depths of Kersey's

villainy—threatening Cate and Elijah, tying them up, stealing the sword, which she'd dedicated her life to finding. But Elijah had revealed every detail. He didn't care that Kersey was their distant cousin and that they'd grown up as family. He'd wanted Penn to know the truth and that Elijah would do whatever necessary to keep Cate safe. Penn was glad his sister was married to such a man.

"Is this another case of stealing an artifact, like my grandfather and the heart?" she asked.

He knew that bothered her, that she was conflicted about wanting to protect and support her grandfather's memory, but that she didn't like the idea of people just taking artifacts. He didn't disagree, which was why he sought to share them with the public in a museum instead of profiting from them. "My sister had planned to give it to the Ashmolean. Like me, she thinks these sorts of objects should be studied and available to all people."

"But the Order stopped that," she said with a hint of derision. Oh, he liked her more and more all the time. "Where is it now?"

"Somewhere safe." But he might have to use it to make their next move. "I may need it to persuade Kersey to help us."

"And you think he can help us get to Foliot?"

He noted she said "us," but he had no intention of allowing her anywhere near Foliot. The man wasn't above killing people to achieve his ends. Elijah's brother had been killed by Camelot in their pursuit of the tapestry that had ultimately led Cate to finding the sword.

"He's the only lead I have. I do believe Septon when he says I can't just arrive at Foliot's house and simply ask whether he possesses the White Book of Hergest and your grandfather's dagger."

"No, I don't suppose you can." The coach slowed as they arrived at Elijah's town house. "Do you know how to find Kersey?"

That was the problem he faced. Kersey had gone into hiding, probably somewhere in Wales, and right now, the only thing Penn could think to do was lure him out with the sword. But first he should speak with his father. There was a chance he'd know Kersey's location, or at least have some insight. Father had always gone out of his way to treat Kersey as a member of their family, knowing that Kersey's own father was so horrible.

Penn was anxious to continue the hunt, and if he were alone, he would. But he wasn't alone, so they'd leave first thing in the morning.

The door to the coach opened, and Penn climbed out. He offered his hand to Amelia. "Would you care to change and join me for dinner?"

She gave him a smile that sent heat all the way through his toes. "I insist upon it."

∼

*A*melia should have been exhausted, but she was energized. She couldn't help but feel excited. It was like reading an exceptionally engaging mystery novel—each day, they learned new things that took them closer to their goal. A goal she wasn't entirely sure she understood anymore, and yet she didn't care.

She wanted to find her grandfather's dagger, but instead of keeping it for herself, she wanted it to be in the museum alongside the heart. Assuming the heart was real. She wasn't sure what she believed, not after all she'd seen and heard.

But most perplexing—and yes, exciting—of all was the

person she was sharing this adventure with. From the moment she'd trained her pistol on Penn Bowen, something within her had broken free. It was as if she'd come out of the dark and was now basking in the light.

She shook her head to banish such ridiculous thoughts. *Focus on our objectives, not Penn.*

Amelia smoothed the dark green skirt of the only formal gown she'd brought, the one she'd worn for dinner at Septon House. Culley, who'd traveled with her from Septon House, came forward with another hairpin. "You've got one errant lock back here," she said, tucking the hair up and pinning it in place.

"Thank you." Amelia hadn't wanted to redress her hair. It wasn't as if she were going to a dinner party or a ball. Still, dinner in an earl's London town house was almost intimidating. And maybe it would have been if the earl had been in residence.

She made her way down to the dining room and stopped at the threshold. The table and set-up was much more formal than the one at Septon House. The room was quite large, with a long table running its length. One end was set with sparkling silver and crystal and immaculate linen.

Penn stood near the chair at the end wearing the same suit of stark black that he'd worn at Septon House. However, tonight, he sported a dark blue waistcoat shot with gold thread. As with the other night, his shirt and cravat were impossibly white, particularly against the dark tone of his skin.

"It's hardly fair that gentlemen can simply swap out a waistcoat and change their costume. We have to pack far too many things," she said.

"Egg arrived while we were out. He insists on packing this 'fancy' waistcoat in case I meet the Prince or someone else of import. Believe it or not, this was stuffed in one of our saddlebags when you met us."

Amelia laughed. "Egg is quite useful."

"He's also a damn blighter on occasion." Penn smiled as he held out her chair.

Two footmen attended them, pouring wine and serving the first course. Amelia picked up the thread of their earlier conversation. "Where are we going tomorrow, Wales? You didn't say precisely."

He paused in eating. "Not Wales. Not yet, anyway. I need to go to Oxford first, and you could meet Burgess. "

Amelia was warmed by his thoughtfulness. "That would be wonderful, thank you. Beyond finding out anything he can tell us about my grandfather's search for the heart and the dagger, I'll just be glad to talk to someone else who knew him."

Penn smiled softly before sipping his wine.

Amelia focused on her meal for a moment, her mind formulating the things she wanted to talk to Burgess about. Did he know about the Order? Did he know why her grandfather hid the dagger instead of just giving it to the Ashmolean as he did with the heart?

"You were quite close to your grandfather," Penn said as the footman replaced the first course with the second. "What about your parents?"

"My mother died when I was young and my grandmother six years later. I was quite close to my father and grandfather. When my father passed a few years ago, I went to live with my grandfather. He was starting to decline, so he needed my help." That was a close enough approximation of the truth. Her grandfather *had* been starting to decline. That she'd needed a place to live wasn't something Penn had to know.

"There's no mention of your husband in there," he said quietly but inquisitively.

"You didn't ask about him." And she certainly wasn't going to offer any information about Thaddeus Forrest.

He picked up his wineglass and peered at her over the rim. "I'm asking. If it's not too forward of me."

"There isn't much to tell. We married, we had no children, he's gone." She bent her head toward her plate and took a too large bite of fish.

"I'm sorry for all your losses. You seem to be faring well in spite of them."

Yes, well, she was nothing if not a strong and self-reliant person. At least that was what she tried to be. She'd been so upset—first despondent about her future and then angry—when Thaddeus had left. He'd run up so much debt that he'd had no choice but to flee their creditors. One had tried to collect from Amelia, and she'd had to give them the contents of their house. Destitute, she'd gone back to her grandfather, who'd been more than happy to welcome her. And join her in damning Thaddeus. That had been five years ago.

"What about your family?" she asked, eager to divert the conversation away from herself. "You've spoken quite warmly of your parents and your sister. And it sounds as if you all share a passion for antiquities and hunting for them."

"We do. As you know, my father is a scholar. My mother met him when she brought him a rare book to evaluate. It turned out to be the key to finding a remarkable treasure—not in the sense of a sword or a heart, but in words. It was a manuscript, which, of course, meant more to my father than any artifact. None of it meant as much as my mother, however."

"It sounds like a grand love story. And they had two children to continue their legacy."

"Actually, I'm not their son, not by blood. I came to live with my father when I was eight."

Amelia stared at him a moment. "I'm surprised to hear that."

"Why, because I'm so fond of them? They're the only parents I've ever known. I remember my mother—the woman who birthed me—but not my father. I've no idea who he was, actually."

He said all this quite matter-of-factly, which was also surprising. She imagined it wasn't easy not to know who your real father was. And yet, it sounded as though he had a father he admired and loved. Did anything else matter?

The footman removed Amelia's plate and promptly brought the next course.

"How did you come to live with the Bowens?" she asked.

"My mother was dying. She knew Rhys Bowen to be a good and trustworthy man, and she asked him if he'd foster me. She had saved money to send me to school, but my father—Rhys—made sure I went to Eton and Oxford."

"So he took you in and adopted you as his own?" Amelia's heart warmed as she thought of the young orphan in need of love and family and finding both to a degree that so many people never did.

"He did." Penn took a bite of pheasant and washed it down with a swallow of wine. "And there's no wife in my history, in case you were wondering."

She stifled a smile. "I wasn't, but thank you for telling me."

"Oh, come now, you weren't a little curious? I find you vastly interesting—and a bit enigmatic. Plus, there's that... thing between us that you don't want to discuss."

She sent him a look of caution. They'd had a nice day and were having a nice evening. Did he need to mess things up with talk of *that*?

Even so, her pulse picked up, and heat spread through her limbs, then pooled in her belly. He was incredibly handsome and charming when he wanted to be. He was also intelligent and committed to his family and discovering the truth. She'd wager he wouldn't find himself over his head in debt and running out on his wife. If he'd had one.

"Do you plan to wed?" She hadn't meant to ask that at all, but the question had shot from her mouth like an arrow at a target.

"I have no plans. Which isn't to say I wouldn't. If I met the right woman." His gaze seemed to darken, the blue of his eyes glowing like sapphires beneath the brilliant candles flickering above them in the chandelier. Goodness, that was a great deal of expense and trouble for two people to have dinner.

"Why are we eating in here?" she asked, abruptly changing the subject to something far safer.

He looked around the room and then up at the dozens of candles. "That is an excellent question. I am not familiar with the workings of this house as I am at Septon House. I should have asked for us to eat in a smaller room."

"There wasn't time," she said. "We arrived and left nearly immediately."

"I suppose you're right, and we won't be here tomorrow." He scooped up a bite of potatoes. "Next time, we'll find the breakfast room."

"You keep speaking of next times."

"Maybe I have plans after all." His lips curved up just before he put the potatoes in his mouth.

What the hell did that mean? He planned to what? She took a long drink of wine. "Do stop flirting."

"You're the one who drew attention to my speaking of the future."

"But you're the one actually doing it," she said. "Speaking of the future. The future for us is tracking down my grandfather's dagger and proving that the heart in the museum is real. That is our future."

"And maybe it will bring us back here to London, and we'll have occasion to eat in the breakfast room. That's all I meant."

She didn't believe him for a moment. He wasn't just flirting with her, he was teasing.

She stood up abruptly. "I think I'm finished."

Before she could turn and leave, he jumped up and came to her side. His hand lightly cupped her elbow. "My apologies. I'm having fun—I thought you were too. Yes, I'm flirting, but I can't help it. You're exceptionally attractive to me in every way, and despite my intention to keep things professional between us, I find myself swept away when I'm in your company."

"So it's my fault if you're boorish?"

He laughed softly. "Boorish? Is it that bad?"

She suppressed a smile. Maybe it *was* fun. And maybe she could allow herself to *have* fun. "No."

He was very close. She could see his ink-dark lashes and how ridiculously long they were, spiking out from his alluring eyes. It would be so easy to sway into him, to allow that protection he'd so easily offered that afternoon. She'd shivered in the coach when he'd promised to keep her safe. He'd meant it, and she believed him.

She held herself back. What good could come of an affair? Plenty, whispered a lonely voice in the back of her mind—a voice she chose to ignore. "This is a professional relationship, but we are friends. And nothing more."

"I'm not sure I can agree to that."

The heat flaring through her intensified at the promise in his gaze. She continued to ignore her body's reaction. "Then perhaps we should end things."

"I *definitely* can't agree to that, but for now, I am more than content to remain friends."

More than content. And she didn't want to end things. For so many reasons. "I'll see you in the morning."

"Good night, Mrs. Forrest."

His mouth curved into a seductive smile, and her resolve wavered. She wanted to know what it would be like to kiss him...

"Good night, Mr. Bowen."

She turned and fled.

CHAPTER 8

The scent of polished wood and old paper filled Penn's nose as they waited in the vestibule outside Carlton Burgess's office at Oxford. Yesterday had been a long day of travel, and they'd arrived at Penn's house rather late. After taking a small dinner, Amelia had gone directly to bed, her exhaustion overriding her initial protests about staying in his house.

He'd argued that she was a widow, chaperoned by a maid, and safe from his advances. Never mind that all three of those arguments were quite flimsy.

Not that he *would* make an overture, such as a kiss. But he'd be damned if he wasn't thinking about it.

They'd indulged their weariness and slept a bit late, and now here they were in the early afternoon awaiting their audience with the Keeper of the Ashmolean.

Burgess opened the door to his office and gave them a wide smile. "How delightful to have you back, Penn." He turned his attention to Amelia. "And this must be Miss Gardiner."

"Mrs. Forrest," she corrected. "Thank you for seeing us."

"Of course, of course. Come right in, please." He stood to the side, presenting his profile, which included a rather pronounced belly. Burgess loved sweets and port to excessive degrees.

He closed the door once they were inside and gestured for them to join him in a seating area arranged in front of the fire. He moved to stand near the wingbacked chair, which Penn knew to be his preferred seat. In fact, Penn had never seen him sit anywhere else, and the chair reflected the wear to prove it.

Penn waited for Amelia to sit on the small settee before dropping down beside her. "We'd love to hear about how you came to know Mrs. Forrest's grandfather. Would you mind sharing that story?" Penn knew he wouldn't—Burgess loved to talk. In fact, Penn sometimes worried he would accidentally betray a secret. However, it was now apparent that Burgess was capable of protecting information over great periods of time. Penn was surprised, and pleasantly so.

"Not at all," Burgess said with an enthusiastic grin. "Your grandfather and I were good friends for many years, Mrs. Forrest. He was an excellent transcriptionist—that was how I met him. As you know, he copied books from French, Latin, and Old English into modern English. While I was studying at Oxford, I took manuscripts to him for transcription. We shared a passion for medieval stories. And fine port." He chuckled.

Amelia folded her hands in her lap. "It's odd that we've never met before now."

"It is, it is. I regret that I didn't visit Jon in the last few years. I don't travel much myself—terrible gout. But we did maintain our correspondence."

"Yes, I know. I read many of your letters." This didn't surprise Penn, particularly if she was trying to learn about her grandfather and about Burgess. "Mr. Bowen gave me the letter my grandfather wrote to you in 1809. I would love to know why he trusted you with the location of the dagger and not me."

Burgess's jovial manner dimmed a bit. "He felt the knowledge could be dangerous. He didn't even tell me until after he passed, you know. Not until you sent me his letter."

Penn decided to cut right to the heart of the matter. "Did he think it was dangerous because of the Order?" He saw the flicker of caution in Burgess's gaze. "She knows all about the Order. Gardiner mentioned it in his journal." He turned his head toward Amelia. "What did it say again?"

Amelia glanced from Burgess to him before reciting the entry, *"The Order will stop at nothing to find the treasures. Why? They proclaim they are protecting them, but there is something off. If only I'd been able to read the book. I feel certain it would provide the answers I seek."*

Burgess's eyes widened briefly, and he lost a bit of his color.

"This was written after the heart was already in the museum," Amelia said. "In 1754. I don't know, however, if the dagger was in his possession."

Burgess shook his head. "It was not. Are you aware of how he found the heart?"

Amelia was completely fixated on Burgess. "No, but I should like to know, if you can tell me."

"Your grandfather was a bit obsessed with the tale of Ranulf and Hilaria. He was a student of medieval romances, but that one was his favorite, probably because it was so rare, I think. He became equally obsessed with the objects from their story: the heart and the dagger. Everyone told him they didn't exist, but he believed they were real." Burgess chuckled again, softly. "I don't know what made him think that. I can only surmise that he was a terrible romantic. Is that true of the man you knew?"

Amelia's lips curved into a slight smile. "It was."

Burgess nodded as he continued, "Jon went to see the White Book of Hergest at Wynnstay. The family was kind enough to allow scholars into their library from time to time. The story was recorded into the White Book by Lewys Glyn Cothi. He studied at the St. John Priory at Carmarthen. Jon went there to learn more about him, and that's where he found the heart."

"Did he say how?" Penn asked. This interested him most since he was convinced Gardiner had found a fake. But he wasn't going to tell Burgess that.

"He didn't, and I did ask. Pity that secret died with him."

For the first time, Penn wondered if it was possible that Gardiner had fabricated the heart that was sitting down the street in the museum. Why would he do that? Penn didn't know much about the man, but he seemed a scholar and a man committed to finding these objects that had come to mean something to him. He wouldn't have created fakes. It also seemed unlikely that he was aware they *were* fakes. If Penn's instincts were accurate.

"Have you any idea how he found the dagger?" Amelia asked.

"Now that is the strangest part," Burgess said, punctuating the air with his index finger. "Someone from Carmarthen brought it to him. Jon was told someone was looking for it, and this person didn't want it falling into the wrong hands. So he took it to Jon, knowing he'd found the heart years before. And before you ask, I've no idea who this person was. Jon never said."

"When was this?" Amelia asked.

"Oh, let me see. About forty years ago—1777 or 1778, I think."

"How long had the dagger been hidden in that cave?" Penn wondered aloud.

"Since about that time. I can't say for sure. Jon wrote to me about the man bringing it to him. He asked what he should do with it. I said he should bring it here, to the Ashmolean, of course." His brow darkened. "But someone ransacked his house shortly after that. Jon was certain they were looking for the dagger. Hearing about his journal entry from twenty years before that, it's clear he knew about the Order of the Round Table."

Amelia frowned. "It's also clear, at least to me, that he didn't trust the Order."

Burgess nodded in agreement. "It certainly sounded that way from the journal."

Amelia glanced at Penn, but her question seemed to be for Burgess. "Do you think the Order ransacked his house looking for the dagger?"

"It's possible," Burgess said with a shrug. He looked at Penn. "You know as well as I do the Order is unpredictable. I've no idea what they would and wouldn't do—it seems to change depending on who's in power."

"Do you know who that is?" Amelia looked between the men.

"We don't." Penn had tried to find out, but it was, perhaps, their most closely guarded secret. If Septon was to be believed, even *he* didn't know who the Prime Chevalier was. Penn turned his attention back to Burgess. "Is that when Gardiner hid the dagger?"

"I don't know exactly when he did that. I only know that he never brought it to the museum. When I asked him about it, he said it had been lost. I didn't know if that meant someone had stolen it or..." His voice trailed off. "I didn't hear another word about it until I received your letter, Mrs. Forrest."

"In which he told you exactly where it was located. But not why." Her tone was edged in frustration.

"That's correct. Another mystery that's lost to us now, I suppose."

Penn didn't like unsolved mysteries. His mind turned back to the book. He just knew Foliot had it, that he'd stolen it during the fire ten years ago. "I'd like to talk about the book for a moment—the White Book of Hergest. Gardiner wrote in his journal about his frustration at not being able to read it. I'm convinced that's the book he meant. What do you suppose that means? Was there something in a language he didn't know? Or was it something else?"

"I've no idea," Burgess said. "And unfortunately, the book is lost now. It burned in a fire in London some ten years ago, I think?" He looked from Penn to Amelia and back again.

"Yes, we're aware of that." Penn darted a glance at Amelia, silently communicating not to say anything. It wasn't that he didn't trust Burgess. He didn't trust the factions at work here—the Order or Foliot and his Camelot group. Gardiner had been afraid that knowledge could be dangerous, and Penn didn't disagree.

"Can you think of anything else I should know?" Amelia smiled at Burgess. "I do appreciate your time."

"Of course, my dear. I was quite fond of Jon." He pushed himself up from his chair and went to the bookcase behind his desk. Scanning the shelves, he selected a slim tome and went to hand it to Amelia. "I'd like you to have this. Your grandfather transcribed it for me. It's a collection of French poems from the fifteenth century."

Amelia opened the volume carefully. Her lips curled into that soft, devastatingly beautiful smile again, and Penn's gut clenched.

She looked up at Burgess. "Thank you so much. I will cherish it."

He beamed down at her, clasping his hands behind his back. "I'm delighted."

Penn stood. "Thank you for your time this morning, Burgess."

"My pleasure, my boy. I'm terribly sorry about what happened with the dagger. Is there any chance at all of recovering it?" He gazed at Amelia with sympathy. "I'm sure it pains you to have lost your grandfather's artifact."

"It does."

Penn offered his hand and helped her up from the settee. "I'm not certain we'll be able to get it back, but we will try."

"If anyone can, it's you, Penn." Do let me know if there is anything I can do to help."

"We will, thank you." Penn guided her from the office and outside into the bright sunshine. He steered her to the left down Broad Street.

"I'm more confused than ever about my grandfather," she said, frowning.

Penn wasn't sure what he'd expected to glean from Burgess, but he'd come away from the appointment with even more questions. He tried to be optimistic in the face of his own disappointment. "We did learn a few things. I think we can surmise he used whatever he found in the White Book to find the heart."

"And yet there was something in the book that he felt held answers. Answers he wanted to find. What could that be?"

"I don't know. We need that book." Determination hardened inside him. It was a familiar sensation that drove him on every one of his quests. This would be no different. Except for the fact that the book was likely in the possession of a dangerous group.

He paused and looked up and down the street before escorting her across.

She looked at him quizzically. "Where are we going? We missed Ship Street."

"I'm taking you to see the heart."

Her lips rounded into an O before forming a soft smile. "I've seen it. My grandfather brought me here when I was ten."

Penn suffered another stab of disappointment. He'd been looking forward to showing it to her. And yet, he got to see that smile again. "You light up when you think of him—when a memory comes to you, I think. He was an important figure in your life."

"He was, especially the last few years. With my parents gone and my grandmother gone, we were all each other had."

He stopped with her outside the museum, the warm summer day shining all around them. "And now he's gone, and you're alone. I'm so sorry, Amelia."

Her green eyes shimmered brightly. "You shouldn't call me that," she said quietly, her gaze never leaving his.

"Probably not, but I like the way it feels on my tongue." He was certain he'd like the way *she* felt on his tongue. He kept that prurient thought to himself.

Her nostrils flared, and he wondered if her mind had gone in the direction of his. "You're flirting again." That answered his question.

"Unintentionally. What can I say? I like you, *Mrs. Forrest.* Shall we go inside?"

They went into the cool interior, and he led her to the exhibit where the heart was kept. It sat atop a column, cradled in a specially made device that allowed extreme visibility. Those viewing it were kept a few feet back from the display by rope fastened to posts. One could walk entirely around the heart to see it from all sides.

"I don't remember the ropes," she said.

"They were introduced about ten years ago. Too many people were touching it, and there was concern it was becoming degraded."

"Weren't you concerned someone would try to steal one of the gems? Or the heart itself?"

"Yes, that too. We do have guards that supervise the museum, and the heart is locked away at night."

She gazed at the artifact. "I wish I could touch it. I didn't back then."

"You will."

She turned to look at him, her eyes sharp.

He smiled. "Tonight. I have access to where it's locked up —because I'm the Keeper's assistant. After dinner, we'll come back here to my office."

"I get to see your office?" There was the hint of that smile again, and his body heated. "I'm looking forward to it."

So was he.

~

The late August night was warm and still as they walked from Penn's house on Ship Street to his office at the museum. Over dinner, Penn had told her all about Oxford, and more than ever, Amelia wished she'd been able to attend university.

His house wasn't much larger than her cottage outside Bath, but it was spread over three floors, plus a scullery downstairs. Aside from Egg, he had a housekeeper and a caretaker, and it was a neatly kept abode, if rather stuffed with books and artifacts. His office also served as a library, but it simply wasn't large enough to hold everything, which was why things had spilled into the other areas. Even her bedchamber had a bookcase, and one wall was covered with a large, somewhat tattered but very beautiful medieval tapestry.

"Your house is charming," she said as he unlocked a door at the back of the museum.

He arched a brow at her as they entered the sconce-lit corridor. "Charming? That's kind of you, but probably an exaggeration."

"Not at all."

He gave her a skeptical look. "It's cramped. But then I'm not home long enough to care." He led her up a creaky staircase.

"That doesn't bother you? To travel so much, I mean."

"Not at all. I become a bit anxious when I've been in one place too long. I think it stems from my childhood. Before I went to live with my father, my first mother and I moved around a lot. We never stayed in one place longer than half a year." He turned into a corridor and stopped in front of a door, which he unlocked.

"Why is that?"

He paused, turning his head to look at her before moving inside. "I'm not entirely sure. I don't remember too much about her, but she was a nervous person."

"I'm sorry. That you didn't have a home," she clarified softly, aching for the boy she hadn't known.

He shrugged. "There's nothing to be done about it, and things turned out all right in the end. I know she loved me— that I remember."

Amelia smiled at him. That was really all that mattered.

"Welcome to my office," he said grandly, sweeping his arm around the room as he turned toward her.

She could barely see a thing since it was dark, and the sconce from the stairwell didn't lend nearly enough light. "Am I supposed to be impressed?"

He laughed, and she heard him striking flint. Soon a lantern on his desk was ablaze, splashing light around the cluttered space. It was an extension of his home, with a small fireplace, two mismatched wingbacked chairs flanking it, a long table shoved against one wall covered with artifacts, bookshelves, stuffed to overflowing, along the other wall, and a desk in front of them, stacked high with papers.

"Now that you can see it, you won't be impressed at all," he said with a healthy touch of humor.

"On the contrary. It looks like a scholar's haven. When he's weary of traveling, which apparently doesn't happen often."

He stared at her. "You understand me completely."

She wasn't sure about *that*. The intensity of his gaze unnerved her. But in the best possible way. Breaking the connection between them, she went to the table and studied the array of items scattered atop the wood. "What is all this?"

"Things I've found that need to be catalogued or studied."

"You've found all this?" She reached to touch a bronze disk but stopped, thinking that she probably shouldn't.

"Most of it. I should clarify—people also bring me things, but the bulk of it is mine."

The sound of him moving something caused her to turn. He stood at the fireplace clearing off the mantelpiece. She watched as he lifted the top off the wood, making the mantel look like a long, slender box.

She walked toward him. "Is that a box?"

"Indeed it is. A secret box, so you mustn't tell anyone."

"You trust me with your secrets?"

He pulled a sword from the mantel and pivoted toward her. "I do."

She gasped. "Is that Dyrnwyn?"

"It is." He brought it toward the desk, letting the light from the lantern better illuminate the weapon.

"It's beautiful. It looks heavy."

"Ridiculously so, actually. I worried that box wouldn't hold it, but I made sure it was reinforced." He transferred the hilt into her hand. "Here."

She closed her fingers around it, and her arm instantly dropped. "My goodness, is it made of lead?"

He laughed softly. "No, something else we likely aren't aware of. Apparently, it weighs nothing when Kersey holds it —or seems to anyway." He took it back from her, for which she was grateful.

"Extraordinary."

He set it on his desk and went back to the mantelpiece, arranging everything the way it was before. "It amused me to store it here at the museum when the Order was so intent on keeping it away from here."

She grinned, appreciating the irony. "Well done."

He flicked her a smile as he finished up, then went to a trunk in the corner. Opening it, he pulled a blanket from the interior. "We'll wrap it in this."

He'd mentioned using it to persuade Kersey to help them. "Do you really think we need it? I worry about losing it again."

He came back to the desk, carrying the blanket. "No one knows I have it."

"Septon does."

After laying the blanket out, he picked up the sword and set it on top of the wool. He turned his head to look at her. "You really don't trust him, do you?"

"I've no reason to."

He nodded and was quiet a moment before wrapping the sword with the blanket. "He won't try to take it. I may be skeptical about his honesty and whether he's told us everything he knows about the Order and their potential involvement with your grandfather, but in this, I trust him."

She touched his arm briefly, drawing him to straighten and turn toward her. "I don't want you to give up the sword. You said your sister spent her life looking for it, and you both believe it belongs here."

"And yet, how can I deny it also belongs to Kersey?" He gave her a small smile. "Anyway, I hope I won't have to. But if I do, I'd rather it go to him."

"I'm confused about Kersey. Is he a friend or foe?"

Penn blew out a breath. "That's a bit complicated. Until a month or so ago, I would've said friend. We grew up together —he's just a few years younger than me—because our fathers are second cousins. My father liked for us to spend time with him because his father is such an ass."

"That would be the Earl of Stratton?" she asked.

Penn nodded. "A worse excuse for a father doesn't exist. In a way, I understand how Kersey took a wrong step here and there. Especially since he lost his wife not so long ago. She died shortly after they married. He was devastated."

Amelia's chest tightened. "How tragic."

"Looking back, Kersey suffered a host of tragedies. His mother left him when he was nine or ten."

To be with another man—she chose Septon over her son. Yes, that qualified as a tragedy in Amelia's opinion. "Around the same age when your own mother died."

His gaze flickered with a bit of surprise and something else, maybe gratitude. "Yes, but I had my parents after that. Whereas Kersey had his father, such as he is." Penn shook his head. "My father made sure Kersey came to visit every summer, but Stratton put a stop to that when Kersey was about fourteen. We kept up a correspondence, however, and when he came to Oxford, I took him under my wing. I thought we were friends—in addition to being cousins, of course—but when I learned he stole the sword from my sister, I had to question the man I thought I knew. I *want* him to be a friend, but I don't know."

She moved a half step closer to him. "Maybe you'll determine that when we find him."

"I'm not sure I want to take you with me on that leg of the journey."

She squared her shoulders. "We're in this together. All this is a gamble."

"It is." He also moved closer, until they nearly touched. "Life is full of risk. That's what makes it worth living." He lifted his hand, and going very slowly, gently traced his finger along her jaw from cheek to chin.

Her belly tightened. They'd traveled this path before, coming very close to a kiss... Only to be interrupted by Septon. Would someone or something else come between them this time? She hoped not.

She did?

Yes, life was full of risk—and joy and wonder—and that *was* what made it worth living.

"Are you going to kiss me now?" she asked, sounding breathless to her own ears.

"If you'll permit me."

"Yes, please."

His eyes slitted but didn't fully close as he leaned forward. "Since you asked so prettily, how can I refuse? The truth is I can't. I've been longing for this moment for quite some time."

His words abruptly ended as his lips captured hers. His arms clasped her waist, and he pulled her against him.

She twined her arms around his neck, bringing her body flush to his. His mouth moved over hers, coaxing her—not that it took much effort—to kiss him back. She angled her head, sinking into him as heat raced through her body.

His fingers pressed into her back, and she responded by clutching his neck, her fingers delving into the hair edging his nape. He pulled back for a moment, and her eyes fluttered open in confusion. She'd rather hoped it would go on longer.

And then it did. He dipped his head once more and kissed

her with a deeper hunger, his mouth opening against hers and his tongue licking along her lower lip. She gasped softly and allowed her tongue to meet his. His hold grew tighter, the desire in her veins more intense. This was more than she'd imagined, more than she ought to indulge. What happened to keeping their relationship professional?

She eased her hands from his neck, sliding them down to his chest. He ended the kiss, pulling away slightly.

"So much for being professional," she murmured.

His lips spread into a lazy, seductive smile that did nothing to douse her passion. "That was professionally outstanding."

She cocked her head to the side. "What are you saying?"

His eyes widened. "Not that you're a professional at *that*. Good God, no." Color rose in his cheeks, and she had to smile at his reaction. "My apologies. I was attempting a jest. A very poor one."

"Are you trying to compliment me?"

"*Yes.* With every fiber of my being. You are extraordinary."

She pulled her hands from his chest and took a step back. "And you like to flatter me."

"Only with the truth. Wait here while I get the heart."

So she could touch it as he'd promised her that afternoon. "It's not necessary. We should probably return to your house since we're leaving early in the morning."

"It's absolutely necessary. We're taking it with us."

"We are?"

"I think we must. We may need it. I'll leave a note for Burgess that I'm borrowing it. That will satisfy him." He handed her his key. "Lock the door behind me. I'll be right back."

He was gone just a few minutes, during which she tried looking at the collection of artifacts on his table but was instead consumed with thoughts of his kiss. Everything would be different now.

Or would it?

Their attraction to each other had been simmering practically since they'd met. Did acting upon it change anything or simply embrace it?

A soft knock on the door interrupted her thoughts before she could answer, which she wasn't sure she could. She went to the door and whispered, "Penn?"

"Yes."

She unlocked the door and let him back inside. He was smiling a rather silly smile. "You called me Penn."

Damn, she had. "It seemed...appropriate now. And yes, you may call Amelia when we're alone."

"Excellent. I shall hope we are alone quite often." He leaned forward and pressed a swift kiss to her lips before depositing a heavy object—though not nearly as heavy as the sword—into her palm.

She looked down at the heart cradled in her hand and imagined her grandfather's joy at finding it. Moving to the lantern, she studied it, seeing where the paint was chipped. "How can you tell it isn't tourmaline?"

"I can't for certain, but it isn't the same color as the illustration in de Valery's manuscript." He picked up the sword. "Which was written using the sixth-century poem my parents found."

"Does tourmaline come in many colors?" she asked.

"At least a few. I've seen pink, which is the color in the illustration, and green."

If this were the real heart, she should be able to use it to make someone—Penn even—fall in love with her. *If* she was a descendant, which she wasn't since Dyrnwyn was so heavy. "You said you tried it on someone, and it didn't work. Isn't that because you aren't a descendant? What if we gave this to Kersey and he tested it?"

"Another excellent reason to find him as soon as possible." He looked at her shrewdly. "You're quite good at this."

Pride swelled her chest. "Thank you. I am a member of the Ladies' Antiquary Society after all." At least she thought she was.

"Indeed you are," he said with admiration. "Come, lady antiquary, let us be on our way."

He extinguished the lantern, plunging them into darkness once more, and a moment later, they were outside his office as he locked the door.

"Ready?" he asked.

She clutched the heart tightly in her fist. "Never more."

CHAPTER 9

*T*he journey through the Cotswolds was beautiful, and though Penn had made it dozens of times, he felt as though he were seeing it through new eyes with Amelia. When they'd stopped for a brief refreshment, he'd convinced her to join him in his coach. Since then, the day had passed quickly as their conversation had mostly focused on Penn's travels and exploits.

Egg was serving as coachman for the trip, a job he sometimes undertook on the rare occasion they took a coach instead of just horses. Penn typically preferred to travel lightly and quickly. The former ensured the latter.

However, this journey was different. He was content not to be in a rush and to enjoy his companion's company. What the hell was wrong with him?

He should be eager to talk to his father about the dagger and the White Book of Hergest—and he was. Yet, he was also eager to spend this time with Amelia.

And that was troubling.

Why, because he'd dreamed of her the night before? Yes. When he dreamed of women, they were faceless, nameless, completely without an anchor in reality. Amelia was quite real and sitting next to him as they pulled into the yard of The Falcon.

As the coach rumbled to a stop, Penn realized he hadn't discussed the particulars of their stay with Amelia. He turned to her as she yawned and stretched.

She blushed faintly. "My apologies. I'll be glad to be out of the coach."

He yawned in response, quickly covering his mouth with his fingers. "I will be too." He grinned. "I stay here quite often as I travel between Oxford and my parents' home in Monmouth. Mr. Jessup runs an excellent facility. There are four rooms, and I'll ask for two of them." He watched for her reaction, but there was none.

What had he expected? Disappointment? Did he think she'd wanted to share a chamber with him? Hell, *he* was the one dreaming of *her*, not the other way around. At least as far as he knew. She'd seemed to enjoy kissing him. Perhaps it wasn't too far-fetched to think she might dream of him too—

"Penn?"

He realized, belatedly and embarrassingly, that he'd gone completely lost for a moment. "Sorry, what was that?"

"I asked if it would be improper that we're traveling together."

"Not at all. You have your maid, and since you're a widow, I daresay there will be few eyebrows raised." Honestly, he paid a minimum amount of attention to societal guidelines. He had no need for them in the life he led.

"I suppose that will suffice."

Penn stepped out of the coach into the early summer evening. The scent of roses and sweet pea clung to the air, as did the chirps of a family of birds and the gentle wings of some flying insect. He turned to help Amelia down, then escorted her into the inn.

Mr. Jessup came from the back, his face splitting into a wide grin. He was short of stature with a balding pate and a generous sense of humor. "Good evening, Penn. It's good to see you." His gaze darted to Amelia.

"Allow me to present Mrs. Amelia Forrest," Penn said, reluctantly taking his arm from hers. "She is traveling to Monmouth with me on an errand of intellectual investigation."

Jessup's dark brows collected over his eyes. "I see." He executed a quick, smart bow. "Pleased to make your acquaintance, Mrs. Forrest. Do you have a maid with you? If not, my daughter could provide any assistance you may need."

Amelia gave him a warm smile. "My maid is just outside, but I do thank you for your hospitality, Mr. Jessup."

The innkeeper's gaze moved past them to the door. "Ah, this must be her now." He looked back to Amelia. "I've just the room for you. Cozy and inviting with fresh flowers Henrietta just cut." He called out for his daughter. "Etta, come show our guests to their rooms.

Etta came from the kitchen, wiping her hands on her apron. She smiled at Penn. "Good to see you, Penn."

"Good evening, Etta," he said. "This is my associate, Mrs. Forrest."

Etta dipped a brief curtsey. "Welcome to The Falcon."

"Etta, please show Mrs. Forrest and her maid to the room overlooking the garden."

"Of course. Right this way." She turned and went to the stairs in the back right corner of the room.

"Come and have an ale with me in the kitchen," Jessup offered. "I should keep an eye on things while Etta's upstairs." He turned without waiting for Penn's reply. Likely because Penn never refused his invitations to join him for ale.

Penn trailed him through the doorway that led to the kitchen at the back of the inn. Jessup stirred something on the stove before fetching tankards of ale for the both of them. He handed Penn his cup and offered a toast. "To a blessed summer."

Penn lifted his ale in acknowledgment before taking a long, deep draught. He closed his eyes briefly. "Still the best ale in England. And Wales."

"But not Scotland, eh?"

"Scotland too," Penn said with a chuckle.

"On your way home, then?" Jessup asked. He was well acquainted with Penn's travel patterns and knew that Penn spent a great deal of time on the road.

"For a bit."

Jessup sipped his ale. "And your companion… She really just an 'associate'?"

Penn ought to have expected that question. He and Jessup were friendly enough. He bit back the surprising answer that leapt to his mouth: *for now.* "Yes. I'm on the hunt for something."

"As usual," Jessup put in.

"As usual," Penn agreed with a nod. "Mrs. Forrest has an interest in the same artifact, and we've been working together to find it."

"Never seen you with a woman before. What does Egg think about that?"

"Egg is naturally disgruntled. You know that." Penn flashed a grin before taking another drink of ale. "In truth, I think he might like her. She did tend a wound for him. As it happens, she knows a bit about healing."

This gained Jessup's attention—his brows pitched up, and he leaned slightly forward. "Does she? I wonder if she has any remedies to offer for my joints. Last winter, they ached terribly."

"You can certainly ask her," Penn said.

"I may do that."

Etta came back into the kitchen and went directly to the stove to stir whatever was cooking there. "What do you plan to ask Mrs. Forrest, Papa?" she asked softly.

"About my joints. Penn says she's a healer."

"She knows some remedies," Penn said. "I'm not sure she'd call herself a healer." He wasn't sure and made a note to ask her more about that. He decided he should wash up before dinner. Excusing himself, he took his ale up to his regular room, where he washed his face and decided to don a new cravat.

A knock on the door caused Penn's fingers to fumble, and the silk slipped out of his grasp. "Bloody hell," he muttered. "Come in!"

Egg walked in, closing the door behind him. "Did you change your cravat?"

Penn frowned into the glass as he tried to focus on his task. One of the reasons he liked this inn so much was because he didn't have to share his room with Egg. Jessup had a nice, warm place in the stable, which suited Egg just fine.

Egg came over and swatted Penn's hands away. "Let me do it."

Penn scowled. "Ow. Careful of my wound." The back of his hand had healed nicely due to Amelia's salve, but it was still a bit sensitive.

"Now who's the infant?" Egg smirked while he quickly and efficiently tied Penn's cravat into a neat and stylish knot.

Penn turned his head back and forth as he surveyed his reflection. "How the hell do you do that?"

"You know I'm good at knots."

"Yes, with ropes. The fact that you can also tie an impeccable cravat is astonishing. Careful, I may promote you to valet."

"Try to give me that title, and I'll reinjure your 'and," Egg said with a glower.

Penn laughed as he turned from the glass.

Egg handed him his coat. "You don't want a valet any more than I want to be one."

"That's true." Nevertheless, he allowed Egg to help him don the garment. "Why are you here?"

"Just to tell you dinner's ready."

"And to apparently save my toilet. Thank you."

"We still leaving early tomorrow?" Egg asked.

"Yes. Why would things have changed?"

Egg shrugged. "I wasn't sure if you and Mrs. Forrest might want to linger here a little longer."

On his way to the door, Penn turned, narrowing his eyes at Egg. "What are you implying exactly?"

"Nothing, really. You and Mrs. Forrest just seem quite…friendly."

He was the second person to ask after his relationship with Amelia. What were they seeing? Yes, they'd shared a kiss, but that was all. "Yes, we're friendly. What would you rather us be?"

Egg snorted. "Not obtuse, but never mind that. You're adults."

Penn rolled his eyes. "I'm leaving now." He went downstairs into the small dining room and found that Amelia was already seated.

She looked up at him, and it seemed her gaze took in his combed hair and his tidy cravat. He was suddenly grateful for Egg's intrusion. She held up a tankard. "Mr. Jessup insisted I try his ale. It's quite good."

"My favorite, actually." He realized he'd left his empty vessel up in his room. Then his gaze fell on the fresh one set at his place. "I see Mr. Jessup has thought to provide one for me as well."

"I asked him to. I hope you don't mind."

"Not at all." Penn took his seat. "Their food is excellent as well."

"I look forward to it."

Etta appeared with their dinner plates. "Two courses," she said in her usual soft tone. Sometimes Penn had to strain to hear her. "Here's the first. Duck with carrots and potatoes."

Penn's mouth watered at the food. "It looks splendid, thank you."

Etta's cheeks flushed a pale pink as her eyes met his. "I hope you enjoy it." Then she was gone, leaving him alone with Amelia once more.

"I trust your accommodations are acceptable?" he asked.

"More than. I can see why you come back here again and again."

"That and the Jessups are good people. Speaking of Mr. Jessup, he has trouble with his joints—they bother him in the winter. I mentioned that you have some experience with healing remedies and may be able to help him."

She swallowed her bite of duck with a nod. "That's not uncommon at his age. My grandfather suffered from the same sort of aches. Willow-bark tea with ginger will help him quite a bit. I can write out how to make it."

"I'm sure he'd appreciate that."

They ate for a few minutes before she paused to take a drink of ale. She peered at him over her tankard and, when she replaced it on the table, asked, "I'd like to confess something."

That sounded serious. He set his knife and fork down. "What's that?"

"I'm...nervous about having taken the heart from the museum." She picked up her fork and poked at a carrot. "It just feels wrong somehow. Perhaps because my grandfather found it and put it there. I don't like thinking I'm undoing his work."

Penn didn't like her feeling unsettled, but he wasn't sure there was anything he could say to reassure her. She still believed the heart upstairs in his room was real. At least he thought she did. "Do you still think it's the real artifact?"

Her eyes widened briefly as her gaze latched to his. She took a moment to respond, and when she did, she surprised him. "I'm not sure." She pressed her lips together. "And I hate that."

Penn's frame relaxed against the chair as her words sank in. She'd begun to come around. He chose his next words carefully. "Maybe that's where your anxiety is coming from."

"Probably." She frowned down at her plate, then took another sip of ale. "I don't know what to believe." She raised her gaze to his once more, and he saw determination in their depths. "I do know I want to find the truth, and that means recovering the White Book of Hergest. Do you really think we'll be able to?"

He leaned over the table slightly and lifted his lips in a confident smile. "I'm very good at what I do."

She stared at him a moment, then rolled her eyes. "Your arrogance emerges at the oddest times."

Laughter shot from his mouth. "Arrogance? I prefer to think of it as being self-assured."

"Call it whatever you like. You're as bold as they come. But I suppose you have to be."

"I would paint you with the same brush."

Her brow curved into an elegant arch. "You think I'm arrogant?"

"Self-assured," he corrected. "And bold. And tenacious. How else could you have nearly shot Egg's ear off and traveled all over southern England with me?"

Now she blushed, and he appreciated the sparkle in her

eye that accompanied it. She went back to eating again, and a few moments later, Etta returned with the second course, replacing the first, then taking her leave once more.

"Jessup's mushroom sauce is divine," Penn said, slicing into his venison and working to scoop up as much sauce as possible. "Or perhaps it's Etta's, I really don't know."

"How long have you known the Jessups?"

Penn thought back to what had first drawn him to the inn. He'd been a student at Oxford. "Close to fifteen years. I was on my way home through Little Witcombe when I saw Etta very high in the oak tree that sits in the corner of the yard near the road. I'm not sure what made me stop, but I did, just to make sure she was all right. She was all of eight years old."

"Was she all right?"

Penn shook his head as he swallowed a bite of parsnips. "No. She was stuck and wasn't able to shout loud enough for anyone to hear her. She's always been painfully shy and soft-spoken."

Amelia's eyes creased with concern. "How horrid—not that she's shy, but that no one could hear her."

"I climbed up and managed to get us both down without falling. Honestly, I'm still not quite sure how I accomplished it."

"She's lucky you came along."

He waved his fork in nonchalance. "Someone would have found her—she hadn't been up there long. In any case, they insisted I stay, and that is how I came to know the Jessups and their delightful inn." He grinned at her before cutting another delicious piece of venison.

"And there are no other Jessups? She doesn't have siblings?"

"Unfortunately, no." He winced at the memory. "I met Mrs. Jessup that first time I stayed. She was with child. It was a difficult birth, and both she and the child were lost. It was a terrible time for them."

"How tragic." She lifted her tankard and murmured, "To Mrs. Jessup."

Penn raised his cup as well. "To Mrs. Jessup." He eyed Amelia as he drank. She had a kind heart. His sister would like her. Would they meet? He wasn't sure if Cate and her new husband planned to stop back in Monmouth after their wedding trip. And even if they did, it was likely he and Amelia would have moved on. He was keen to find the White Book—and the true heart.

They finished their meal, and before Penn could ask if she wanted to have a nightcap, she tried to stifle a yawn and failed.

"I'm afraid I'm ready to retire," she said apologetically.

"I'll escort you upstairs." Watching her yawn made him tired too. Nevertheless, his body was still contemplating that it might be nice to escort her all the way to her room and see if she offered an invitation. He inwardly grimaced.

Maybe he *was* arrogant.

"Thank you." She started to rise, and he rushed to pull back her chair.

He offered her his arm and tried to ignore the rush of anticipation her mere touch incited. Guiding her up the stairs, he paused at the landing and gestured down the corridor opposite his room. "Down there?"

"Yes, at the end."

He walked her to the door and waited until she removed her hand. When it took a second or two longer than necessary, he wondered if he ought to feel encouraged. "We'll leave early, taking breakfast with us. Unless you'd rather stay."

"No, I'd prefer to be on our way as soon as possible."

He laid his hand against his chest. "Your eagerness speaks directly to my heart."

"And now you're a poet?"

"My father would be delighted to think so."

Her soft laughter sang in the dim corridor. "I'm looking forward to meeting your parents."

"I'm sorry I can't meet yours." She sobered, and he wished he hadn't said that. "I didn't mean to make you melancholy."

"You haven't. I like thinking of them." Her gaze found his, and a connection between them gathered and held.

"May I kiss you again?" He hadn't meant to ask, but it suddenly seemed as though he must.

She didn't break eye contact, and she didn't blink. "Yes."

Again, she surprised him. He gently cupped her face and lightly brushed his lips across hers. Their first kiss had been a rush of sensation. This one would be an exploration, a deepening of what they already knew of each other. And he knew enough to realize he was sliding into the promise of something that would bring them both pleasure.

Hell, maybe he *was* a poet. A bad one, anyway.

Her lids dropped closed as he tipped his head and pressed his mouth more firmly against hers. Her hands moved under his arms to clasp his back.

He caressed her nape, then trailed the fingers of one hand down her spine. His movement necessitated she move her arm over his, and she did so with alacrity, her palm flattening against the side of his neck just above his cravat so that her flesh and his connected.

The contact caused a shiver that started at the back of his neck and fanned out to every part of him. Before he could recover, her tongue sought entrance to his mouth, and the control he was clinging to faltered.

He surrendered to her kiss, pressing her tight against him as rapture built within him. Kissing Amelia was like nothing he'd ever known. It was sweetness and fire blended with audacity and seduction.

He cradled her head with his left hand, pulling it back slightly as he tasted her mouth. They were close to the door. In fact, she pushed her back against it and pulled at him, her hands clinging tightly to his coat and his nape.

To keep his hand from being pinned between her back and the door, he skimmed his fingers under her arm and over her rib cage. His knuckles brushed the curve of her breast, and he simply couldn't refuse the temptation.

He tried to cup her from beneath, but her corset prevented such intimacy. Instead, he brushed his hand up to where her flesh peeked above the dainty lace edge of her gown. He ran his thumb over her bare skin and felt her reaction as she withdrew her tongue from his and a low sound formed in her throat.

Emboldened, he slipped his fingers into the top of her gown. She thrust her breasts forward, seeking his touch. It was all he could do to keep from tearing her gown away and feasting on her.

But he wasn't a brute. Nor did he want to rush this moment. He wanted to savor every touch, every taste. Taking his mouth from hers, he nipped at her chin before kissing along her neck, his tongue and lips sampling her sweet, sensitive flesh.

She gasped softly as her fingers moved into his hair at the back of his head and pressed against his scalp. He needed no further urging. He trailed his mouth down along her collarbone, then lower still until he reached the rise of her breast. He longed to set it free, to find her nipple, to increase her pleasure. Her breathing was rapid now, matching the frenetic beat of his own heart.

He clasped her waist, kneading her through the layers of her clothing. She arched forward again, this time with her pelvis. He groaned quietly, just managing to keep himself in check. But only barely.

Her hand moved down his back and she clutched at his backside, pulling him flush against her. His cock, pressed neatly against her core, pulsed with desire.

This was the moment he'd ask to take her into her room. The moment they'd come together and spend an evening of mutual bliss. But after that evening came the morrow and, with it, the parting.

Only they couldn't part. Nor did he want to.

His lips stilled against her breast. What the hell was he doing? It was now clear that Amelia was different from any other woman he'd encountered. And what did that mean?

He couldn't embark on a liaison with her. She was more than that. She was a woman one married.

But he *couldn't* do that. His life didn't allow for a wife or a home or a family. She deserved all that and more.

Penn removed his arms from her and took a wobbly step backward.

Her eyes came open, and they were bemused. Her kiss-swollen lips parted, but she didn't say anything. She simply stared at him as if she were trying to regain her bearings. Which was precisely what he was trying to do.

"I didn't mean for that to get so..." What? Intense? Passionate? Reckless? *All of those.* "I should bid you good night."

She nodded, her eyes flickering with a touch of wariness. "Good night, Penn."

"Good night, Amelia."

Turning, she opened the door and went inside without a backward glance.

He wondered if her maid was inside or if she was lodging somewhere else. It was a good thing he hadn't tried to go into her room. If the maid had been there...

He shook his head and ran his hand through his hair,

chastising himself. None of that mattered. They were supposed to be acting professionally.

Pivoting on his heel, he stalked down the corridor toward his room. As he passed the stairs, he nearly crashed directly into Etta.

She let out a soft cry and seemed to teeter on the top stair. Penn reached out to grab her lest she lose her balance. Clasping her around the waist, he held her tightly. "I've got you."

Her warm brown eyes were round as dinner plates for a moment before her features began to relax.

He realized she held something in her hands. "What do you have there?"

"My father wanted me to bring you some whiskey." She held up a bottle and a tumbler between them.

"That was very thoughtful of him." Before he let go, he searched her expression. "Do you have your footing, then?"

She blushed and looked away, a small smile teasing her lips. "Yes, thank you."

He removed his hands and took the whiskey and the tumbler from her. "Now I don't have my hands free to rescue you, so look sharp." He winked at her.

Holding up her hands, she wriggled her fingers. "My hands are free now. Mayhap I'll rescue you. I do owe you—twice now, I suppose."

"You do not owe me anything, Etta. It was my pleasure to take you down from the tree all those years ago." He lowered his voice to a conspiratorial tone. "It makes me feel a bit like a hero."

She nodded enthusiastically. "Because you are. You're *my* hero." She stepped onto the landing with him and before he realized what she was about, she kissed him.

And it wasn't a quick brush of her lips against his. No, she pressed her mouth to his and laid her hands against his chest.

Shock froze him to the spot, and since his hands were full, he couldn't very well push her away. Not that he wanted to do *that* given he'd just saved her from tumbling down the stairs. *Pull yourself together,* he admonished himself.

He took a small step backward. "Ah, Etta. Miss Jessup," he amended, thinking they'd been far too familiar over the years.

Scarlet flooded her face, and she pivoted so that she presented her profile. "Forgive me, I thought you might like me to do that." She shook her head vigorously. "No, I wanted to do that." She turned back to face him. "I've wanted to do that for some time."

Apparently so. She'd called him her hero. Hell, had he encouraged her somehow? "Et—Miss Jessup, I apologize if I've given you the wrong impression. You are quite, er, young for me." That was certainly true. Or it seemed to be—in his mind, she would likely always be the young girl he's rescued. "I care for you a great deal, as if you were part of my family— like a sister."

Her features fell as if he'd just told her that her dog had died. Penn felt terrible. But if Jessup found out about this… Penn straightened. "Let's keep this between us, shall we? No one need know you gave me a thank-you kiss for saving you. Twice now."

Now she looked relieved. "That's an excellent idea. Thank you." She tipped her head to the side. "Twice? Does that mean I should give you a second kiss?"

Penn stepped back again, moving so quickly, he almost dropped the bottle and tumbler. "No, that won't be neces- sary. Your gratitude is quite noted. And appreciated." He smiled and held up the items in his hands. "Thank you for the whiskey. Good night."

Then he turned and fled to his room as quickly as he could. And locked the door for good measure.

*A*melia surveyed herself in the glass. She looked calm and serene, her hair perfectly dressed by Culley, who was now packing up the last of their things.

Inside, however, Amelia was a tumult of emotion.

After Penn had pulled away from their kiss last night, Amelia had gone into her room with a sense of relief. However, the desire he'd awakened in her had quickly chased that relief away. Deciding she *did* want to be a bold adventurer, she'd turned and opened the door intent on inviting herself back to Penn's room—that would have been a necessity since Culley would be sleeping on a pallet in her room.

Only Penn had no longer been in front of her door.

Peering down the corridor toward his room, she'd seen him at the top of the stairs, his hands clasping Henrietta Jessup rather intimately. Then she'd given him the bottle and cup she'd been holding only to put *her* hands on *him.*

Then she'd kissed him.

And that was all Amelia had been able to tolerate. She'd closed the door—quietly so as not to alert them to the fact that she'd opened the door in the first place. She regretted it entirely.

What had she expected? Penn's reputation with women was apparently well-known. Culley had told Amelia all about it after hearing quite an earful from Penn's housekeeper. It seemed women flocked to him, finding him irresistibly attractive. For the most part, he kept to himself, but he was a man, after all, and conducted discreet liaisons from time to time.

Had he turned to Henrietta after deciding it was best to keep his relationship with Amelia professional? It was her own fault for insisting they do that. Except, she'd made light of it when he'd kissed her in Oxford, and… And what? They hadn't discussed any expectations and whether they would kiss again. Then he'd asked her last night, and she'd felt certain they were of a similar mind.

Apparently, she'd been wrong. Or he'd changed his mind. Perhaps she was just really skilled at driving men away.

Gritting her teeth, she turned from the glass. Culley had just finished buckling up her valise. She gave Amelia a bright smile, blissfully ignorant of the turmoil rattling in Amelia's head.

"Ready, then?" Culley asked.

Amelia took a deep breath to cleanse her frustrating thoughts. "Yes. I imagine someone will fetch our luggage—whoever brought them up."

"That was Egg," Culley said.

Giving Culley a nod, Amelia departed the chamber and made her way downstairs. As she descended, her body tensed. She didn't particularly want to see Penn this morning. Perhaps she could go directly to her coach. He did say they wouldn't be lingering for breakfast.

But no, there he was standing near the door speaking with Mr. Jessup, his hair combed back from his handsome face, and his shirt and cravat almost blindingly white against his dark tan skin. He smiled at something the innkeeper said, and Amelia's insides twisted with want.

Damn him.

How many times had she thought that curse in reference to Thaddeus? *Too many.* But at some point, she'd realized she was better off without him, even if his abrupt departure had been devastating for a time.

A thought occurred to her—she ought not carry on any sort of liaison with Penn Bowen. She was, legally, still a married woman. Thaddeus had to be missing seven years to be declared dead, and it had only been five.

Did any of that really matter? It wasn't as if her marriage to Thaddeus had turned out all that well. Aside from the fact that he'd left her, their union hadn't been the grand love affair she'd hoped it would be. He'd swept her off her feet when she'd been barely twenty-one, and for the first few months, she'd believed he loved her in return. Then he'd stopped coming home at night. Then he'd stopped coming home for days at a time. Then he'd stopped coming home at all.

Then the creditors had come and taken most of what they'd owned.

Oh, she knew marriage could be a happy estate—her parents and grandparents had demonstrated that. Still, she wondered why hers had gone so horribly wrong.

Grandfather had said she chose poorly. Well, she didn't mean to do *that* again.

Penn's gaze found hers, and his mouth lifted at the corners in a half smile. It didn't reach fruition, however. Instead, his eyes darkened and his brow creased.

Perhaps because she hadn't returned his expression of happiness.

Extricating himself from Mr. Jessup, Penn came over, his gaze now wary. "Good morning." The greeting held a bit of a question.

"Good morning," Amelia said, hoping she didn't sound as stiff as she felt. She didn't want things to be awkward since they had to work together.

He lowered his voice to a near whisper. "Are you upset with me?"

She blinked at him and kept up an air of nonchalance that was quite at odds with the thundering of her heart. "No. Should I be?"

Yes.

He hesitated before slowly answering. "I hope not." He

pressed his lips together. "I apologize for last night. I got carried away, and that wasn't well done of me."

Just as she suspected, he regretted it. "Yes, well, we won't do that again. We've behaved professionally for the majority of our association, and I expect we can do so again." She squared her shoulders. "Are we ready to depart?"

"Nearly. I'm just waiting for Henrietta to bring our breakfast so we may take it along with us." His gaze tripped past her toward the back of the inn. "Here she comes."

Anger flared in Amelia's chest. Rather than turn and see the woman Penn preferred to be kissing, she said, "I'll be outside." She stalked quickly from the inn. Outside, the summer morning was bright and warm. She inhaled deeply, willing the scent of grass and wild rose to banish the ire burning through her.

Their two coaches were ready and waiting in the yard. Amelia's coachman, Horatio, stood speaking with Culley, while Egg leaned against Penn's coach, eating an apple.

Penn came from the inn, a basket in each hand. He frowned slightly as he approached her. "Are you sure you're not angry? You looked angry."

"I'm not angry." She tried to sound blithe. "I simply didn't wish to come between you and Henrietta saying your goodbyes."

After a flicker of surprise in the darkness of his eyes, they narrowed slightly. "What does that mean?"

Amelia shrugged. "I thought you and she shared a special...connection." She tried to keep the acid from her tone, but failed. How she hated sounding like a shrew.

Understanding dawned in his features. "You saw... You're jealous."

Apparently. "I am not." She hated sounding like a liar even more.

He smiled then, taking her off guard. "Henrietta does

have a tendre for me, as it happens. I believe she has a bit of hero worship from the time I saved her all those years ago." He shook his head. "I never knew. Last night, she kissed me. It was…awkward. I'm afraid I crushed her sensibilities. I felt terrible."

Now *Amelia* felt terrible. "I'm sorry to hear that happened. It's just…"

"I kissed you, then left abruptly." He cocked his head to the side. "How did you happen to see me with Henrietta?"

Heat rose up Amelia's neck, and she hoped the blush didn't spread to her face. She wasn't going to tell him why she'd really opened her door again. He might not have been willfully kissing Miss Jessup, but the entire event had given Amelia more than enough reason to recall that their relationship was supposed to be strictly professional. "I forgot to ask you about the plan to retrieve the dagger. I know we're going to see your father for help regarding the White Book of Hergest, but how will that point us toward the dagger?"

"That will depend on what we learn. You've reminded me that we should discuss how I will introduce you to my parents."

She blinked at him. "As your partner in recovering the dagger. How else would you introduce me?"

"No other way." He searched her gaze for a moment before handing her one of the baskets. "Here is your breakfast. Jessup tucked a small bottle of ale inside."

"How thoughtful of him."

"Are you sure you're not angry? Or jealous?" The last seemed to carry a hopeful tone.

"I assure you I am not. You are correct in that we were carried away last night, and we mustn't let it happen again."

"I rather liked kissing you," he said softly. "But I didn't wish to take advantage."

"I appreciate your behavior. You're a true gentleman, and

I'm glad I can trust you." She offered him a bright smile as a butterfly flitted over their heads. "As nice as kissing you has been, I think it best if we return to our original arrangement. We have an important objective, and we should be focused on that." She sounded so convincing that she almost believed herself. And yet, a part of her, the romantic that had hoped for the grand love affair with her husband, sagged with disappointment.

"As you wish," he said, his tone now a mixture of disappointment and frustration. "We'll be in Monmouth early this afternoon. Enjoy your journey."

"You too." She turned and went to her coach and wondered if a return to their original arrangement was even possible. Despite what she'd said, she couldn't help but think of his lips covering hers, his hands caressing her, his hips thrusting forward...

Amelia opened her basket and found dark brown toast inside. A smile crept over her mouth as she realized only Penn could be responsible for that. Damn, she couldn't even have her breakfast without him intruding.

She took a large bite of the deliciously scorched bread. Best to keep herself occupied, or it was going to be a very long trip.

CHAPTER 10

*T*he familiar face of his childhood home—well, part of his childhood—greeted Penn as his coach rumbled to a stop in the drive. His father called Hollyhaven a cottage, but it was rather larger than that. With its mullioned windows and ivy-covered stone, it was the most charming home Penn had ever seen. When he'd come to live here, he'd thought he'd been transported to a fairy tale.

But then his father had been the real reason for that. Followed quickly by his mother, since they'd wed soon after his arrival. No matter how old he was or how far he traveled, he always looked forward to coming home.

He didn't wait for Egg to open the door before stepping out of the coach. Already, the door to the house opened to reveal his smiling mother, her honey-blonde hair still devoid of any white or gray.

Instead of hastening to the entry, he went to Amelia's coach. He didn't care what she'd said that morning. She *had* been angry, and he was willing to wager she'd been jealous too.

However, any pleasure he might have felt at her

emotional response was tempered by her insistence that they return to their original arrangement—that of professional partners and nothing more.

And why was he upset by that? *He* was the one who'd put an end to their embrace last night. *He* was the one who was terrified of settling down.

Wait, terrified?

Before he could answer that thought, Amelia's coachman helped her down, beating Penn to the door. Penn awaited her descent and couldn't help but think she was even lovelier now than she had been that morning. Blonde curls peeked from beneath the rim of her bonnet, and her green eyes shone like gemstones in the bright afternoon sun.

He offered her his arm. "Come, I'll introduce you to my parents."

Guiding her to the door, Penn saw that his father had joined his mother. Rhys Bowen was tall, dark eyed, and dark haired with the same dark Welsh complexion as Penn. They looked enough alike that no one questioned whether Penn was his blood son. Indeed, among the handful of people who knew the truth, most of them commented that Penn looked as though he was. Though Penn knew it was impossible, it still gave him comfort.

Margery Bowen smiled broadly as they approached. "Penn, we're so glad to see you." Her gaze moved to Amelia. "Welcome." She glanced toward her husband and murmured, "It seems our children keep bringing home members of the opposite sex..."

Penn's sister, Cate, had brought her now-husband, Lord Norris, here several weeks ago. Apparently, he'd assured the Bowens that his relationship with Cate was purely nonromantic. Clearly, that had been a lie. In this case, however, Penn could make the same claim and be assured that it was, at least right now, completely accurate.

"Mother, Father, allow me to present Mrs. Amelia Gardiner Forrest." Penn included her family name on purpose.

As expected, Father's brows arched with interest. "Gardiner? As in Jonathan Gardiner? Did your…grandfather, I would think, discover the Heart of Llanllwch?"

She nodded. "He did, indeed." She dipped a curtsey. "I'm pleased to meet you both."

"Come in, come in." Mother stepped to the side and gestured for them to move into the coolness of the entry hall.

"Would you prefer to rest, or can I tempt you to join us for tea in my study?" His father's hopeful tone matched the anticipation in his gaze.

Penn looked toward Amelia in question. He'd join his parents, but he wanted her to do as she pleased.

She smiled at his parents. "Tea would be lovely."

Father led them into his study, which was situated just off the entry hall. It was a large room dominated by a long table that was always covered with books or manuscripts or odd ends of paper as his father completed translations.

Amelia's gaze roved the bookshelves climbing the walls, the ornate desk at the opposite end, and, of course, the table in the center. "My grandfather would have loved this," she said softly, almost reverently.

"I'm sorry I didn't know him, or I would have invited him to visit," Father said. "We'll sit over here for tea." He indicated the furniture arranged in front of the window that faced the drive.

Amelia didn't immediately move to sit down. Instead, she surveyed a medieval manuscript that lay open on the table, its illuminations vividly striking.

Father stood next to her. "This is from the fourteenth century."

"Is that Welsh?" she asked.

"Medieval, yes," Father said, flicking a glance toward Penn. "My son can translate it for you, if you like."

She darted a look at Penn, and he saw the question there. He gave an infinitesimal nod.

"How wonderful to be able to read that." Her tone was rather wistful. "I'm afraid I can only read and speak French."

"I have many French romances, if you'd care to read them," Father offered. He was always keen to share his library. "It might be slightly challenging if they're older, but Penn or I could help."

"You came here very quickly," Mother said as she sat on the settee in front of the window.

Confused, Penn blinked at her. "What do you mean?"

Mother's eyes showed a flash of surprise. "You didn't receive our note?"

"I did not."

Father turned from the table. "Ah, well, we can discuss that later. Penn, tell us what brings you and Mrs. Forrest here." He smiled warmly at Amelia and waited for her to take a chair near the settee before sitting down beside his wife.

Penn took the chair at the other end of the settee. "You're aware that Jonathan Gardiner found the Heart of Llanllwch. He also found the dagger that counteracts it."

The anticipation in Father's gaze heightened. "And you have it now?"

"No, but I did." Penn hated disappointing his father. "It was stolen from us, and now we are on the hunt to recover it."

His mother looked between him and Amelia. "You both found it?" Her eyes narrowed perceptively. "How long have you been working together, and how did that come about?"

The tea arrived then, and Mother dismissed the housekeeper immediately so they could continue their conversation.

Penn exchanged a look with Amelia, whose eyes widened briefly. She had to be wondering if Penn planned to tell his parents that she'd threatened to shoot him. "We, uh, happened to stumble upon it at the same time." That was true enough. "Her grandfather had asked her to find it, but unfortunately didn't leave her with enough information. What he did was write a letter with the dagger's location, which he sent to Carlton Burgess."

"Naturally, Burgess sent you to retrieve it," Penn's father said as he helped himself to a biscuit from the tray.

"But who stole it?" his mother asked. "And I trust you're all right?"

"Yes, though Egg sustained a minor injury. Which Mrs. Forrest was kind enough to tend with a homemade salve. He's fine now."

His mother looked at Amelia with a hint of admiration. "Thank you, Mrs. Forrest. Egg is dear to us, despite his sometimes sour demeanor."

"You were telling us who stole it," Father prompted.

Penn continued. "We aren't certain, but I would wager it was the Camelot group. Septon insists it wasn't the Order."

Penn's father leaned back against the settee and stretched his arm out along the back behind Penn's mother. "You've already seen Septon?"

"We went there afterward. I wanted to consult his library."

"But not him?" his mother asked. Unlike her husband, she didn't entirely trust Septon. Not since the Order had attacked them all those years ago.

Penn shrugged. "His library usually provides the answers I need."

"In this case, Septon proved helpful," Amelia said. "We were looking for the origin of the Ranulf and Hilaria story."

"It's in the White Book of Hergest," Father said immediately. "Unfortunately, that book is lost. But the tale was copied in many other books."

Penn poured himself a cup of tea. "We know. However, the White Book may not be lost. We tracked it to the book-binder in London. After speaking with them, I believe it was stolen during the fire—and that the fire was set as a diversion to make it look as though the book was lost."

His father's eyes widened. He pulled his arm back to his side and leaned forward. "You can't be serious."

Mother elbowed him gently. "Of course he is, dear. He's our son." The note of pride in her voice warmed Penn's heart.

"I am going to find the White Book because I believe it holds the key to finding the real Heart of Llanllwch."

"You still believe the one in the museum is fake?" Father asked.

Penn pulled it from the pocket of his coat where he'd stashed it that morning at the inn. "I do."

His mother gasped. "You stole it from the museum?"

"Borrowed it," Penn clarified.

Father's dark brows gathered over his darker eyes. "Why are you so convinced the White Book holds the key?"

"My grandfather was especially interested in it," Amelia answered. "He went to see it at Wynnstay."

Penn's mother shook her head. "My apologies, Mrs. Forrest. I should've offered to pour your tea. Forgive me. We are swept into conversations of this nature quite easily, I'm afraid."

Amelia smiled softly. "I understand. I've started to do the same thing since becoming acquainted with your son. He's quite passionate about antiquities. And, perhaps more importantly, the search for them."

Mother chuckled as she poured tea for Amelia and then herself and Father. "Yes, that's Penn. As you can see, he poured his own tea without missing a step. We usually just help ourselves."

Penn felt mildly embarrassed. He hadn't even thought to offer Amelia tea before pouring his. As was often the case, his social skills were a bit lacking. But then they weren't typically necessary in the life he led.

Father diverted the conversation away from any discomfort. "I never had a chance to see the White Book." His voice held a note of regret. "How will you find it?"

"Foliot has it." Penn awaited his father's negative reaction and wasn't disappointed.

"And just how in the hell do you think you'll get it from him?" He shot an apologetic glance toward Amelia. "Forgive me."

"I'm hoping Kersey will help us," Penn said, anticipating another reaction, but not entirely sure what it might be. Like Penn, Father was torn between fury at him for how he'd treated Cate and stolen the sword and love for the person they'd known for years, and in Father's case, Kersey's whole life.

"You're in luck, because he's likely on his way here," Mother said, surprising the hell out of Penn.

Penn looked from her to his father and back again. "He is?" He suddenly recalled what she'd said when he'd arrived, commenting on how quickly he'd come. They'd summoned him home for some reason. Had they done the same to Kersey? That made absolutely no sense. What made even less sense was Kersey listening to them. Penn shook his head. "I can't imagine he'll come. How did you even know where to find him?" Kersey had ridden off to parts unknown after giving Cate the sword.

Father lifted his shoulder in an enigmatic shrug. "I know Gideon quite well."

Penn wasn't sure what to make of that statement but

didn't have a chance to ask. Amelia abruptly stood. "If you'll excuse me, I think I'd like to go upstairs for a respite before dinner."

Everyone else jumped to their feet. "Of course," Mother said. "I'll have Mrs. Thomas show you upstairs." She guided Amelia from the study. At the door, Amelia cast a glance back at Penn, but her expression was unreadable.

He had no idea where things stood between them. That wasn't true. They were partners and nothing more.

"You're frowning," his father said.

Penn blinked and turned his attention to his right, where his father was plucking another biscuit from the tray.

"What's going on between you and Mrs. Forrest?" Father asked.

"Nothing." Penn realized he answered a bit too quickly, but it was the truth.

Father gave him a knowing stare. "That look you just gave her wasn't nothing."

"What look?" Mother swept back into the study and landed back on the settee next to Father. "Are you discussing Mrs. Forrest?"

"*He's* trying to," Penn muttered.

"And Penn is trying to tell me there's nothing between them."

"I'm not sure I doubt that." Thank goodness for his mother's sense. "At least as far as Mrs. Forrest is concerned. I didn't catch any indication they share anything more than a professional acquaintance." She turned her head to her husband. "But then I missed whatever 'look' you just mentioned."

"He frowned as she left. That was after she looked back at him. I couldn't tell if she was trying to say something. Without saying anything."

Mother nodded. "I know what you mean." She turned to Penn. "Interesting."

Penn rolled his eyes and picked up his teacup, taking a deep drink before clattering it back on the table. "Is this how you discuss me when I'm not here?"

"Somewhat." Mother laughed softly but then sobered rather quickly. She looked back to his father, and Penn's neck prickled.

"Why did you send for me to come home? And Kersey too?"

His parents exchanged another look, the kind they always shared when they were worried about one or both of their children. And this worried Penn.

It was his father who spoke first. He angled his body toward Penn and gave him an earnest look followed by the slight curving of his lips. He seemed to be trying to impart a sense of supportive concern. Penn's worry intensified.

"The Earl of Stratton has died."

Penn exhaled. "I can't imagine anyone will mourn him."

"Gideon might—at least a little," Mother said.

That was true. After his mother had left, Kersey had only had his father, such as he was. They'd developed a close relationship for a while, until Kersey had come to realize just how horrid his father was.

"Is that why you asked me to come?" Penn asked. "To be here for him?"

Father shifted uncomfortably, appearing as though he were sitting on sharp rocks and not a settee. "Not, uh, exactly."

Mother stood from the settee and came around the low table where the tea tray sat. She knelt beside Penn's chair and took his hand. The apprehension he'd just dispelled came roaring back.

Penn's heart began to pound. He couldn't imagine why they were acting like that. "What is this about?"

Father took a deep breath and looked Penn square in the eye. "The Earl of Stratton wasn't just Gideon's father. He was also yours."

It was as if the world around him faded to gray. Penn wasn't aware of his parents, of the chair beneath him, of the roof over his head. The face of his mother—the woman who'd given birth to him—floated before him. He saw the fear that had always lurked deep in her gaze, even beneath the love she'd had for him. He recalled the secrecy she'd incessantly employed in his youth, telling him to never give his name to strangers and not to talk to Quality at all if possible. The name Will drifted up from the recesses of his mind—she'd called him that a few times when he'd been very young. He remembered that Stratton's first wife had disappeared and was found dead.

"His first wife didn't die, did she?" Penn asked in a barely audible voice. In fact, he wondered if he'd actually spoken aloud.

"Not until later. After she brought you here. To me." The anguish in his father's voice did nothing to soothe the confusion and distress tumbling through Penn.

The room—and his parents' concerned faces—came back into focus. "Why did she bring me here?" Penn was vaguely aware of his mother squeezing his hand.

"Because I was the only family she trusted. She wanted you to have your birthright some day—after Stratton was dead."

Dread filled Penn's soul. "What are you saying?"

"You're the Earl of Stratton now."

Hell no. *Hell* no. "I can't be. No one even knows I exist. Kersey—Gideon—sure as hell doesn't know."

His father winced. "That's true—about Gideon.

However, the vicar who recorded your birth is very much aware, and he's protected the legal proof of your birth for over thirty years. As directed by your mother, he'll come forward now and provide the proof necessary for you to claim the title."

Penn stood, dropping his mother's hand and awkwardly stepping around her. "I don't want it."

An earl? What the fuck was he supposed to do with that? He hadn't the slightest notion how to be an earl, nor did he want to be. A future of being tied to a title loomed before him like an executioner's axe.

His father's face was grim, his mother's lined with sorrow. "You don't have a choice."

They'd lied to him for years. They'd allowed him to cultivate a life that had nothing to do with an earldom, knowing that someday it would come to an abrupt and necessary end.

"You didn't think how this would affect me?" He hated how broken and angry he sounded, but he couldn't help it. And he wouldn't. They deserved his rage.

"I've thought of little else," Father said, rising from the settee and helping his mother to stand.

She gave him a tentative smile. "Penn, we'll work through this. It will be all right."

"Tell that to Gideon when he arrives. I'm sure he'll be just as thrilled as I am. You've ruined two lives today, and for what?"

His father's features were a mix of regret and resolve. "For your birthright. You *are* the Earl of Stratton."

"Not if I can help it."

Penn stalked from the room and left through the back of the house, heading straight for the woods behind the sloping yard. It was the place he'd always gone when he'd first come to Hollyhaven—it had been his haven.

And for the first time in years, he needed a refuge. For the first time in years, he felt alone and abandoned, as if his world would never be right again.

~

*A*melia walked downstairs for dinner at seven. They'd pushed dinner back an hour for some reason she didn't know. She was surprised to find the dining room empty upon her arrival. Was something amiss at Hollyhaven?

There'd been a strange air in the study that afternoon—something between Penn's parents. She'd excused herself thinking the family needed some privacy. Now the feeling that she was somehow intruding intensified.

"Good evening, Mrs. Forrest."

Amelia turned at the sound of Penn's mother's voice.

"Good evening, Mrs. Bowen."

The older woman smiled briefly—too briefly. "Please call me Margery."

"I couldn't."

Penn's mother waved her hand in dismissal. "I insist. I don't know the nature of your relationship with Penn, but if he brought you here, he must think quite highly of you. He never brings anyone here."

That made Amelia absurdly pleased. "We've become friends," she said cautiously. She didn't want to disclose anything Penn would prefer to keep private. But was there really anything to hide? She'd told him that morning that they were going back to where they'd started. Well, not quite where they'd started. She had no intention of pointing a pistol at him anytime soon.

No, never that. In fact, she'd begun to regret telling him she wanted to just be partners again. Because she didn't really. The truth was that she *had* been jealous.

"I'm not aware of Penn having any women friends,"

Margery said. "I'm glad, because he could actually use a friend right now."

Her words alarmed Amelia. "What happened?"

"Will you sit and have dinner with me? I'm afraid it will be just us. My husband is too upset to eat and begs your pardon for being absent."

"Of course. Where's Penn?"

"I'm not entirely sure." Margery gestured toward the table. "Shall we sit?"

Amelia took one of the two places with a setting. She hadn't noticed there were just two when she'd entered.

Margery sat at the end of the table to Amelia's left. A young footman served them soup and then departed.

Amelia grew anxious waiting for Margery to explain Penn's absence. "Is Penn all right?"

Picking up her spoon, Margery stared at her soup a minute. When she raised her gaze to Amelia's, it was filled with apprehension. "I don't know." She gave her head a shake. "That's not true. No, he's not all right. We gave him some upsetting news."

Amelia grasped at what it could be. "Does this involve Kersey?"

"Yes. Somewhat. His father, the Earl of Stratton, died three days ago."

The flash of relief Amelia felt was momentary. Clearly, this affected Penn somehow. "Why is Penn upset about this? I had the impression he didn't care for Stratton."

"*No one* cared for Stratton," Margery said derisively. She gave a delicate shudder. "Which is one reason this news was so upsetting for Penn." She looked at Amelia with a sad gaze. "Penn is the earl's firstborn son. Stratton was abusive and horrible, and Penn's mother fled when she was with child. She orchestrated her own fake death to protect her son."

Shock froze Amelia for a moment. "If she was supposedly dead, how can Penn be the earl?"

"There's a vicar who helped Penn's mother escape. He housed Eleanor until she gave birth and bore witness, recording Penn's birth in the church registry."

Amelia's heart sank. There was proof he was the heir. "Penn doesn't want to be the earl."

"You know my son very well."

"Where is he now?" Amelia could only imagine what he was feeling. If she found out her parent was a horrid person and that she suddenly had responsibilities she'd never conceived… He was an adventurer, an explorer, not a lord.

"He left. He often spent time in a small lean-to in the woods behind the house when he was a boy. I suspect that's where he went. He could be back by now." Margery looked down at her soup. "I suppose it's gone cold by now."

Amelia took a taste and found it was still warm. Only she wasn't very hungry anymore. Forcing herself to sip a few spoonfuls, she noticed Penn's mother seemed to be trying to do the same.

Thankfully, the footman rescued them a moment later, removing the dishes. Of course, he only brought the next course, which was about as appetizing as the first.

That wasn't fair. The fish did look delicious, and Amelia told herself she ought to eat.

Margery took a few bites and set her fork down. "I'm afraid I'm not that hungry. Don't let me interrupt you, however. I'm happy to have a bit of company. It's quiet here now that Cate is married. Did Penn tell you about his sister?"

Amelia swallowed a bite of fish. "Yes. I understand she is newly married." To an earl. Amelia had told Penn she'd never met an earl. Apparently, last night, she'd kissed one.

She set her fork down. "I'm not particularly hungry either. I blame all the food the inn sent for my journey."

There had been an excess, really, and every bite was delicious. But she knew that wasn't the reason for her loss of appetite.

She wanted to ask about Penn and how he'd come to live with them, but decided she preferred to hear that from him. If he wanted to talk to her. First, however, she would keep Penn's mother company. "Since we don't seem to be interested in eating, would you like to show me your husband's study?"

Margery's eyes lit with interest. "Oh yes, let's. That will be a welcome distraction." She stood, and Amelia joined her.

Later, after Amelia had heard the exciting tale of how Penn's parents had met, she stood in her bedchamber as Culley put her clothing away. "Culley, do you happen to know where Mr. Bowen's—Penn's—chamber is located?"

Culley snapped her head around in surprise. "I believe it's the one next door."

Good, that would decrease the chance of her being noticed.

"Are you going to…visit him?"

Amelia didn't see any reason to lie, not to Culley. "He's had some bad news, and as you know, he and I have become friends. I'd like to make sure he's all right."

Culley's expression softened. "You've a kind heart. I won't say a word, of course."

"Thank you. I really am just paying a visit." Amelia didn't know why it mattered. She was a widow and not the slightest bit concerned about ruining her reputation. She was, however, a guest in the Bowens' home, and she meant to behave respectfully. She doubted Penn's parents would mind her checking on him, especially not if it helped.

As she made her way from the room into the corridor, she wondered if she were doing the right thing. What if he didn't want to see her? Well then, he wouldn't open the door.

Assuming he was even there. She hoped so. She hated thinking of him outside in the dark. Alone. Upset.

Relying on the audacity he claimed she possessed, she knocked on his door. When she heard nothing—no response and no movement—she said, "It's Amelia."

When there was still no sound from the room, she knocked again and repeated herself, but a bit louder—as loud as she dared.

Not willing to give up, she reached for the latch. If he wasn't inside, she'd wait for him. The door wasn't locked. She pushed it inward. And nearly fell flat on her face.

Strong arms caught her as she pitched toward the floor. The door had moved quickly, and she realized now it was because someone had been opening at the same time she'd pushed.

She looked up into the dark blue, tortured gaze of Penn.

His grip on her waist was tight and...electrifying. He didn't immediately let go, and she basked in his touch. Alas, he finally released her.

"What are you doing here?" he rasped.

She closed the door, plunging them into darkness without the light from the sconce in the corridor. "I came to see you."

"Well, that's obvious. Why?"

She followed him into the room and promptly stubbed her toe on something. "Ow. Do you suppose you could light a candle?"

A moment later, she heard flint, and a candle sputtered to life. She took in her surroundings—Penn's bedchamber. She'd stubbed her toe on the chair set in front of a writing desk. The candle sat on a nightstand on the other side of his bed. He sprawled in a wingbacked chair set in front of a dark hearth, his long legs stretched before him. He drank from a glass dangling from his fingertips.

Tightening the tie of her dressing gown, Amelia ventured farther into his room. There wasn't a chair for her to sit in, unless she wanted to pull the desk chair over to the hearth. Which she might, *if* he gave her any indication he wanted her to stay. Right now, she assumed he was moments from banishing her.

She took up a position near the corner of his bed, less than a couple of dozen inches from his bare feet. He wore only his breeches that stretched just past his knees and a shirt that had been pulled from the waistband and was, of course, open at the neck absent a cravat. She was seeing far more of Penn Bowen than she ever had before, and her body was well aware of it, reacting with heat and desire. She shoved it aside. Now was not the time for such distractions. "Your mother told me about the Earl of Stratton."

His gaze, still dark and tormented, lifted to hers. "You mean me?"

"No, I meant the prior earl."

"But the issue is me, isn't it?" He tipped the cup back into his mouth, draining whatever was inside. Then he set the empty tumbler down onto the hearth to his left.

"Yes. I can imagine—"

"Can you?" he snapped. "Can you really imagine how this feels? My entire life has been upended. Hell, my entire life is a bloody lie." He jumped to his feet and prowled past her.

She turned as he walked by, her body tense and on edge as she witnessed this new side of him. He'd always been genial and unflappable—even when they'd been tied up by brigands. But this was something wholly different, and she knew it.

"I know," she said quietly. "That's why I can only imagine how this feels. And what I imagine is that you're devastated."

He paced on the opposite side of the bed but said nothing. Just when she was about to move toward him, he came around the bed in a flash, stopping right in front of her. "Devastated is a good word. Also furious. And heartbroken. My parents knew all this time and never told me."

Heartbroken. Hearing him say that twisted her heart too.

"I'm sure they had a good reason."

He let out a derisive snort. "Can you think of one?"

She could but wasn't sure he really wanted her to answer. "They wished to keep it a secret from Stratton? He doesn't sound like a very nice person."

"Yes, that's their reasoning. But why not trust me with this life-altering, future-changing secret?" His eyes blazed with anger as he leaned toward her. "Why let me create a life as a scholar and an adventurer knowing I was going to have to cast it all aside to become a fucking earl?"

His crude language jabbed at her, but she didn't blame him. It only made her want to soothe him even more. Before she could say a word, however, he continued his ranting. "I don't want that life. I want the life I already have. I *like* that life. Especially since you came into it."

His fury melted into something else—a heat she felt into her bones as he stared at her with desperation. She touched his face, feeling the scrape of his beard emerging along his jaw. "Penn—"

"That's not even my name." His voice was rough and sad. "It's William. My mother changed it to some place we visited —Pennard. I'd forgotten that until today."

"You shall always be Penn to me," she said softly, caressing his cheek.

"Penn, your partner?" he asked huskily.

She dragged her hand along his jaw and brushed the pad of her thumb over his lips. "My partner. My friend. My lover." She infused the last with a bit of a question, holding her breath as she waited for his response.

His gaze speared into hers before he drew her thumb into

his mouth, licking her flesh with his tongue. Then his hands came around her waist, and he pulled her to his chest. He released her thumb from his lips. "You're certain? Because I am on the edge of so many emotions right now. Rejection is not something I want to contemplate."

She brought her other hand up between them and cupped his face. "I've never been more certain of anything." And it was true. She wanted him with the ferocity she saw reflected in his gaze. "I don't think I could handle rejection either—if you recall, you're the one who pulled away last night. *I'm* the one who opened my door to hopefully persuade you to change your mind."

"Bloody hell, I mangled that," he whispered. "Not tonight. Tonight, I'm yours. Completely."

"Then I shall take you."

CHAPTER 11

*A*ll the anguish and anger and despair washed away the moment her lips touched his. Penn crushed her against him, desperate to feel every part of her. He stabbed his tongue into her mouth, also desperate to taste her. He relented slightly, thinking he mustn't be so…savage.

But her hands curled around to the back of his neck, her fingers digging into his flesh. Her tongue slashed against his with its own fierceness, encouraging his ardor.

God, how he wanted her. He hadn't realized just how badly until that moment. Or maybe because of that moment. He didn't think he'd ever needed someone more. Not just any someone, *her*. She'd come to him when he needed her most and was now offering herself as a balm.

Wait. He couldn't take her like that.

He dragged his mouth from hers. "Amelia," he breathed, trying to slow his thundering heart. "I can't—"

"Are you rejecting me? I thought we said we weren't doing that."

He saw frustration spitting in the depths of her gaze. "I appreciate what you're trying to do, truly."

She cocked her head to the side. "And what is *that?*"

In the face of her anger, he felt uncertain. "Making me feel better?"

Her brows angled over her eyes in a deep V. "Pennard Bowen, if you think this is about making you feel better, you're incredibly obtuse. This is about *me* wanting *you*. *Desperately.* And I thought it was about *you* wanting *me*."

Desperately? Oh God, he hadn't been prepared for that. For her.

"How much more plain do I need to be?" She took her hands from around his neck and slipped them down between them. His breath caught in expectation, but she only untied her dressing gown. Still, watching the garment slide from her body to the floor was enough to make his cock go completely hard. She stood before him in her thin nightgown, the slope of her breasts and the dip of her waist tantalizing in the candlelight. Then she did the unthinkable. She lifted the hem of her gown and drew it over her head, baring herself completely to his starving gaze.

Arching her brow at him, she gave him a seductive half smile. "Do you have any questions now?"

He let his gaze devour her, feasting on her creamy breasts tipped with dark pink nipples and drifting lower to the plane of her abdomen to where it met the thatch of blonde curls cloaking her sex. His mouth went dry.

Why? No, he didn't want to ask that. He knew they wanted each other, and that was enough for tonight. He shook his head as he reached for her, splaying his hands against her back and drawing her against his chest.

Her breasts connected with him, and he groaned softly before kissing her again. She opened her mouth beneath his as she clutched at his shirtfront, her fingernails grazing his chest as she fisted the linen. Her tongue met his with eager strokes as they explored each other. There were no barriers tonight, no uncertainty, just blissful connection and mutual need.

He moved her around the end of the bed, steering her to the side of the mattress. She was warm and soft against him. And he was wearing too damn many clothes.

As if she'd heard his thoughts, she pushed her hands up under his shirt and skimmed her palms over his abdomen. His muscles tightened in response, and he deepened their kiss.

She curled her fingertips into his chest, then flattened her hands over his nipples. Sensation sparked through him, and he hastened to pull his shirt over his head and cast it aside.

With the kiss broken, she bent her head to his torso and licked at his flesh. With a growl, he turned her and guided her backward onto the bed. She lay before him, her body gleaming and beautiful in the candlelight.

Her eyes slitted as she looked up at him. Her lips were parted, beckoning him with a silent siren's song. But he didn't want her mouth. Not just then.

He bent over her and took her nipple between his lips, sucking softly before he licked gently. She arched up off the bed with a moan. He clamped down hard, taking what she offered. What she seemed to know he needed.

He cupped her other breast, using his thumb and forefinger to tease the nipple into a hard, delicious point. Desperate to taste that one too, he moved his focus, her soft cries and moans a sensual accompaniment to his feast.

"*Penn.*" She said his name. Then again. Then a thousand times. He didn't know. He only knew how she felt, how she sounded, how she tasted.

He trailed his lips and tongue down her abdomen, licking a path between her ribs and over her navel, darting his tongue inside briefly before he continued toward the greatest prize.

He stroked his fingers over her sex, teasing the silky folds before using his thumb to press on her clitoris. She cried out as her hips thrust into his hand. He blew on her heated flesh, his fingers parting her.

"Penn?"

He was vaguely aware that his name was a question. "Hmmm?" He licked at her clitoris, and she bucked up, surprising him.

"What are you doing?" she asked sharply, pulling him from his sexual haze.

He clasped her hip and massaged her flesh as he looked up at her over the peaks and valleys of her torso. "Giving you pleasure. Have you not done this before?"

She shook her lifted head.

He shouldn't think ill of the dead, but her husband was a selfish prick. Not to mention an idiot for denying himself one of life's greatest joys. He gave her an encouraging smile as he traced his fingertips over her mound, staying to the outside but circling inward bit by bit. "Do you mind if I kiss you here?"

"I— It seems scandalous."

"Of course it is. Anything that feels this good is scandalous, isn't it? Will you trust me to give you pleasure?"

She hesitated briefly before nodding.

"Oh good. I promise you won't regret it." He smiled wickedly before swirling his thumb over her clitoris and licking her deeply. As his tongue flicked inside, her hand clasped at the back of his head. Her legs, tense a moment ago, relaxed briefly before tensing again. But this time, he knew it was for a different reason. He could feel the pleasure building inside her, in the movement of her hips and the intensity of her cries.

He reversed his hand and mouth, spearing his finger into her sheath as he sucked at her nub. Moving between her legs, he positioned them over his shoulders and buried his tongue deep inside her. She arched up, thrusting against him. He held on to her with one hand and used the other to coax her orgasm. She was so close, he could taste it.

And then she was there. Her muscles clenched around him, and she made a sound that was nearly inhuman—a high-pitched keen that made him smile. She thrust up, and then he felt her body relax. Light quivers danced along her thighs as she recovered.

Penn stood up and peeled his breeches away. She rotated on the bed, lying lengthwise, and reached for him. He lay down next to her, his body eager. But he wanted to give her a moment. He could wait. He'd wait as long as necessary.

She cupped the back of his head and drew him down to kiss her. Sliding her tongue into his mouth, she hesitated briefly, likely tasting herself, but then plunged forward. He found her nipple with his fingers and tugged gently at her flesh before rolling it and pulling once more.

Then her hand closed around his cock, and logical thought fled his brain. She stroked his length, loosening and tightening in perfect succession as she moved along his flesh. At the base, she squeezed, her fingertips grazing his balls. God, he was going to explode like a green boy.

"Amelia," he murmured.

"You'll take precautions?" she asked.

Precautions…yes. He was glad she mentioned it. He always did, but damn, he was completely lost in her.

Her hand wrapped around the stem of his cock, she gently urged him toward her. He moved over her, settling between her legs, which she bent up as she guided him to her sex. She was hot and wet, and he could barely wait to drive inside her.

Somehow, he went slowly, sinking into her flesh inch by inch until he was seated to the hilt. She wrapped her legs around his waist and ran her hands up his back to clasp his shoulders. "*Move.*"

Her single command sent blood rushing to his cock. He needed no further urging. Withdrawing, he thrust back in. She took him deep, her legs clenching around him.

"*Faster.*"

He tried to keep control, to set a pace that wouldn't scare her.

"Penn, I want you to *move.*"

Apparently, she knew far better than he did. He gave up trying to hold back and let himself go. He snapped his hips into hers, driving hard and fast. His control was lost, his desire spiraling beyond his grasp. She met him stroke for stroke, her hips rising off the bed. Her sheath constricted around him as she came again.

Rapture pushed him to the very edge of sanity. Before he tumbled into the darkness, he remembered to pull out. He shouted as his orgasm tore through him, and he spilled his seed on her belly.

Out of breath, he rolled to her side, gasping. It took him a moment to find his voice. "Sorry. For the. Mess."

She stroked her fingers along his bicep. "I never conceived with my husband, but we weren't even together a year. I thought it best to be cautious."

"You're a very smart woman. But that's one of the reasons I like you so much." He rolled from the bed and went to his dressing area. Behind a screen was a dresser with a basin. He poured water into it and dampened a cloth before returning to the bed.

"Here." He handed her the linen to tidy herself and turned his back to offer her some privacy.

"You don't have to turn away," she said. "After...*that*, I don't think I can be shy."

"You're a remarkable woman, Amelia." He rotated and

took the cloth from her when she was finished. After cleaning himself and disposing of the soiled linen behind the screen, he returned to the bed.

"I suppose I should return to my room," she said softly.

He lay down on his side and reached out to smooth a strand of hair that had come loose from her braid away from her forehead. "Do you regret coming?"

"Not at all."

"What I should have asked is if you regret staying."

"My answer is the same." Her brows gathered, and she scooted closer to him. Smoothing her fingertips over his forehead, she whispered. "Try to sleep. I know there's a tumult inside your head, but there's nothing to be done right now. You can seek your answers tomorrow."

Answers. He wasn't sure there were any. Just horrible, immutable truths. He leaned over and kissed her, their lips gently touching. "Thank you. Will you stay? For a little while?"

"For a little while." She worked to pull down the covers so they could slide between them. Once they were nestled inside, he drew her close against him and brushed his lips against her hair. She'd bathed earlier.

"You smell like honeysuckle and sunshine." Happiness.

She inhaled. "You smell like grass and pine."

"I was outside for quite a while."

She nuzzled closer against him. "Did it help?"

"Yes." But not as much as this. As her.

That thought stuck with him as he drifted to sleep.

～

*C*onsciousness stole over Penn with the languor of a kitten stretching in the sunlight. He was warm with contentment, his lips curving into a smile as he recalled last night with Amelia. Reaching for her, he felt nothing but the cold bed next to him.

His eyes flew open, and he sat up straight, the covers dropping to his waist. His heart, which had started to beat faster at finding her gone, began to slow. Of course she was gone. She couldn't exactly wake up in his bed this morning.

And it was morning, wasn't it?

He threw the covers back and stepped out of bed, crossing to the window and peering through the slit in the curtains. Yes, morning, but early.

The rest of yesterday—the bad part—rushed over him like a massive wave on the Cornish coast. He was a bloody fucking earl.

He thrust the thought away, willing himself to think of Amelia instead. He washed and dressed before prowling down the backstairs to the kitchen. He'd taken that route more times than he could count—more times than he'd taken the stairs he ought. But this morning he wasn't avoiding detection so he could sneak to the larder for a sweet. He wanted to avoid seeing his parents because he was still furious.

Unfortunately, the moment he stepped into the kitchen, that objective was utterly smashed.

His father stood at the worktable in the center of the room, his head snapping up and his dark eyes focusing on Penn. A blend of regret and relief mixed in their depths. "I'm pleased to see you. I hope you slept well, but I suspect you didn't." There was no relief in that statement however, just a heavy sadness.

Penn had slept better than he ought, because of Amelia, but he wouldn't tell his father that. "I don't know what I'm supposed to say. If you're looking for absolution, I'm afraid you won't find it from me."

His father nodded slowly, his expression tight and pained.

"I don't expect to. You're angry, and you've every right to be, but someday I hope you'll understand that I was only protecting you. And following your mother's dying wish."

Penn pointed upstairs. "*She's* my mother." And he couldn't believe she'd gone along with it.

"Would it help you to know that she wanted to tell you?"

It did, a little. But again, he wouldn't give his father any satisfaction. Not now. "The fact remains that neither of you did, and now I find myself wondering what the hell I do next. I don't want to be a *goddamned earl.*" Penn couldn't keep his lip from curling as the anger he'd felt last night returned with brutal force.

Father winced. "I know."

"You know? How could you know? If you had, you would have managed this differently. My entire life feels like a lie. Do you understand that? I'm not Pennard Bowen, scholar and adventurer, I'm William Kersey, Earl of bloody Stratton." Just saying the title made him shake with rage and, if he was honest, a bit of nausea.

"You remembered that name?" his father asked softly.

Penn pivoted from the table and from the intense remorse in his father's stare. "What happened to her, really?"

"She was ill, just as she told you, and she died a few months after you came to live with me, which I also told you."

"So that much was true."

"Yes."

"And when did she take me away from Stratton?"

"You weren't even born. Stratton was a terrible man. She didn't want him raising you, and she was right to keep you from him. You've seen what he's done to Gideon."

Hell, Gideon. Penn's *half brother.* As angry as Penn was, how would Gideon react? He'd suffered his father and his mother's abandonment, and now his birthright had been

stripped away. Not only that, but if his mother hadn't actually been married to his father, he was *illegitimate*. Penn
turned his head to glower at his father. "Why was I spared
Stratton's parentage and Gideon was not? You protected
me and not him. And you're still doing it. Exposing this
secret doesn't just make me the earl, it makes Gideon a
bastard."

Father paled as he opened his mouth, then closed it again,
his jaw working. "I...tried. I tried to include him in our
family as best I could, but you must know there was no way
on earth Stratton would let anyone take his son from him.
Why do you think your mother—the woman who gave birth
to you—ran? She knew it was her only chance to keep you
from him. So she faked her death with the help of her
parents and the vicar of their church, and that vicar ensured
your birth was recorded and hidden."

"To be uncovered at the appropriate time." Penn swore
under his breath before turning his body toward his father
and crossing his arms over his chest. "Why does this vicar
need to come forward? Why not let Gideon be the earl? He's
been raised to the title. I have not, nor do I want it. What of
my position at Oxford? I have a *life*, Father."

His father came around the table then, and Penn dropped
his arms, ready to flee if necessary. "I know you do!"
Emotion ripped across his father's features, and tears welled
in his eyes. "But there is nothing to be done. The vicar made
a promise to Eleanor Kersey and to her parents that you
would be the earl."

Why hadn't his grandparents taken him in? He feared he
knew the answer. "Are my grandparents still alive?"

Father shook his head. "I'm sorry. They died before you
came to live with me."

He'd expected that, but also realized that even if they
hadn't, his mother might not have given him over to them. If

she had, Stratton might have found him. "I never met them. At least not that I can remember."

"Eleanor broke with everyone from her life after you were born. I imagine it was painful for her and for your grandparents."

"You *imagine*?" Penn asked.

"She didn't reveal too much when she came to ask me to care for you."

"Enough to persuade you to take me in."

A bittersweet smile curled his father's lips. "It wasn't difficult. At the time, I had no marital prospects, and the idea of a son appealed to me."

Because of the close relationship he'd shared with his father. Penn had heard of him so much that he sometimes felt as if he'd known his foster grandfather.

"Penn, being the earl isn't all bad. You'll be free to do whatever you choose—Stratton was a very wealthy man."

"Free?" A hollow ache started in Penn's chest. "What of my responsibilities to the title, to the estate, to the tenants, to my seat in the Lords? All that will take time away from my occupation, my *passion*." The word brought Amelia to his mind, where she lingered for a moment and took some of the sting away. "I'll be anything but free."

His father's forehead creased into deep furrows. "There will be a way to manage it all. I know there is."

"Because you have so much experience being an earl?" Penn asked, not caring if he sounded cruel.

"No, because I know you, and I've no doubt you'll excel in this as you do in everything." His father's gaze was full of admiration and pride.

Penn allowed a soft grunt to push past his lips. He didn't want his father's pride right now. And he sure as hell didn't want this nuisance. He was supposed to be hunting the White Book of Hergest and the real Heart of Llanllwch. "I came here on a mission," he said with more than a bit of irritation. "Not to be an earl."

"And no one will interrupt that. When Gideon arrives—"

Penn cut him off. "He'll be devastated. And furious. I can't imagine he'll stay to help me get the book, and I wouldn't blame him."

His father flinched. "We'll work it out. Penn, I'm so sorry for this. Even if I'd told you before, it wouldn't change things. You are who you are. You're still Penn, as well as William Kersey, Earl of Stratton."

Again, the name and title grated, like the edge of a blade scoring his flesh. "Maybe if you'd told me sooner, I could've learned to be." If he'd known he was to inherit a title, he would've done things differently. He wouldn't be working for the Ashmolean, and he wouldn't be chasing antiquities.

Was that true?

Penn thought back to the first Roman coins he'd found as a young boy. He'd been six years old, living in a town near the Welsh border. Digging in the yard of the small cottage where they'd been staying, he'd found five coins, which he'd later identified as Roman with the help of a man in the next place they'd lived. That man had given Penn a few other coins and shared with him his own meager antiquities collection—some pottery, more coins, and a spectacular bronze dagger that Penn had coveted.

A spark for discovery and knowledge was kindled that day, and so when Fate delivered him to an academic with a passion for medieval manuscripts, Penn had felt a connection. Losing his mother had been excruciating, but he'd thought he'd found a place where he belonged. A place where he could be the man he wanted to be and lead the life he craved.

He was fooling himself if he thought he could've changed who he was meant to be. He was an antiquary. A scholar. An adventurer. A protector of history. He lifted his gaze to his father. "You're right about that—I am who I am. I am not an earl. And I'll be damned if I let Gideon be a bastard."

Penn turned and left the kitchen without getting anything to eat. His mind was far too heavy with plans for what to do next.

he press of lips against Amelia's temple roused her from sleep. A smile curved her lips as she inhaled Penn's scent. Rolling to her back, she opened her eyes. Her vision filled with his handsome face as he bent over her. Then his mouth found hers, and she closed her eyes again, sighing contentedly into his kiss.

When he pulled away, her lids fluttered open, and she blinked toward the window. "What time is it?"

"Early still," he murmured. "But I need to leave, and I wanted to see you first."

She pushed herself up to a sitting position, and he perched on the edge of the bed next to her. "Where are you going?"

He took her hand in his and rubbed his thumb over the backs of her knuckles. "I need to deal with this earl nonsense."

Amelia rubbed the sleep from her eyes. "What does that mean?"

"I need to find the vicar who will provide proof that I'm

William Kersey. Then I'll convince him to destroy it and forget I ever existed."

"Can you do that?" She considered everything she knew of him, particularly his charm. She'd detested him on sight, and now look at them... "Never mind, of course you can. How long will you be gone?" She liked seeing him with a purpose—the spark was back in his gaze after yesterday's shock.

"Hopefully no more than two days. I'm not entirely sure where the vicar is located, and I don't want to ask my father. He'll likely try to persuade me not to go. Besides, I'm still angry, and I don't want to talk to him." He sounded a bit like a belligerent boy, but she couldn't blame him. His entire world had been turned upside down.

"If you don't know where to go, how will you find him?"

He grinned, and her heart skipped. "You must know by now that I'm exceptionally good at finding things. And that includes people. My mother, that is, the woman who gave birth to me, left me enough clues. I believe this vicar is located in a village near the English border. We skirted it several times, and I was sure she met with someone on a few occasions. In retrospect, I think she visited this vicar or perhaps her parents."

With his free hand, he tucked an errant hair behind her ear. "Will you wait here for me so that we may continue our quest when I return?"

Wait here with his parents with whom he was angry... That wouldn't be awkward. "Perhaps I should go with you."

He shook his head gently. "Egg is already preparing our horses. We'll leave shortly and, if we're lucky, return late tonight. You'll have all day to peruse my father's library, and he will undoubtedly relish the opportunity to share it with you."

"I don't know," she said uncertainly. "I suspect everyone may be too upset to behave as if nothing's wrong."

His jaw tightened, and he glanced away before stroking her hand once more. "It will be fine. I promise. I have to do this. You understand, don't you?"

She brought his hand to her lips and pressed a kiss on the back. "I understand you want your life to remain as it is. I'm not sure you can accomplish that feat, but I support your endeavor. Please know that—I will support you no matter what." Support him? What did that mean? She had feelings for this man. She cared for him, reveled in his company, admired him… But she'd no idea where it would lead. The most she could promise, and the most she could expect in return, was friendship.

"I appreciate that more than you know." He leaned forward and brushed his lips against hers. "I wish I had more time," he said softly against her mouth as his hand caressed her nape.

Delicious shivers raced down her spine and along her arms. "I wish you did too."

He pulled away from her with a frustrated groan. "Someone will likely bring you a breakfast tray shortly. I should go before I'm discovered."

She withdrew her hand from his. "It wouldn't do for an earl to be caught trying to seduce a house guest."

He grumbled low in his throat. "Another reason to avoid this bloody title. Nobody cares what Penn Bowen does." He arched a dark brow at her. "In any case, I'm not *trying* to seduce you, my love. If you recall, I was quite successful."

She swatted at him, and he stood with a soft laugh. "Maybe I was the successful one," she said smugly.

"Indeed you were." His eyes glimmered in the early morning light. "One more thing. I'm leaving the heart with you." His gaze strayed to the table next to her bed upon which sat the, probably, fake Heart of Llanllwch. "You'll keep it safe." It wasn't a question, but a confidence in her ability. "I hope to see you tonight." He blew her a kiss and departed, leaving the stamp of his presence long after he'd gone.

Some time later, a housemaid delivered a tray, and Amelia finally roused herself from bed. She went to the small table near the window, and her gaze immediately caught a slip of paper tucked into the corner of the tray. It had to be a note from Penn. Smiling, she plucked it up and opened the parchment. Her good humor fled as she read the missive.

Mrs. Forrest,

I was acquainted with your grandfather, and I know how much the White Book of Hergest meant to him. I am in possession of this book and will trade it to you for the Heart of Llanllwch. You must meet me where the River Monnow meets the River Wye at dusk this evening.

It is imperative you come alone. If Mr. Bowen accompanies you, there will be no trade. In fact, you are advised to keep this entire affair from Mr. Bowen if you prefer to ensure a smooth transaction.

Amelia's hands shook as she reread the short note. She turned it over in her hands searching for the author's name, but there was no indication of who'd written it.

Immediately, she considered it must be from the Order, or more specifically, from the Camelot group. Foliot purportedly had the book. Had he penned the note? Why go to the trouble to steal the book in London several years ago and decide to trade it now? Unless the heart was just that important to him.

She turned her head to where the stone sat on her bedside table. How did he—or whoever had written the note—even know she was in possession of the heart? Somehow, they were aware that Penn had taken it from the museum.

Penn.

It didn't even occur to her to abide by the author's threat. Of course she would tell him. If he was still here.

She dressed hastily without assistance and made her way downstairs. In the hall, she encountered Thomas, the butler. "Excuse me, has Mr. Bowen—that is, Penn—departed already?"

The butler's gaze reflected a mild surprise, but he covered it quickly. "I believe so."

"You knew he was leaving?" Rhys Bowen's voice from the doorway of his study drew her to pivot in his direction.

She saw no reason to lie. "Yes."

"And you know where he went and why?"

Unsure if Penn's father knew, she hesitated before answering, "I think so."

Mr. Bowen gave a slight nod. He looked tired. Defeated perhaps. She briefly considered telling him about the note but decided Penn wouldn't want that. At least not right now. That she felt a loyalty to Penn ought to have surprised her, but they'd forged a relationship that went beyond what she would have expected.

"We're glad to have you here," Mr. Bowen said. "Please excuse my wife and me—we'll try to be engaging hosts, but this is a difficult time."

"I understand," Amelia murmured. What a tangle. She understood Penn's anger but also saw the regret etched into his father's expression. "I think I'll just take a walk outside. Please don't trouble yourself over me."

He nodded before retreating to his study. Amelia turned and walked toward the back of the house, eager to see this place in the woods where Penn went. Perhaps being there would help her decide what to do, since she couldn't talk with him.

She stepped outside, where the late summer morning held a touch of crispness. The temperature would creep lower and lower as the days shortened, but for now, she lifted her face to the cloud-dappled sky and closed her eyes while the sun's rays heated her cheeks.

Taking a deep breath, she mentally chastised herself for leaving her bonnet inside, but then she hadn't planned to come out here. She walked toward the wooded area beyond the yard.

As she picked her way into the canopy of trees, the temperature dropped, and she shivered. Wrapping her arms around her chest, she took a few more steps before her eye caught a small shelter nestled into the trees ahead.

Curious, she increased her pace until she arrived at the small lean-to. A bench was built against the only wall. Carvings on the wall drew her to move inside and study what had been written—or drawn. There were what looked like Celtic symbols as well as foreign words. Welsh, she thought. She bent and read the one word she could definitively read, carved just above the bench: Penn.

Again, she wished he hadn't left. She'd tucked the note into a small pocket in her skirt and now removed it. She scanned the lines again and realized she'd nearly memorized it.

"Find something good?"

The deep masculine voice startled her, and she let out a squeal before turning around, her heart in her throat.

The gentleman leaned against a tree just outside the lean-to. "My apologies."

Amelia willed her heart to slow as she stiffened her spine. Folding the paper in one hand, she slipped it back into her pocket. "I believe you're trespassing."

"Actually, I was going to say the same thing to you."

She narrowed her eyes wondering if this man could be...

"I'm Kersey," he said, affirming her suspicion.

She exhaled, relieved he wasn't a brigand. Given her past experience with the dagger and now the note she'd received earlier, she wasn't sure what to expect. "I'm Mrs. Amelia Forrest, an associate of Mr. Bowen's."

Kersey's brow arched with interest. "Have you brought a medieval manuscript for him to review?"

"No, not that Mr. Bowen. Mr. *Penn* Bowen."

The interest in his gaze deepened. "Penn is here?"

"Er, no."

Kersey was a bit taller than Penn, but their frames were similar with broad shoulders and narrow hips. He was perhaps a few years younger than his half brother, and while their hair was a similar dark brown, Kersey's eyes were a storm-heavy gray instead of Penn's striking blue.

"He's not here and yet you are. Why would he arrange to meet you here instead of at Oxford?" Kersey shook his head. "I suppose it's none of my affair."

Her mind warred with itself over what she knew and what she ought to disclose. It certainly wasn't her place to tell this man about Penn's parentage or where he'd gone. She could, however, talk with him about the White Book. That was, after all, what she and Penn had come here to do before everything had fallen to pieces with the Earl of Stratton's death. Penn would want her to pursue their quest, she was sure of it. "Actually, it *is* your affair. I came here with Penn in the hope of finding you."

Kersey's eyes widened briefly, and the gray lightened with surprise. "Perhaps that's why I was summoned. The note from Rhys didn't say specifically."

It wasn't, but again, it wasn't her place to enlighten him. She neither confirmed nor denied his assumption. This was a pivotal moment—she could become the seeker that Penn had groomed her to be, pursue the hunt her grandfather had started and been unable to finish. Or she could say nothing and await Penn's return.

There wasn't really a choice at all.

"My grandfather was Jonathan Gardiner." This elicited another flash of surprise in Kersey's expression. "Penn and I are looking for the White Book of Hergest. We believe Timothy Foliot has it in his possession and that you can perhaps help us obtain it."

All that was rather moot, she realized. Or at least it could be since she had a clear path to the book—if she believed the note. And yet, she couldn't go to this meeting at dusk on her own as the note demanded. Only a fool would embark on such a dangerous folly.

How she wished Penn hadn't left!

It took Kersey a moment to respond. "I'm familiar with this book. However, I can't help you get it. I'm probably the last person Foliot would care to see," he said wryly.

"Right. Because you stole that sword from Penn's sister."

He flinched slightly. "You heard about that."

"I did. I understand you may not be entirely trustworthy, but you're the only hope we have."

He studied her a moment, his eyes narrowing shrewdly. "It sounds as though you and Penn are quite close."

"We're working together to find the White Book of Hergest."

"Why? What's so special about this book? I know who your grandfather is, so I wonder what it has to do with the Heart of Llanllwch."

She didn't necessarily want to get into the specifics—Penn's belief that the heart was fake, the theft of the dagger, or anything else. Especially if Kersey couldn't help them.

"Since you can't provide assistance, I'm not sure there's any point in my telling you."

"You're a cunning thing, aren't you? I see why Penn would like you." He pushed away from the tree and took a step toward her. "Perhaps I *can* help. I'm familiar with Foliot and his...organization. Which I'm not particularly proud of." His gaze darkened. "But there's a lot I'm not particularly proud of," he added softly.

Somehow, she'd been thrust into the thick of this family, and she wasn't sure what she thought of it.

"Ah well, I can't change the past. I can only do my best to repent." His gaze flicked to her skirt. "What was the paper you found?"

Her pulse quickened. "I didn't find it."

"Yet you were reading it out here." He lowered his voice dramatically. "Is it a secret? Maybe a love note from Penn?" He smiled to show he was teasing. At least she thought he was teasing.

"It isn't from him," she said.

"You didn't answer my question about why you're meeting Penn here. If you've been working together, why isn't he here?"

She fumbled for an excuse but could only think to say, "I didn't meet him here. We arrived together. He's gone on an errand with Egg."

"And left you at Hollyhaven with his parents." He cocked his head to the side. "I'd say he set out to do something dangerous and didn't want you to accompany him. Perhaps he went to find the White Book on his own."

"I don't believe that's what they're doing." She prayed Kersey wouldn't ask.

"Well, since I am here and you and Penn are in need, perhaps I can assist you. I suppose we must wait for Penn to return."

Except if she really wanted the White Book, she could trade the heart for it at dusk. And that was what she and Penn wanted, what her grandfather had wanted. However, her grandfather had also found the heart. Could she really turn it over to the Camelot group? She realized she wasn't entirely sure it wasn't fake. It seemed Penn had impacted her in many ways.

The adventurous spirit he'd sparked in her begged for action. She wanted to make this trade, and standing in front of her was a person who could possibly help. If she could trust him.

She stared at him closely. "Did you mean what you said about repenting?"

"I did," he said cautiously. "Why?"

"Because I am in need of assistance, and Penn isn't here. I'm wary of trusting you, but I don't think Penn will return in time." Doubt crept over her. Perhaps she should have asked Rhys.

"I can see you already regret asking me to help. Let me put you at ease. I owe Penn and his family, and I would appreciate the opportunity to repay their kindness and care. They were there for me in…dark times. I repaid them with villainy."

"That all sounds rather epic," she said drily. "The note you saw me reading arrived in my room this morning." She probably ought to have asked the maid where it came from. Penn would've known to do that. Again, she wished he hadn't left.

"From whom?"

"I don't know, but I suspect someone in the Camelot group." She withdrew it from her pocket and handed it to him. As he reached for it, she pulled her hand back. "Do you swear I can trust you?"

"You can."

She pinned him with a threatening stare. "You should

know that I'm a fair shot, and I don't appreciate being betrayed."

"Thank you for the warning." He placed his hand over his heart. "I swear on my life you can trust me."

She gave him the note and watched as he scanned the lines. "Do you recognize the hand?"

"I don't," he said, frowning. "But this has to be from the Camelot group since they are in possession of the book. Unless the author is lying and looking to dupe you."

"I considered that, which is why I won't go alone."

He returned the note to her keeping. "Would you have asked Penn if he were here?"

"I would."

Kersey grinned. "Smart. I'll say it again—I see why Penn likes you."

Heat threatened to rise in her cheeks, but she kept it at bay. "Do you think it's worth trying to make this trade?"

He looked at her intently. "Do you have the heart?"

"I do."

He blew out a breath. "The author of this note knows that."

She fingered the parchment before shoving it back into her pocket. "Clearly."

"Which means you've been followed and your actions supervised," he said. "But then you probably knew that too."

Actually, that hadn't occurred to her, but of course that was the only way anyone would know. Her neck pricked with unease. How long had they been followed? And why hadn't they tried to steal the heart from them when they'd stopped at The Falcon in the Cotswolds? Perhaps this person was afraid of Penn, and that was why they didn't want him aware of tonight's transaction.

Tonight's transaction.

That phrase made it seem as though she'd made up her

mind. And she supposed she had. She wanted that book, and if the heart really was a fake—as Penn was certain it was—trading it away wouldn't matter. "How do we do this if I'm supposed to go alone?"

Kersey crossed his arms over his chest. "I can hide in the trees—there's a copse near where the rivers meet. Or I can disguise myself and go as your groom. They can't object to you having a groom."

She was skeptical of his ability to fool someone who might be acquainted with him. "Disguise yourself how? What if this person—or people—knows you?"

"I suspect they do," he said without a shred of concern. Was he fearless or naïve? She doubted it was the latter. "I can make myself look different. Trust me."

It appeared she had no choice. "I am. And don't let me down." She narrowed her eyes at him and pressed her lips together, trying to look imperious.

He bowed. "On my honor, of which I still have a bit, I will not." He straightened. "I think it best if I don't accompany you back to the house. Can you meet me here an hour before dusk? I'll have a horse for you. I assume you ride?"

"Yes." Well enough that Penn could've taken her with him. But then she wouldn't have been here to receive the missive. She made a mental note to ask the maid where it had come from.

"Excellent. I'll see you back here later. Until then, adieu." He bowed again and took himself off, cutting through the trees away from the house.

Why had he come here instead of going to the house? She wished she'd asked, but decided it didn't matter. As she watched him go, all she could think was how he would react when he learned the real reason behind Rhys's summons. As upset as Penn had been about the revelation of his father, Kersey's reaction could be far worse. He'd mentioned "dark times." She knew his mother had abandoned him, and his wife had died. This was going to be a blow, and though they'd just met, she rather liked him.

She shook the dreary thoughts from her head as she turned back toward the house.

It was possible she'd have the White Book in hand when Penn returned. He would be so thrilled. And if he was able to stop the vicar from revealing his sire, things could perhaps continue as they'd planned. They'd have the book, find the real heart—

The smile starting to curve her lips faded. This wasn't what she'd planned. She'd planned to protect her grandfather's name and prove Penn wrong. If they found the real heart, her grandfather's legacy would be tainted.

Book and heart aside, what would become of her relationship with Penn? With their quest finished, would they part ways? What else could they do?

She wasn't free to marry. Not yet anyway. She'd have to have her husband declared legally dead, and she wasn't sure what that entailed.

Besides, she and Penn hadn't discussed a future, and until they did, all this was useless thinking. Better to keep her focus on the book and the heart.

As she neared the back of the house, the back of her mind asked, *what of* your *heart?*

CHAPTER 13

*a*fter arranging with Culley to take dinner in her room, Amelia had instructed her maid to inform the household that she planned to retire early—if the household even asked. She'd kept to herself all day, which hadn't been difficult. With Penn gone and, more importantly, due to the reason for his absence, a pall of gloom had settled over the house.

With about an hour until dusk, Amelia stole from the house and made her way to Penn's lean-to. She'd brought Dyrnwyn with her, and the sword was even heavier than she remembered when she'd picked it up at Oxford. After a few yards, she had to drag it along the ground.

Kersey waited with two horses. At least she thought it was Kersey. The man, dressed in an oversized costume of indeterminate age, hunched at the shoulders and wore a wide-brimmed hat that shaded his face.

As she approached, he looked up, and she breathed a sigh of relief. "I almost didn't recognize you."

"Then I've done well." He straightened to his full height. "I was just practicing my stoop."

"Very effective."

"It changes my height and body shape, while averting my face as well. I didn't have time to obtain fake facial hair. A gray beard would've helped."

"You put a great deal of thought into this," she said.

"It's an important endeavor, and I mean to be successful." The determination in his tone was evident, and Amelia was glad she'd decided to trust him.

"Should I ask where you obtained the horses?"

"One is mine, of course, and the other I borrowed from an inn near town." He cocked a brow at her. "Did you think I'd stolen it?"

"No." Maybe.

His gaze dipped over her. "I didn't realize you'd be in disguise as well."

She glanced down at her men's costume—the one she'd worn when she'd met Penn. She'd brought it along on their journey to London, suspecting it might be useful. "It's rather difficult to dash about looking for antiquities in a gown."

His gaze turned apologetic. "I'm afraid I brought a sidesaddle."

She silently cursed, but offered him a smile. "It's my fault. I didn't think to mention what I would be wearing. I'll manage."

"And, ah, what are you carrying?"

Unsure of what they might be facing, she'd decided to bring the sword, as well as her pistol, which was tucked into her waistband. "It's a sword."

"That's not just any sword," he said darkly.

"No, it isn't. I suspect you recognize it."

"How did you get it?"

"From Penn. I thought it prudent to bring it along, particularly if it...activates its power for you." Just saying that made her want to shake her head. She still didn't quite believe it, and if she were honest with herself, she'd brought it to see if it did in fact *flame*.

"That was well considered of you," he said with a nod. "I can attach it to your saddle."

"Shouldn't it be on your saddle? And, er, it's rather heavy."

He took it from her, lifting it with ease. "Not for me. I'll put it on mine." He moved around his horse and fastened it to his saddle. "You have the heart?" he asked.

She patted her chest where she'd hastily stitched a pocket that afternoon. "Let us be on our way." She placed her hand on the saddle, and he boosted her up. A few minutes later, they were on their way from Hollyhaven.

They arrived at the junction of the Wye and Monnow Rivers with plenty of time to spare before dusk. The Monnow Bridge with its gatehouse loomed over the Monnow River, casting a shadow across the water from the setting sun.

Kersey dismounted, then helped her do the same. "I suspect he won't be alone."

"But I'm supposed to be. What if they see you and decide to forgo the meeting entirely?"

"That's a possibility, but I don't think that will happen." He adopted his hunch. "Whoever wrote that note wants the heart. What is more concerning is if there are a large number of them. If that happens, we should leave immediately."

Her pulse picked up speed, and she nodded as she worked to remain calm. How she wished Penn were here.

The minutes stretched as the sun dipped lower over the horizon until it was nothing but a wash of color to the west. The temperature dropped, and the breeze picked up. Expecting someone to arrive at any moment, Amelia tensed. But no one came. Her tension turned to frustration.

"It's going to be dark soon," she said urgently but keeping her voice low.

"I have a lantern," Kersey said. "I won't light it quite yet."

"I don't like this. What if they plan to accost us in the dark? Maybe we should go."

Before she could answer, she heard the cock of a pistol and a deep masculine voice that was eerily familiar. "You were supposed to come alone."

Amelia whipped around to see a man in a hood standing ten yards away. Two large, rough-looking men flanked him. How had the brigands crept up on them so quietly?

"Surely you can't fault me for bringing a groom." She worried they would hear the fierce thundering of her heart. For a moment, it was all she could hear as apprehension seized her.

"I suppose not. Do you have the heart?" That voice skipped across her flesh and made the hairs stand on end.

"I do," she said cautiously. "Do you have the book?"

"I do. Come forward, away from your groom."

Amelia flicked a glance toward Kersey, who nodded slightly. She took a few tentative steps but stopped when she was still several yards away.

"Closer, please," the familiar voice urged.

Who the devil was this? Why did she know him? Fear made her movements slow and unsteady. She took a deep breath and willed herself to relax. She could do this. For the book. For her grandfather. For Penn.

When she was just two yards from the man, she stopped. "Show me the book before I come any closer."

The man pushed his hood back, and Amelia gasped as recognition slammed into her. "Thaddeus!"

Her husband's mouth spread into a lazy smile, reminding her of why he'd caught her eye in the first place. He was attractive, though not nearly as handsome as Penn. Where Penn made her heart skip with anticipation, seeing Thaddeus filled her with dread. He'd failed her in every way possible.

"Good evening, Amelia. May I say, the years have been exceptionally kind to you." His gaze traveled over her slowly, making her skin crawl.

She couldn't find any words to respond. How was he here? Where had he been? Why had he left? At last, she blurted, "Are you part of the Camelot group?"

Thaddeus took a few steps toward her, his dark eyes narrowing. "You've learned quite a bit in my absence."

Anger finally surpassed her shock. "What should I have done, crawled into a hole and awaited your return?"

"Oh, my dear Amelia, I never planned to return. Surely you must know that?" His condescension cloaked her like a moldy, bug-ridden blanket she longed to cast aside. Just as he'd done to her.

"I'd hoped," she said. "In fact, I'd rather hoped you were dead."

He clucked his tongue. "I suppose I deserve that." He moved even closer, and Amelia took a step back. Her elbow connected with something, and she glanced over her shoulder to see that Kersey had crept up behind her. His proximity made her feel marginally better.

"I can see I made a mistake," Thaddeus continued. "You are lovelier than I remember. More spirited too." He tipped his head to the side. "How did that happen?"

"One might argue you didn't take the time to know me." That was certainly true. They'd been married less than a year before he'd disappeared.

"And I'm the poorer for it. Ah well, it's not too late, and you are still my wife."

Revulsion slithered through her. "In name only." What did he mean to do? "Show me the book. Let us complete this transaction and go our separate ways."

"I don't know," he drawled slowly. "The law says you are my property. I think perhaps I'd like to have the heart *and* you." He took a few more steps, until he could almost reach out and touch her. At this distance, she could see the familiar cleft in his chin, the dark sweep of his lashes, the arrogance in his stare.

Amelia flinched, and Kersey touched her arm reassuringly. "*Show me the book.*" The words came out as a near growl through her clenched teeth.

Thaddeus expelled a tired breath. "I didn't actually bring it with me, silly. What I *do* have are two friends who will ensure you—and the heart—accompany me. Come along, then." He pivoted slightly as if he simply expected her to join him.

"I'm not going anywhere with you."

Kersey leaned down and spoke close to her ear. "Pretend to go. I need the distraction."

When she hesitated, he whispered urgently, "*Trust me.*"

She had no other choice. The other two men had also advanced, and they each carried a pistol. Wait, she had a pistol too! She brought her hand up and lightly grazed the section of her coat that covered the weapon hidden in her waistband.

"Where would you take me?" she asked.

"To my house." He chuckled. "Don't look so surprised. I'm not destitute as I had you believe. The debt was simply a sound reason for leaving. I live just west of Glastonbury. It's two days' ride, I'm afraid. But you look well accustomed to riding." His gaze dropped to her breeches, and his mouth twisted into an appreciative smirk. "We'll need your horse, however. Groom, fetch her horse."

Amelia turned her head as Kersey trudged back to the horses. He limped, and his fake hunch was quite pronounced. She wouldn't have guessed he was a man in his prime.

The horses! More accurately, the sword! Her heart began

to beat faster again, but this time with excitement. She needed to give Kersey the distraction he needed.

She closed the gap between herself and her husband. Her stomach turned, but she ignored the reaction. "You have a house?" She fluttered her eyelashes at him. "Is it large? I had to move in with my grandfather after you left, and that's where I currently reside. It's rather dreary."

A light of anticipation glowed in his eyes, and again, her insides roiled in disgust. "It's larger and better appointed than the one we shared. There are sheep grazing nearby and a tall, stately oak that provides the best shade on a summer day." Was he actually gloating about leaving her and finding a better situation? His smugness was intolerable, but she would go along to meet her own ends. "You'll be quite comfortable there. With me."

"And the book is there?" she asked sweetly, offering him a smile laced with acid if he cared to look closely enough. Thankfully, the darkness was coming fast.

"Yes."

"Where's the heart, love?" he asked, curling his hand around her waist.

She struggled not to pull away. "In my coat." She slipped her hand inside the new pocket and withdrew the stone.

Kersey walked her horse toward the brigands. Where was the sword? Had he transferred it to her saddle? Amelia wondered what he planned to do. If he could take on the two brigands, Amelia could use her pistol to drive Thaddeus away.

Just as she'd used it against Penn and Egg. She knew she could shoot if necessary, but could she injure Thaddeus...or worse? More importantly, would she? She'd missed Egg, but she'd realized she'd done so on purpose—she didn't really want to harm anyone. She wasn't sure she could. But this was a different matter entirely. There was no way she would accompany Thaddeus anywhere.

She uncurled her fingers to reveal the stone filling her palm. Thaddeus sucked in a breath. "That's it." He picked it up, and again, she had to fight to keep herself still. Every instinct she possessed screamed for her to clutch her hand around the heart and train her pistol on her villainous husband.

At that moment, light flooded the area. Kersey had taken the sword from its scabbard, and it glowed with an eerie blue flame. The shouts of the brigands filled the air, and Thaddeus swore.

Amelia lunged for the heart but knocked it from Thaddeus's hand. She heard a loud *clack* and looked to the ground. The heart had fallen against another rock and split in two.

"The key!" Thaddeus cried out, dropping to his knees.

Amelia pulled the pistol from her belt and cocked the hammer, aiming the barrel straight at Thaddeus. "Move away from it."

He turned his head to look up at her. "Bloody hell, Amelia, you aren't going to shoot me."

"You don't know that. Don't try me." She curled her lip as power surged through her. "Get away from the heart." Wait, he'd called it a key? Why?

A loud shriek drew them both to look toward where Kersey fought the two henchmen. One writhed on the ground and the other ran away. Instead of following him, Kersey stalked back toward Amelia. "Does he really not have the book?" he called out.

Amelia looked down at Thaddeus. "If you have the book, give it to me, and we'll let you go."

Fear glazed his dark eyes as he looked up at her. "I don't have it. Let me go, and I'll get it for you."

"You think I would trust you?" Amelia sneered.

"I never would've taken you for such a heartless bitch." He reached for the heart then, his fingers scrabbling over the earth.

Apprehension buzzed over her, and she squeezed the trigger. Thaddeus's sharp cry rent the air. "You shot me!"

Kersey was upon them now, the flaming sword still lighting the way. He scooped up the two halves of the heart and thrust them at Amelia. "Come on!" He ran for her horse, and she followed, the heart clutched in one hand and her spent pistol in the other.

At her horse, she tucked the pieces of the heart back into her coat.

"I'll take that." Kersey took her pistol and thrust it into his pocket. Then he boosted her up and took off toward his own horse. "Ride for Hollyhaven as fast as you can!"

Thaddeus had stood and now staggered toward his fallen man.

Amelia guided her horse back the way they'd come. Her mind churned with everything that had just happened. Thaddeus was alive and well and apparently part of the Camelot group. What did that mean? Had he always been a member? Was that why he'd married her? Or had he somehow fallen into that group after meeting her grandfather? Wait, did she think her grandfather was somehow attached to them?

She felt sick. And disappointed. And utterly foolish.

It was several minutes before Kersey rode up alongside her. "I think we can slow down a bit," he called out.

Amelia eased her mount to a trot and glanced over at him. "They aren't following us?"

"No. I'm sure they've gone to lick their wounds."

Oh God, she'd *shot* Thaddeus. She'd all but pushed that from her mind. Now his yelp of pain slammed into her brain, and she saw him recoil and grab his right arm. "I shot him," she whispered. "Do you think he's all right?" she asked more loudly.

Kersey shot her a quick look. "Your... Thaddeus or the other fellow?"

"Thaddeus, and I hope he's suffering. He deserves to."

"He's your husband?" At her curt nod, he added, "I take it you're quite shocked to see him?"

"He abandoned me five years ago."

"He's clearly an imbecile."

"And a member of the Camelot group." She looked over at him again as they turned onto the road that would take them to Hollyhaven. "Do you know him?"

"I recognized him, but we'd never been introduced. I can tell you he's one of Foliot's inner circle," he said grimly.

The questions crowding her mind grew louder. Had Thaddeus been part of that inner circle when he'd married her? Had her entire marriage been a farce?

She began to understand how Penn might have felt yesterday upon hearing about his father. The feeling that her marriage had been a lie blossomed in her chest and grew outward until she felt as though she might suffocate. To think she'd been used... Well, it didn't bear thinking.

And yet she couldn't wipe it from her mind.

~

*F*rustration pitched through Penn as he stalked through the near darkness toward the house from the stable. They hadn't been able to find the vicar. He'd left the village for some unknown "errand." It might've been unknown to the man's wife and rector, but it wasn't to Penn.

Egg had gone off in pursuit while Penn had returned to Hollyhaven. He'd been incredibly torn. While it was vital he stop this vicar from proving Penn's birthright, it was also imperative he continue his quest with Amelia.

He entered the house through the back and headed straight for the stairs. As soon as he walked into the hall, his parents came from his father's study.

"We saw you ride to the stable," his father said cautiously. "I was hoping you would look more at ease."

"I was hoping I'd *feel* more at ease. Pardon me, I need to speak with Amelia."

He started up the stairs and heard his mother say, "She's already retired for the evening."

Penn wasn't about to let that stop him, and right now, he didn't give a damn if his parents knew it. He needed to see her, to bury his hurt and disappointment in her embrace.

He arrived at her chamber and rapped on the door. When no answer was forthcoming, he knocked a bit harder. Still nothing. Was she really asleep?

He'd just take a peek... Easing the door open, he stepped inside. Light from behind him splashed into the chamber, and he could see the bed was devoid of her presence. As was the rest of the room. What the hell was going on?

He closed the door and ran back downstairs. His parents were no longer in the hall, but the door to Father's study was open. Penn crossed to it with long strides and went inside. His father stood near the table, his mother caressing his arm. They both looked at him at the same time, and both immediately registered his annoyance.

"Where is she?"

Mother stopped stroking his father's arm. "What do you mean?"

"Amelia is not in her chamber. You said she retired early."

"That's what her maid reported," Mother said, her voice edged with concern. She looked up at Father, who shook his head.

"I don't know where she could be, Penn."

Penn swore under his breath. Why would she leave? And if she hadn't left, where was she?

"Should we search the house?" Mother asked.

"Yes, let's." Father took charge, leaving the study.

Penn overheard him giving instructions to Thomas. Weariness stole over Penn, along with a stinging sensation of defeat. Where was she?

A moment later, voices in the hall shook him from his stupor.

"She's here," Father called just before Amelia stepped into the study. Her cheeks were dark pink, her hair mussed as she removed her men's hat with its wide brim. She wore the costume he'd met her in. Why?

Gideon came in behind her. He was also garbed strangely. His clothing was old and too large. And he carried Dyrnwyn.

"How the hell did you get that?" Penn demanded.

"I gave it to him," Amelia said. "We needed it."

"Why?" Penn's gaze strayed to Gideon, anxiety tumbling through him. Why were they together?

"I think I'll let her tell the story." Gideon set the sword atop the long worktable, then shrugged out of his oversized coat and draped it across the back of a chair. He sat down and looked from Penn to Amelia and back again, his demeanor reflecting none of the tension Penn felt.

Penn turned his gaze to Amelia and registered the apprehension he'd missed a moment ago. He was a self-involved ass. In two steps, he was in front of her, taking her hands in his. "Are you all right?"

She nodded. "Yes. I received a...note this morning with my breakfast. A boy delivered it to the kitchen and asked that it be given to me."

Penn didn't like the sound of this, particularly knowing

the end result of this note somehow involved Amelia looking upset and Gideon wielding the flaming sword.

Amelia's gaze softened as she looked at him. "You'd already left; otherwise, I would've told you about it. Despite the note warning me not to."

Anger—directed at himself—rose in his throat. He should've been here with her. "Where is this bloody note?"

She let go of his hand and pulled a small piece of parchment from her coat. He took it and quickly read the lines.

When he looked back at her, he couldn't keep the incredulity from his tone. *"You went to meet this blackguard?"*

"Not alone," she said with a defensive edge. "Kersey came with me."

Penn's father broke in, looking toward Gideon, "When did you arrive?"

"This morning. I met Mrs. Forrest outside, and she shared the note with me." He turned his head to Penn. "She would have shared it with you, I assure you."

Penn reined in his temper—he wasn't typically an angry sort. He was levelheaded and composed. It took quite a bit to ruffle him. Apparently, this was precisely that. He took a deep breath and looked intently at Amelia. "You're sure you're all right?"

"Yes."

"Did you get the book?" A bead of anticipation worked its way up Penn's spine. To have the book…

Her brow creased. "No."

His anticipation crumbled away like a dried-up biscuit. "The heart?"

"I still have it." She pulled it from her coat and winced as she transferred it to his palm. "We dropped it."

He looked at the two pieces and felt only a mild disappointment. "Good thing it's not the real one."

Her lips curled into a faint smile. "I thought you might say that."

"Who wrote the note?" Penn asked, already thinking how he might find the villain and ensure he never bothered Amelia again. In fact, why had this person sent *her* the note? They'd clearly known she—along with him—was in possession of the heart, which meant they'd been followed from Oxford.

Amelia exchanged a quick look with Gideon. Something was off...

Gideon stood and stepped toward Penn. "Real heart or not, that stone is more than what you thought."

Penn looked down at the two pieces and moved his fingers, turning the stone in his palm. He lifted his gaze to Gideon and then Amelia. "What do you mean?"

It was Amelia who answered. "Apparently, it's a key."

CHAPTER 14

*R*elief surged through Amelia. She sent a brief, grateful look toward Kersey. He gave her an infinitesimal nod.

"A key?" Penn turned to the table and set the two pieces of the heart down on the wood.

Rhys went to the hearth and picked up the flint to light a lantern, which he set down near the stone. "A key to what?"

Everyone huddled around the table. Rhys next to Penn and Amelia on Penn's other side. Margery sidled up beside her husband, and Kersey stood near Amelia's elbow.

Penn leaned over and picked up a piece, holding it to the light as he turned it over in his fingers. He narrowed his eyes and used his other hands to pick at the paint that had chipped from where the stone had split. "I can't tell, but there may be something etched here."

Using his thumbnail, he pushed a bit of paint away. It flaked off and floated to the table. He continued until he'd exposed a small area. Holding the rock to the lantern, he sucked in a breath. "It looks like a coded message."

Rhys pitched forward and studied the piece. "Indeed it does. There has to be a cipher."

"I think I know where it is," Kersey said, and all eyes turned to him. "The White Book of Hergest."

Rhys turned toward him, his gaze intense and almost… hungry. "How do you know that?"

"I saw it a few times at Foliot's. I suspected it may be a palimpsest."

"You know how to recognize that?" Rhys's question was tinged with admiration.

Kersey squared his shoulders. "I paid attention when I spent time with you in my youth. I didn't share my suspicions with Foliot or anyone else, and I don't think they realize what it is."

Amelia had no idea what they were talking about. "What is a palimpsest?"

Penn turned to her. "The easiest way to explain it is to show you. Father?"

Rhys left the table and went to one of his bookshelves. He selected a volume bound in dark brown leather and brought it to the table. He opened it in front of Amelia, but it was Penn who spoke.

His long fingers traced over the text. "You can see what's written here, but if you look beyond the words, you'll see that something else was on this paper before. The paper was reused. In most cases, it's simply a matter of needing parchment and using what's available. However, sometimes the palimpsest hides secret information. Do you see the traces of what was there before?" He scooted the lantern closer to the book.

She bent down and blinked, clearing her sight to peer past the writing. "Yes!" She looked over at Kersey. "You detected this in the White Book?"

"I did."

Amelia studied the book again before straightening. "Remarkable."

"I don't suppose you recall what the palimpsest said?" Penn asked Kersey.

Kersey shook his head. "I wasn't able to study it. As I said, I only suspected it was there, but it was behind the story of Ranulf and Hilaria, so that seems to fit."

Excitement curled through Amelia, and when she looked at Penn, she saw the same anticipation reflected in his eyes. "We need that book," Penn said determinedly.

Something tickled the back of Amelia's mind. "When my grandfather was ill, he mentioned something that I attributed to the ramblings of a dying man. He spoke of a hidden text. When I asked him if I should find a book for him, he said no it was hidden *text*. I didn't understand what he meant."

"You think he knew about the palimpsest?" Rhys asked.

"We know he saw the White Book at Wynnstay. So I think it's possible. He said that a hidden text was the key to everything." She couldn't believe she hadn't remembered that until now. But now was precisely when it was important, and that was all that mattered.

"We need that book," Penn repeated.

Amelia's gaze fixed on the two pieces of the broken heart. "If that heart holds a clue, then it really is a fake." She'd gotten so wrapped up in the hunt that she'd forgotten her initial pledge to preserve her grandfather's legacy.

Penn put his arm around her and gave her shoulder a squeeze. "If your grandfather knew of the palimpsest and said it was the key to everything, it seems likely that he knew it was fake."

Yes, it did. But she had so many questions. That would likely go unanswered. An overwhelming wave of sadness washed over her. Penn perhaps sensed that as he drew her tight against his side and brushed a kiss along her temple.

It took a moment for his actions to sink into her brain. She glanced at the others. Kersey was fixed on the heart, but Penn's parents quickly looked away, as if they'd been caught staring at something they shouldn't.

Amelia inwardly winced. She doubted they'd be able to categorize their relationship as just professional any longer. And here she was, a married woman.

Suddenly, she wanted to get away from all of them, to run from the sensation of the walls closing in around her. Her life had drastically changed in the course of a day. Last night, she'd lain with Penn, hopeful for a future they might have together. A future that, for now, would never be.

"I can get the book," Kersey said.

She was grateful for the intrusion on her thoughts and for the distraction from Penn's solicitude.

Penn dropped his arm from her shoulders. Had he realized his faux pas? He angled himself toward Kersey. "How?"

"I'd rather not get into the specifics, *but* I know Foliot." He said the last rather darkly and with more than a hint of remorse.

"How is that exactly?" Penn asked. "I'd like to know how you came to know him."

Kersey exhaled, then moved from the table to a chair at the end. He sprawled into it before answering. "He approached me several years ago—when I was at Oxford. Preyed on me is perhaps a better description," he said wryly. "He knew my father was interested in antiquities, especially books, and that Stratton was woefully uneducated about them. He offered to tutor me, and I accepted."

"That is how the Order grooms potential members," Rhys said, taking a few steps away from the table. "Septon explained it to me once because I asked. I wondered why I hadn't been approached."

Penn turned his head toward his father. "And why was that?"

"Because I didn't exhibit sufficient interest in Arthurian legend specifically."

"Neither did I," Kersey said.

Rhys's gaze softened, and his lips curved into a slight smile. "But you're a descendant of one of the knights. Your interest in Arthurian legend or even antiquities isn't required."

Amelia found that a bit odd. "At all? If a person didn't even show a passing curiosity, why would the Order think they would care?"

"They make contact to ascertain whether the descendant might develop an interest, if not a passion," Rhys said.

Kersey made a sound that was part grunt and part scoff. "That sounds like precisely what Foliot did with me."

"Only Foliot is more than just a member of the Order," Penn said. "He's the leader of a villainous faction inside it."

"Which I didn't know." Kersey didn't say this defensively, but as a matter of fact. "He never told me I was a descendant —merely hinted that I may have a connection. I didn't know for sure until I picked up that sword." His gaze flicked to the weapon lying on the table.

"Is there a chance Foliot doesn't know for sure?" Rhys asked.

Kersey shook his head. "Not anymore. The men we met tonight saw me wield the sword. They'll undoubtedly report that back to Foliot."

Amelia tensed, waiting for Penn—or anyone else—to ask about the men. She didn't want to talk about Thaddeus right now. She didn't want Penn to learn about him in front of his parents.

She still couldn't believe he'd shown up. Had he written that note? She hadn't recognized the handwriting, but she honestly couldn't say if she'd know it if she saw it. Had he been following her and Penn from Oxford or perhaps even longer? Her skin crawled thinking of that.

"I'm not convinced you should get the book," Rhys said with grave concern. "It will be dangerous, and I don't trust Foliot."

"I could go," Penn said.

Fear constricted Amelia's chest. She knew Penn did dangerous things, but she couldn't let him. Before she could protest, his mother beat her to it. "No, you can't." Her gaze darted to Kersey. "And I don't want you to go either."

Kersey arched a brow. "Because my father is dead, and I need to assume the earldom? That can wait a few days."

And that was Amelia's cue to leave. None of what needed to be spoken next was her business. "I am suddenly quite fatigued. I'd like to retire."

Penn gave her a knowing look, his eyes burning with intensity. She had the sense he wanted to say something, to do something. But he'd already done enough. It had to be evident to everyone their relationship went much deeper than finding a treasure.

Too bad it had to end.

On that despondent note, Amelia said good night and fled.

⁓

*P*enn watched Amelia go with an ache in his heart. He longed to follow her, to hold her, to make certain she was safe. He sure as hell didn't want to talk about the bloody earldom.

His father went to the sideboard and pulled out the whiskey bottle. "Who wants to join me?" Penn, Gideon? Port for you, my dear." He poured her a glass of her favorite after-dinner drink and handed it to her.

"Yes, please," Penn said.

"And for me." Gideon made to stand, but Father waved him back down.

He poured the drinks and delivered a glass first to Penn and then to Gideon. "How did you hear of your father's death?"

"The steward at Westerly Cross." That had been Gideon's mother's father's estate.

"So you've been staying at Hardy's cottage?"

Gideon took a sip of whiskey and nodded.

Penn recalled that Hardy's cottage was on the Westerly Cross estate and was where his parents had found the glass device that had been created to decipher the de Valery code. The estate had passed to the new baron. "Your cousin allows you to stay there?"

"Second cousin, and yes. My grandfather made a provision for it in his will. He wanted the cottage to belong to me, and the current baron has no quarrel with it."

"I'm sorry you felt you had nowhere else to go," Mother said softly. "You are always welcome here."

Gideon's eyes widened then. "Even after what I did to Cate?"

"She explained everything," Mother said. "We understand what drove you, especially hearing what you said today about Foliot seeking you out. I can certainly grasp why you might respond to a father figure."

Penn's gut clenched. He'd always felt bad for Gideon, for the father he'd been stuck with. Penn had been far luckier with a man who wasn't his father. And now to know the truth...

Father took a drink of whiskey and went to sit next to

Gideon at the table. "There's more to your father's death than you know."

Mother sat down on Gideon's other side, and Penn remained standing. Apprehension tripped through him as he waited for his father to deliver the blow.

Gideon looked between them, his brow darkening. "This should be a happy occasion. I think we're all pleased he's dead."

"You know of his first wife," Father said slowly.

Gideon's hand paused as he lifted the glass toward his mouth. "Yes." He took a sip and set the tumbler back on the table.

"I met her a long time ago," Father said. "She didn't die—at least not when she was purported to. The report of her death was falsified so she could escape your father."

"Can't say I blame her for that. At least she didn't abandon her son with him." Derision dropped from his tone and burned the air like an acrid smoke.

"No, she took her son with her—in her belly. Then, years later, when she became ill, she gave him to me." His sad gaze flicked to Penn, and in that moment, Penn forgave him. It had never been a question. He'd just needed his anger to wane. Rhys Bowen had done what he thought was right. In truth, he'd been dealt an impossible situation, and he'd done the best he could.

Gideon's jaw twitched, and his eyes narrowed to steely slits. "What are you saying?"

"Penn is William Kersey, now the Earl of Stratton."

Once again, Penn flinched at the name, hating the sound of it. That wasn't who he was, who he wanted to be.

Gideon turned his gaze on Penn, his lip curling. "After all these years, you want to claim this title?"

Penn shook his head as his body twitched with distaste.

"*God no.* I don't want it. I left early this morning to try to find the vicar and destroy his proof."

"I told you that's where he went," Mother said, looking at Father.

Father turned to Penn. "Did you find him?"

"No," Penn said bitterly. "Egg is on the hunt, however. I wanted to get back here to find the heart."

His mother gave him a look of understanding. "To Amelia."

Hell, he should've expected that. He'd all but declared his feelings for her in front of them when he'd touched her and kissed her and demonstrated his unabashed concern. And what were those feelings exactly… He couldn't think of that now, as much as he might want to. His entire being yearned to go to her, but there would be time.

"Why is Egg hunting a vicar?" Gideon's voice was cold, detached, almost emotionless.

"He recorded Penn's birth and agreed to keep it quiet until Stratton died," Father said. "It was paramount to Penn's mother that Stratton never knew of his existence. I kept her secret until yesterday."

Gideon's gaze swung to Penn again. "You didn't know?"

"I didn't. You must believe me when I say I don't want it. You've been raised to be an earl. I'm a scholar and an adventurer. If I had to manage an estate and sit in the House of Lords, I'd go mad." He threw back half his whiskey, relishing the trail of fire it burned down his throat, then set his tumbler on the table. He stared at Gideon and promised, "I will not let you be known as a bastard."

The edge of Gideon's mouth lifted into a bitter smile. "That won't change the truth. I am what I am." His echo of what Penn had said to his father sent a chill down Penn's spine. "And if Egg doesn't find this vicar in time?"

The question hung in the room like a hangman's noose.

"He will," Penn said, clenching his jaw. He wouldn't accept anything else.

Gideon tossed down the rest of his whiskey and stood. "Well, I suppose my future is in Egg's hands. Here I thought I was an earl... All this time, I've held the courtesy title, and I wasn't even a viscount either, but a bastard. It's no more than I deserve after the way I've behaved. Probably best for me to go off and live the life of a hermit." Was he trying to bring humor to this dismal situation? He certainly wasn't reacting the way Penn had.

Mother stood and touched his arm. "It is *not* what you deserve. And you won't go and be a hermit. You are not alone anymore, Gideon. You never were."

He gave her a half smile. "You did always try. All of you." He looked around the room. "But my father was a blackguard and a scoundrel, the very worst our species has to offer, and he raised me in his image."

"You are not like him," Father practically growled.

"I'm *trying* not to be. If you'll excuse me, I'd like to retire too." He turned and started toward the door.

Penn called after him, "Take the sword."

Gideon slowly pivoted. He stared at Penn in question but didn't say a word.

"Take it. It's yours."

Gideon went back to the table and picked it up in the middle of the scabbard, demonstrating that for him, it clearly weighed far less than for the rest of them. "Since learning I was a descendant, I'd hoped that maybe Stratton wasn't my father, that perhaps I was a by-blow. My mother has already demonstrated her proficiency for infidelity. However, I see now that the line isn't through my father, but my mother." He looked at Penn. "Otherwise, this sword would work for you too."

Penn hadn't considered that. "You're correct."

"I wonder if my grandfather was aware of that connection?" Gideon tipped his head toward Penn's father.

Father had met Lord Nash on several occasions—he and Mother had been quite fond of him. "I don't think he was, but I daresay he'd be thrilled. And proud of you."

Gideon gave a slight nod, then clutched the sword more tightly as he sent Penn an earnest stare. "Thank you, brother."

Then he turned once more, and just before he left, Father called after him, "We'll decide what to do about the book in the morning."

Gideon raised his free hand in silent response before leaving and closing the door behind him.

Everyone was quiet a moment. Father sipped his whiskey, then inclined his head toward Penn. "That was the right thing to do."

Penn picked up his whiskey. "Earls need swords."

Mother looked at him with worry. "Do you really think Egg will be able to find this vicar? And how will he stop him?"

After taking a sip of his drink, Penn shrugged. "I expect he'll kidnap him and bring him back here."

Mother's gasp pierced the air. "He won't."

"He might. But more likely he'll just steal the register so the vicar no longer has written proof."

"He's tracking him to London?" Father asked.

"Yes, but the vicar won't get that far. Egg will catch up with him tomorrow or the next day at the latest."

"I'm surprised you left this matter to him," Father said softly, exchanging a look with his mother.

"Finding the real heart is more important."

"Or is it Mrs. Forrest?" Mother asked. "Please don't try to prevaricate. We aren't blind, and we remember what it was like to work together and the...emotions that can come from such an association."

"I'd rather not discuss that, if you don't mind. I think there are far more urgent matters at hand, namely how we will recover this book. We'll meet at breakfast to develop a plan." He finished his whiskey and set his empty glass on the table. "Good night."

As he walked toward the door, his mother touched his arm. He paused, and she pressed a kiss to his cheek. "I hope you know how much we love you. Whatever happens, you are our son, and nothing will change that."

Penn gave her a fast, warm hug. "I know." He dropped a kiss on her head and looked over at his father. "I love you too."

He hurried from the study and went directly to Amelia's room, uncaring what anyone thought. What did it matter now since it seemed their secret was no longer a secret?

He paused outside her door. Was what they shared a secret? What exactly did they even share?

His mother had spoken of emotions. Penn certainly had several where Amelia was concerned. He'd hated being away from her today. He'd wished she'd come with him, despite what he'd told her that morning. He realized he wanted to face adversity with her as well as celebrate their victories. Warmth and anticipation bloomed in his chest as he knocked on her door.

A moment later, she opened it, and he couldn't wait for an invitation. He pushed inside and closed the door behind him. Then he drew her against his chest and cupped her face just before he pressed his mouth to hers.

The kiss was short but ravenous, their lips moving together in hungry strokes. "I've been waiting all day to do that," he murmured against her. Then he claimed her mouth once more, caressing her face and neck.

She wrapped her arms around him and held him close, kissing him back with a fervor that matched his own. Need raced through him and washed away the pain and frustration. Whatever happened with the bloody book and this damn earldom, he had Amelia. Together they would surmount anything.

He needed to feel her, touch her, taste her. He steered her toward the bed, his lips and tongue devouring her eager mouth. She clutched at his cravat, tugging the ends free from his waistcoat, then pulling it loose and tossing it aside. Next, she pushed at his coat, and he twitched his shoulders, helping her strip it from his body.

Then her fingers were at the buttons of his waistcoat, pushing and pulling to get them free. He untied the sash of her dressing gown—thank goodness she'd already disrobed —and slid his hands inside to clasp her waist.

She shoved his waistcoat off and tugged the hem of his shirt from his waistband. He pulled at the fabric and tore it over his head, briefly breaking their kiss, before pushing her dressing gown to the floor.

The touch of her hands against his bare chest elicited a groan deep in his throat. He didn't stop kissing her but licked at her tongue with his. Her fingertips curled into him, the nails digging into his flesh. But there was no pain, just a scalding desire to possess her and be possessed.

He guided her backward until her thighs met the bed. He gentled the kiss as he slid his hand beneath the hem of her night rail. He grazed his fingertips along her flesh, seeking that sweet, hot place between her thighs.

Finding her curls, he stroked her folds. She parted her legs, welcoming his touch. Her hands moved up around his neck and clutched him tightly.

He lifted her and set her on the bed. Then he took his mouth from hers, but only to cascade kisses along her cheek and jaw and down her neck. He tugged the neckline of her night rail down, stressing the fabric as he worked to pull it past her nipple. When it was just barely free, he lowered his mouth to lick and suck at the tight point.

She cupped his head, her fingers digging into his scalp as her low cry cloaked him with seductive promise. He slipped his hand beneath her night rail once more, skimming over her thigh to find her core. She was wet and ready for him, her flesh silky and warm and so inviting.

He brought his head up and brushed his lips against hers. "I want to bury myself inside you." He stroked his finger inside her, and she let out a soft moan.

Her hands fell to his shoulders, and she pulled back slightly. "No."

He blinked, his ardor cooling at the sound of her denial. "Is something wrong?"

She swallowed as she pulled her hands to her lap. "Yes. We need to talk."

CHAPTER 15

*T*he tightness in her throat was almost unbearable as Amelia worked to keep the tears at bay. She'd been so glad to see him, then he'd kissed her, and she'd been lost. But she couldn't allow them to continue as if her husband hadn't reentered her life today.

"Yes, I suppose we should." He ran his hand through his hair, mussing it to a terribly attractive degree. He smelled of late summer berries carried on the wind and tasted of sharp whiskey. He was a feast for her senses, and she nearly lost the battle to keep her emotions in check.

His face was grim. "I didn't find the vicar. But Egg is after him, and I expect he'll find him tomorrow or the next day."

He thought she wanted to hear about the earldom, about what had happened downstairs after she'd left. Good, perhaps that would give her a moment to settle her nerves. "How is Kersey?"

Penn shook his head, blinking with disbelief. "It's the damnedest thing, his reaction wasn't nearly what I would've expected. I daresay he took it better than I did, which I never would have guessed."

"Perhaps he didn't want you to see how deeply he's affected."

"I suspect that may be it. Egg is going to stop the vicar—and I'm going to ensure Gideon is the earl."

He sounded so confident. She almost believed that he could do anything by sheer force of will. But of course, not everything could be fixed. "Why didn't you go with him?"

He cocked his head to the side, his lips tilting into a half smile. "I should think that would be obvious. Because I prefer to be here with you, to continue our quest."

If only it was just the quest. But it was more than that. And it was more than just wanting him, though she did—desperately. She was in love with him. The realization burned and brought the tears back up her throat.

She swallowed convulsively and took a deep breath. "I have to tell you about the man we met today."

His eyes lit with interest. "Yes! I forgot entirely. I want to hear all about that." He stepped forward, reclaiming the space they'd shared a few moments ago. "After. First, I want to take you in my arms."

He leaned forward, and her heart fairly beat from her chest as she slid to the side, evading his touch. "He's my husband."

She wrapped her arms around herself in an effort to keep from crumpling into a terrible mess.

He pivoted toward her, his thigh pressed against the bed. He blinked, his long, dark lashes, briefly masking the intensity of his cobalt gaze. "Pardon me?"

Amelia took another deep breath, but it didn't really help. Her heart seemed to crash even harder against her rib cage. "The man we met today was my husband."

"I thought your husband was dead." His voice was low and full of gravel.

"He left five years ago. I never thought to see him again."

"*He* sent you that note?"

"He must have, though I didn't recognize the hand."

Penn's tone was even and sure, giving her no clue what was going on in his head. "So he knew we had the heart."

She nodded slowly. "Somehow. I don't know. He's a member of the Camelot group."

Penn bent and retrieved his shirt. When he'd pulled it over his head, he perched at the end of the bed, far away from her. "Tell me everything. How you met, why you married, why he left."

Now he sounded coldly angry, but she didn't blame him. "We met at an assembly in Bath. It was a rather short courtship—just a few weeks." He was the first man who'd paid her attention, and he was handsome and charming and in possession of a decent income. "My father endorsed the union, and we wed."

He folded his arms over his chest. "That's it?"

"What do you want to hear, that I fell madly in love with him? I thought I had. Now I know—" She'd been about to say she knew the difference. But she wouldn't burden him with her feelings. "Now I know better. It was infatuation. I was young and foolish."

"Yet your father allowed you to wed, so he must have had something to recommend him. You say he left you because of debt?"

"That's what I thought. He gave me the impression today that wasn't true. Or perhaps he went into debt on purpose. I know there were creditors—they took everything."

"Or they weren't really creditors, and they simply took his things to wherever he went."

Amelia's jaw dropped. She'd never imagined such cruelty, such viciousness. And yet seeing him today, she realized it was not just possible, but likely. "That is probably true." Foolish didn't begin to describe how she felt.

His gaze softened. "I'm so sorry, Amelia. You say he's a member of the Camelot group. Everything we know about them says they're ruthless in the extreme. Is it possible he courted you to gain access to your grandfather?"

She thought back, and shame engulfed her. "Grandfather never liked him, and my father changed his opinion too. They didn't think he was good enough for me. I never thought he'd come back. I certainly hoped he wouldn't. I planned to have him declared dead so that I could truly be a widow."

"But he's not dead, and he wants the heart. Did he bring the book to trade, or was that a lure to get you there?"

"He didn't bring it."

"I wouldn't expect that he did. I wouldn't have gone to this meeting. I would have gone and watched to ascertain who showed up, then I would have developed a plan." He stood up from the bed. "Which changes nothing, of course. Your husband is very much alive and has apparently been watching you. I wonder for how long?"

Nausea swirled in her gut. To think Thaddeus had been spying on her all this time made her ill.

"That was a rhetorical question," he said. "I can see how distressed you are, and I'm sorry for it. I wish you'd told me the truth about this. Why didn't you?" He looked hurt and upset, and she longed to smooth the lines away from his forehead and kiss the tension from his mouth.

"I didn't think it mattered. I thought he was gone forever —maybe even dead," she said hopefully. "I certainly never imagined he would turn up in this fashion." She stood and smoothed her night rail down. "I don't know how we continue from here. I thought I would be free—"

She stopped. They'd confessed nothing, promised nothing. And yet it felt as though they had. To her, at least. She had no idea what was in his mind.

"But you are not."

Penn picked up his waistcoat and shrugged it on, then he scooped up his coat and cravat, draping them over his left arm. He gave her a smile that was devoid of humor and full of sadness and regret. "Here I thought being an earl was the worst thing that could happen to me. Turns out I was wrong."

Anguish tore at her, and she clapped her hand over her mouth lest she allow a sob to escape. She blinked against tears.

"Don't cry, Amelia," he said softly. "You couldn't have known. Anyway, I'm a traveler, a man without a true home. I am, unlike you, eternally free, and that's the way I like it. God willing, I'll get to continue that way, and Gideon will be the earl." He inhaled sharply and straightened his shoulders.

"In the meantime," he continued, "we'll devise a plan to recover the book and solve the cipher to find the real heart. Then our association will have reached its fruitful end."

Amelia wasn't sure how she could go back to the life she'd led before she'd met Penn. She didn't want to. But Thaddeus had given her no other choice. Thaddeus might even try to reclaim his marital rights. Dread pooled in her belly, and she had to work to keep herself from completely falling apart.

Somehow, she found her voice, though it was wobbly at best. "Yes, we will. I'm sorry, Penn. I wish things were different." So badly she wished they were different.

He nodded but didn't say another word before he left, closing the door behind him with a soft click that reverberated in her chest like a physical blow. Then she went thoroughly and horribly to pieces.

∼

*T*he night passed even worse than the previous. Penn had barely slept, and now that it was morning, he simultaneously yearned to see Amelia and wasn't sure he could bear it. Knowing her husband was alive and involved in their quest filled him with anger and despair. He'd wondered at what kind of future he and Amelia might have with the life he led, but all that was moot now that he knew she was still wed. They had no future.

And neither did the life he enjoyed. The moment he'd learned he was an earl, he'd felt doomed. Making Amelia his countess would have been a shining beacon, transforming a disaster into something he could not only tolerate but maybe, just maybe, anticipate.

However, he couldn't take a wife who was already married.

A voice in the back of his mind reminded him of Septon —a baron who openly lived with his mistress who was married to someone else. *Had* been married to someone else. Penn wondered if they would marry and, if so, would it change how Society viewed them? Septon wasn't entirely ostracized, but he also wasn't accepted amongst the most elite. Lady Stratton, however, had been almost universally shunned. She never went to London and nearly the only social gatherings she attended were the ones she hosted with Septon. Could Amelia be content with a life like that if they chose to be together in spite of her marriage?

Disgust roiled in his gut. He couldn't ask her to do that.

And what of your children, another voiced asked, *they would be bastards.* That hadn't been an issue for Septon and Lady Stratton as they hadn't had children. Penn had every reason to expect he and Amelia might. He couldn't do that to them.

The dismal thoughts churned in his mind as he made his

way to the dining room. His parents were already seated as he walked to his chair.

"You don't look as if you slept very much," his mother said worriedly. "I'm sorry about everything on your mind." She'd always done her best to ease Penn's troubles, and he imagined it was difficult for her to see him in distress. He wouldn't tell her that she didn't even know the half of it.

Gideon came in then, and Penn was saved from having to respond. His cousin—no, his half brother—took the chair opposite Penn's. He looked slightly better than Penn felt, which wasn't saying much.

The only open space left was next to Penn, which meant Amelia would sit beside him. He tensed as he awaited her arrival. And then she was there, garbed in a peach-colored gown with a wide, cream-colored sash. She looked fresh and lovely, and his heart ached at the sight of her.

Her gaze landed on the vacant chair to his left, and her reaction was barely detectable—just a slight flaring of her nostrils and parting of her lips. He knew her well enough to recognize her discomfort. He also knew her well enough to conclude that she would rise above it.

Penn, his father, and Gideon stood as she made her way to her seat, and Penn held her chair while she situated herself at the table.

"Good morning," Mother said with a warm smile. "I trust you slept well."

"Fine, thank you," Amelia said evenly. At this distance, Penn could see the faint streaks of purple beneath her eyes. She was a decent liar.

Thomas served as footman this morning, piling their plates from the sideboard with the items they chose from the offerings. When he was finished, they began to tuck in. It was Gideon who spoke first as he picked up his fork.

"I think I have a good plan for obtaining the book."

All eyes turned to him. Penn was eager for something to take his mind off the bleak prospect of his future. "Let's hear it."

Gideon shot Penn an anxious glance. "Just bear with me while I lay it out. We know where the book is—at a house outside Glastonbury, which is where Foliot has an estate. I'd wager this house is on the estate. Foliot likes to keep his people close. I've stayed with him on several occasions."

"That's useful," Penn said, suspecting where Gideon might be heading and not liking it one bit.

"The man in possession of the book—Thaddeus—we can distract him and steal the book—"

Penn dropped his utensils. *"No."* Gideon had gone precisely where he'd feared. "She's not doing that."

"Who?" Penn's father, seated at the end of the table to Penn's right looked from Penn to Gideon and back to Penn again.

"Me," Amelia said. She dabbed at her mouth with her napkin before continuing. "Thaddeus is my husband." She paused, registering the exchanged look of surprise between Penn's parents, but only briefly. "We weren't married very long before he left me. I thought it was because of debt, but it seems he was tasked by the Camelot group to obtain the dagger—and anything else they might be able to learn—from my grandfather. When he wasn't able to get anything, he left."

She gave her attention to Gideon. "I'll do it. Just tell me what I need to do."

Penn angled toward her. "You can't."

She turned her head to look at him. "Why not? He's my husband. I'm the best—perhaps the only—person to distract him while you and Kersey steal it."

"She can take care of herself, Penn," Gideon said. "She did shoot him after all."

Penn blinked at her, surprised but then not. She had come close to doing the same to Egg. "You did?"

She nodded. "I actually wanted to hit him, not like when I missed Egg."

Penn almost smiled. "We would need to scout the place—if it's too large, this won't work."

"I propose we hire a hack in Glastonbury," Gideon said. "I'll pose as the coachman and deliver Mrs. Forrest to the house. While she distracts Mr. Forrest, Penn will sneak in and nab the book. When you have it, come to the coach, and we'll signal for Mrs. Forrest to leave. She'll come out to tell me—the coachman—I can leave, but in actuality, she'll leave with me. And you. And the book."

"Well, that sounds rather neat and tidy," Father said. "I was going to offer to come along, but what role would I play?"

That earned him a reproachful stare from Mother.

"I think we can handle it," Gideon said with a slight smile. "If Penn is in agreement. It seems as though Mrs. Forrest is up to the task."

Amelia nodded. "I am."

Penn had executed exercises such as this before, but never when it would endanger someone other than Egg. And never when it would endanger the woman he loved. Yes, he loved her. Beyond expectation. Beyond reason. He couldn't put her at risk, even if she *could* take care of herself.

He abruptly stood and looked down at Amelia. "May we take a walk, please?"

She blinked up at him, her green eyes brilliant in the morning sun streaming through the windows. Without answering, she rose, and he moved to pull her chair back for her.

He glanced at the table. "Please excuse us."

Gideon looked up at him, but only briefly before going

back to his breakfast. His parents, on the other hand, watched them depart the dining room.

Penn escorted her to the back of the house and into the morning room, through which they exited into the yard. He didn't stop there, but motioned for her to walk with him toward the wood where he went to think.

"Are we going to your lean-to?" she asked, surprising him.

He stopped and turned toward her. "Yes. How do you know about that?"

"I went there yesterday after you left. It's an excellent place to go for reflection and solitude. But I suspect we aren't going there for either, so why don't you say what you want to say right here?"

She was angry. He could feel the emotion rising off her in waves. Well, he was angry too. And scared and so frustrated at his lack of control, he could scream. They were still in view of the house—if anyone went to the morning room— and that wouldn't do.

"Just please come with me?"

Her eyes narrowed, and she pursed her lips. "Fine, but I'm not changing my mind."

$\mathcal{T}$he coolness of the tree canopy was a welcome balm to the irritation rioting through her. Amelia didn't stop her purposeful march until she reached the lean-to, where she turned and crossed her arms over her chest. Her body, taut as a drum, hummed with myriad emotions—anger, frustration, hurt. And determination.

"You aren't changing my mind." It bore repeating.

He came into the lean-to and put his hands on his hips. "You can't do this."

"I *can't?*"

He blew out a breath. "You *can*, but you shouldn't. A thousand things could go wrong, and we've no idea what Forrest is capable of. You shot him—why didn't you tell me you shot him?" He didn't wait for her response before saying, "Clearly, you thought him a threat."

"I didn't keep it from you on purpose. Last night was... difficult." If she thought about it too deeply, she'd lose herself again. Her emotions were far too close to the surface. "He had two men with him, and it was just Kersey and me. Kersey took on the other two while I distracted Thaddeus. He tried to take the heart, and it fell. I didn't want him to get it, so I shot him in the arm."

Penn stared at her a long moment. "I don't want you to do this. We can't control the situation when you're alone with him. I don't like it." He clenched his jaw. "Unless you're considering going back to him."

"No!" Why was he behaving like an imbecile? "Of course I don't want to go back to him. I *want* the book and the heart—the real heart, assuming the book will lead us to it and it actually exists. I am in this hunt until the bitter end."

She paced from one end of the lean-to to the other. "I thought about my grandfather all night." Not *all* night. Only when she hadn't been thinking of Penn, which was a fair amount. "I think it's likely he knew the heart and the dagger were fake. If he believed the White Book was the key—"

"Then he'd have to think it was the key to something, and what else besides the real heart, especially since the fake heart contains a clue. Assuming it *is* a clue. I keep thinking it could all be a ruse. Until we get the book, we can't know."

She'd stopped when he interrupted her. "Yes, we *need* the book. Gideon's plan is the best chance we have, and you know it. He will be with me in the coach, right outside the house. And you'll be there, *in* the house. I trust you both to keep me safe."

He took the one step that separated them, then lifted his hand to her face. His fingertips caressed her cheekbone and trailed down along her jaw. "I promise to always keep you safe, no matter what the future holds. You may not be mine, but I will always wish you were."

The dam inside her broke, but not in the way it had last night. Instead of sadness and despair, she gave in to her anger and frustration at her situation.

You may not be mine, but I will always wish you were.

His words fed the hunger in her soul and pushed her to

take what she wanted, and not what she should be content to receive.

She clutched his lapels and pulled him to her until they crashed together—lips, chests, pelvises. He kissed her hard and fast, his tongue lashing at hers. She poured every emotion she had into the embrace, curling her arms around his neck, and pushing her body against his.

He clasped her back, his hands running up and down her spine and sides without stopping. If they'd been in a bedchamber, she envisioned them tearing at each other's clothes. But they weren't in a bedchamber.

She drew back with a gasp and stared at his kiss-reddened lips. "I'm sorry."

"Don't be. Do you want to stop?"

"Shouldn't we?" She glanced at their surroundings—a narrow bench that spanned just half of the lean-to's wall. It couldn't support their weight.

His gaze speared into hers, dark and intense. "If you want to."

"No. I mean, I don't want to stop, but it seems rather impossible to continue. Here."

He gave her a slow, seductive smile. "You know I enjoy a challenge." He clasped her waist and lifted her farther into the lean-to, until her back was against the wall. "Put your leg up here." He gestured to the bench.

She positioned her foot securely onto the wood, and his hand delved beneath her skirts. His fingers danced across her thigh before tangling in her curls. She clutched his shoulders, holding on to him for balance.

"You can lean against the wall," he murmured against her ear as he teased her sex with languid caresses. "In fact, I suggest you do. I'll be using it to support our...activities shortly."

His mouth covered hers in a searing kiss. She moaned

into him as need spiraled through her. He slipped his finger inside her, and she bucked against him.

He tore his mouth from hers with a groan and kissed along her neck. She dug her fingers into him as her legs tensed. She wanted more, needed more.

"Penn. I want—"

He kissed her again, his mouth ravaging hers. She couldn't get enough. Then there were two fingers pumping into her again and again. Pleasure built, and she wasn't sure if she could sustain herself.

Suddenly, his fingers were gone, and her skirt fell. She blinked at him as he bent his head. She dropped her gaze and saw him unbuttoning his fall.

When she lowered her hand to help him, he grunted softly. "Lift your skirts."

She did as he bade, tugging the volume of fabric up to her waist, exposing her flesh to the air and to him.

"So beautiful," he murmured, as his cock sprang free of his clothing. His gaze found hers. "Hold on to me."

He put his hands beneath her clothing and clasped her waist, lifting her from the ground. Her back, already against the wall, pushed against it, as he brought his hand down the back of her thigh, pulling her leg around his waist.

She understood and wrapped herself around him. Bracing her against the wall, he guided his cock into her sex, and she was instantly overcome with a wave of stunning rapture. He filled her completely, then pulled back only to drive into her again. Two strokes and she was gone, her climax tearing through her with a ferocity she never thought possible. But hadn't he already shown her that what she thought was impossible wasn't?

That was the last rational thought she had as he thrust deep inside her, his body pinning her—deliciously—against the lean-to. He filled her so completely, and the pleasure… It never seemed to ebb. Even after the climax, it began to build again immediately. She was going to come a second time, and surely *that* was impossible...

He buried his face in her neck, kissing and nipping at her flesh. She raked her nails along the wool of his coat and wished it was his bare back.

He slammed into her again, and she felt his hips twitch with the onset of his climax. Then hers was upon her, proving that nothing was impossible—at least not with Penn.

She cried out, and he kissed her hard and fast, trying to muffle his own exclamation. She tipped her head back against the wall as their harsh pants filled the small space of the lean-to.

After a moment, when they were slightly more in control of their breathing, he withdrew from her. "Hell, I meant to pull away."

She hadn't even considered it. She'd thought of nothing but coupling with him, of appeasing the ache inside her. "I'm sure it's fine," she murmured.

He guided her wobbly legs to the ground, letting her skirt fall down around her legs. Frowning, he tucked his slackening shaft into his clothes. "I have nothing to help you clean up."

She flashed him a brief smile. "That's what excessive undergarments—namely petticoats—are for." She turned to the side and took care of her situation before facing him again. "How awful do I look?"

"You look beautiful." He traced his hand along her hairline, smoothing the strands from her face and gently kissing her lips.

She turned and presented her back. "And from this angle?"

"A bit of dirt here and there, I'm afraid. I'm sorry."

She turned back around to see the remorse in his gaze. "I

wouldn't trade it for anything. Thank you—for that. I shall never regret anything between us."

"Nor will I."

"I'll go directly to my room." She smoothed her hands over her skirts, trying—hopelessly—to erase the wrinkles they'd caused. "Tell the others I needed some time to think."

He cracked a half smile. "It won't be hard to convince them of that."

"And you'll finalize the planning with Kersey? We should leave as soon as possible. I can be ready in an hour. Actually, tell them I've gone upstairs to pack."

His forehead creased. "You really want to do this?"

"Yes." She exhaled and gave him a reassuring smile. "It's the only way. We've come too far to let them win." This had started as a quest to find her grandfather's dagger, but it had become so much more. The stakes were higher and more complicated than she ever could have imagined. She couldn't have walked away if her life depended on it. Her life did depend on it—this was all she had. All she wanted.

She kissed his cheek. "I'll be ready in an hour." She'd explain to Culley and Horatio that they could stay here in her absence.

She started to move past him, but he clasped her hand and drew her to turn. "If I could think of a way for us to be together, I would." His voice was low and intense. "But with your husband... I can only think of Septon and Lady Stratton. They might be together, but I can't subject you to that level of disdain."

She hadn't even thought of them. And while she wanted Penn, she didn't think she could live like that. "I appreciate you saying so. I wouldn't want that either." What's more, she wouldn't do it to him. He was an earl—probably—and he needed a legitimate countess. She couldn't be that for him.

She turned and went into the house, eager to be on their

way as apprehension and sadness stole the bliss he'd given her.

She'd been wrong before. Some things *were* impossible. She and Penn might want a future together, but they'd both have to accept that it just wasn't meant to be.

$\sim$

*P*enn waited a few moments before he followed Amelia inside. He needed to catch his breath.

What the hell had he been thinking?

He *hadn't* been thinking. He'd been *feeling*. And surrendering to those feelings.

He'd been foolish and reckless, and he couldn't do it again. That knowledge burned through him. He closed his eyes and dropped his head, then massaged the back of his neck as if he could drive the tension away.

Except he couldn't.

Focus on the book.

Lifting his head, he inhaled sharply and dropped his hand to his side. Yes, he needed to focus on obtaining the book and solving the code so they could find the real heart.

They. His association with Amelia wasn't finished yet. He still had to watch her divert her husband while he found the book. That would be pure torture.

But not as awful as when he had to say good-bye.

Shoving the thought aside with a curse, he stalked into the house. When he arrived in the dining room, three pairs of eyes looked up at him. They'd finished their meals, and Penn's had been covered to preserve it for when he returned. Only he wasn't really hungry.

"Where's Mrs. Forrest?" Gideon asked, glancing behind Penn.

"She's gone upstairs to prepare for the trip. We'd like to leave immediately."

Gideon leapt to his feet. "Excellent. I'm glad she convinced you of the integrity of the plan—she'll be fine. You'll ensure it."

Of course he would. Penn said nothing.

"I'll have the horses prepared," Gideon continued. "I think we should ride. A coach will slow us down. As I said before, we'll hire one in Glastonbury for our needs."

"I agree," Penn said.

Gideon nodded, then left.

Penn's mother didn't waste time in broaching the subject of Amelia. "Penn, I don't wish to overstep, but I would be remiss if I didn't ask you about Amelia. It was evident last night that your relationship is beyond that of mere professional associates." There was concern in her gaze but also something else—was it sadness?

Penn had considered—briefly with all that was going on —what he might say in the event his mother asked this. He didn't want to go into too much depth. It was all moot anyway. "It turns out the husband who left her years ago has returned, so our relationship—whatever it was or might have been—is that of friendship and nothing more." Never mind what had just occurred in the lean-to. They shouldn't have done it, but neither would he regret it.

His father coughed and dipped a glance toward Penn's throat. "Son, your cravat is askew."

The meaning was clear—they'd drawn their own, not inaccurate, conclusions about where Penn and Amelia had gone. Or, more importantly, what they had done during their absence from the dining room.

Penn silently swore as he adjusted his neckcloth. He was probably cocking it up even further, so he gave up almost immediately. Where was a glass of whiskey when he needed it?

His mother laid her hand on the table, reaching toward him. "Penn, it's none of our concern, but we care for you and don't wish to see you hurt. When I thought there might be... something between you, I was overjoyed. To think you had finally found someone who would make you happy, someone for whom you might settle down..." She winced. "I'm sorry you can't pursue it."

"Well, he *could*..." His father drawled.

His mother gasped and sent him a sharp look. "Rhys! He most certainly cannot."

"It works for Septon and Lady Stratton." Father tipped his head to the side. "Do you think they'll wed now?"

Mother rolled her eyes. "Septon allows many things that most would not. His association with that awful Order should be proof enough. You can't think to infer Penn is the same."

Father straightened. "No." He shot an apologetic smile at Penn. "I wish there was a way for you and Mrs. Forrest to be together—if that's what you both want."

That was what *he* wanted. Would she want the same if she were free? She hadn't said. But again, it was moot. It was perhaps better if he didn't know.

"As an earl, you should consider taking a countess," his mother said. "But there'll be time for that. Or not. I'd never planned to marry, and if I hadn't met your father, I would likely be a spinster. There's nothing wrong with being unmarried."

Penn stood from the table, anxious to put an end to this disquieting conversation. He wanted to focus on obtaining the White Book of Hergest. That was something he could control, something he could achieve.

"I won't be the earl, Gideon will. Even now, Egg is

perhaps on his way back with the proof so that we may destroy it. Or perhaps he already has."

"And if he doesn't?" Father asked with a grimace. "You need to think about the possibility that you *are* an earl."

Bitterness rose in his mouth. "I've thought of little else." Until he'd learned of Amelia's husband. For a brief while yesterday he'd actually come to terms with being the earl, if it meant Amelia would be his countess. Without her, he didn't want it. Hell, without her, everything seemed far less palatable.

His heart had started to pound. He took a deep breath to calm himself. He wasn't angry with his parents, but with the situation he found himself in. "My apologies," he said. "I know you both have my best interests at heart."

Father stood and came around to his side of the table. He clapped his hand on Penn's shoulder. "We certainly do. And I deeply regret not telling you about Stratton sooner. I'm, ah, surprised at how well Gideon is taking this."

Mother left her chair and joined them. "I've been wondering about that too. Do you think he's all right, or is he just hiding how he really feels?"

Penn wasn't sure. "I'll find out on our journey."

Father didn't look convinced. "If he'll tell you. He can be rather enigmatic. Very unlike his father—Stratton's thoughts and opinions were never a mystery."

"He couldn't possibly keep anything to himself." Mother shuddered. She turned a bright smile on Penn. "Please take care of yourself. And Gideon. And Amelia."

"I will." He kissed her cheek, then embraced them both. "Watch for Egg, and tell him I'll be back soon. We'll send word when we have the book and let you know what we plan to do next."

CHAPTER 17

*T*hey arrived in Glastonbury the following afternoon after spending the night in Ston Easton at a tiny inn. He and Gideon had shared a chamber, and when Penn had attempted to discuss the earldom, Gideon had feigned exhaustion.

Penn hadn't believed him, but neither had he pressed the issue. In truth, he didn't particularly want to talk about it either. He didn't even want to *think* about it. He just prayed Egg had found the vicar.

Gideon led them west of the town toward Foliot's estate, and presumably Forrest's cottage. Though Gideon was somewhat familiar with the estate, it took him a little while to find what he thought was the right place. He motioned for them to join him near a stand of trees.

"That looks like what Forrest described, doesn't it?" Gideon inclined his head toward the cottage at the base of a gentle slope.

Amelia nodded. "Yes. There are sheep grazing, as he said, and a tall oak tree. It's also nicer than the cottage we shared."

Penn ignored the pang of jealousy that shot through him.

"I see the front door. Presumably, there is a window or a door for me to enter in the back. I'll find something."

She looked over at him from beneath the brim of her bonnet. Her riding habit, a dark bottle green with gold trim, intensified the color of her eyes. Or perhaps that was just his whimsy. Whenever he looked at her, he felt like a man dying of unquenched thirst.

"What if you don't?" she asked. "How will I know if we need to abort the plan?"

"I'll use the signal we discussed earlier," Gideon said. He'd demonstrated a birdcall that would be easy to discern, even from inside the cottage.

She didn't appear entirely mollified. Her gaze fixed on Penn. "And will I know if you're able to get inside?"

"Hopefully not. I try to be quieter than air." He winked at her, hoping to put her at ease even though his own insides were a combustive mess.

Gideon cleared his throat. "Let's review this one more time. Amelia and I will go to the inn to hire the coach and change our clothing. Penn, you'll stay here and scout your entry point.

"We'll return in an hour or so. While Amelia distracts that imbecile, I'll wait with the coach. Penn will have found his way inside and will nab the book. When he arrives at the coach, I'll give the signal. Amelia, you'll extricate yourself from the cretin and come to the coach. Once you're inside, we'll leave immediately."

Amelia exhaled. "Then we'll drop Penn here at his horse and take the coach back to the inn."

"Where Gideon will obtain your horses, and we'll meet at that abandoned cottage we found outside the north end of town," Penn said. "Then we'll solve this bloody riddle and find the heart."

"It all sounds so neat and tidy." Amelia sounded nervous. "You seem to have thought of everything."

Penn wanted to take her in his arms to reassure her. "I try to do that in these situations—it's how I'm so successful."

Gideon snorted. "Is that what you were when the dagger was stolen from you?"

They'd related that story to him last night over supper. Amelia was sorry she likely wouldn't get the dagger back, but finding the "key" her grandfather had mentioned and solving this mystery would be enough. Or so she'd said.

Penn glowered at Gideon in response, which only made his half brother smile.

"Shouldn't we get going?" Amelia asked. "I'd like to get this over with."

"Yes, let's." Penn was eager to have the book in his possession and Amelia away from Forrest. It was going to take every ounce of self-control he had not to pound her husband into the floorboards.

"One more thing," Gideon said. "The heart."

"I'll bring it with me to the cottage." The two halves were nestled in Amelia's saddlebag. They'd written down the code, then altered it on the stone just in case she had to give it to Thaddeus. Penn really had thought of and planned for everything.

Amelia turned her head toward him and gave him a soft smile. "Be safe."

He nodded and watched as she and Gideon rode east toward Glastonbury. When they were out of sight, he put his mind to the task at hand—finding a way in to Forrest's cottage.

Then he would wait.

～

*T*hough she'd reviewed the plan in her mind a dozen times, anxiety pulsed through Amelia's frame. She smoothed her hand along her skirt, finding the slight bulge of the small pistol she had hidden in her pocket. It made her feel marginally better. She'd shot Thaddeus once before, and she could do it again.

Maybe this time, he'd do her the courtesy of dying so that she could get back to the life she wanted.

She winced, hating herself for thinking such a thing. But really, contemplating a future in which she was tied to Thaddeus Forrest was enough to make her want to open the carriage door and retch.

The vehicle they'd obtained was a chaise. It was small and open at the front with a single horse drawing it, which Gideon—he'd instructed her to call him by his given name since he was no longer Viscount Kersey, at least as far as they knew—was riding postilion.

As they traveled down the lane that led to the cottage, her apprehension increased. It was a mild afternoon, but it might have been scorching hot given the beads of sweat trickling down the back of her neck.

She couldn't show Thaddeus that she was nervous. She had to convince him she wanted to start fresh. No easy feat since at their last meeting, she'd shot him.

The vehicle slowed to a stop in front of the cottage. It really was a charming abode, with flowers blooming in front and a gable on one side. Their house had been smaller with a thatched roof and a single room upstairs—their bedchamber —accessible by a rotting staircase.

Nausea roiled in her gut. Why had she thought of their bedchamber?

Gideon climbed from the horse and came around to help her out. "Are you ready?" he asked quietly. "It's not too late to change your mind. Penn and I can come up with another plan."

She stared at him with pursed lips. "Now you sound like him. I don't need to be coddled. I'm quite ready." Maybe if she said it enough she'd believe it.

No, she could do this. She *would* do this. She'd had plenty of nerve when she'd pulled her pistol on Penn and Egg. Goodness, that seemed a lifetime ago now.

She picked up her reticule from the seat, and the pieces of the heart clacked together inside. Placing her hand in Gideon's, she stepped down from the chaise. Lifting her chin, she walked to the door with far more aplomb than she felt.

Before she could lose her courage, she rapped sharply. A few moments later, an older woman opened the door. She had a kind face and a warm smile. "Good afternoon," she said cheerily. "Can I help you?"

"Yes, I'm here to see Mr. Forrest."

The woman's brow darkened. "He wasn't expecting anyone. I'm afraid he's not receiving visitors at present."

Amelia summoned her grandest smile. "I'm certain he'll see me. I'm *Mrs.* Forrest." She gave the woman a conspiratorial wink.

"Oh!" The woman's dark eyes widened, and her lips parted. "I had no idea. Please forgive me."

"It's quite all right," Amelia said. "We've been…estranged. However, I saw him recently, and he invited me to come." None of that was untrue.

"Come in, come in, dear." She opened the door wide and ushered Amelia inside. "I'm Mrs. Jones, Mr. Forrest's housekeeper. And cook. My husband is the caretaker. We live not too far from here." She chuckled. "Just listen to me go on. You don't care about any of that." She peered at Amelia intently. "Or perhaps you do if you're here to rejoin your husband. Hopefully, your presence will improve his disposition. He's been in a terrible state since day before yesterday. He sustained an injury to his arm, and it's made him quite disagreeable."

Good. Amelia stifled her glee. "How unfortunate. Is that why he's indisposed?"

"Yes, I believe he's sleeping, but I'll wake him. As you said, he'll want to see you, I'm sure." She looked Amelia up and down. "Aren't you a pretty thing? I can't believe he never told us about you." She clucked her tongue before taking herself off toward a staircase at the back of the hall.

Mrs. Jones turned at the base of the stairs. "Forgive me. Make yourself at ease." As soon as the housekeeper disappeared up the stairs, Amelia burst into motion.

To her right was a small sitting room and to her left was a larger room with several chairs and a settee—all from their house. Penn had been right about the creditor story being a ruse.

Fury bit at her as she moved inside and saw that the chamber opened to another room at the back. She crept toward the doorway and almost shrieked when she saw Penn climbing in through the window. She couldn't meet Thaddeus in this room. She needed to "make herself at ease" in the other sitting room across the hall.

Except she didn't get that chance.

Heavy footfalls sounded on the staircase. She reached for the door and drew it nearly closed, but stopped as it creaked. Damn, it was still ajar.

"Amelia?"

She briefly closed her eyes and conjured the nerve and composure she required to face Thaddeus.

Just before she turned, Penn met her gaze. He gave her an encouraging look. That was all she needed.

Pasting a smile on her lips, she spun about. "Thaddeus."

He wore breeches and stockings with a pair of slippers.

His shirt was open at the collar and was rather wrinkled, as if he'd been sleeping in it, which she supposed he had. It looked as though he'd hastily donned a waistcoat. The buttons weren't properly fastened, with one extra button at the top and an extra hole at the bottom.

He didn't look pleased to see her. On the contrary, his mouth pitched into a frown, and his brow furrowed. "What the devil are you doing here? Came to finish me off?" He went directly to the sideboard, where he poured himself a glass of something. Gin, she assumed. That had always been his drink of choice.

She noticed he used his left arm for everything, leaving his right arm bent at the elbow. She couldn't discern his wound or any bandages beneath the volume of his sleeve.

She took a few steps away from the door at her back even as she strained to hear what Penn might be doing. "How is your arm?"

He threw himself into a chair near the hearth and glowered up at her. "You bloody shot me."

She'd prepared a response for that. "*You* abandoned me." She narrowed her eyes at him and crossed her arms over her chest—this part wasn't an act. "The creditors took nearly everything. I was humiliated. I had to return to my family in shame."

He sipped his gin and let the glass dangle from the fingers of his left hand. "I am sorry for that. I truly didn't mean to hurt you."

"Then why did you do it? Why marry me in the first place if you planned to leave?"

"I didn't *plan* to leave." He shrugged. "But your father and grandfather were intolerable, and it was simply easier to bid you adieu."

"Except you didn't. You left while I was visiting my grandfather. I came home to an empty house. You didn't even leave me a note. For all I knew, you could've died." After a time, she'd begun to hope so.

He took another drink of gin, then set his glass on a table beside the chair. Leaning forward, he blinked at her. "Did you love me so much, then?"

No, she hadn't loved him at all. She'd been infatuated by his charm and looks at first, but marriage to him had quickly proven to be anything but a happy ever after. He drank to excess, stayed out late—and sometimes didn't come home at all—and spent too much money. How much money she hadn't realized until after he'd left. He'd supposedly worked as a translator, but she rarely saw him work.

She couldn't tell him the truth, not when she was trying to convince him she wanted to be with him again. She swallowed against the revulsion rising in her throat.

"I've missed you," she said, avoiding his question about love. "I'm sorry I shot you. I was just so angry that you'd left me. And it seems you used me into the bargain. Did you marry me just to learn my grandfather's secrets?"

"You're far more astute than I gave you credit for, but then you're several years older now." His gaze traveled leisurely over her body. "More than just your mind has improved."

She nearly gagged at the lascivious look in his eye. But then his gaze turned dark. "Still, you shot me, and the wound could fester." He sniffed.

Feigning concern, she took a few steps toward him. "I'm terribly sorry. I wasn't thinking clearly—can you blame me?"

"I suppose seeing me *was* quite a shock for you. But damn, woman, I'd no idea you could shoot like that. Just nicked my arm, but it was enough to make me bleed like a damned gutted pig." He picked up his gin and drank the lot, then held up the glass to her without a word.

This was something she remembered well—pouring him

gin. She went to the sideboard and filled the glass as much as she dared. Perhaps she could get him drunk enough to lose consciousness, and then she and Penn could find the book easily and be on their way. However, if memory served, Thaddeus was particularly good at holding his drink.

She handed him the gin and tried not to flinch as his fingers grazed hers. Thank goodness she was wearing gloves.

He sipped the gin and narrowed his eyes as he contemplated her. "You going to stand all day?"

She pivoted and sank onto the settee, angling herself so she could see the partially open door to the other room. Thankfully, she'd closed it enough that they wouldn't be able to see anyone moving around inside. They could, however, perhaps hear something if Penn wasn't careful. And the door *had* creaked.

Suddenly, she wished she had a glass of gin. Maybe it would calm her nerves. No, she needed her wits about her.

"You seemed to know of the Camelot group," he said, eyeing her speculatively. "How?"

"My grandfather told me about them," she lied. She'd discussed various lines of conversation with Penn and Gideon last night so that she would be prepared. "They stole his dagger from me."

"I heard it was from Penn Bowen, that damn treasure hunter. I followed you with him—first to London and then to Oxford." He took another drink of gin. "You seemed quite…close."

"He was a means to an end," she said flippantly. "He knew things that could help me find what I sought. As you said, he's a treasure hunter. Probably the best."

Thaddeus snorted. "Probably. But not any longer. Where is he now?" His expression turned smug, and Amelia had to fight not to laugh.

Right under your bloody nose.

"Tell me, my darling, what is it you seek?" His endearment sickened her, but she kept her expression placid.

She didn't want to say the book, for fear he'd go looking for it while Penn was trying to steal it. "I'm not certain anymore," she said, trying to draw out their conversation. What was taking so long? That room Penn was searching wasn't *that* large. Surely he should've found it by now.

Unless it wasn't there. Which was why this plan had been launched in the first place. In the event Penn couldn't find it, she'd have to flush it out.

She wanted to be sure to give him enough time. "How did you become involved with the Camelot group?"

"It was before we met. I was in Bath, and I met the man in charge of the group. He presented me with an offer I was loath to refuse." He gave her a sad look. "I'm sorry to say it involved you. As you surmised, he wanted me to marry you so that we could get close to your grandfather and his secrets. I insisted courtship would be enough, but Foliot— Camelot's leader—said I would need longer than that to gain your grandfather's trust." Thaddeus sipped more gin, then gave a hollow laugh. "Turns out no amount of time would have earned me that. Gardiner despised me."

"Yes, he was quite pleased when you left." She saw no reason to lie. "So your objective was merely to learn his secrets?"

"Specifically to find the dagger—we knew he probably had it. We just didn't know where. Took a while, but the group got it in the end."

"Where is it?" She couldn't keep herself from asking. If it was here, she'd take it if she could.

He gave her a coy look and then laughed. "You want that dagger, don't you, my sweet? Unfortunately, I don't have it, but perhaps I can get it for you." He set his gin down on the table again, then tapped his finger against his lip. "There would be a price."

Her gut clenched as she imagined any number of prices she'd be forced to pay—all of them lurid and revolting. "What would that be?"

"Well, I already expect you've come back to resume your place as my wife. But that won't suffice. Foliot will never relinquish the dagger, not without gaining the heart. He needs both items, you see. Rather, he needs something that's on both items. Once he has that, I imagine he won't care if you take the dagger back."

This was excellent information. She wondered if Penn could hear it. "I would be most grateful. I miss my grandfather very much, and having his most prized possession would be a balm for my grief."

"Did you by chance bring the heart?"

She picked up the reticule, which had been perched on her lap, and jangled the contents. Curling her lips into a saucy smile, she said, "I did."

His gaze glowed with appreciation. "How cunning of you."

He leapt up suddenly, surprising her, and snatched the reticule from her grasp. "Now, we just need the book to go with this, and I can take it to Foliot." Nervous energy fairly pulsed from him, but he paused to stare intently into her eyes. "Thank you. You've saved me quite a bit of trouble. Come, we'll take it straightaway. His house isn't far—just a mile south." He clutched the reticule and started walking toward the back room.

No! He was going to get the book. He couldn't do that!

She jumped from the settee and grabbed his elbow. "Where—"

He howled in pain and swung around with a vicious

glare. "Careful! That's where you shot me." He rolled up the sleeve of his shirt to expose a thick white bandage.

She winced. "I'm so sorry."

He grunted in response, then turned back toward the room where Penn was searching. Why hadn't he found the damn thing yet? This was moments away from utter disaster. She had to warn him.

"Are you going into that room to fetch the book?" she asked rather loudly.

He paused, then pivoted to face her, his expression confused. "Yes," he said slowly. "But I've just remembered that it's in here." He rolled his eyes, then tapped his finger against his temple. "Mind's a little befuddled from the laudanum the physician gave me for the pain."

Laudanum *and* gin. It was a wonder he was still conscious.

He went to a desk in the corner near the front window. His gaze strayed to the window facing the drive. Shooting her a glance, he asked, "Is that your chaise?"

"Yes."

"Why is it still here?"

She was ready for that question too. "I wasn't sure if you'd allow me to stay. I did shoot you, after all."

He turned from the window and gave her a seductive look. "It seems we both have things to repent for. I shall look forward to it."

Thankfully, he turned his attention to the desk, because Amelia wasn't able to entirely suppress the shudder that racked her frame.

He set the reticule down on top of the desk and opened the top drawer. Then he withdrew a book bound in white leather.

Amelia didn't have to ask what it was. "The White Book of Hergest." For a moment, all her apprehension and tension evaporated. This was what her grandfather wanted to find. The key to everything.

She realized she may not have spoken that loudly enough, so she repeated with more volume, "Is that the White Book?"

"Indeed it is. Foliot entrusted it to me a few years ago when he became concerned that someone would trace it to him. Now we shall take it, along with the heart, to Foliot directly so that he can put them together with the dagger and do whatever it is he's wanted to do." He tucked the book under his arm.

No, that wouldn't do. She needed to take the book and leave without him. Perhaps she could shoot him again...

He reached up and touched his bare neck. "Damn, I suppose I should dress." He turned toward the hall. "I'll be but a moment. Unless you'd care to help me." He leered at her, and she could see the gin had settled in to take effect. His eyes were less focused than they'd been a few minutes ago.

This was her moment. Shoot him and attract the attention of Mrs. Jones and Mr. Jones, assuming he was here. Or, find some way to get the book out of Thaddeus's hands and get him upstairs.

Unfortunately, she could think of only one way to do that.

Swallowing her loathing, she sauntered toward him with a sultry smile. "Why don't I help you dress?" she offered. "Or undress..." She took the book from his grasp and set it on the table next to his glass.

His eyes narrowed to lecherous slits, and before she knew it, he'd put his arms around her waist and pulled her to his chest. "I like the direction of your mind." He lowered his mouth to hers and kissed her. His lips were parted, and she could taste the gin on his breath.

She suffered his kiss for what seemed an eternity before gently pushing him away. "Come, let's go upstairs," she announced loudly, taking him by the hand and pulling him toward the hall.

He followed with alacrity, stumbling slightly when they started up the stairs. Dear God, please let him fall unconscious from the gin and laudanum.

If he didn't, she'd have to come up with an alternate plan or find herself in dire straits indeed.

CHAPTER 18

*P*enn opened the door slowly and only until it
started to creak. Then he stopped and wedged
himself through the space and stepped into the room Amelia
and Forrest had just vacated. Anger and worry raged through
him, and he had to stop himself from going after them
upstairs. If Forrest laid a hand on her...

Hell, he already had. Penn had watched him kiss Amelia
through the gap in the door. He'd nearly dashed into the
room and thrown the blackguard to the floor. But they were
so close.

And there it was—the book—sitting innocently on the
table. Penn picked it up and flipped open the cover. A
detailed illumination leapt from the page, making his heart
race faster than it already was.

He glanced about and saw Amelia's reticule on the desk.
Why leave the heart with Forrest if they didn't have to? He
plucked that up and crept toward the hall, listening for any
movement from the opposite corner of the house where the
kitchen was located.

From his earlier reconnaissance, he'd ascertained there

was a housekeeper and another retainer, perhaps her husband based on the way they'd spoken to each other. The man had left a while ago, but there were two other men who were of far greater concern. They were big, rough looking, and armed with pistols. Camelot henchmen, he guessed. Both had left on horseback shortly before Amelia and Gideon had arrived, but they could return at any moment.

Penn stepped into the hall and looked toward the stairs. He stood still as a statue, straining to hear the slightest thing, but only silence greeted his ears.

Perhaps he ought to go up. It wasn't the plan, but the thought of leaving Amelia alone with Forrest was enough to make him shake with agitation.

The sound of a door closing and a singsong voice humming prompted him to dash for the front door and make his exit. He ran to the chaise and leapt inside, dropping the book and the heart on the seat.

Gideon, who'd been standing near the horse, came around to the side, his gaze falling on the White Book. "You got it."

"Yes. But she's upstairs with that snake. If she's not down here in one minute, I'm going up. Give the damn signal." His body thrummed with energy. He stared at the house, specifically the window in the gable. He'd no idea if that was where she was, but it was close enough.

Gideon's birdcall rent the air.

They both watched the house, waiting. Images of Forrest kissing Amelia as he had downstairs filled Penn's head. Along with Forrest touching her, undressing her…

Penn sprang out of the coach with a curse.

Gideon grabbed his arm. "Wait! Give her a moment. She'll come."

"What if she can't?" Penn pulled his arm from Gideon's grip.

Penn stared at his half brother, frenzied to make sure Amelia was safe. Gideon nodded. "Go."

As he turned to go to the door, it opened, and Amelia stepped out, closing it carefully behind her. She rushed forward, her face a bit pale. "Let's go! Mrs. Jones thinks I'm going back to town to fetch my things. That's what she'll tell Thaddeus when he wakes."

Penn helped her into the chaise as Gideon mounted the horse. She picked up the book and her reticule and set them in her lap as Penn climbed in beside her.

"When he wakes? What happened?" he demanded.

"He's been taking laudanum for his wound—the one I gave him," she said with pride. "Then he drank quite a bit of gin. All it took was me pushing him over, and he lost consciousness. I'd forgotten how much I hated his snoring." She shuddered and brushed at herself from shoulder to knee. "I'm so *glad* to be out of there."

Gideon drove the chaise up the lane as fast as he dared, causing Penn and Amelia to lurch forward a bit. She nearly dropped the book, and he reached to catch it, his hand covering hers.

She turned her head, and their gazes connected. Relief and joy and love surged through him. Unable to stop himself, he leaned forward and kissed her. It was brief but wonderful, their lips clinging to each other for a delicious moment.

"I'm glad you're out of there too."

Amelia shot a glance back toward the cottage. "I don't think he'll follow us. He's not capable."

"There were a couple of Camelot henchmen hanging about earlier," Penn said. "But I haven't seen them return."

"Do you think we can alter the plan and all go to the inn to retrieve our horses and things?" she asked. "We could look at the book there."

Penn considered that. "We could, but I always find it best

to keep moving in these kinds of situations. They may not follow us, but they'll come looking, and I'd rather not be in Glastonbury when that happens."

Gideon steered them to the copse of trees where Penn's horse stood. When the chaise came to a stop, he turned to look at them. "I agree. We should continue as planned."

Amelia looked to Penn. "Did you hear what he said about the dagger? We need it and Foliot has it."

"Yes, I heard." Penn had been so distracted by Amelia's safety—as well as jealousy, if he was honest with himself—that he'd forgotten that bit. "It certainly sounded as if we won't be able to complete our task without it."

"I'll get it," Gideon said without hesitation. "You drive the chaise back to town and fetch the horses and our things."

Penn leaned toward Gideon. "You can't mean to go to Foliot's on your own?"

Gideon shrugged. "Why not?"

"Isn't he angry with you for not delivering the sword?"

"Perhaps, but Forrest didn't deliver the heart either, and he was fine today, wasn't he?"

"Yes," Amelia said. "But he was clearly agitated about Foliot. When he learned I had the heart, he was quite pleased —relieved, actually. Said I saved him a great deal of trouble."

"I have the sword." Gideon inclined his head toward the bottom of the chaise where he'd fastened Dyrnwyn before they'd left the inn. "I can dangle it in front of him. He'll be thrilled."

Penn frowned. "You can't give it to him."

"I don't mean to." When Penn opened his mouth, Gideon held up his hand. "Will you allow me to do this?" It was less a question and more a demand. "I've much to atone for. I will get the dagger—and I won't have to forfeit the sword to do it. It may take me some time, however." He stroked his chin a moment. "Instead of meeting at the abandoned cottage, go to

Wells. There's an inn on the west side of town—The Stag and Hare. Go there and wait for me. It'll be far more comfortable."

Penn appreciated Gideon's determination or bravery or whatever it was. It didn't alleviate his concern, however. "How long do you suspect?"

"Depends on if Foliot is home, which he usually is. He prefers to have minions do all the work of the Camelot group." He dismounted and walked toward Penn's horse, stroking the animal's neck. "I'll go with the sword and tell him I'm back with the group. He'll likely invite me to dinner, then he'll disappear with one of his mistresses for a bit. That's when I'll get the dagger."

"*One* of his mistresses?" Amelia asked.

"He's not as uncouth as my father was, but they share many of the same appetites." He climbed onto Penn's horse. "I wouldn't expect me before midnight. But it may be later than that. Try to get the room in the corner. It's the nicest and easily accessible from the backstairs. If not, I'll find you regardless."

Penn climbed out of the chaise and looked up at Gideon. "You might be good at this treasure hunting."

A short laugh escaped Gideon's mouth. "We'll see. Don't get separate rooms. It's best if you're together." With a nod, he turned the horse and set off in a trot.

Penn turned back to the chaise. "This is frustrating."

Amelia set the book and reticule on the seat beside her. "Why, because you can't go with him?"

"Yes. He's doing what I do. It's as if our roles have already reversed, and I'm stuck being the bloody earl on the periphery of all the excitement."

"Some would argue that being an earl is plenty exciting," she said softly. "But not for you."

His gaze found hers, and he felt a pull to go to her. But he didn't. "No, not for me."

The air grew thick around them, and everything seemed to fall away. She was the one who broke the spell. "Can we go? I'd like to get as far away from Thaddeus as possible."

"Yes, of course." Penn climbed onto the horse and drove the chaise toward Glastonbury. All the way there he wondered how in the hell he was going to inhabit a single room with her at an inn and keep his hands to himself.

~

*B*y the time they walked into their room at the inn, Amelia was a bundle of nervous energy. She was anxious to look closely at the White Book. She and Penn had discussed it earlier, and both were excited to find the palimpsest and see what they could make of it.

But it was more than that. There was a current of tension stretching between them. It was neither good nor bad, but it felt as if they were each waiting for something to happen. She supposed it was normal for them to feel awkward after everything that had occurred. And given the way their future had been altered by Thaddeus's appearance. Again, Amelia regretted that her bullet had only wounded him.

And again, she admonished herself for such awful thoughts.

"I'm sorry to have made you wait to investigate this," Penn said as he set the book on the table situated near the window. "I'm afraid I was ravenous for dinner."

"It's fine. I was too." Plus, dining downstairs had postponed the inevitable—the two of them sharing this small space.

Gideon had said it was the inn's nicest room, and it was quite charming, with a well-dressed four-poster bed, an armoire they wouldn't use, and a decent-size table that would allow them to complete their work. Two lamps lit the space, and Penn had obtained a third from the kindly innkeeper who believed they were husband and wife, which he'd set on the table.

Next, he fetched parchment and a pencil along with the paper on which they'd written the code from the broken heart. He set these on the table and waited for Amelia to take a seat before he joined her. They sat on adjoining sides of the table with the book set at an angle near the center between them.

They both stared at the book, neither moving.

"You should open it," she said.

"No, you should. For your grandfather."

She took a deep breath and opened the front cover. A brilliant illumination greeted them, and she smiled. "He would have loved this. I know how much he liked illuminated manuscripts."

"He would've loved my father's library."

"Yes, he would." Amelia looked at Penn askance, wishing she'd had more time to investigate Rhys Bowen's shelves.

She carefully turned the pages, going slowly so they had time to study each page. All the while, she was incredibly aware of Penn's presence. Thankfully, he wasn't close enough to touch her. It was good they weren't right next to each other, and the sides of the table weren't long enough to support that.

Nearly halfway through, they came across the tale of Ranulf and Hilaria. Amelia's pulse sped, and the concerns weighing her mind faded to the background. "There it is."

"My father said this is the earliest recording of it—as we know it now. Every extant version is based on this." He leaned over, bringing his head close to hers. "It was written by Lewys Glyn Cothi."

"That was the monk at St. John Priory in Carmarthen?"

Penn nodded as he scanned the page. He brought the lantern closer to the book, and light splashed over the page. He squinted, then lowered his face to the parchment. "I see it," he breathed. "It's Old Welsh. I don't find this terribly often."

"Can you read it?" She knew he could read Middle Welsh.

"Yes." He was silent another moment, during which her anticipation crested.

"Penn?"

He gave her an apologetic smile. His eyes were so animated, his excitement so palpable, she would've forgiven him anything. She probably would've forgiven him anything anyway. Wasn't that what you did for those you loved?

"Sorry, I'm afraid I got wrapped up reading it," he said. "Let me translate. It says the heart was hidden because it caused too much pain. The fake heart was created along with a dagger and the myth that a witch had designed it to counteract the heart, thus nullifying the power of the heart."

"That seems like a great deal of trouble when they could just have destroyed the heart."

"They didn't want to. The Order—of course it was them —sought to preserve it, so they hid it and created the false objects as well as the tale of Ranulf and Hilaria."

"So the story I grew up loving is a creation of the Order?" That left a distinctly bitter taste on her tongue.

"So it would seem. Which means Lewys Glyn Cothi was either a member or, at the very least, associated enough with them that they had him create the tale." He looked over at her. "I'm sorry. That does rather take the charm out of it." He bent his head once more and continued. "The location of the heart is encoded on the objects that were created."

He leaned even closer to the paper. "There, I think that's

the cipher." He nudged the book toward her and pointed to a spot near the bottom of the page.

She could barely make out the palimpsest. What she could see looked like a jumble of letters. In a completely foreign language. "What does it say?"

"It says heart at the beginning. I think they've used a keyword—in this case—*heart* to set up the alphabet. Then I see 'left five.'" He lifted his head as a broad smile split his handsome face. "That's the cipher."

His glee was infectious, and she couldn't contain her laughter. "I have no idea what that means."

"Let me show you." He pushed the book away from him and picked up the pencil and parchment. After scrawling what looked like an alphabet, he repeated it underneath. Only the second version was slightly different.

He pointed to the top line he'd written. "This is the Old Welsh alphabet. And this"—he pointed to the line beneath it —"is the alphabet with the keyword. The keyword is 'heart,' which makes sense, and this is the Old Welsh word for it. Those letters have been taken from the alphabet and moved to the front for the cipher. The rest of the letters follow in order, minus the letters that were moved."

She began to understand. "Do these alphabets then match up against each other as a key?"

He stared at her in obvious admiration, causing her to blush. "You're rather brilliant, you know. It's one of your most attractive qualities."

The blush spread through her, heating parts of her body that were better left forgotten as they sat here together. *Alone* together.

"So yes, you'd use these two alphabets to decipher the code. But we're missing a step."

She recalled his translation. "The 'left five.' Whatever that means."

"It's a cipher Julius Caesar used. Since this employs two different kinds of ciphers, we must take another step. We must shift each letter in this bottom alphabet to the left five spaces."

He scratched the pencil over the parchment, writing the new alphabet at the top of the two lines he'd drafted previously, rearranging the letters as he described. "Now, we can use this to decipher the message on the heart."

She reached for the paper with the message and set it closer so he could see it, anxious to see what it read. "Well, what are you waiting for?"

He lifted the pencil again, then paused, turning his head to look at her. "There is no one I would rather share this discovery with than you. In fact, I'd never considered sharing discoveries with anyone. Now..." He didn't finish but dropped his head to focus on his work as he deciphered the letters from the broken heart.

Broken heart.

Yes, that described this situation perfectly. The two pieces of that stone could very well be the ruptured halves of her own heart.

He set the pencil down with a pensive look.

"What does it say?" She could hardly stand it and found his reticence frustrating. "Don't keep me in suspense."

He turned his head with a twinkle in his cobalt eyes. "The Vale of Neath."

"Where is that?" she asked, hoping it wasn't terribly far.

"The valley of waterfalls. It's the most beautiful place in the world." His tone was rapturous, his gaze equally so. "It's about two days' ride from here, maybe three if the weather doesn't cooperate."

"That is where the heart is?"

"So it would seem. The vale is quite large, however, so

we'll need to decipher whatever is carved onto the dagger to define the exact location."

She thought of Gideon's quest to obtain the dagger and hoped he was all right. "I hope Gideon can find it. And that he's safe."

Penn's forehead pleated with concern. "I hope so too. I should have gone with him."

She put her hand over his forearm. "I'm glad you didn't."

His brows arched briefly, and she removed her hand. She shouldn't touch him.

"It's all right for you to court danger, as you did this afternoon with Forrest, but I am not to do the same?" His tone held a playful edge, but she wouldn't let his teasing go unanswered.

"It was dangerous for you too. I had to stop Thaddeus from going into that room. He would've seen you for certain."

Penn's gaze took on a steely glint. "I wouldn't have minded. Would've given me an excuse to fight him."

Gone was his lively tone and replaced with something darker. Stress speared through her, and she worked to hide it from him lest he only grow more upset.

He turned his chair, angling his body toward hers. "What will you do, Amelia? With Forrest?"

"Do? Nothing. Hopefully I won't see him again."

"He's your husband. He may decide he wishes to claim his rights—"

She jumped up from the chair and paced toward the bed. "Must we discuss this?" Anguish spiraled from her belly, prompting her to wrap her arms around her midsection.

Turning, she startled to find Penn just a foot away. He'd moved so quickly. And silently.

"No," he said. "But I can't help it. I'm in agony thinking of what your future may hold."

She was too. And in that moment, she didn't want to shoulder that burden alone. "Penn," she asked softly. "Can we pretend to be what the innkeeper thinks? If just for tonight."

He looked momentarily confused, his brows pitching over his eyes before realization struck and his pupils narrowed. "You want to be my wife."

She nodded, unable to speak as emotion poured through her.

He lifted his hands to her face and stroked her cheeks with his thumbs, dragging them down to her lips where they met in the center. She opened her mouth and drew them inside, her tongue sliding over the thick pads.

He inhaled sharply as his lids drooped. He pushed one thumb farther inside. She closed her lips around him and sucked hard. He slipped his free hand around to the back of her neck and began pulling pins from her hair. When the mass was loose around her face, she relinquished his thumb. And he immediately replaced it with his mouth.

The kiss was rough and desperate, a perfect expression for how she felt inside. If she couldn't have this night with him—just one more time in his arms—she thought she might perish.

She wouldn't, of course, and even thinking such melodrama was the height of idiocy. But she was helpless. He'd talked of her future, and right now, it was a dark, hazy unknown. Tonight, she wanted light and comfort, to bask in the knowledge of what she knew to be true—that Penn was the only man she'd ever loved, and the only man she ever would.

He explored her mouth with deep thrusts of his tongue and excited her with nips and sucks, tugging on her lower lip until she gasped with want. Then he began to strip his clothes away with great urgency. She helped, untying his cravat and unbuttoning his waistcoat.

She still wore her riding habit, which she'd put on after returning to the inn in Glastonbury. It, like the gown she'd brought and worn to Thaddeus's cottage, could be donned and removed without the assistance of a maid. Since, of course, she'd left Culley at Hollyhaven.

When he went to the chair to remove his boots, she unbuttoned her jacket and tugged her arms free of the snug-fitting garment. After hanging it on a hook, she began to unfasten her skirt.

Penn had returned, clad only in his shirt and breeches. "Let me," he murmured, covering her hands with his and working, effortlessly, to remove her skirt.

He helped her step from the fabric, then hung it on the hook with her jacket.

She drew her shirt over her head, and once more, he provided assistance. Again, he took great care with her clothing, hanging it up with the rest.

"You could be a ladies' maid," she said.

"Only yours." He drew her against his chest and renewed their kiss. This time was gentler, slower. They took their time studying each other's reactions and offering up new methods to drive the other to distraction.

She pulled away to tug his shirt up over his head. When she made to hang it on the hook beside hers, he said, "You needn't take the same care with my things."

She hung the garment and gave him a saucy stare. "I'm doing what a wife ought."

"*Amelia.*" The word was part growl of desperation and part heartfelt plea.

She knew what he wanted. She wanted it too.

They moved more quickly, removing the rest of their clothing until they were bare to the other. He stared at her a long moment, as if he were memorizing every inch of her flesh. She thought so, because that was what she was doing to him. From the muscular plane of his shoulder to the flat expanse of his abdomen to the jut of his shaft to the slope of his thigh, she would remember him always.

She lunged for him, unable to be apart from him for another moment. He caught her against him, kissing her soundly as he swept her into his arms and carried her to the bed. It wasn't far, and he laid her gently on the mattress before climbing up beside her.

She turned on her side and they lay facing each other. He stroked her collarbone and trailed his fingertips down to her bicep before cupping her breast. Sensation bloomed from his caress, making her breasts feel heavy and her sex pulse.

He lowered his head and licked at her nipple, softly at first, then he closed around her and sucked, just as she'd done to his thumb. She gasped and thrust her fingers into his hair, holding him to her. Nothing had ever felt so good, so right. She clung to the moment, to the sensation, to Penn.

His mouth didn't leave her, but his hand traveled down her side, leaving a trail of heat and want until he found her sex. He stroked along her folds, but their positions didn't allow for her to open her legs. And she wanted to feel him inside her.

Pushing on his shoulder, she flattened him to his back and rolled on top of him. As she rose up, he was forced to relinquish her breast. He stared up at her with curiosity and intense desire.

"You seem to have a plan of your own."

"Not particularly." She'd never been on the top, but she knew it was done. "You'll have to show me." She straddled his hips and moaned as soon as his cock grazed her sex.

"Are you certain? You seem to be doing quite well on your own."

She'd closed her eyes briefly, but now opened them again

to see what she should do. He watched her, his eyes slitted, as he clasped her hips.

"It's not all that different from riding a horse," he said.

A laugh spilled from her lips in spite of the intensity of the moment. "I should hope it is. I don't ever plan to ride a horse without clothing."

"You don't want to reenact the tale of Lady Godiva? Remind me to show you the copy of the book, in which the story is contained, by Roger of Wendover in my father's library."

She instantly sobered, thinking again that she wouldn't be spending time in his father's library. He seemed to realize it too, for he curled his hand around her back and drew her down. "Kiss me."

She did, opening her mouth over his and spearing her tongue inside. She liked this angle. She was very much in control and in command. He seemed to like it too, if his moans were any indication. Along with the rise and thrust of his hips. With each pulse, his cock stroked her sex, and she whimpered with need.

She drew back enough to whisper. "Show me."

He put his hands between them and gripped his cock. "Guide me inside. Sit up so I can watch."

She straightened, looking down at where his hand was wrapped around the base of his shaft. Putting her fingers over his, she lifted her hips and brought him to her entrance.

He let go of his cock and stroked her folds, opening her as he pushed inside with her assistance. "Bring yourself down on me." His voice was tight and strained, echoing the extreme urgency she felt.

She pushed down, going slowly as he filled her sheath. She gasped when she was flush against him, his length buried inside her body.

"Now move."

She looked at his face, still awash with delicious tension. His eyes were still open and focused on where their bodies joined.

"How?" she asked, sounding breathless as pleasure spread through her. She was content to just be like this, having him a part of her.

"However you want." He rotated his pelvis, gently thrusting. "Slow like that. Or fast." He held her waist as she withdrew part way, then snapped his hips up, driving deep. Lights danced behind her eyes.

"Oh." She decided this could be a *bit* like riding a horse. She pulled up, lifting herself off his shaft, then bore down again, taking him as far as she could. Over and over, she repeated the motion, relishing not just the acceleration of pleasure but the feeling of control.

"Faster." His fingers dug into her hips. "Please."

She increased her speed, but incrementally, after a handful of strokes. His hands skimmed up her ribs and cupped her breasts. He ran his thumbs over the tight nubs, then squeezed his fingers around them. There was no pain, just a delicious burst of sensation and a sudden urge to *move*.

She rose and fell more quickly now, grinding down against him as he massaged her breasts. She'd never been more aware of how his touch could make her feel. Beautiful. Rapturous. Powerful.

He began to urge her on with words, commanding her speed and her direction, extolling her beauty and prowess. Then his thumb was on her sex, stroking that most sensitive place at the top—her clitoris—and she was lost. Her muscles tightened as her climax crashed upon her. She cried out and moved in a frenzy to satiate the desperate need inside her.

In a fluid movement, he pulled her down against his chest, then flipped her to her back. "My turn," he murmured before taking her mouth in a long, wet kiss.

She clasped at his back and wrapped her legs around him. She dug her heels into his backside, never wanting him to leave her.

But he did. Just barely and only to drive home once again, his cock filling her and prolonging her orgasm. The sensations rioting through her were mad and wonderful. She gave in completely to the need to feel everything he would give her, putting her mind and body utterly in his power.

He took it. And with the greatest care. He slowed for a moment, letting them both catch their breath. He ended the kiss so that he could kiss along her jaw and nip at her ear. She felt spent, but not for long. He began to move more purposefully again, and soon, pleasure began to build once more.

"Move to your side." His words against her ear didn't make sense.

"How?"

"Roll slightly." He guided her to her left side, pinning her left leg beneath him. "Bend your leg." He clasped her right thigh and showed her what he meant.

She brought her knee toward her chest and this opened her to him in a way she never imagined. The position brought him against her mound, sparking a delicious sensation that prompted another climax. Her keening cries filled the room, but she was incapable of stopping herself.

He pumped into her again and again, sending her so far over the edge of reason that she wasn't sure she'd find her way back again. His shout joined her chorus, and she was aware of his thighs tensing between hers. Ecstasy claimed them both as he rode her into the storm.

It was several minutes before calm returned. She felt boneless but wonderful as he rolled from her and sprawled on his back. Amelia stayed on her side while a smile of satisfaction curved her lips.

She was suddenly so tired. A yawn assaulted her, and she brought her hand to her mouth.

"We can sleep for a while," he said, pulling back the coverlet and helping her slide beneath it.

She ought to clean up, to put a night rail on at least, but she was too exhausted. Too sated. And far too comfortable as Penn drew her against him. He lay on his back, and she curled into his side, her hand splayed over his chest.

Floating between consciousness and sleep, dreams began to invade her mind. "Maybe I can divorce him."

Lips pressed against her forehead. "That would be difficult, my love."

"You still couldn't marry me," she murmured. "An earl can't have a divorced countess."

"I won't be an earl."

She sighed. "You don't know that."

"We could leave Britain." His voice sounded so far away, as if she stood on top of a tower and he was at the base. They were a prince and a princess in a fairy tale.

Only theirs didn't have a happy ending.

CHAPTER 19

*T*he sound of their door opening drew Penn to full wakefulness. He sat up, rubbing his eyes, and blinked at the figure in the doorway. "Gideon?"

His half brother closed the door and moved into the chamber. "Get up. We don't have much time. I can only stay a few minutes."

Amelia stirred beside him. He leaned down and kissed her temple. "Gideon's here. We need to get up."

"I'll turn my back," Gideon said, positioning himself in front of the hearth.

Penn left the bed and pulled his clothing on as quickly as possible. He pulled Amelia's chemise from the hook and handed it to her. "Do you need help?"

She shook her head. "I'll manage."

Penn went to the chair and sat down to pull on his stockings and boots. "How late is it?"

Gideon slid him a weary glance. "Nearly morning."

"Can I assume from your urgency that you have the dagger?"

Pulling the blade from his coat, Gideon tossed it onto the

table next to the book. "I'd write down the code before you go, just in case you lose it. Better to have two copies."

Penn noted he said "you" not "we," but perhaps it was a slip of the tongue. "We solved the code," he said. "I'll just decipher it now, and then we'll know where we're going."

Gideon's eyes flashed with admiration. "Well done. But then I'm not surprised."

Penn finished pulling on his boot. "The words on the heart said the Vale of Neath."

"Waterfalls and gorges and caverns," Gideon said. "Your father took us there one summer."

"You remember." That had been their very best summer together, or so Penn had always thought. "It's one of my favorite places."

"Mine too. I haven't been back."

Penn smiled up at him as he turned toward the table and picked up the pencil. "Well, you will now."

Gideon shook his head. "I'm not going with you. One of Foliot's men followed me here. I need to go now and divert his attention."

Penn copied down the code from the dagger, checking it twice before handing the weapon back to Gideon. "Here, take it. And the heart. We don't need them. I'll return the book to the Williams-Wynn family. After my father spends a few days with it first," he added with a half smile.

"I don't need any of it." Gideon's gray eyes were dark as iron. "I only want the real treasures—*all* of them."

Penn frowned. "What happened with Foliot?"

Gideon shook his head. "There isn't time. Just find the heart and keep it safe, please."

"I will."

Amelia pulled on her jacket as she came toward them. "What does the dagger say?"

Penn quickly deciphered the letters. "Sgwd yr Eira. It means waterfall of snow."

"That's where you'll go?" Gideon asked.

Penn stood. "Meet us there."

"I will if I can. But I won't let Foliot or his men get to you. Only you can find the heart. I may be good at planning, but you're the treasure hunter, Penn."

"And you're the earl—I'll make sure you are, Gideon, even if I have to leave Britain."

Gideon's lips spread into a fast smile. "I don't care anymore. I *have* a birthright. I'm a descendant of Gareth. The Thirteen Treasures are *my* responsibility—not the Order's, *mine*. I will ensure they're found and protected."

"What if you aren't the only descendant of Gareth?" Penn asked. "Someone in the Order may challenge you on that."

"Let them try." Gideon turned and stalked toward the door. "I have to go. Wait a bit before you leave so that I can lure them away."

"Them? It's more than one?"

Gideon shrugged. "I'm not sure. Be wary when you go, just in case someone lingers and catches your scent."

Penn went to his half brother and clasped his hand. "Be safe. And come to Hollyhaven when you can. I'll have good news for you."

"You're such a bloody optimist."

"My father taught me to be." Penn winced as he realized his father was really Gideon's father.

"And mine taught me the opposite." The disgust in Gideon's tone sliced into Penn as surely as that rock had carved into his hand the day he'd found the dagger. The day his life had irrevocably changed. His gaze strayed to Amelia, who stood quietly near the table.

"Be well, Penn. And find a way to marry her." He inclined his head toward Amelia. "Whatever you do, don't subject her to what Septon did to my mother. No woman deserves that."

What he really meant was that no child deserved to lose their mother in such a way. Penn agreed. At least in this instance, there wasn't a child.

As far as he knew... He hadn't been particularly thoughtful tonight, nor had he been the other day in the lean-to.

With a final nod, Gideon turned and left the chamber, closing the door firmly behind him.

"I wonder what happened with Foliot," Amelia said, echoing what was rooted in Penn's mind.

"I don't know, but Gideon seems to have a new purpose."

"It sounds like a good one," she said softly.

Penn agreed. And he'd do everything he could to help him, including finding the heart. He went to the window and looked out into the predawn. It would be light in the next hour. "We can leave soon." He turned from the window to see her staring at him with a sad expression.

He moved toward her, asking quietly, "What is it?"

"You know." She shook her head. "Let's not speak of it. We'll find the heart, and then we'll return to Hollyhaven."

"Where Egg will be waiting with the proof that I'm the earl. Then you'll help me burn it."

She smiled, but it was tinged with regret. "And then I'll go back to my grandfather's house, and you'll return to Oxford."

"Or you could come with me," he said. "If I'm not an earl, no one will care if we're together. It's not as if your husband is a notorious earl. You can be a widow. In fact, we could marry—"

"Penn!" Her eyes were wide, and her lips parted briefly before she clamped them shut. "What would happen to your reputation if people learned I had a living husband? You're a respected scholar, and I won't endanger that." Her gaze softened, and she gave him a pleading look. "Can we please not discuss it? There's no point, and I'd rather enjoy the time we *do* have together."

An aching despair rooted in Penn's gut and spread, leaving him feeling hopeless and angry. "I may murder him yet," he muttered as he pulled on his waistcoat.

"You won't," she said with certainty. "And that's why you're better than him."

Being better wouldn't make him happy. No, that was the woman standing in front of him. Maybe, just maybe, he'd find a way to change their fortunes.

❧

*T*he weather hadn't cooperated, and so it was that they found themselves finally approaching the village of Pontneddfechan on the third day after leaving Wells. Amelia hadn't minded because that had meant two more nights with Penn instead of one.

He'd stopped trying to talk about the future, for which she was grateful. It was painful enough knowing their parting was coming. She preferred to bask in the joy of their union while it lasted.

There'd also been no talk of love, but she felt it between them. She longed to tell him so, but couldn't form the words for fear she would fall to pieces and never recover.

"There's an inn," Penn said, gesturing ahead. "I'll ask them to stable our mounts while we take our walk." He looked up at the sky with a grim expression. "I hope the rain stays away."

They'd endured quite a storm on their first day out. By the time they'd stopped at an inn, they were both drenched and miserable. They had, however, grown quite warm together in front of the fire that night. She smiled at the memory, glad for it now and to have it for the future.

They rode into the yard at the inn and dismounted. Penn handed her the saddlebags that held her things as well as the book and other artifacts.

"You're sure you want to leave them here?" she asked. They'd discussed it at length last night—whether to take the items with them to the waterfall.

"I think it's best. I would feel terrible if the White Book were damaged."

She smiled at him. "I am beginning to think the heart will pale next to the book."

He laughed softly. "No. It's different. But yes, rediscovering this book is exceptional."

Because he was anxious to present it to his father so that he could study it for a few days before returning it to its owners. She understood because that was precisely how she would feel if her grandfather were alive, and she could give him the heart.

Well, not *give* it to him. They were going to give it to Gideon.

Penn spoke with the innkeeper, renting a room for the night and stabling the horses. He carried the saddlebags up to their room, where Amelia changed into her men's costume and Penn organized what they would take with them.

He draped one bag over his shoulder diagonally and prepared to do the same with the next one.

"I can carry that," Amelia offered. "Let me be Egg."

Penn let out a sharp laugh. "You could *never* be Egg. You are far too attractive and pleasant."

Amelia stuck her lower lip out and grunted. "I can be disagreeable."

He went to her and kissed that lip, making her withdraw it with a giggle. "Please don't. I love you just the way you are."

Love? She lost all semblance of humor and stared at him.

He seemed to realize what he'd said. Their eyes connected for a moment before he averted his gaze. "You can carry it if you want." He held it out to her, careful not to touch her hand.

She took the bag and draped it around herself as he had done. It was a bit heavy, but nothing she couldn't handle. "Everything you think we'll need is in here?"

"Except your pistol." He looked at her in question, and she patted her waistband in response. "Good. I have mine, and—" He withdrew the small knife she'd withdrawn from his coat the day they'd met and placed it in her hand. "I want you to carry this."

"What if you need it?" she asked, hating this distance that was growing between them, but knowing it was necessary if they were going to survive their inevitable separation.

"You'll give it to me." His lips quirked up briefly before he turned and stalked to the door. "Let us be on our way."

When they entered the common room, the innkeeper approached with a small bundle, which he handed to Amelia. "I've packed a bit of food for you along the trail, if you become hungry."

"Thank you." She took the bundle and tucked it into her bag, while Penn accepted a flagon of ale from the innkeeper, which he tied to his belt.

"Where are you headed?" the innkeeper asked.

"To look at the waterfalls," Penn said. "I saw them once and would like to share them with Mrs. Bowen."

Mrs. Bowen.

She'd inhabited that name for the past few days, and she didn't want to give it up.

The innkeeper eyed Amelia's breeches with a mix of curiosity and disdain. "Before you go, I recommend you stop and speak with Mr. Hughes. He's mapped all the waterfalls and would be an excellent source of information. He lives just down the lane in a small cottage with a thatched roof and a crimson door."

"Thank you, we'll consider that." He said good-bye to the innkeeper, then held the door open for Amelia.

They walked out into the cool, gray afternoon. Amelia shivered but knew she'd warm up quickly when they started to walk. "Should we stop in and see Mr. Hughes?"

Penn looked conflicted, his gaze moving down the lane toward what she assumed was the man's cottage—it looked like what the innkeeper had described. "I'm not sure I want to take the time. We need plenty of time to walk to the falls, search for—and find—the heart, and get back before nightfall."

They could wait until tomorrow. That would give them one more night. However, they were both eager to find the heart. This was the culmination of their journey together.

Culmination meant the end. A lump lodged in her throat, and she struggled to swallow past it. Perhaps they *should* wait…

Before she could voice her concern, Penn took a step toward the lane. "Let's visit him. When I came here in my youth, we started at Ystradfellte, which is north of here, so he may have useful information. We'll be brief."

And they were on their way.

It was a short jaunt to the cottage where Penn knocked on the door. The man who opened it was squat and thick. Not fat, but well muscled. He reminded Amelia of a less grizzled version of Egg.

"Good afternoon," Penn said. "We're going to walk to Sgwd yr Eira, and the innkeeper said we should visit with you first."

The man looked up at Penn, scrutinizing him for a moment before inviting them inside. "Come in, come in."

Penn glanced at Amelia. "We shouldn't stay long."

Mr. Hughes waved his hand as he led them to a sitting area. "You've plenty of time to walk there and back before nightfall." He turned to face them. "Unless you're planning to spend some time at the waterfall?" Something about the question struck Amelia as odd. It wasn't an innocuous query but gave her the impression he was searching for information.

Her hackles rose, and she paused just behind Penn, then reached out to touch his arm.

The older man's gaze flicked toward Amelia's movement. She withdrew her hand as Hughes stuck his out toward Penn. "I'm David Hughes."

Penn shook his hand. "Penn Bowen, and this is my, er, wife."

Hughes's eyes widened briefly. "Mr. Bowen! Well, of course I've heard of you and your illustrious father." He bowed to Amelia. "Pleased to make your acquaintance, Mrs. Bowen. What brings you to the waterfall?"

"We're on our honeymoon trip," Penn said smoothly. "I visited here in my youth, but we came from the north."

Hughes nodded. "Ah, from Ystradfellte." He peered at them with a bit of skepticism, and again Amelia's senses pricked. "You're a treasure hunter, Mr. Bowen. Are you certain you aren't looking for something? The Heart of Llanllwch, perhaps?"

Penn took a step back so that he was even with Amelia. "Who are you?" he asked in a low, fierce tone.

"I'm a bit like you," he said. He turned his attention squarely on Amelia. "Is there a chance you're related to Jonathan Gardiner? You've a bit of the look of him—it's your eyes."

Amelia edged forward in surprise and anticipation. "You knew my grandfather?"

Now it was Penn's turn to touch her arm. He moved closer to her side.

"I did," Hughes said. "You are not the first people to search for the Heart of Llanllwch. And you won't be the last."

"But my grandfather didn't find it," Amelia said.

Hughes's gray brows shot up. "Didn't he?"

"That one was fake," Penn said flatly. "And he didn't find it here, but near Carmarthen, which I think you know. You're a member of the Order. Don't deny it. I know you watch over the Thirteen Treasures, and that's what you do here, isn't it? You're one of their watchers."

"Very astute of you, Mr. Bowen, but then I would expect nothing less. Indeed, I'm a tad surprised it took you that long." His eyes glowed with mirth, but Amelia wasn't amused. What was this man about?

"Help me understand," she said. "How did you know my grandfather?" He'd doubted that the Order truly wanted to protect the treasures, and yet he'd apparently met one of their watchers.

"He went to Carmarthen looking for the heart. I used to live there. When he found it, we let him take it."

"The fake, you mean," Penn said.

Hughes gave him a pointed look. "Yes, that's why we let him have it. We hoped it would stop others from looking for the real one." His expression softened as he looked to Amelia. "You appear confused. Let me reassure you. Your grandfather was on a quest to find the heart, but more importantly, to find answers. He grew to understand what the Order was about and even agreed with our purpose. For that reason, he was given the dagger to keep it safe."

Amelia tried to make sense of what Hughes said. It was wonderful to know what had happened, but it didn't help her confusion regarding her grandfather. "Was he part of the Order?"

Hughes shook his head. "No. He was what we called a Friend of the Order." He shot a glance toward Penn and smiled. "Like your father."

Amelia watched the confusion she felt bloom on Penn's face. Just as quickly, it evaporated when he said, "I don't think my father would characterize it that way. He might go along with the Order, but he doesn't necessarily agree with you."

"Yes, well, that has been a struggle for us over the centuries. We don't expect everyone to understand." He nodded toward Amelia. "But your grandfather did—eventually. He didn't trust us at first, but over time he grew to appreciate our efforts. He took the dagger and kept it safe. Although I understand it's been stolen."

"It was, but it is back in my possession."

Hughes looked pleased. "And now you're both here to find the heart. Alas, I can't let you take it."

Penn chuckled softly. "I mean no offense, Mr. Hughes, but I don't think you'll be able to stop us."

"Not on my own perhaps, but you won't be allowed to take it."

Frustration grated through Amelia. They'd come all this way, and now they'd have to turn back empty-handed.

Penn took a step toward the older man, all humor gone from his face. "That heart belongs to the descendants of Gareth, and as it happens, I'm going to deliver it to one so he can keep it safe."

Surprise flashed in Hughes's eyes. "That's what we do in the Order. We protect the treasures from being used for malevolent purposes."

"In darker times, I understand why the Order would have felt that was necessary. But the Order is no longer the peace-seeking organization it once was. There's a dangerous faction gaining power. Surely you're aware of the Camelot group."

Hughes's brow creased, and he looked away. "They're a blight on all of us."

"I don't disagree," Penn said. "I can't let them find the heart, and they're doing everything they can to do so."

Hughes was quiet a moment as he stared off toward the wall. When he turned his attention back to them, he looked a bit...defeated. But then determined. "I won't stop you; however, I need to know the identity of this descendant."

"Gideon Kersey. He already possesses Dyrnwyn—and it flames in his grasp."

"Indeed?" He sounded a bit euphoric, his gaze sparking with delight. "How I should like to see that. I'll need to write to the Order."

"Do what you must, just as we will," Penn said.

Hughes gave a perfunctory nod and walked them back to the door. "Continue down the lane until the path veers off. Follow that to where the River Mellte meets the River Hepste, then go a mile east to the falls. Good luck to you."

"Thank you." Penn's hand grazed the small of Amelia's back on their way outside. They were silent as they walked to the path Hughes had described.

"I'm not sure what to make of that," she said at last.

"Nor I. The Order is so damned enigmatic. Are they good, are they bad?" He shook his head. "Sometimes I can't decide."

"It's apparent my grandfather changed his opinion after what he wrote in his journal. I doubt I'll ever know why."

Penn looked over at her, his eyes full of empathy. "Is it good to know at least that much?"

"It is."

They fell silent again as they followed the path. The area was breathtaking, with moss-laden branches stretching overhead and birds sounding their presence from all around them, along with the occasional croak from a frog.

After some time, they reached the junction of the rivers then had to climb up an incline to the path that headed east toward the waterfall of snow. The path followed the River Hepste, descending as they approached the fall, a sheet of water spilling gracefully over the rock.

"It's so beautiful." Amelia had never seen anything like it. "But how will we find the heart amidst that?"

"I'm not sure, but in my experience, there is usually a clue or two to be had." He waggled his brows at her, and she could feel his excitement.

"I think I understand why you do this. The thrill of imminent discovery is a singular emotion."

"Yes, it is." He clasped her elbow as her heel slipped on a patch of mud. "Careful."

The entire area was damp—from the falls and likely from the rain that had fallen that morning. She was quite glad she'd decided to change into her men's clothing.

They descended all the way to the falls, and the spray coated her in a fine sheen of water.

"Come, we can walk beneath it." He took her hand and led her beneath the curtain. They stopped in the middle and looked through the water.

"This is astonishing," she breathed. She'd never imagined she'd see such things, or experience all she had since meeting Penn. She turned to him. "Thank you. For this. For everything you've shown me."

He faced her. "Thank *you*. For everything you've shown me."

Overcome, she looked past him. Then she squinted. "Penn, is that a drawing on the rock?"

CHAPTER 20

"What?" Penn swung around and looked at where she pointed. There on the rock was a pattern of lichen that looked suspiciously like…a drawing. He stalked to the rock and stared at the pattern.

Amelia stood beside him. "It looks like several waterfalls. Why draw a picture of waterfalls beneath a waterfall?"

Penn opened his bag and found the small cleaning brush. Lifting it to the rock, he gently scrubbed the lichen away. In so doing, things became much clearer. The lichen collected at the bottom of the drawing fell away to reveal letters.

"Amelia, hand me the paper." He'd been sure to bring that just in case the code from the White Book would be necessary to find the heart.

She handed him the code. "You were smart to bring this, but then you are the smartest man I know."

He shot her a look of amusement. "Your flattery will not go unremarked." Quickly deciphering the letters, he looked down at what he'd written. "Sgwd Clun Gwyn. Fall of the White Meadow."

"Another waterfall?" she asked.

"Two, actually. There's a lower and an upper falls." He looked at the drawing again. "That is definitely the lower falls. They're four smaller falls and pools between them. Excellent for a swim on a summer's day. The upper falls are far more majestic—a single fall of water at least forty feet tall."

"So this is pointing us to the lower falls?"

"That's my guess." He felt vaguely unsatisfied, as if he were missing something. He brushed his hand over the rock, feeling the grooves. With a curse, he gave the paper back to Amelia. "Hand me a fresh piece of parchment and a scrap of charcoal."

She dug around for what he needed and gave them over one at a time.

Flattening the paper over the rock, he used the charcoal to make a relief of the carving.

Amelia leaned in close to him. "A rubbing?"

"A trick I use quite often." He finished and stared at the paper. But it was Amelia who saw it first.

She pointed to the top of the falls. "There! It looks like a tiny heart."

He turned with the paper, holding it to the light filtering through the falls. Excitement swelled in his chest. "Yes, that's a heart."

She grinned widely, mirroring his elation. "*The* heart. We know where to go."

"Indeed we do, back out to the River Mellte and then north."

She hugged him with glee. "We almost have it!"

They turned on the path and started back along the waterfall, walking quickly in their excitement. As soon as they emerged from behind the fall, Penn stopped short.

Standing above them on the path was Amelia's husband and four other, larger men. One of them Penn recognized from outside Forrest's cottage. All of them drew pistols, and Penn rushed to do the same.

Trailed by the henchmen, Forrest came down the path, his pistol trained on Penn. "I wouldn't try that. If you shoot me, the others will take you down faster than you can say, 'Please, don't shoot.'" He slid his gaze toward Amelia. "Don't bother with your pistol either, you Amazon. One of you disarm them!" he yelled over his shoulder.

One of the henchmen rushed forward and relieved both Penn and Amelia of their pistols, tucking one into his belt and handing the other to another of the men.

"You were a bit difficult to track, but not impossible, as you can see," Forrest said smugly. His eyes narrowed at Penn's hand, and he took a step forward. "What's that?"

Penn wadded the parchment and threw it into the center of the river, where it rushed downstream.

"Goddammit!" Forrest cocked his pistol and aimed it directly at Penn's heart. "What *was* that?"

"Nothing," Penn said calmly, aching to throw the man into the river after the paper. In fact… "Would you like to go after it? I'd be happy to help." He gave the man a malevolent smile.

Forrest sneered. "I ought to shoot you. I think I will."

Amelia leapt in front of Penn, putting herself between him and Forrest's weapon. "No! You can't shoot him. He's an earl."

Bloody hell, what was she doing? Penn put his hands on her hips. "*Amelia*, don't."

Forrest looked momentarily surprised, then laughed. "An earl? No wonder you like him, sweetling. That would be quite a step up from me." He exhaled with exaggerated regret. "Alas, we are still married."

"Only as long as you live," Penn growled.

"Yes, well, at present, that looks to be longer than you will."

"You can't kill him, please," Amelia begged. "I'll go with you. I'll take you to the heart."

Forrest blinked at her. "You know where it is?"

"It was on the paper," she said.

Penn dug his fingertips into her hips and held her against his chest. He whispered against her ear. "Amelia, please don't."

"You'll come with me willingly?" Forrest asked skeptically. "And not just to get the heart. We'll get the heart, and we'll go back to my cottage together, as husband and wife."

Fury raged through Penn. He longed to pummel the blackguard. "Why do you want her now, Forrest? Is it because she's only attractive to you when she wants someone else?" He nuzzled Amelia's cheek to needle the man.

She elbowed Penn in the gut, shocking the hell out of him and nearly causing him to lose his balance. She stepped away and turned furious eyes on him. "I don't want you either. I liked being *alone*. However, if my choice is to get the heart and return with Thaddeus, so be it."

Forrest's laughter filled the gorge. "You'd choose me over an earl? Too bad for you, Bowen." He reached out and took Amelia's hand, pulling her to his side. "Keep an eye on him," he shouted to his cohorts before turning his head to his wife. "How can I trust you? I suspect you've been whoring yourself with this…earl. Why would I want you back?"

"Because you do," she said softly, sweetly.

Penn's heart clenched under the stress. He watched, horrified, as she kissed him, her lips sliding over his. Penn could almost feel her doing the same to him, and he had to stifle an angry cry.

She pulled back and gave Forrest a brilliant smile. "Now, let us go and get the heart. It's at the top of the Fall of the

White Meadow, a magnificent fall—forty feet tall, he said." She flicked a cold glance at Penn, but now he understood her ruse.

She was talking about the upper falls. Not where the heart was. God, she was amazing, and he'd never loved her more.

He masked his relief and managed to grit out, "You deserve each other."

"Tie him up," Forrest said, taking Amelia's hand and turning to head back up the path.

"Wait." She pulled away and turned back to Penn. She took his hand, and he realized she held his small knife. "I'm sorry it had to end this way. The heart is the most important thing to me. You've always known that." She curled his hand around the knife, then went back to Forrest.

Amazing maybe didn't adequately describe her.

He watched her walk past Forrest and continue up the path. He knew exactly where to find her—and he would, just as soon as possible.

The largest of the henchmen took a length of rope from his pack and approached Penn.

"Where would you like me?" Penn asked affably.

"Take his bag and tie him to a tree," Forrest said. "A very rough one. Wouldn't want him to be too comfortable. Then catch up with us." He smirked at Penn. "I'm sure someone will come to find you, Bowen. Someday." With a gleeful whistle, he turned and followed Amelia up the path.

The ruffian grabbed Penn by the arm and dragged him toward a tree. Penn carefully slipped the knife up his sleeve and prayed the villain wouldn't find it.

"Nah, this one's too smooth," the man said, shoving Penn to the next tree. "This one'll do."

Penn winced as the rough bark bit into his back, and he nearly let the knife slip from his sleeve.

The ruffian pulled the pack over Penn's head and dropped it to the side. Penn considered sticking his knife in the man's gut, but if he wasn't successful, his options would be limited. Better to use the knife to cut himself free and come up with a plan to dispatch the brigands and rescue Amelia.

Expelling a grunt, the man jerked Penn's arms around the tree. Then he looped the rope around Penn and the trunk, binding him tightly so the rough bark pressed uncomfortably through his clothing. The rope went around his chest and arms but didn't sit as low as his wrist. It was going to be the devil to contort his hands to get the rope cut. He hoped he didn't drop the knife. Perhaps he should've stabbed the man.

Seizing the moment, Penn coaxed the knife into his hand, then shot his arm forward, slicing awkwardly at the villain's chest as he pulled at the slack rope. Occupied with tying the rope, the man was taken completely off guard. He stumbled back with a cry. Eager to keep him from sounding the alarm, Penn dove toward him and knocked him to the ground. He rose over him with the knife, intent on killing him if necessary.

However, it wasn't necessary because the sound of the man's skull striking a rock made Penn cringe. The brigand's head lolled to the side, and his eyes drooped closed. Penn leaned over and listened for breathing.

He wasn't dead. Penn expelled a sigh of relief. He'd just as soon *not* kill anyone if he could avoid it. He stood and grabbed the rope, then dragged the man to the tree where he tied the villain's thick wrists together. Lastly, Penn used the rope to secure him to the trunk.

Picking up his bag, he pulled it over his head and settled the pack against his hip. Then he stashed his knife in his coat and started up the path. He was eager to catch up to Amelia, but he needed to be smart and careful. If they saw him coming, they could just take aim.

Instead, he'd creep off the path through the trees and the shrub and look for an opportunity.

Traipsing through an untraveled area took more time, but he reasoned it was worth it. At least he hoped so. When he neared the junction of the two rivers, he slowed and took stock of his surroundings. He climbed up a steep hill to his right and used it as a vantage point to see the path.

One of the henchmen stood sentinel at the junction. He looked out over the rivers and periodically turned in a circle as he surveyed the area.

Penn climbed back down and picked his way to a tree that was closer to the junction. He picked up several rocks and shoved them into his bag before shimmying up the trunk. Crawling carefully out to a branch that gave him a good perspective, he reached for one of the rocks. He wouldn't have many chances to hit his mark before the man found him. And then he'd have to worry about evading the brigand's pistol shot.

Twice the size of a duck egg, the rock would do significant damage if Penn was able to hit his mark. He took a deep breath and hefted the weapon before pulling his arm back and letting the object fly.

He didn't wait to see the result before pulling another, slightly smaller rock, from the pack. The first missile struck its target, but the man didn't go down. The rock hit him square in the shoulder, prompting him to look around frantically.

Penn clenched his jaw and threw again. This time, it struck the villain in the neck. He lifted his hands, gasping as he staggered backward. He lost his balance and tumbled down the ravine toward the river.

Scurrying back down the tree, Penn ran to the junction

and looked down. The henchman lay in a heap at the bottom and appeared to be unconscious. Even if he wasn't—or if he awoke—he wouldn't be able to climb back up without assistance. He'd have to follow the river and hope to find another way up to the path.

Turning on his heel, Penn followed the track for a bit before reverting to the brush to avoid being seen. He passed the lower falls of Sgwd Clun Gwyn, and things became difficult as the slope became more vertical. The walk along the beaten path would be strenuous enough. Here, amongst the plants and trees of the forest, it was a bloody challenge.

Then he heard a sound that terrified him to the bone: a single gunshot.

Swearing, he ran to the path and gave up his plan of being quiet. He had to get to Amelia, and he had to do it *now*.

CHAPTER 21

"**You** imbecile!" Thaddeus screamed at the man who'd tripped on the slope as they neared the top of the falls and accidentally discharged his weapon.

"He shot me," the other man said in disbelief as he pivoted toward Amelia, who stood just in front of him on the path. Crimson began to spread up his shirtfront, and he sank to the ground.

"Help him!" Thaddeus demanded of the man who'd fired.

The culprit scrambled to his feet and promptly slipped again. Swearing, Thaddeus moved past her and pulled the injured man up the path and off to the side in a small, muddy clearing near the top of the falls. While he labored, Amelia considered how she might escape. However, without a pistol with which to shoot Thaddeus or the other henchman, she doubted she'd get very far.

Thaddeus dropped the man and cursed again. "That hurt my bloody arm!"

Amelia stared at her husband, wondering what she'd ever seen in this pathetic, unscrupulous man.

The henchman who'd fallen staggered into the clearing covered in mud, then rushed to kneel by the other man's side. "I'm so sorry, Bertie, 'twas an accident."

Bertie groaned, and his eyes fluttered closed.

The other man blinked up at Thaddeus. "We need to get him some help."

"And how do you propose we do that?" Thaddeus snapped.

"I'll carry 'im."

"It's miles back to the village."

"There's another one that way." The man pointed up the path past the falls. "That's what the man in the village said, remember?"

Thaddeus scoffed. "We're getting the heart first. Leave him for now."

Bertie groaned again, and he'd lost every bit of his color. Amelia hated seeing him in pain, but it was one less obstacle for her and Penn to deal with.

Penn. She prayed he'd been able to escape his bonds. And where was the henchman who'd tied him up? And the man Thaddeus had stationed at the junction to wait for him?

Thaddeus wrapped his hand around her elbow. "Let's go, it's starting to rain."

He was right. A fine mist had begun to fall, quickly coating them in dew.

"Now where is this heart? You said the top of the falls, but where the hell would we find it?" He walked beneath a canopy of trees and moved close to the river's edge where the sound of the water spilling over the falls filled the air.

Amelia looked down. It was quite a drop. But not a straight fall as she'd thought. There was a ledge partway down that broke the fall. If they crossed the river, they could make their way down to the ledge where the rock would be slick, and he might slip...

"It's down there on that ledge—hidden behind the water."

Thaddeus stared down at the outcropping. "You can't be serious."

"Why wouldn't they hide it somewhere that's difficult to reach? It makes perfect sense to me."

"Bloody hell," he muttered. "We'll need to cross the river." He glanced at her legs. "Good thing you're dressed like man again, but that will stop when we get home."

Amelia gritted her teeth but said nothing.

"Bertie's unconscious," the other henchman said with grave concern.

"Are you sure he's not dead?" Thaddeus asked.

Amelia sucked in a breath. "When did you become so uncharitable?" she asked crossly, uncaring what he thought of her irritation.

"When people behave like idiots and endanger our mission." He rolled his eyes before looking down at the man. "Come on, Price, let's get the heart, then we can get Bertie out of here." He gave Amelia a taunting stare. "Better?"

She didn't respond before turning and walking along the river to find an area that was calm enough to cross. This took several minutes as there was a fair bit of rapidly moving white water at the top of the falls. Thankfully, the river wasn't very deep, and she was able to ford it with a minimum of water hitting above her boots.

Aware of splashing behind her, she reached the other side of the river and turned to watch Thaddeus and Price cross. It was no wonder Price had slipped on the path. He was incredibly unbalanced as he made his way over the slick bottom of the riverbed.

At last they joined her, and Thaddeus gestured toward the falls. "Lead the way, then."

She started back along the riverbank, which was mostly flat, slick rock. It sloped slightly down as they neared the falls, and she had to work to keep her balance. The sound of the rushing water combined with the excessive apprehension she felt at having to climb down to the ledge.

When they reached the top, she veered to the right to a place where they could easily—well, as easily as possible— make their way down to the ledge. She stopped before climbing down and caught her breath.

Thaddeus joined her and studied the falls. "You're sure it's there?"

"As sure as anything," she lied. Now that she was here, she began to panic. The heart *wasn't* there. What would he do when he couldn't find it? "I'll wait here," she said.

He shook his head. "No, you're coming with me. And it better be there." He looked up at Price. "Hold your pistol on her. If the heart isn't there, shoot her."

Amelia swallowed. And prayed Penn would arrive in time.

~

*P*enn came upon the man lying off to the side of the path. He was pale and cold. And quite dead. Without pausing to ponder what had happened, he relieved the poor fellow of both his pistol and Penn's. He said a silent prayer, then hurried up the path, crouching low as he looked toward the top of the falls.

His heart leapt into his throat as he saw them—Amelia was climbing down a slope of rock to the ledge partway down the falls with Forrest following behind her. The other, and thankfully last, henchman stood at the top with his pistol directed at Amelia.

Penn scanned the river, looking for where they'd crossed. Seeing a slower portion just up the way, he hurried along the path, keeping himself as low as possible in the hope they wouldn't see him. He was grateful for the excessive foliage on this side of the river, and not just because it was keeping him partially dry. The rain had started a bit ago and while it was only a mist, it was the kind that soaked you over time.

Not that he cared. He'd brave a thousand storms and climb a thousand canyons to reach Amelia.

He made it to the other side of the river without being seen. This next part would be trickier because there was nothing to shield him on that side of the water. He had to hope the brigand would keep his focus on Amelia. Who Penn couldn't even see right now, and that drove him mad.

Moving as quickly and quietly as possible, he hastened along the slick bank of mostly rock. As he neared the top of the falls, his foot slipped. He wobbled and dropped one of the pistols. His breath caught, but it didn't go off. Still, it was enough for the man at the top of the falls to turn and look.

"Forrest!" The man brought his arm around and fired his pistol at Penn.

Penn dodged to the right but felt a burning sensation in his left bicep. He rushed forward and raised his weapon, squeezing the trigger. The bullet hit the man square in the chest. He wove for a moment from side to side, then fell gently backward, disappearing over the fall.

Amelia's scream rent the air, and Penn ran to where the man had fallen. Now he could see her. She stood on the ledge near the fall. Forrest had a hold of her, one arm wrapped around her waist and the other pointing a pistol at Penn.

"I can easily shoot you and throw her over the falls," Forrest yelled over the sound of the rushing water.

Penn could barely breathe. If he lost her… He struggled to find words that could somehow defuse the situation. "You'll never find the heart, then."

"It isn't here?" Forrest moved his hand up and tossed the hat from Amelia's head. He thrust his fingers against her scalp and gripped her hair. "You lied to me. Give me one good reason not to throw you over right now."

"Wait!" Penn cried. "I can get the heart for you. This is the wrong place. Don't blame her. I told her the wrong falls. I'd planned for us not to find it and leave. Then I'd come back and have it for myself."

"You expect me to believe you were both trying to cheat each other?" Forrest let out a hollow laugh. "You must think me incredibly stupid."

Yes, actually. But not stupid enough since he held the woman Penn loved and was completely in command.

"No. But the heart isn't here. It's at the lower falls. Let me take you there, and we can find it."

Forrest pushed Amelia toward the edge but didn't let go. She let out a sound that was half sob and half shriek, putting her hand up and trying to grab his wrist.

"I'll push you, my darling. Please don't make me. I'd hate to see your beautiful face splattered below."

Fear sliced through Penn. He started to make his way down the rock face to the ledge.

Forrest cocked the pistol. "Don't come any closer, Bowen."

Then everything happened very quickly. So quickly that Penn barely had time to react.

Amelia turned and brought her knee up into Forrest's groin. She grabbed his right arm and squeezed. Forrest screamed in pain and dropped the pistol. It clacked against the rock and bounced over the waterfall.

Free of him, Amelia took a step backward. That was the moment Penn dashed down the rock face, nearly slipping over the falls himself.

"You bitch." Thaddeus sneered as he lunged forward. Amelia danced backward, evading his grasp.

Thaddeus grabbed air and realized his mistake. He'd

overextended himself, and he pitched forward, falling onto the slick rock. He tried to find purchase but slipped to the edge. "Help me!" he cried, as his legs swung out over the fall, dangling in the air. He grabbed at the rock, but gravity had other ideas, and he simply fell over the side and tumbled down to the river below.

Amelia wasn't out of danger. She'd lost her balance as she'd worked to stay clear of Forrest. Penn moved as quickly as he dared, sticking close to the rock face and away from the edge. "Take my hand!" He reached for her as she started to slip.

Just when he thought he was going to lose her, his fingers met hers. He clasped her hand and pulled her hard against him. They fell back against the rock, and he fought to keep them upright.

Her breath came hard and fast against his chest as he wrapped his arms around her and held her close. "I've got you," he said, kissing her temple. "I've got you."

She dug her fingers into his shoulders and clutched his coat so tightly that it pulled around him, reminding him that a bullet had grazed his arm. But he didn't care. He'd endure anything for her.

"Is he...?" Her voice was muffled against his chest. "I can't look."

Penn couldn't look right now either, but he couldn't imagine anyone would survive the fall with the rocks below. "I can't verify anything, but I think we can assume he's dead."

A shudder racked her body. Penn held her more tightly and brushed his lips across the top of her head. "I'm sorry," he murmured.

"Can we get off this ledge, please?" she asked, still without lifting her head from where it was tucked into him.

"Yes, let's." He positioned her between himself and the rock face as he slowly led her back to the incline.

She climbed up with him holding and guiding her from the back. He scampered up after her and, well away from the edge, drew her into his embrace once more. "You're safe now."

She twined her arms around his neck, her body still shaking. He held her close, stroking her back and whispering words of calm and care. The rain continued to mist around them, and he moved his hat to her head.

Blinking, she pulled back and looked at his arm. "You're bleeding."

Penn winced. "That last brigand shot me." He studied her, looking for a wound he couldn't see. "What about you? I heard a gunshot earlier."

"That was an accident. Price—the one you shot—slipped on the path, and his pistol went off. He injured another of Thaddeus's men, Bertie. Did you see him on your way here? We need to help him."

Penn shook his head, his mouth pressed into a grim line. "No, we don't."

Amelia lifted her fingertips to her lips and briefly closed her eyes. "I feel terrible that any of this had to happen."

Penn brought his hands to her face and cupped her cheeks. "None of this is your fault. The Camelot group is evil and will stop at nothing to achieve their ends. They need to be stopped." He thought of Gideon and again wondered what had happened between him and Foliot.

Thinking of Gideon prompted his next question. "Are you ready to go find the heart?"

She breathed deeply. "After I look at your wound."

"It's fine. Barely a scratch. You can tend it when we get back to the inn."

"You must at least let me wrap your cravat around it." Her tone brooked no argument.

He pulled his coat from that arm, with her assistance,

wincing with the effort. "You're behaving like a wife again."

"Is that a proposal?"

"Hell yes. Marry me, Amelia."

She rolled up the sleeve of his shirt and looked at his wound. "You may need a couple of stitches." Reaching up, she tugged his cravat free, then wrapped it tightly around his lower bicep. "What is it with everyone getting shot in the arm?" she murmured.

As she helped him get his coat back on, he said, "You didn't answer my question."

"I'm still thinking about it." She gave him a saucy smile. "You have to kiss me first."

He couldn't contain the smile that spread across his lips. "Have I told you how much I love you? No, I don't think I have. I've been too afraid to speak the words with the future—"

"Shhh. I love you too. So much." She stood on her toes and put her mouth to his.

He held her tight and lost himself in her embrace.

She pulled away and looked up at him with a fiercely determined gaze. "Now, let's find that treasure."

∽

The mist stopped, and none too soon, because Amelia was cold to her very bones. She supposed that was to be expected, given the traumatic series of events she'd just survived. As thrilled as she was to hopefully find the heart at last, she looked forward to a warm fire.

And Penn's arms around her.

He was ahead of her on the path as they descended to the lower falls, which allowed her to stare at him as eagerly as she liked. And apparently, she'd be able to stare at him in the days and weeks and years to come.

Did he really want to marry her? She didn't doubt his emotions, but he was still Penn the adventurer for whom home was a transient place. She could accept that because for her, home would be wherever he was.

And yet, she didn't want him to feel trapped. He'd talked of being free and liking it. If he could manage to avoid being the earl, would he really want a wife?

Penn paused, then turned slightly, holding his left hand back for her. "Come walk with me."

She took his hand and came abreast of him. A moment later, they came upon the clearing with the body of Bertie. Her throat clenched, and she squeezed Penn's hand.

"When we get back to Pontneddfechan, I'll make arrangements to have the bodies recovered. The man who tried to tie me up should be fine. He was unconscious when I left him tied up. The fourth man fell down the ravine to the river, and I've no idea where he could be."

"Thank you for taking care of things," she said. "I'm sorry the others are dead, even Thaddeus."

They'd found his body trapped between some rocks, and Penn had dragged him to the shore. Seeing him lifeless had made her sad, even with all the grief he'd caused her. But there was also a sense of relief because for so long he'd been an unfinished chapter in her life, something she wasn't sure would ever be completed. After feeling trapped for so many years, she was able to look to the future.

"I am too. However, if the choice was them or you, there was no choice at all." He brought her hand to his mouth and pressed a kiss to the inside of her wrist between her glove and the hem of her sleeve.

The lower Fall of the White Meadow came into view. "Do you think the heart is at the top of the first fall in this series?" she asked.

"That would be my guess based on how the map was marked."

"And it was on this side?" At his nod, she exhaled with relief. "Good. I don't think I could cross the river again."

He squeezed her hand again and led her to the edge of the path near the top of the first of the four small falls. "Now we look for anything that will help us find the heart." He let go of her hand and walked off the path. "It wouldn't be out in the open. I'm thinking it's in something."

Amelia walked to the nearest tree. There was a V in the trunk where two branches started. "In something like this?"

Penn joined her and looked over her shoulder. "Perhaps. But I suspect it's in a vessel of some kind. This is a rough place to keep something of value. With the falls and all the rain, there's a great deal of humidity. That would be very damaging over time."

"Except to a rock." Amelia looked at the rock around and beneath the river, over which the water tumbled to the pool below. "Unless the rock was in the river." Then it would erode or be washed away.

She turned from the river and studied the other side of the path. There were trees draped with moss, and ferns blanketed the ground. Crossing over the path, she stepped into the undergrowth. To her left was a particularly large oak, larger than the others around it. Lichen coated much of the trunk, but there was one area where it looked a bit like a pattern, reminding her of the map they'd found at the fall of snow.

Calling out to Penn, she traced her fingers over the subtle pattern and found the shape of a heart. He arrived at her side with a soft exhalation. "What did you find?" The astonishment in his voice spurred her heartbeat.

"Do you see what I see?" she asked, tracing over it again.

"Yes." He moved toward the trunk and felt along the bark.

For some reason, Amelia looked down. She crouched low, brushing her hands along the trunk and then moving the ferns at the base. The moss was thick here, growing in fat clumps.

She plucked at a bit of it, and a piece tore off in her hand. Beneath, there was ground and the edge of something that wasn't dirt. She pushed at the moss and uncovered the edge of something pale and brilliant.

Moving the moss aside, she exposed it entirely—a small, pink, heart-shaped stone nearly the size of her palm. She picked it up and wiped the rest of the moss and dirt away. "Penn," she said softly. "Is this tourmaline?"

He turned and looked at the stone in her palm. "I believe so." His lips spread into a wide grin. "It's certainly heart shaped."

She lifted her gaze to his. "Is this it?"

He nodded. "It has to be."

"How can we know for sure?"

He tipped his head to the side. "I don't suppose you can use it to make me fall in love with you—that's already happened." He smiled again, and she laughed in response.

"Assuming this is the real artifact with whatever enchantment these thirteen treasures possess."

He looked at her in surprise. "Now you're doubting if this is real?"

"No, I'm sure it's real, and that it's likely enchanted, unlike the faux heart and the dagger." She tipped her head to the side. "We can't test it, of course. It will only work for Gideon and others like him—descendants."

"That's true. I suppose he can try it out, then."

She ran her thumb over the beautiful stone. "What a dangerous thing, to meddle in matters of love. What if someone like Thaddeus had this and was able to use it to make me love him?" She shuddered. "I may understand why the Order seeks to keep these treasures hidden."

Penn was quiet a moment, his brow creasing. "It is a concern. I should hate for them to be used for evil purposes. For that reason, I'm glad to turn them over to Gideon. Perhaps he'll be able to find a way to keep them safe. Hopefully, we can see him soon to discuss it."

Amelia looked up at him. "We? Does that mean you wish me to accompany you?"

"Of course. I'm still waiting for your answer to my question." He curled his arm around her waist and drew her against his chest. She held the heart between them. "I don't ever want to let you go. Do you think you can put up with being an adventurer's wife? I can promise it won't be boring."

"No, I can't imagine it would." She looked down at the heart briefly, then lifted her gaze to his. "Are you certain this is what you want? You like your freedom, and if you aren't an earl, you'll still have that—"

He gazed at her intently. "Amelia, *you* are my freedom. You're the home I never knew I wanted, the one I think I was trying to avoid. The only home I've ever known is with my parents. Before that, I didn't belong anywhere, and since then, I think I've been...restless. Searching, but not for treasure. For you."

Her heart swelled with joy. She stood on her toes and gave him a brief but satisfying kiss. "I will be your wife whether you're an adventurer, a scholar, an antiquary, or an earl."

He picked her up and swung her around with a laugh. Then he kissed her soundly before setting her back to the earth again. "We should hurry back before it gets dark."

She tried to hand him the stone, but he curled her fingers around it.

"You keep it," he said. "In your pack. You've worked very

hard for this, and your grandfather would be exceedingly proud."

She hoped so.

Later, after she'd applied a salve to his arm and properly dressed his wound, they lay in bed at the inn, a fire sparking in the hearth and the treasures they'd collected displayed on a small table. The dagger, the fake heart, the White Book of Hergest, and the Heart of Llanllwch. It was quite a haul, as Penn had noted earlier.

"When I went down to fetch our dinner, the innkeeper said he and Mr. Hughes would take care of the bodies in the forest."

"Is the innkeeper part of the Order, then? He did encourage us to see Mr. Hughes."

"I'm not sure," Penn said. "And he may not tell me if I asked."

Amelia snuggled against his side, laying her head atop his shoulder. "Do we need to leave terribly early for Monmouth? I'm rather exhausted." She yawned to punctuate her statement.

He rolled over on top of her, surprising her and eliciting a gasp from her lips. "Mrs. Bowen—"

She narrowed her eyes playfully at him. "I'm not Mrs. Bowen yet."

"The innkeeper thinks you are, and I prefer to keep to the charade. *Mrs. Bowen*, if you think you're exhausted now, just wait until I'm finished with you."

"Is that a promise, Mr. Bowen?"

"One I intend to keep until my dying breath." He kissed her, his tongue delving deliciously into her mouth. After a moment, he paused. "On second thought, I intend to keep it forever because one lifetime simply won't suffice."

He kissed her again, and Amelia wondered if even forever would be enough.

*B*ecause it was rainy and cool, Penn and Amelia took two days to travel from Pontneddfechan to Hollyhaven. Also because they took their time enjoying their newfound joy.

As they rode into the stable yard, they'd barely dismounted before his parents came dashing from the house. Following at a more sedate pace behind them were his sister, Cate, and her new husband, Elijah.

Penn put his hand at the base of Amelia's back as they greeted his mother and father, and he introduced Cate and Elijah.

"Well, did you find it?" Cate stared at him in eager anticipation.

"I take it Mother and Father told you what we were doing." He'd dispatched a note to them from Wells informing them they were going to the Valley of Neath to find the heart.

She pursed her lips at him. "You're keeping up the suspense on purpose, and it's beastly of you."

Amelia reached into the pocket of her habit and opened her palm to display the Heart of Llanllwch.

Cate sucked in an audible breath as she moved closer. "Can I?"

"Of course." Amelia placed it in Cate's hand.

"It's beautiful," Cate said. She lifted her gaze to Penn and grinned. "Well done."

Penn inclined his head toward Amelia. "Tell that to my fiancée. She found it."

"Fiancée?" This came from Penn's mother, who also came forward to look at the heart. She snapped her gaze to Penn. "What about—"

Penn interrupted her. "That is a very long story that we will tell you in due time. Suffice it to say that Amelia is free to be my lawful wife."

Mother's eyes widened briefly, then she gave a slight nod. "I see." She looked to Amelia. "Should I be sorry for your loss?"

"Not at all. I'm sorry for what happened, but I am eager for the future." She moved closer to Penn, and he squeezed her waist.

"Let's not stand around here all day," Father said, glancing up at the sky. "It's going to rain again soon."

Cate handed the heart to their mother, who was anxious to see it more closely. Looping her arm through Amelia's and pulling her from Penn's side, Cate guided her toward the house. "Are you sure you want to marry my brother? He's rather arrogant."

"Yes, I'd noticed that, but I daresay he grew on me, and I learned to look past it."

"Well, you'll need to keep him in line." She threw a dazzling smile at her often stoic new husband. "Isn't that right, Elijah?"

"I am entirely at your service, as you well know." He

arched a brow at her, and Penn detected a note of mischief in the man's gaze. Perhaps he wasn't as buttoned up as Penn had thought. Or perhaps he was merely shirking the role of military officer as he adjusted to his new position as earl. Or, and this was the most likely, Cate was provoking him to madness.

Penn walked over to him. "It turns out I may need your advice." He glanced over at his father. "Has Egg returned?"

Father shook his head with a grim expression. "I'm afraid not."

Nearly a week ago, this would have sent Penn into a dark mood of despair, but instead of pretending to be optimistic about things, he actually was. He still didn't particularly want to be an earl—he didn't know the first thing about it—but with Amelia at his side, he was ready and willing to face anything. Plus, he had a brother-in-law who'd unexpectedly inherited an earldom and seemed to be coping just fine, as well as a half brother who'd been raised to be an earl who could certainly show him the way. Once Gideon finished whatever quest he'd decided he needed to pursue.

"What sort of advice do you need?" Elijah asked, falling into step beside Penn and his father as they trailed the women to the house.

"How to be an earl. Turns out I'm the firstborn son of the Earl of Stratton. I'm hoping I don't have to actually fulfill that title, but it all depends on finding a vicar who has proof of my birth."

They paused outside the house, and Elijah looked from Penn to his father and back again. "This sounds complicated. Does Cate know about this?"

"Not yet."

Elijah's gaze lit with mirth. "I know something she doesn't? Oh, this will be fun."

They went inside to Father's study, where they ate and

drank while Penn and Amelia related the tale of how they'd found the heart.

Mother had paled during certain parts, and both Penn and Amelia took great care to leave out the intimate details. They sat together on the settee, their thighs touching as they relived their adventure, and he marveled that he didn't think he could love her more, and yet each moment he was with her proved that thought wrong.

When he'd finished, Father stood and went to his desk, where he picked up a piece of parchment. "This arrived yesterday from Gideon." He handed Penn the letter to read, but shared the basic contents. "He's committed to destroying Camelot for good."

"I'm not surprised," Amelia said. "Something happened when he obtained the dagger."

Father's mouth dipped into a pensive frown. "Yes, I should like to know precisely what happened there."

Penn exchanged a look with Amelia. "As would we, but he didn't have time to tell us."

Their gathering was interrupted by the arrival of Egg. Penn leapt up from the settee upon seeing his assistant. "Egg! Tell us your news." His heart thumped in his chest as he waited anxiously for Egg to speak.

But Egg didn't reflect Penn's excitement. In fact, he looked rather disappointed.

"It isn't good. News that is," Egg clarified. "The vicar's gone missing. I tracked him to Gloucester and into the Cotswolds. But then he seemed to vanish. I stopped in every inn in every village all the way to Oxford. Then I employed Charlie to go to London and see if the vicar showed up to petition the Lord Chancellor. He's keeping a watchful eye."

Charlie lived in Oxford and helped Penn with translations and copying documents from time to time.

Penn sagged back down onto the settee, where Amelia immediately took his hand and murmured, "I'm sorry."

"Didn't you say you could come to terms with being the earl?" Cate asked. They'd discussed Penn's surprise inheritance before sharing the tale of the heart—Elijah had been far too eager to tell his wife that he knew something she didn't. Having grown up with Cate and her insistence to know everything, Penn had appreciated the man's glee.

"Yes, I can. I will." If he had no choice, and right now it certainly seemed that way. But what the bloody devil had happened to the vicar? "I'd like to remain who I am. Not just for me, but for Gideon too."

Elijah let out a distasteful snort. He'd not entirely forgiven Gideon for endangering Cate. And yet, he'd gone to great peril to save Gideon's life. Gideon may have had a terrible father, but in this room was a group of people who supported and loved him.

"We'll find him yet," Egg said. "Can't see myself working for an earl." He wrinkled his nose as if he smelled something horrid, prompting everyone to laugh.

"Any earl would be lucky to have you," Penn said. He reached over to the table in front of him and picked up the Heart of Llanllwch, then tossed it to Egg. "Catch. We found it. The real one."

Egg's jaw dropped as he held it up to the light streaming through the window behind Penn. "You were right all along. The one in the Ashmolean was a fake."

"Yes, but a valuable artifact all the same. Without it, we couldn't have found the real treasure," Amelia said.

Penn turned his head toward her. "Well, that is certainly true. But I daresay the dagger was the most important piece."

Amelia looked at him in confusion. "The dagger, why?"

"Because it's what brought me to you, and *you're* the real treasure."

"I think we should all toast to that," Penn's father said.

When everyone had a drink, Father lifted his glass. "To my son and his bride. May your life together be the most exciting adventure you'll ever take." He looked over at Penn's mother with a broad smile. "Just like ours."

Penn drank to his future wife while she smiled at him and whispered, "It already is."

I hope you enjoyed Lord of Fortune! Read on for the exciting conclusion to the series, Captivating the Scoundrel, featuring Gideon, a descendant of one of King Arthur's knights who must partner with a bold and brilliant young woman in a quest to save his legacy--the Thirteen Treasures--from a nefarious secret society led by her father.

THANK YOU!

Thank you so much for reading Lord of Fortune! It's the fourth book in the Legendary Rogues series. I hope you enjoyed it! Don't miss the rest of the series:

The Legend of a Rogue
Lady of Desire
Romancing the Earl
Lord of Fortune
Captivating the Scoundrel

Would you like to know when my next book is available and to hear about sales and deals? Sign up for my VIP newsletter at https://www.darcyburke.com/readergroup, follow me on social media:

Facebook: https://facebook.com/DarcyBurkeFans
Twitter at @darcyburke
Instagram at darcyburkeauthor
Pinterest at darcyburkewrite

And follow me on Bookbub to receive updates on pre-orders, new releases, and deals!

Want to share your love of my books with like-minded readers? Want to hang with me and get inside scoop? Then don't miss my exclusive Facebook groups!

Darcy's Duchesses for historical readers
Burke's Book Lovers for contemporary readers

Need more Regency romance? Check out my other historical series:

The Untouchables
Swoon over twelve of Society's most eligible and elusive bachelor peers and the bluestockings, wallflowers, and outcasts who bring them to their knees!

The Untouchables: The Spitfire Society
Meet the smart, independent women who've decided they don't need Society's rules, their families' expectations, or, most importantly, a husband. But just because they don't need a man doesn't mean they might not *want* one...

The Untouchables: The Pretenders
Set in the captivating world of The Untouchables, follow the saga of a trio of siblings who excel at being something they're not. Can a dauntless Bow Street Runner, a devastated viscount, and a disillusioned Society miss unravel their secrets?

The Phoenix Club
Society's most exclusive invitation... Welcome to the Phoenix Club, where London's most audacious, disreputable, and

intriguing ladies and gentlemen find scandal, redemption, and second chances.

Wicked Dukes Club
Six books written by me and my BFF, NYT Bestselling Author Erica Ridley. Meet the unforgettable men of London's most notorious tavern, The Wicked Duke. Seductively handsome, with charm and wit to spare, one night with these rakes and rogues will never be enough...

Secrets and Scandals
Everyone has secrets and some of them are a scandal . . . six sexy, damaged heroes lose their hearts to strong, intelligent women in the glittering ballrooms and lush countryside of Regency England.

Love is All Around
Heartwarming Regency-set retellings of classic Christmas stories (written after the Regency!) featuring a cozy village, three siblings, and the best gift of all: love.

If you like contemporary romance, I hope you'll check out my **Ribbon Ridge** series available from Avon Impulse, and the continuation of Ribbon Ridge in **So Hot**.

I hope you'll consider leaving a review at your favorite online vendor or networking site!

I appreciate my readers so much. Thank you, thank you, *thank you*.

I chose to set this story in and near Wales both because of the subject matter and because my grandmother, Selma Rita King Finney was born in Cardiff in 1916. I still have family there and was fortunate enough to visit several years ago. It's a beautiful land with charming people, and while the Welsh language is difficult to pronounce, I find it lovely—probably because I can still hear my great-uncle Alec singing it.

The thirteen treasures of Britain are mythical objects that appear in various legends. They have been used in countless stories and in many ways (Harry Potter's Deathly Hallows are somewhat based on them). I adapted them for this series and added the Heart of Llanllwch as well as the dagger for purely narrative purposes. The White Book of Hergest did go missing at a bookbinder in London and was possibly lost in the fire depicted in this book. The problem with the water pipes and not being able to put out the fire quickly was also real. The Tale of Ranulf and Hilaria is not.

The Order of the Round Table and the subgroup of Camelot is a completely fictional group, but is based on the myriad secret societies that have existed for centuries.

Edmund de Valery and Anarawd are fictional characters as are the documents they produced.

Of course there is no proof that King Arthur, his knights, the Round Table or any of Arthurian legend is real. I'd like to think it's a little bit history with a dash of embellishment and a lot of great storytelling.

ALSO BY DARCY BURKE

Historical Romance

Legendary Rogues

The Legend of a Rogue
Lady of Desire
Romancing the Earl
Lord of Fortune
Captivating the Scoundrel

The Phoenix Club

Invitation
Improper
Impassioned
Intolerable

The Untouchables

The Bachelor Earl
The Forbidden Duke
The Duke of Daring
The Duke of Deception
The Duke of Desire
The Duke of Defiance
The Duke of Danger
The Duke of Ice

The Duke of Ruin

The Duke of Lies

The Duke of Seduction

The Duke of Kisses

The Duke of Distraction

The Untouchables: Spitfire Society

Never Have I Ever with a Duke

A Duke is Never Enough

A Duke Will Never Do

The Untouchables: The Pretenders

A Secret Surrender

A Scandalous Bargain

A Rogue to Ruin

Love is All Around

(A Regency Holiday Trilogy)

The Red Hot Earl

The Gift of the Marquess

Joy to the Duke

Wicked Dukes Club

One Night for Seduction by Erica Ridley

One Night of Surrender by Darcy Burke

One Night of Passion by Erica Ridley

One Night of Scandal by Darcy Burke

One Night to Remember by Erica Ridley

One Night of Temptation by Darcy Burke

ROMANCING the EARL

"...A fast paced story that was exciting and interesting. This is a definite must add to your book lists!"

-Kilts and Swords

"Once again Darcy Burke takes an interesting story and...turns it into magic. An exceptionally well-written book."

-Bodice Rippers, Femme Fatale, and Fantasy

LORD of FORTUNE

"If you love a deep, passionate romance with a bit of mystery, then this is the book for you!"

-Teatime and Books

"I don't think I know enough superlatives to describe this book! It is wonderfully, magically delicious. It sucked me in from the very first sentence and didn't turn me loose—not even at the end ..."

-Flippin Pages

CAPTIVATING the SCOUNDREL

"I am in absolute awe of this story. Gideon and Daphne stole all of my heart and then some. This book was such a delight to read."

-Beneath the Covers Blog

"Darcy knows how to end a series with a bang! Daphne and Gideon are a mix of enemies and allies turned lovers that will have you on the edge of your seat at every turn."

-Sassy Booklover

ABOUT THE AUTHOR

Darcy Burke is the USA Today Bestselling Author of sexy, emotional historical and contemporary romance. Darcy wrote her first book at age 11, a happily ever after about a swan addicted to magic and the female swan who loved him, with exceedingly poor illustrations. Join her Reader Club newsletter for the latest updates from Darcy.

A native Oregonian, Darcy lives on the edge of wine country with her guitar-strumming husband, incredibly talented artist daughter, and imaginative son who will almost certainly out-write her one day (that may be tomorrow). They're a crazy cat family with two Bengal cats, a small, fame-seeking cat named after a fruit, an older rescue Maine Coon with attitude to spare, and a collection of neighbor cats who hang out on the deck and occasionally venture inside. You can find Darcy at a winery, in her comfy writing chair balancing her laptop and a cat or three, folding laundry (which she loves), or binge-watching TV with the family. Her happy places are Disneyland, Labor Day weekend at the Gorge, Denmark, and anywhere in the UK—so long as her family is there too. Visit Darcy online at www. darcyburke.com and follow her on social media.

facebook.com/DarcyBurkeFans

twitter.com/darcyburke

instagram.com/darcyburkeauthor

pinterest.com/darcyburkewrites

goodreads.com/darcyburke

bookbub.com/authors/darcy-burke

amazon.com/author/darcyburke